The Nightmare We Know

THE DARK ABYSS OF OUR SINS • BOOK TWO

The Nightmare We Know

THE DARK ABYSS OF OUR SINS • BOOK TWO

KRISTA D. BALL

REGRETS OF THE SOUL

LORD GOD ALMIGHTY, please forgive me. None of this was my intention. I had not meant for the demon gates to even form, much less for them to open. Yet, it happened, and I was useless to stop the onslaught and consequent slaughter of your innocent children.

Lord God Almighty, I know you will judge me harshly. Rightfully so, if I do not atone for my transgressions. I need your guidance. They do not know I am a mage, let alone an elemental wielding the power of the demon gates. If I reveal myself and my knowledge, sparse as it is, my influence and access will be altered. My abilities will be cursed and reviled, and I will be persecuted for nothing more than having been made in the image of my Lord God.

Deep within my soul, I know I must correct the path. How, though? I lack control in times of extreme tension. Were not the months at Borro Abbey the apex of anxiety? Will it become worse at Orsini? What about the travel to get there? What if I create them on the inside of the carriage while I sleep? I must exercise great caution, for I shall not be burned at the stake alongside so many of my brethren and sisters. I will fix what I have broken.

Perhaps this is your plan, Lord God Almighty. You wish me to use my abilities and bring the elementals together, hand-in-hand, with the normal. Together, we will bring down the demons, be they the ones with wings that attack us or the creeping darkness within our own hearts.

I see it now, Lord God Almighty. Thank you for revealing it to me. I see your plan. I see why you gifted me with the ability to form marks. I see now that you protected me at the abbey. I survived the flames so that I could enact your will. Yes, of course. I see it all now. Yes, Lord God Almighty. You are ever all-knowing and all-seeing. My doubts were formed out of weakness.

Lord God Almighty, I am your humble servant. I will follow your plan and I will bring about the final peace that you so desperately want for your people.

CHAPTER ONE

East of the Ruins of Borro Abbey

THEY'D BEEN RUNNING for six days now. Six long, brutal days of dodging General Bonacieux's men. Six days of evading frightened farmers and laborers who were very willing to shove a pitchfork into any stranger. Six days of Allegra's swollen ankle slowing them down.

Six days of demon attacks.

"Um, Cram?" Dodd said, his voice pinched. "I think they see us."

Dodd was crouched near some underbrush with his spyglass. He had a decent vantage of the trail below. Though wet from the melting snow, Dodd could spot demons or Bonacieux's stragglers, who weren't any better than the demons.

"We're kinda busy here, Dodd," Walter said.

"Almost there," Allegra said. "Just hold on, Dodd."

"Almost," Walter agreed.

"That doesn't stop them from seeing us," Dodd said. They were all hungry, and patience was in short supply.

Allegra threw stones at a smallish-sized demon to pull its attention away from Walter. Her elemental fire was so unpredictable that she was more likely to burn another building down on their heads than be helpful. Dodd was still sore about the church she'd accidentally burned down. How was she supposed to know that some demons could inhale elemental fire and breathe it back out? Up until last year, she didn't even believe in demons.

"Oh yeah, they've definitely spotted us," Dodd shouted at them as he scrambled to his feet. "Shit, hurry up, Cram!"

"Free feel to deal with this on your own, Dodd," Walter said through clenched teeth.

"I'm the brains of this operation. You're the grunt," Dodd said, doing nothing to help with the demon who was now diving toward Walter's unprotected head.

"Allegra! Now!" Walter ordered as he dropped into a crouch.

Allegra blasted the insectoid creature that was no bigger than her head with fire. The detonation of the nearby tree's demon mark ripped the portal opening wider. It pulled on the small demon, which screeched and shrieked as the winds from inside the portal sucked it back into its world. Walter slammed his hand on the tree's trunk from behind, fighting the winds and howls from beyond inside the portal. With a few spoken words, the portal snapped shut. He leaned against the now-mangled, smoking tree for support, breathless and swearing.

Likewise, Allegra sagged against a nearby tree that was also blackened and twisted from the exposure to the demon portal and magic. She tried steadying her breathing, but her heart pounded painfully in her chest. She glanced over at Walter, who appeared uninjured, and said, "I hate demons."

"You're not supposed to like them," Walter said. He was panting, though not nearly as hard as her. He didn't have an injured ankle, true, but he was also in exceptional shape. She was still in a corset and had grown frail over the winter months at the abbey. She would have had angry words for anyone who'd said that to her, but she knew it in her heart. It simply stung her pride to even think it.

"People, I appreciate this bonding time going on, but we *still* have company coming up the ridge. Could you do something useful, Cram? If it's not too taxing, of course. I wouldn't want you to pull a muscle."

Allegra gave Dodd a reproachful glance, but the young man seemed to not notice it. Walter made a weary sound but pushed himself back to his feet. He stepped in front of them and, with a motion of one hand, created a miniature chasm along the path.

Dodd pulled out his spyglass. "That's not going to work, Cram. My arm is longer than that thing is wide."

Walter rolled his eyes and made a punching gesture. Rocks and trees fell and the ground shook beneath their feet. "Is that better?"

Dodd inspected the trail destruction. "I'd have done it better, but I guess it's acceptable."

"Ass," Walter said, though without any real malice. He yawned and shook the hand he'd made the punching gesture with. "It was far easier when everyone was terrified of my magic. Now I got the Pope's man over here telling me to sin on a regular basis. The world makes no sense anymore."

"We all face hardship," Allegra said, giving Walter a small grin. She let out a weary sound. "All right. You were both right. We can't chase every demon that's been let loose."

Allegra's entire body ached, and her various cuts, bruises, and burns tugged at her patience. She'd sprained one of her ankles when she'd jumped from a burning Borro Abbey. It might even be broken, if the swelling and bruising were any judge.

The last food they found was two days ago at an abandoned cabin. They gorged what they could and took what could be carried, but their pockets—and stomachs—were empty again. There was still a significant amount of snow melting this far up the path. Nothing edible could be foraged yet. At their current rate, they'd be dead long before the thaw and first edibles. This plan of hers wasn't working, and Allegra had to admit it.

Her instincts were to go back down the mountain and raid one of the farming hamlets that dotted the Cathedral's Way, the well-maintained highway that connected the countryside with the great Orsini Cathedral. Most until now were empty, and she knew why.

Bonacieux's maundering leftovers made travel difficult, and no doubt they were the reason for the abandoned housing along their path thus far. If they were less recognizable, she'd suggest risking it. Yet, it seemed too close to asking to be captured, a plan born out of desperation and starvation.

Everyone knew Walter Cram, demon lover. Lieutenant Dodd was a part of her personal security and a top officer in the Holy

Father's Own Consorts. He was even still wearing his green uniform. She? Well, she was Allegra, Contessa of Marsina and the Arbiter of Justice. It wasn't like she could pretend to be a peasant woman when she still wore her embroidered satin jacket.

Dodd sheathed his spyglass. "Well, Your Ladyship, what's our next move then?"

Allegra pushed stray strands of hair from her eyes. She dreaded what she was about to say, but the words had to be spoken. "Orsini."

Walter snorted.

"Does the mage committee have a comment?"

Walter brushed the dirt off his stolen jacket as best as he could. Allegra felt guilty about the theft, but Walter wasn't dressed for the cold nights. Walter's argument was that the farmhouse was abandoned, though Allegra pointed out that it was probably because the occupants left due to an army coming down the highway. "Would you rather I freeze to death" had been how Walter had won that argument.

"Committees always have a comment. It's why they are the true evil."

Allegra was too tired to even offer him a smirk. "Dodd, do you know how long it will take us to get to Orsini on foot?"

Dodd tried to give her a supportive smile, but he was clearly as tired as she was. The best he could do was nod at her feet. "I hate to say, Contessa, but it'll take us a month with the way you're hobbling. We're making bad time."

"We'll starve first," Allegra said.

"Not Dodd," Walter added. "He has enough fat on him to get through another winter."

"Oh, fuck off. Sorry, Contessa. He's pissing me off."

"Awww, is the Holy Father's man hungry? Does his belly ache?" Walter said in a sing-song voice.

Dodd replied without bothering to hide the contempt in his voice. "My orders are to protect the Contessa, not you, demon lover."

That made Walter bark out a laugh. "Well, Ally, we need food before Dodd here starts eating his own arm."

"Fuck off."

Allegra didn't bother getting in between the two men. They got along well enough, considering neither could stand the other's guts. Provided they weren't fighting over anything important, she didn't care. Walter Cram would get on anyone's nerves in the best of time, and she'd once been in love with the man. If she couldn't stand him, even back then, there was little hope for anyone else.

"Your Ladyship, I recommend we continue on this path, circling down toward any houses we see. Even a bit of shelter would be welcome," Dodd said.

Walter shook his head. "Bonacieux's scouts will find us."

"So what? You think we should starve?" Dodd demanded.

"Frankly? Yes. We keep this path until we hit the bridge road. If it's clear, duck down to get some food. Otherwise, head north until we're out of Bonacieux's reach, and then keep going east. Circle back down south once we hit the River Three and get to Orsini alive."

"What are we going to eat?" Dodd demanded.

Walter shrugged, completely unconcerned. "There's going to be enough water, with the snow runoff, so we won't die of thirst."

"I'm not sure what to do." Allegra blew on her hands to try to warm them.

"That makes them colder," Walter snapped. "Shove them under your armpits."

"Stop yelling at me! I'm cold and I'm hungry, and my ankle feels like it's going to collapse under me at any moment. And..." Her words caught in her throat. Then, she forced out what had been pressing on her. "I dread going to Orsini and what I face there."

Bonacieux had seen her use fire. She had stupidly used fire magic in hopes of stopping him. She was so exhausted that the most pathetic flame possible had come from her hand; it couldn't even catch the floor on fire. And he'd seen it. He would tell the Cardinals. They would revoke her authority. Soldiers would arrest her. A mob would burn her alive in the courtyard. All of her childhood nightmares were going to unfold now, and all because she'd made such a foolhardy mistake.

"No one will believe Bonacieux," Walter said quietly. "Lex was there, don't forget. He'll lie for you. Assuming he made it out, I guess."

"Lex would've made it out," Dodd said sternly.

Walter gave Dodd a sharp look, a hot word on his tongue. But he seemed to gather himself, and then nodded. "Well, if you say Lex made it out, then Lex will cover for Allegra."

"He will," Dodd said, with total confidence. "Besides, Contessa, think about it. There's no way anyone with a working brain will believe Bonacieux over Lex. Come on, it's Lex. Everyone loves Lex."

"It's the baby-face," Walter said, nodding. Growing serious again, he said, "Bonacieux killed the queen. They will have to believe that simple fact. For him to accuse *you*, of all people, of being an elemental mage after he murdered the queen? No. No one will believe him. So enough of this. It's time to go back."

Allegra held her tongue, for she was uncertain what to say. She knew she did not want to repeat the obvious question: what if Lex didn't make it? That would only open others. What about Stanton? What would her life be like without him, having only just found each other? She didn't want to even think about Nadira or Serafina, let alone Father Michael and Nathan, and all of the Consorts. What about the refugees? Or Borro townsfolk? How many had Bonacieux killed?

"Cram, go easy on her," Dodd said in a cautious tone, trying no doubt to not sound insulting. It still stung her pride. "If it were just me and you here, sure, I wouldn't care. Look at her, man! She can't walk. I don't mean any offense, Contessa, and it's certainly not a comment about your weight, but I'm not keen on carrying you to Orsini."

"What if we're captured?" Walter asked. "I won't be able to protect any of you. If we're very, very lucky, all that'll happen is they'll string us up. I don't even want to think about the not lucky scenario."

"She's going to die!"

Tears of frustration laced with physical pain welled up in Allegra's eyes. She had tried to be strong. She'd tried so hard to keep up with their punishing pace, but she had no physical training or even proper footwear. She could not even take off her corset to let her ribs expand, for the garment was combined into a jacket. To remove the corset was to remove her entire jacket, and she would certainly freeze.

"I am trying my best," Allegra said softly, interrupting the bickering of her companions. She let out a weary sound. "I am in so much pain. I am trying to keep up with the pace Walter wants, but it is making my ankle hurt more, not less. I fear I am going to slip and fall, and then break something. And it doesn't help when the two of you won't stop bickering and bossing me around!"

"Sorry," both men said at once.

She wrapped her arms around her torso, hugging herself tightly against the chilled air. Both Walter and Dodd remained silent. Finally, she said, "I don't even know if…he…if he…"

She could not say the words. Even his name was off limits her to voice. What if he had not made it? What would she do?

Oh, the practical, spinster side of her announced she would dust herself off and carry on. That, in time, she would cherish the moments they'd stolen. But she did not want practical. She wanted love. She wanted Stanton Rainier's arms around her, whispering that he would never leave her.

Walter put a hand on her elbow, an awkward intimacy. "Rainier made it."

A lump formed in Allegra's throat. "What if he didn't? He didn't come to look for us."

"Contessa, I really need you to listen to what I'm going to say," Dodd said in his serious voice. The one he so rarely used. "I know Lex and Rainier are alive because no one has come for us. I know that doesn't make sense, but I need you to believe me. Think about it. If Lex and Rainier were dead, who'd be left in charge? Martin? He's a good guy, don't get me wrong, and I'd trust him to watch my back, but there's no way on the Lord God's green grass that he has enough discipline to get the survivors to safety. He'd have risked sending people to look for us, and any missing mages. But you know Rainier isn't like that. Neither is Lex. Even hurt, Lex isn't like that. But, if one of them weren't alive, you see they might be convinced to waver. But both of them? Together? They're like a giant wall of stubborn. Now, you think about that. They'd follow what your orders would have been, no matter what. What would your orders have been, if you were there?"

"I don't know, Dodd!"

"Get the civilians out," Walter said. "You'd have told them to get the civilians and the clergy out. You'd have said to get as far away from the demons and the army as possible, and you'd stay with the mages to take down the demon."

Dodd nodded. "That's what you would have said if Rainier had come upstairs looking for you. He'd have done it, too. Think about that. Them not coming for us just means they did what you would have ordered. You gotta be alive to follow orders, Your Ladyship."

"I don't know Rainier that well, but I know his reputation. He would have gotten civilians and clergy out first and that's why he's not here. He's looking after them and keeping his green Consorts in line. I bet some of the wet ears he has would have come looking for you, otherwise."

"That's true," Dodd said. "Same with Lex, actually."

"We know they're alive because they're getting the civilians out. It's a good sign."

Allegra gulped back the tears as best as she could, but she still had to rub her eyes with the inside of her wrist. Dirt stung her eyes, even though it was the cleanest part of her body at the moment. False hope was such a dangerous emotion; the delay of grief only increased the finale. However, she also knew what they said had a kind of logic to it. The conflict between her hopes and her worries threatened to rip apart her reasoning and good sense.

Be that as it may, she knew she needed to make a choice. Her previous one had rid the world of a few demons, but it had cost her in pain and suffering. "I would prefer if we made our way back down to the upper road, at least for the next couple of days. I seem to remember there being farmsteads along that route. Perhaps we could request help from someone. We can evaluate what to do next once we run out of road."

"Yes, Your Ladyship. Are you able to make some distance today? I'd like to get ahead of those assholes, if you don't mind my language," Dodd said. He was motioning with his chin toward the distant troops Walter had cut off.

"I'll try my best," Allegra said.

That seemed to impress Dodd. He turned to Walter and asked, "Are you coming?"

Walter kept his disapproval to himself, though Allegra knew him well enough to sense it. "Well, obviously."

STANTON RAINIER TROTTED his horse down the long procession of carriages, heading toward the back of the line. Thank the Almighty the weather was holding, or else the roads would have been a quagmire of muddy ruts and broken wheel axles. And blood. There would be so much blood. There was already too much of it behind them.

Stanton shook off the reflection. The roads were good, and they were making exceptional time. Another day, maximum, and they would reach Orsini's safe walls. Even now, the clusters of frightened farmstead holders along the highway had evacuated either further up the foothills with their herds or had added themselves to the baggage train to continue onward to Orsini's embrace. Often, the wives and children came with the caravan, in hopes that Stanton's soldiers could protect them, while the men and older boys took the flocks into the mountains. The displacement of people had already begun, and this war was only days old.

Still, Stanton asked Serafina to take detailed notes along the way for reimbursement from the Arbiter's accounts once they were in safety. Serafina recorded animal feed, supplies, clothing, medical attention—regardless of how rudimentary—and even if all were offered without reservation or expectation of payment. The Arbiter's office was vacant at the moment, but the memory of her lived on; she'd have wanted them to pay back anything taken. Until Stanton and Serafina received new orders, they would continue as before. It was the best form of respect Stanton could offer at the moment, until such time as he could allow himself to grieve.

Stanton squinted as the sun came out from behind a small cloud. Provided the skies stayed clear, they might even be able to see the Cathedral's spire just before twilight. Stanton longed for its comforting sight, a sign from the Almighty that His hand had guided them thus far, and that His protection would continue to be with them. They needed all of the help they could rally.

He knew the spire's sight would ease the minds of the people he and the Consorts protected. Inside the comforting embrace of the walls and iron gates were hundreds of soldiers and guards who could, and would, be called upon to defend the lives of civilians and clergy alike. The walls and attached towers had a permanent division of archers poised, ever prepared for an assault, a strike, or even a riot.

Once inside, he could get his people proper medical attention and healing. He could then confer with the Holy Father himself, plus the cardinals, and the other guard captains. In unison, they could decide their next move and avenge the life of the Arbiter and every single innocent taken by that Cartossian butcher.

Stanton cleared his throat, even if his thoughts were his own. He did not want his expression to change, and he knew it did at the mere thought of her beautiful, vulnerable, elegant face. He shoved the Arbiter's name, her face, and her voice to the very back of his mind. He could not dwell on her until all of these people were safe. His grief would have to wait. These peoples' lives all hung in the balance and he would not have their deaths upon his soul. This wasn't his first crisis, nor, he feared, his last. He knew what to do, and getting these nobles and clergy, along with the servants and locals, to Orsini and out of harm's way was what he was going to do.

He comforted himself that she would have understood. If ghosts were real, he was certain she would've appeared to him and offered that very advice: grieve when duty is discharged. It was why he did not rush through the flames to get her. It was why he did not abandon these people to comb the mountainside for her. His duty was to these people, and not to his weeping heart. She would've understood. It was why he loved her.

And as for safety, they were far from it. Bonacieux's army was behind them, ever pushing. A small cavalry unit harried them a few times, assaulting the back ranks with arrows and swords. They'd suffered losses from the attacks, but it could have been worse. It surprised Stanton that it wasn't worse.

The General's army moved far slower than Stanton had calculated. They should have been overtaken by at least Bonacieux's full cavalry's might, if not the main force. His army could have marched through the night and cleared the distance. Stanton could not decide if it was arrogance or the beasts that slowed Bonacieux's progress. He decided not to dwell on that point, either. Instead, this was a blessing from the Lord God Almighty and he would take whatever help He deemed to provide.

Stanton had not seen the demon, but he'd heard its screams. As far as anyone knew, Lex had been the only one to escape the battle with the demon. He'd not asked Lex yet what he'd seen, since the poor boy's night terror screams continued sending chills down everyone's spines. A day before, Father Michael had managed to procure a special herb from a humble chapel and had instructed Nathan to keep it flowing in the tea. Lex's first night without nightmares had been a relief for everyone, and Nathan shared the tea with the others who were struggling.

Stanton was happy for the tea, but not about leaving the sisters behind who'd helped them. They reasoned stragglers may need shelter. Bonacieux would not murder innocent sisters, they were certain. Stanton and Father Michael both warned the women, but they were insistent on remaining at their post in the service of the Almighty. In the end, it was Stanton who convinced Father Michael to leave them. Their duty was to the Almighty and they had sworn an oath to service. Their service was different than his, but no less important. He could understand that. Father Michael refused to see it in that light, though he eventually relented.

From atop a carriage, Father Michael waved to get Stanton's attention. He turned his horse around and waited for the bishop's carriage to catch up to him, then he trotted alongside. Next to Father Michael sat one of the stable boys from the abbey, holding the reins in pale knuckles. On the other side of the boy sat the stable master. And curled close to him was a sleeping dirty-faced little girl.

Stanton nodded and said to the boy, "How goes the lesson?"

Miles, the stable master, shrugged. "He's too wee of a lad to handle these horses properly, but he's getting the hang of it enough in case..."

Father Michael put a reassuring hand on the boy's shoulder. "He's picking it up fast. He might be a coachman when he grows up."

"Aye. Good job for the lad in that, too," said Miles. "Molly here is too little still. The reins are too big for her tiny fingers. Isn't that right, my girl?"

Molly gave no answer, hopefully lost in happy dreams.

Miles laughed. "That girl can sleep through anything."

The boy, whose name Stanton didn't know, offered a shaky smile, but went back to concentrating on the reins and the horses. Many of the carriages were doing the same, after the first attack where two men were slaughtered before the Consorts could stop them. They'd taken out the carriage driver and the horses panicked. In the end, they'd lost two carriages and three horses had to be put down due to their injuries. Four people were killed, with six more injured.

"How goes the front?" Father Michael asked. He'd been caught in only his trousers during the attack. He still wore them, despite the small holes where sparks had burned through the fabric. The fire-singed dark trousers did not match the yellow pelisse and patchwork quilt he'd paired with it, but at least it looked warmer than being shirtless.

"The front is as anxious as the rear, Father."

Father Michael smiled, shaking his head. "My dear Captain, the front is closer to safety than us poor souls in the rear."

It was difficult to smile, but Stanton forced one out to prop up the bishop's spirits. "This is why you are a bishop and I am a mere soldier, Father. You have the sense of the people's heart."

A bark of laughter escaped Father Michael. "Those of us tasked with protecting the rear worry. There will be much relief when we can all see the spire, I think. Even the thought of the safety of the Cathedral and its walls gives me comfort."

"Not the Almighty?"

"The Almighty saw fit to ensure the Cathedral's original builders encircled it with stone walls and towers. Celebrating its walls is celebrating the Almighty's hand in our lives. So, how do you fare, Captain?"

"I endure," he said, unable and unwilling to bring any conversation to the Arbiter's disappearance.

If *she* were alive, she would have caught up to them by now. Cram, for all of his faults, would have gotten her here, or would have gotten himself here. Same with Dodd and several of the others who were also missing.

He couldn't keep his mind from spinning the various calculations. If she took the mountain pass, most likely because of Bonacieux's men, it's possible she wouldn't arrive for days or even weeks, if she were on foot. If she were injured, maybe longer. Of course, if she were alone and injured, she'd never make the journey. She'd perish somewhere on those slopes.

If Cram were alive, though. Cram would make it. He'd get her home to him, one way or another. He had to hope and pray and trust.

Father Michael eyed him during the silence. "Captain, be strong. I pray to the Lord God Almighty every hour for not just her safe return, but the return of all of our brave Consorts who are missing. I also pray for those courageous elementals who risked their very lives to allow us the time for our escape. None of us could have taken on a demon from the abyss, and yet they did that for us, their enslavers. Oh, don't give me that look, Captain. I know they did not have to help us, but they did willingly, and without any support or assurance. I believe I shall write to the Holy Father himself when I arrive in Orsini and tell him of the bravery of the elemental mages at Orsini."

"I'm sure Walter Cram would have appreciated that."

"As would have she." Father Michael didn't say *her* name to him, which suited him just fine. Each time someone said the Contessa's name, a dagger scraped across his soul. "I still have hope for Walter Cram's return as well. He was nothing if not an irritating man, who was the cause of at least half of what he complained, but we were the better for him in this world. I do not wish him departed. I fear we still need him."

Desperate to drag the conversation away from anything like mourning or reflection, Stanton said, "It was because of him that we had to arrest one of the brothers over the winter months."

Father Michael rolled his eyes. "As I said, my son, he *is* an irritating man."

Stanton appreciated the emphasis. He said, "I have to check on the rear. May the Almighty be with you, Father."

"We shall make it to safety."

"I hope that is prophetic wisdom, Father."

"I lack that particular talent," Father Michael said, with a laugh. "I can only give an old man's hunch."

"You're not that much older than myself, and I am not old."

"Ah, but you have a full head of hair still, and the hairline adds wisdom as it recedes," Father Michael said. "At least, that is what I use to comfort myself in the mirror."

Stanton laughed and turned his horse around to continue down the caravan. He nodded and waved, shared quick greetings, and answered short questions as he passed by the various carriages and carts that housed people, animals, personal items, and supplies.

His eyes watered in the wind. Still no sign of rain, though, so the wind would keep the roads good and dry. He knew everyone would want to keep going, but the horses were exhausted. They'd been pushing them hard to get this far. At least they didn't have much in the way of livestock with them. He, along with Father Michael, had managed to convince the farmers to take their herds into the mountains. There wasn't much grazing up there, but at least the animals (and farmers) wouldn't be slaughtered by Bonacieux's men.

They still had some chickens, and a couple goats, and all the dogs they could grab from the abbey's stables. Even some cats and kittens were found and stuffed into the carriages with children in hopes to stop the wailing. A traveling merchant and apothecary had joined them, with their donkeys and dogs. Stanton turned no one away. Neither did Father Michael. Together, they represented Arbiter and Pope. Who could stand against them?

His heart suddenly pounded, the rise of old memories causing a pressure in his chest. Stanton managed to gain control before he lost himself in bad reminiscences, from a time when he didn't know what he was doing. More than anyone else here, he knew what was at stake for these people. He'd lived through it before. And no matter what François and the King had always said to him, he'd always felt responsible for the lives lost in that attack so long ago. He would try not to make the same mistakes he's made before; one of those mistakes was wearing out the horses. The other, was resting too long.

Perhaps the reason he'd made so many mistakes was because he wasn't omniscient. That's what *she* had said to him one night in bed.

In due time, he pulled alongside Rahna and Martin. Both were on horseback, keeping watch over the very rear of the caravan. Stanton tried switching out the Consorts as much as possible— rest made for sharper eyes—but he'd been pleased with Rahna and Martin's work. They handled the stress well. Rahna might have been their newest recruit, hired specifically for her ability to act like a living battering ram, but she showed a sturdiness of character that well suited her for the job.

Rahna's face was still covered in scabs and angry blisters, though Stanton was assured by the apothecary that her extreme paleness made them look worse than they were. When she'd come out of the bishop's bedroom with him, her face had been a mask of blood, but it turned out to be mostly tiny splinters from a falling beam. The burns were from the flames that licked the beam as it crashed to the floor. She'd been struck in the face with splinters and flame. She'd have minor scars, of course, but even those would eventually fade away. That was good.

Rahna gave him a twitchy smile. A drop of blood appeared at the corner of her mouth, in one of the cracks between scabs. She winced. So did he.

"Hello, Captain! I was about to swing around the bushes and give Beatrix a hand."

"Good plan," Stanton said. Rahna had dealt with her stress and inexperience appropriately, and he was pleased to see her staying busy and taking initiative. She had taken to scouting, after the last attack, and had been tagging along with the more experienced Consorts.

Once she'd left, Stanton asked Martin, "Any problems?"

"With the caravan? Nothing." He pointed his chin at the carriage. "Lex is bleeding again."

Stanton made an annoyed sound.

"We used the last healing stone on him. I did a check. All of our jackets' healing buttons are used up. One of the viscounts had a healing hankie or whatever. I stuffed that in Lex's guts, but…Lex needs a surgeon and a healer."

"We can't go any faster," Stanton argued.

"Can't we send him on horseback? Let Orsini know we're coming?"

Stanton shook his head. "Lex would bleed to death."

"He might anyway without help," Martin said darkly.

"I heard that," came a thin, but surprisingly cheerful, voice from inside the wooden carriage.

Stanton managed a very stern tone. "You're supposed to be resting, Lex."

The carriage shutter opened. A thin-faced kid stuck his head out, along with three big dogs, tongues all lolling to one side. Lex's cheekbones were always sharp enough to cut leather, but they were far more sunken and gaunt than usual. His eyes had dark circles under them, but his smile was still strong.

"Some of us are trying to not to bleed to death here, but it's really hard when everyone seems convinced it's going to happen."

Stanton smiled. "I wasn't talking about your death. Martin here was. He worries."

"Martin needs to enjoy his role as leader for as long as he can, because it's not going to last as soon as I can fucking stand."

Stanton reached into his saddle bag and pulled out a hunk of cheese. He pulled alongside the carriage and passed the small piece in. "You're hungry. It's making you grumpy."

Lex snatched the cheese before the dogs could and asked, "Got any bread?"

Stanton rolled his eyes dramatically before pulling out a small round loaf. He passed that through the window. "You eat more than I do."

"The dogs are hungry," Lex said. He broke off a piece for each gaping maw before ripping off his own piece. "Besides, I'm injured. I need to keep up my strength. I'm wasting away. I could die. Martin just said so."

"That's what you get for not putting on any weight all these years. I said you were always too thin. Didn't I, Martin?"

"You did, Captain. And did Lex listen? No, sir, he didn't. Now look where we are, sir. Wasting away, sir."

Stanton gave Lex a "well, there" look.

"It's not my fault Dodd was eating off my plate, stealing my food." Lex's features darkened at the mention of his childhood friend. "Bonacieux is going to regret meeting any of us."

"He could still be..."

"Don't."

Stanton stopped speaking. He was doing the same with the Arbiter, unable to even say her name in his thoughts. He had to keep the walls firmly intact, and he understood all too well that Lex needed his own walls up. Lex had to heal. Sobbing over his lost childhood friend would not knit the skin back any faster.

"Sorry, Lex."

"Yeah. Well." A beat passed before Lex brightened his features and, voice back to its usual cheer, though it was a touch forced this time, asked, "Either of you got any wine?"

"No, Lex. I am not carrying bottles of wine with me. And, if I was, I would not share them with you and the dogs."

Lex made an annoyed sound. "Too bad. *Oh.*"

"What?"

"Father Michael's wine cellar is gone, isn't it? That's just...mean."

They shared a look and then burst out laughing. It hurt to laugh. Yet, it felt good because it was the proof Stanton needed that they were still alive. He could not bring back the dead. He would grieve and mourn when it was safe, but for now, it was good to just remember they were alive.

"You know, I think I have the key to the Orsini cellar back in my old desk."

"You are my favorite Captain, sir."

CHAPTER TWO

ALLEGRA FINALLY GAVE into the pain. She announced, voice cracking, that she couldn't go on. Dodd said it was getting dark anyway; worse, the clouds had moved in to obscure the moonlight. Dodd and Walter left her leaning against a tree until they found a suitable evergreen to sleep under. Dodd and Walter helped her to a nearby rock, as tears streamed down her face from the pain. Her thoughts were incoherent. All she could think about was making the pain cease. She struggled to form sentences. She simply wanted a moment's release from the pain.

It felt like an eternity of the two men dragging broken boughs and branches over to a particular majestic spruce tree with wide, low-hanging branches. They swore and bickered as they worked, but they worked. Finally, when they were both satisfied with their bed for the night, they helped her back over, easing her down carefully to the middle of the pile.

"How's that?" Walter asked.

"It's not as cold down here," she said. The wind had picked up, too, and that was a torment on the flesh all on its own.

She eased herself down and rolled on her side like she always did. Dodd took position behind her, rolling away from her to fan out the boughs around them as if it was a natural part of the tree. Walter eased in front of her, facing away, and did the same.

"This is a great spot," Walter said when he finished working. "If you're going to stop, stopping next to uprooted trees is a great spot. Natural wind barrier!"

She tried to laugh, but the sound that escaped her was feeble. The trees groaned and creaked around them. She broke off a piece of tree that scratched at her ear, and the scent of spruce filled the air. As long as she didn't move too much, the little needles didn't poke at her, and made for a surprisingly comfortable bed, considering their circumstances.

She yawned. Exhaustion from the exercise, the stress, hunger, and the ever-present pain in her ankle stripped her of all strength. Yet, her mind was on edge still and sleep was not immediate.

Dodd's stomach made a mournful sound. "Oh my fucking lord, I am so hungry. Why are there no houses around here? My stomach is eating itself, I'm sure of it."

"We're in a forest on the side of a mountain," Walter said.

"That's no excuse! What about the logging cabins? Huh? What about them?" Dodd asked. "I would love a pie right about now. A nice, juicy gammon pie. Contessa? What do you want?"

"I'd love a pound cake," Allegra said. Her stomach made a gurgling sound. "The entire cake. How about you, Walter?"

He sighed, but said, "Soup, with the bone marrow all floating on top. Loads of turnip, too."

Dodd made a disgusted sound. "Potatoes, man."

"Oh, potatoes are good, too, but there's something special about turnip."

"I'd murder a cardinal for some potatoes," Dodd said.

"Which cardinal?" Allegra asked.

That made them all laugh. They shared several more minutes, chatting through all of their current cravings. Pie in all forms was high on the list, as were potatoes, butter, gravy, bread, jam, cake, coffee, tea, sugar in all forms, stew, and turnips for Walter.

Finally, as the laughter began to die down, Allegra said, "To be honest, I'd rather deal with hunger than this horrible pain."

"Do you want another button?" Dodd asked.

"You should take it," Walter said.

She struggled with this every night. Sometimes, she accepted the healing device of Dodd's, but other times, she refused. She did not have any supplies to make any sort of healing device, but even then, she could not be certain of her ability. Walter said he was getting worse at making items, as opposed to improving, and said he'd stopped when the last scarf he'd knitted burnt the owner. Likewise, Allegra worried about what she'd create while terrified and in pain. She could do herself more harm than good.

That left Dodd's buttons. Innocuous as a fashion item, they were one of the special emergency items given to all Consorts. Her concern was a matter of severity. If one of them broke a limb or lacerated themselves, those healing buttons could mean the difference between bleeding to death and holding together long enough to get help.

The choice rubbed Allegra. She hated having to make it every single night.

"There's still some shine in the one from a couple nights ago," Dodd said. "Use that one. I can't sew it back on anyway. All it's doing is keeping cozy in my pocket."

"Allegra, please," Walter said.

The pain won the argument. She accepted the little bobble and reached down to position it as close to her ankle as position. Carefully, she lowered her leg back down and concentrated on keeping her foot still– an easy task since rolling her foot clockwise caused eye-watering pain.

"Contessa, I have a weird question."

"What is it?"

"With Queen Portia dead, who is next in line for the throne?" Dodd asked. "I just realized I had no idea."

"I didn't know you cared about politics, Dodd," Walter said. "The things you learn when you travel with strangers in the forest."

"I mean, I don't give a shit about politics if you want the Lord's truth, but I'm bored and I'm curious."

"I don't believe she named an heir. It's not like anyone expected her death anytime soon," Allegra said. She thought on it and finally said, "I suppose Katherine – Grand Duchess Katherine – will be named temporary regent until the best claimant is determined."

"Wouldn't she have the best claim?" Walter asked.

Allegra closed her eyes as a little warm spot formed on her ankle. It sent a shiver through her spine as it tried to chase out the cold from her bones. "It's arguable, but she's probably the best to keep the ship afloat, as it were. There are so many parties who will come forward that, unless Portia named an heir that no one knows about, it might be years before they straighten it out. They might even need the Cathedral's help to arbitrate."

"Assuming Bonacieux isn't planning a coup," Walter said.

Allegra's breath caught in her throat. She had been wondering throughout this entire process what he gained by killing Portia. Yes, he was a zealot, but why didn't he simply arrest and charge her? A mock trial would give him time to get his own puppet on the throne. Instead, he outright murdered her.

"Contessa?" Dodd asked, concerned.

"I just had the most horrible thought. What if he is waiting for reinforcements? What if his plan was to take the throne all along?"

Dodd whistled. "Then we're probably all fucked."

It came as no surprise to Allegra that she did not sleep soundly that night.

THE CARAVAN'S ARRIVAL at the great Cathedral was every drop the dramatic tableau the court gossips loved, Stanton thought bitterly. Stanton had instructed the coachmen to keep their pace steady to avoid undue alarm. However, as soon as the path widened into the cobblestone road that announced the Cathedral's entrance, coachmen and horsemen alike whipped a hoof-pounding, heart-racing charge for the gates. Safety was inside those walls and none would dawdle for the sake of sensibility and decorum.

"Out of the way!" the lead coachman shouted over pounding hooves. Lollygaggers previously wrapped up in their own concerns jumped out of the way, some falling, some crashing into their own carts, all falling out of the way.

He couldn't condemn the coachmen, since he also spurred his own horse to match the charging speed of the carriages desperate for safety. In the distance, Cathedral guards rushed toward the racing caravan.

Then Stanton was recognized. And the Consorts' green

jackets. And then Father Michael. Then, when no Arbiter appeared, the people knew. The wailing and the shouting began. The convoy charged past the guards. They charged past the merchants and vendors. There was no stopping until they were in front of Orsini Palace itself.

There were gasps and cries when the crowd realized it wasn't just a ragtag group who did not know how to control their horses; these were some of the greatest of Serna's nobility racing through the gates. The crowd gathered about them, pressing, yelling, shouting.

Stanton swung himself off his exhausted horse, shouting as he did, "Martin! Get Lex to a surgeon! Now!"

"On it, Captain!" Martin shouted as he dismounted.

"Rahna! Beatrix! Get the wounded out of the carriages. Carefully, do you hear me? Carefully."

Cries went up from the crowd at the knowledge there were injuries. More shouting, more pressing.

"Get back!" Stanton yelled at those directly in his path. "Out of my way!"

"Where is the Arbiter?" the crowd shouted.

"Out!" Stanton bellowed.

"Out of the way!" That was the Cathedral guards who'd been close enough to help. Those they'd left beyond the gate would still be sprinting to catch up to them. "Make room! Make room!"

To the two guards hurrying down the staircase toward them, Stanton said, "I need to see the Holy Father. Escort me through at once."

The younger of the two guards ignored the demand and blurted out a string of questions. "What has happened? Is that the Bishop of Borro Abbey? Where is the Arbiter? Why is she not with you?"

Stanton ignored her and looked over his shoulder at the argument behind him. He pushed the crowd out of his way until it parted enough for five guards to wedge themselves closer to the carriages. "Billy! Billy! Help Father Michael! Get them out of the carriages, carefully! Carefully! They are injured."

"Injured!" Up went the loud whispers and wails of the crowd.

Stanton ignored the crowd. He pushed back to the guards nearest the grand stairs and asked, "What's your name?"

"Archer Janet, Your Grace."

He ignored the use of his title. "You work with my Consorts to get these people inside into the ballroom. Get the fires lit and the kitchens to send up hot food and wine. Do you understand me? Ballroom. Fires. Food. Wine. Healers."

"Um, the ballroom is being prepared..."

"I don't care," Stanton snapped. He tried not to yell the words, but the crowd grew louder as more guards arrived to form a protective line around the carriage doors. "Do as I order. You. What's your name?"

"Corporal James, Captain."

"Take me to his Holiness. *Now*."

"Yes, Captain," James said.

Stanton trusted the duty of hospitality and medical attention to his junior soldiers, while he sprinted through the hallowed halls of Serna's holiest of places. He spared a quick prayer for help as he passed Tasmin's portrait on the wall, asking she grant him the necessary tact and compassion, alongside swift detail, when he told the Holy Father that his childhood friend was most likely dead, and that war had erupted. She had faced greater trials in her life; may her hand be upon him now.

"Out of the way!" James shouted at various guards near the entrance from the public to private areas. "Captain Rainier to see the Holy Father!"

"This is business that cannot be delayed!" Stanton shouted. He managed to skid to a stop in front of the closed door to the inner wing. "Open this door immediately."

"I'm sorry, Captain. The Holy Father is in conference and..."

"The Arbiter is likely murdered! Let me through, boy!" Stanton bellowed.

His voice boomed through the corridor. Shocked silence echoed painfully around him, as the entire gathered clergy and civilian alike soaked in the news. Then the rumble of whispers and gossip. Several glances at the door from whence they had come;

the world had changed and only now were they being made aware of it.

The guard stared at Stanton, shock rendering him unable to speak.

"Boy, the door," Stanton said, this time not shouting, but his voice clear and determined.

"Yes, Captain," the other guard said, turning his back on them to open the door wide for them to charge through. "The Holy Father should be in the ballroom, Captain. They are preparing for the spring ball."

Stanton had completely forgotten about that. He'd lost track of all time at Borro, where his nights had been filled with Allegra's warmth and his days with a dedication to peace. It had been a long winter, and the thaw wasn't improving matters, but they had survived and thrived. He'd not taken the assignment to fall in love, but he had. And now it was all gone.

He shook his head and gritted his teeth. There was no time for grief. He was about to break the worst news to the Holy Father threefold, and he was not going to be anything but professional.

"Wounded will be coming through here. See that they are led to the ballroom," Stanton said.

"But the..." the younger guard said.

"Yes, Captain," said the other guard. "We'll see to it."

"But..."

"Shut your fucking mouth," the guard said. "Do you know the way, Captain?"

Stanton gave him a curt nod, and he and his escort rushed down the inner sanctum's corridors. He supposed he didn't actually need the escort; he probably knew the way better than James. However, he might need a messenger, and the corporal would be useful.

Stanton skidded into the ballroom and shouted out, "Holy Father? Where is the Holy Father?"

At least two dozen scribes were in the room, along with as many members of the clergy, all in various robes of their orders and appointments. Their bickering continued for a handful of seconds after Stanton's arrival. Some continued to argue, even as silence fell upon the others, as if there was nothing happening beyond their walls. As if an army wasn't soon about to reach their gates. As if the world wasn't on fire.

The Holy Father stepped around the crowd. "Rainier! What in the Almighty's name...what has happened? Look at the state of you. Good God, you're covered in blood. Are you injured? What has happened?"

"Holy Father, the wounded are coming now. The guards have orders to bring them here at once."

"This is *not* the appropriate place…" one bishop began, from the scholar's guild.

"We are clearly busy," said an old mother, from one of the healing orders.

"Excuse me, but I don't give a good goddamn what you think," Stanton said. His curse elicited gasps. His language was simply not done in this place.

"Where is Allegra?" the Holy Father asked, his voice low and commanding. "And explain to me why you are covered in blood."

Stanton realized at that moment that he was wearing the same clothes he'd been wearing when he'd carried Lex out of the burning abbey. He'd used his jacket's enchantments to slow Lex's bleeding. His healing buttons had been spent quickly; Lex was bleeding heavily in those early moments of the abbey's destruction. His jacket had been passed around for the warmth enchantments, to protect the children. Eventually, those wore out, too, and his jacket was returned to him. Just a regular piece of fabric covered in blood.

No wonder they'd all looked so shocked. He must have looked as though he'd faced off with death. Which he had.

The exhaustion suddenly hit Stanton, the gravity of what he was about to say finally. Her name was about to escape his lips. He didn't know if he had the strength for it in front of all these people.

"Your Radiance," Stanton said, now very tired. "We must talk in private. The situation is grave."

"Captain, we are very busy—"

"Silence!" the Holy Father snapped. "Where is Allegra?"

Stanton licked his lips. He took a long, deep breath and said, "I believe she died when Borro Abbey collapsed." The room fell into shocked silence. "Your Radiance, please trust me. What I have to say needs to be said in private."

"How could it collapse? It's a damn mountain." Stanton immediately recognized Pero's voice. He pushed through the stunned clerics and passed his papers to a scribe. He put a supportive hand on his husband's back. "How could it collapse with Allegra inside?"

"Why are you covered in blood?" asked a priest. He recognized her though he did not know her name. Her voice quavered. "There's so much blood. What has happened?"

Stanton did not want to deliver the news like this, but he was exhausted, hungry, and cold. He was nearly in as much shock as the Holy Father appeared to be. He tried to keep his voice low so that the people gawking in the corridors wouldn't hear.

"Captain?" Pero whispered. "What has happened?"

In as low of a voice as he could muster, Stanton said, "Cartossa's General Bonacieux attacked the abbey when a massive demon was brought forth through a portal."

Everyone just stared at him.

"Walter Cram, the elemental rebel, and…the Arbiter organized a group of elementals to take on the fiend. However, Bonacieux's men burned the abbey. The only person from above that made it out was Lieutenant Lex, who is gravely injured and is in need of a surgeon and a healer. However, he has been able to tell us that he witnessed Bonacieux kill Queen Portia. Then, as we were fleeing the burning abbey, it collapsed in on itself. We believe that killed the demon and closed the fissure."

"*What?*" Francois demanded.

It sounded like nonsense even to his own head. Demons? Portals into the abyss? An attack by Cartossa? The murder of a queen? It was all too much, and how he wished it was a terrible dream.

Alas, it was not, and he had to try to explain the horror to these people. Who were planning a ball, of all things. A ball. The world was ending, and they were planning a party.

"*What?*"

"I beg you. We have to talk in private because there is an army coming to attack the Cathedral."

That roused the Holy Father from his shock. "No one would dare attack us! We are..."

"In grave danger, Your Holiness. Trust me when I say that we have perhaps a day or two, maximum, before Bonacieux arrives with his army and may the Lord God Almighty have mercy upon us when that happens."

To puncture the statement, Martin and Rahna burst into the room, shouting orders to guards carrying the maimed and injured. Martin completely ignored the audience of clergy and snapped, "Get them to the back corner. We have a couple hundred people to get inside. To the back."

"But you...Allegra told me there were over five hundred refugees alone," Pero said in a low, almost slurred voice. Like the life was draining out of him.

Stanton nodded gravely. "We took who we could."

"Captain! As soon as we got Lex out of the carriage, he started bleeding bad. We got him wrapped in healing buttons. I'm not sure what the surgeon is going to do, but she's with him."

Stanton nodded his head. "Good work. Get them inside."

That seemed to rouse some of the clergy. The mother with the healing order's insignia on her blue robe said, "Holy Father, may I send for our supplies? We have healing items stockpiled for such an emergency."

"Yes...yes, of course. Please," the Holy Father said, struggling to pull himself out of his daze. "Someone send for the servants. We need food, water, blankets, candles. Wine. Brandy. Run!"

Two scribes dropped their papers and pencils. They ran out of the door, pushing past a guard and a daisy chain of children, all holding hands. It broke Stanton's heart because they weren't weeping. They were stone-faced, the shock finally had fortified walls inside their sweet, innocent minds. One of the sisters stepped out from the group, toward the children, and encouraged them to come along and that snacks were on the way.

"Father…" Stanton pleaded now.

"Get the senior cardinals into my chambers immediately! Do you hear me? I don't care if they are on their death beds. Get them into my chambers *now*. You? Who are you?"

"This is James, he's the guard who helped me through."

"James. Get me the captains."

"Which ones?"

"*All of them.*"

CHAPTER THREE

THE SURGEON UTTERED her surprise that the stitches done by a "backwoods hack" didn't need to be corrected, though more were needed due to, as she put it, "refusing to sit still. Young man, I will tie you to the bed if you don't stay still." Beyond that threat, Lex was ordered on bed rest, and hourly boiled bone and onion broth.

Lex pretended not to hear the pope's personal apothecary's recommendation for wine laced with sleeping powders twice daily, and unlimited chamomile tea. As the surgeon had nodded her approval, Lex knew protesting would be pointless. It might even bring on another lecture from the surgeon.

Lex winced, and even cried out in pain, when the healer and his assistants took over. The assistants held Lex's arms out at his sides, while the healer tightly wrapped Lex's naked torso in a healing cloth. Tears filled Lex's eyes, from both the pain and the embarrassment of intimate exposure, but they went about the business as quick as possible.

"Can you breathe, boy?" the healer asked.

"Not well," Lex answered.

"Good," the healer said. He went back to pinning the cloth into place.

Lex listened to the assistant's story that this was from the vault of healing items for emergencies. The Holy Father himself authorized the distribution of such items, blah blah, fucking blah.

Lex knew the assistant meant well, but it hurt so damned much. It took everything in Lex's power not to slap the assistant and tell him to fuck off to the abyss.

The assistant continued on, explaining how this particular cloth was woven with great care by the Orsini Guild of Mages, clergy mages who devoted their lives to harnessing their magical abilities into potent healing items. These items were normally never distributed to the general populace, and these were kept in case of injury or sickness to the senior cardinals or even the Holy Father himself.

Something about their darkening expression must have clued the healer into the dark thoughts swimming around in Lex's mind because he cleared his throat and said, "The Lieutenant would like some silence."

When Lex didn't offer up a reply, the assistant fell silent.

"Oftentimes, the injured and sick do not wish to hear the prattle of assistants telling them how lucky they are to be receiving treatment," the healer said. He was pinning a new cloth over where Bonacieux's sword had tried to kill Lex, and nearly succeeded.

"Not to put too fine of a point on it," the surgeon said while she inspected the bandages, nodding her approval as she did, "You were lucky you did not bleed to death, child. Thank the Almighty you'd put your jacket on that day. That is the only reason you managed to crawl to help."

Lex did not feel lucky. Nor did Lex appreciate the *child* comment. Normally, those comments didn't rankle Lex. Some of the priests called Rainier *child*, and he was in his mid-thirties. But today, the word crawled deep under the skin and was an irritant. Lex already felt like an invalid; the *child* comment just rubbed it in.

Finally, the assistants pulled a clean, crisp tunic over Lex's head. There was an immediate sense of relief being covered up once more and not exposed to an entire room of strangers. Though, Lex did have to admit that they recognized them all by sight, and actually did know the surgeon. Even so, Lex was never comfortable with the forced intimacy of medicine, and this was no exception. Of course, it also didn't really matter what Lex felt. When one's guts are visible through one's skin, the surgeons don't seem to give a rat's kiss what the patient wants or feels.

Finally, the gaggle of medical professionals left—how did they all fit into the room? —and Lex was forced to face the silence alone once more. The apothecary said he would have wine and some bread brought up to the room, while the kitchens prepared the endless supply of restorative broth that would be needed for everyone. Lex was instructed to rest and, finally, they were left alone.

Of course, it would be impossible to rest without the sleeping powder. Father Michael had acquired some on the journey and thank the Almighty for that. Without wine or hard spirits, there was nothing Lex could use to drown out the nightmares. Lex knew in their heart that the powder was needed, even as Lex hated the idea of needing it.

That first night in the carriage, when both the pain and the nightmares were unbearable, Father Michael stayed with them. Lex didn't want Rainier to see them like that; Lex wouldn't have even wanted Dodd to see. They were in a bad way, in those early first days. There was something about Father Michael, though. He was a priest, and he was gentle when he spoke. His voice always put Lex at ease.

"Lex, my boy," Father Michael would say. Father Michael's accent would draw out the word *boy* and it always made Lex smirk back at the abbey. In the flight from the abbey, though, it was a balm. Like, someone was listening to every single word spoken. Lex needed that as their own body warred infection.

Then Father Michael told Lex war stories. The stories weren't all the priest's, Lex was certain, but likewise, some of the stories were too personal, too detailed, to be anyone other than Father Michael's. He never distinguished the stories, though. He just told them. Talking about the confessions he'd heard over the years, of soldiers who couldn't look at their own hands because the memories of blood were etched into their skin.

Lex was acutely uncomfortable during many of the stories. Yet, Lex also couldn't stop listening. That first night felt like a death vigil, and it most likely was. The bleeding just refused to stop. Lex developed a fever. A few times, Lex was too exhausted to speak and was mistaken for asleep. The others talked, either through the window as they traveled or whenever the caravan stopped to rest and water the horses. Father Michael had told Rainier to prepare himself; that Lex would not make the night.

But Lex did make that night. Nobles and clergy alike, complete strangers to Lex, handed over every single trinket they had. Some even suffered their own painful injuries to give up their healing stones for Lex's guts to stay put. And what did Lex's brain do to reward them? Screaming night terrors of a mangled demon crushing the heads of their friends. Of killing innocent children. Of nobles and clergy and chambermaids falling through collapsing floors, to be engulfed by the flames. Of being ripped limb from limb.

Lex closed their eyes, gulping down the rising of bile and panic. It faded into the back of Lex's mind, the comfort of Father Michael's words echoing over the sounds of a demon's shrieks: *People say the Lord God Almighty never gives us more than we can bear. I never believed that. I believe sometimes he misjudges and does gives us more than we can carry. That is why we have friends. Let your friends carry the burden, my son. Hold my hand and we will carry this burden together.*

Lex's heart wanted to weep, but their body was too exhausted for tears now. All that was left was the exhaustion and grief, the pain and the nightmares. Dodd wasn't coming back. New friendships did not come easily to Lex; while others preferred plenty of tight friends, Lex preferred a small net of one or two very close friends inside a circle of acquaintances. Now, that net was empty. The Contessa was gone. Dodd was gone. Lex was alone now.

Regret pulled at Lex. There had been times where Lex wondered if maybe, just maybe, something might happen with Dodd. Where friendship might cross over to another path. Lex had never told anyone, but one of the reasons Lex had never formed any serious attachments was because every single man Lex had met fell short of Dodd. Dodd had become Lex's standard.

"Oh, Lord God," Lex whimpered into the darkness of the room. "He's gone."

The bindings around Lex's torso were too tight, cutting off the air supply. Lex tried to claw at them, but accidentally hit the wound. Spots formed in Lex's vision, cutting off the panicked state into a haze of pain.

As the worst of the pain faded, a knock at the door startled Lex. A grim-faced Rainier stepped into the room, illuminating the darkness with his lantern. Behind him followed an unnecessary gaggle of cardinals. Lex pulled the patchwork blanket tight and stared at the sober expressions. The Holy Father came in last, and he looked so exhausted that he'd probably not even flinch if a demon offered him a cup of tea and some scones.

When no one spoke, Lex asked, "Is it a cancerous tumor?"

That seemed to break the tension. Pope François offered a light chuckle at the joke. It seemed forced, but at least he was trying. "The surgeon, the healer, and the apothecary all assure me that you will make a full recovery."

Lex nodded. "The Captain's looking worried. I thought maybe the surgeon said I was dying. I'm glad they weren't lying to me."

"Not at all. Given time, bed rest, and broth, you will soon be on your feet," Pope François said.

"*Strict* bed rest," Cardinal Giso said.

"*Hourly* broth," the captain corrected.

"Ah, yes. Mistress Nadira is *en route* to the kitchens now, to yell at them for not having broth on the boil already," the pope said. "Serves them right, too, for being unprepared. A place this large should always have broth on the boil. But, no, Lieutenant, it's nothing of that nature to concern yourself. By the Almighty's hand and the strictest adherence to surgeon orders, and you will mend. Alas, we are here because we need you to recount the final scenes at the abbey, upstairs in that vile moment."

Lex flinched and instinctively pulled the blanket tighter.

"I am aware of the grave difficulty of my request. Normally, I would never have allowed this conference nor forced this confidence. However, I believe our safety relies upon your knowledge. You are the only one to have survived the main battle with the demon. We need your help to survive whatever comes next."

Lex tucked the blanket under their chin, suddenly aware of how they were wearing only a sleeping tunic in this crowd of purple-robed cardinals. Lex wanted to crumple in on themselves, to form a ball of protection. However, the gash Bonacieux cut in Lex's guts made that impossible. It was difficult to sit up without a servant. A ball of limbs was impossible.

Lex had avoided reliving the tale until now. Rainier had hinted once, and Lex had turned him down. Lex wasn't ready, and Rainier had accepted that with grace. But as they looked at the gathered cardinals, Lex knew it was time.

Lex blew out a breath and nodded. "Yes, Your Radiance. I will try."

"Thank you," he said gravely.

"Some of it is a blur now. I remember situations, but I can't say if I'm remembering them in order or not. A lot happened, and I was badly injured for some of it."

"Do your best, Lex," Rainier said.

Lex nodded and ignored the sour taste in the back of their mouth, as bile rose. "Well, I don't know where to start, Your Graces. What do you want to know?"

"Start with how you ended up in the Queen's suite," the pope said.

"Right. Well, Cram was the one who got me that morning. Walter Cram, the elemental mage? He said we needed the Contessa because a demon had come through Queen Portia's bedroom wall."

"Why did that rabble-rouser have intimate access to the Arbiter's personal guards?"

Lex knew exactly what Cardinal Vanida was asking; The Contessa ranted endlessly about the man. "I don't know what you are asking, Cardinal."

Vanida puffed out a breath. "I'm asking why he was even allowed to speak to you without being arrested!"

"I don't think Walter Cram is important to this story," the Holy Father interjected. "Lieutenant Lex, please continue."

Lex decided not to correct the pope by saying that Cram was annoyingly important to the story; that would just get the cardinals all frothing at the mouth. They might as well wait for that part.

A knock interrupted them, and the apothecary walked in, surprised by the sight of a room full of cardinals. "My apologies,

Your Graces, Your Radiance. I have brought my patient bread and wine, until the broth is ready."

He handed Lex the double-handled mug and said, "Drink all of this. Try to eat some of the bread, too."

"Thank you," Lex said. They sipped the wine and winced at the bitterness. There was enough powder in it to sedate a horse. They took a bite of bread. Thankfully, that wasn't laced with drugs.

"So, what happened next? After you were fetched," the pope asked.

"Well, see, Cram explained about the demon, and by the time we all got to the Queen's bedroom, there were already several elemental mages working to contain the beast. I don't know how they got there or how much time has passed. I guess Cram sent for them, but I don't remember."

Lex let out a hiss of pain and winced. They used the opportunity to take a moment to regather and collect their thoughts. It was hard reliving the scene. That demon haunted Lex's nightmares, as did Queen Portia's screams, and the sword skewering Lex's body. A chill gripped their spine, and Lex blew out another breath, forceful and deliberate.

"Take your time, my son," Pope François said. "I understand."

Lex nodded, grateful for both the acknowledgment and that it wasn't a long, drawn out discussion about feelings and nightmares. Lex wasn't ready for that; Lex was never ready for that. The only person who could even trick Lex into *that* kind of conversation was never coming back.

"So, anyway, Cram helped the mages to control the demon. I guarded their backs, since they obviously had their hands full. During all that, that's when…Well, I'm not sure how to say this part."

"Just say it," Rainier said.

"Well, see, Queen Portia was an elemental mage. She helped them fight the demon." There was a collective gasp. Lex interjected before the others could interrupt. "She was really scared. The Queen, I mean. But Cram and the Contessa told her she needed to help, so she did. They needed her help, too. That thing was…something else."

"Are you saying the Contessa already knew?" Cardinal Vanida demanded. His face was growing redder by the second. "Are you saying the Arbiter *knew* the Queen of Cartossa was an elemental mage?"

Thankfully, the drugs hadn't started working yet. There was no way Lex was getting in the middle of Vanida's twisted world while they still had their undrugged wits about them. "I never said anything of the kind, Your Grace."

"If the Arbiter knew Queen Portia was an elemental mage, she broke the law in not reporting her," Cardinal Vanida said. "We should censure her."

"She might be dead!" Cardinal Giso said in a scandalized tone. "Let's put the politics aside for once, Vanida."

"The rules are the rules," Cardinal Vanida said loftily, like his opinion mattered to Lex.

Lex lifted a hand to interject. That got the others a stern look from the pope and Giso bit back his reply. "*Actually*, Your Grace, the Contessa granted safe passage to any elemental mage living at Borro Abbey or in the town. They couldn't be arrested just for being elemental mages. So even if she knew, the Queen was still doing well within the Arbiter's rules for life at Borro."

"She broke the law, too!" Cardinal Vanida exclaimed. "Are you people listening to this?"

The pope raised his hand. "Let's focus. Lieutenant Lex, what happened after Queen Portia joined the fight?"

"No! I will not focus. This entire situation could have been avoided if Lieutenant Lex and the Arbiter had done their job and arrested all of the mages!"

Lex pulled back a little from that. How dare this pompous ass of a cardinal think he had any clue what it was like in the abbey? They survived the winter because the Contessa had granted mages immunity. That was why they weren't burnt alive in their beds long before Bonacieux's men showed up with their torches.

Lex raised their voice, hoping to cut off the stream of bile coming from Vanida's mouth. "Without the mages—"

"Those mages are murderers!" Cardinal Vanida roared.

"They saved us!" Lex shouted back, an action that brought a racking cough. "They're the only reason—"

"They're the only reason the demon was there in the first place!" Vanida shouted.

"Let the poor boy speak! He's on his death bed, you old fool!" Giso bellowed.

"I'm not dying..." Lex protested.

"This *poor boy* is a senior Consort who...who...did not do his duty!" Vanida's spittle hit Lex in the face.

"That is a lie!" Rainier roared in a voice Lex rarely heard come from the captain. It was a deep sound that announced imminent danger. "How *dare* you accuse one of my men of dereliction of duty, Your Grace? How dare you!"

"Enough!" the pope finally shouted over them all. "Enough!"

After they settled into merely glaring at each other, and Vanida was no longer in danger of a stroke, the pope added, "I apologize, Lieutenant Lex. Our manners seem to be running away with our fears today. Please, continue. And *no one* will be interrupting you this time."

Lex gave the Cardinals a moment to interject, but they clearly knew their own chain-of-command, too. The cardinals listened intently as Lex tried to relay the details without emotion. Just the facts. Mages fetched. Mages fought. Bonacieux stabbed. Lex escaped.

After those basic details were laid out, it was the time to add in the little half-truth. "Your Radiance, I'm afraid that Bonacieux plans to tell everyone the Contessa is an elemental mage."

"Why would you say that, Lex?" Rainier asked. They'd not rehearsed the story, but Rainier was a smart chap.

"I agree. Why would you think that?"

At that moment, Lex *knew* Pope François absolutely knew that his childhood friend was an elemental mage. The man needed a better card face because Lex was not buying the fake surprise. "The Contessa had been throwing lit pieces of wood at the demon. She isn't an elemental, of course, but we'd all seen that the demon reacted to fire. So, she used the tools at hand to attack it."

Lex didn't move their gaze away from the pope, who held Lex's eyes with his own. An unspoken understanding took place between them. Another person was brought into the pact to keep the Contessa's secret safe.

"What happened when Bonacieux showed up?" the pope finally asked.

"Well, my back was turned, you see, so I'm not completely certain. I know the Contessa had already collapsed. I think Cram said the demon had swiped at her or something like that, but it's all a haze to be honest. A lot was going on at the time. A lot of people were hurt or…dead…by that point."

Lex knew lies would be too complicated to remember, especially now that the wine was starting to work. *I don't remember* and *I didn't see it* were great weasel words.

"This is what I remember clearly. She was on the floor and had dropped one of the pieces of kindling she'd been using. Bonacieux murdered Queen Portia and shoved her into the portal. Then," Lex shuddered, "he stabbed me. The Contessa tried to throw her piece of wood at him, but she was too hurt. I remember seeing sparks and it honestly looked like she was casting a spell at him. But it was just that piece of kindling sparking. Bonacieux called her a bunch of horrible names and then said he was going to tell everyone what she was. Then he left us to burn to death. Or, me to bleed to death, I suppose. Asshole."

One of the very wrinkled cardinals asked, "Are you saying that the Arbiter caught the Abbey on fire?"

"No. The building was already on fire. We could smell the smoke upstairs."

"Why didn't do you anything?" someone asked.

"Because there was a giant fucking demon in front of us. Excuse my language, Your Radiance."

"Under the circumstances, please do not feel the need to edit your words," the pope said.

"Witnesses say Cartossian soldiers caught the abbey on fire. Do you believe that?" asked Cardinal Giso.

The Contessa always spoke well of him, but Lex wanted to be cautious. So, Lex offered a shrug and the truth. "I have no idea, Your Grace. I was upstairs with the demon and the mages."

"Why *were* you there? Are you a mage?" Cardinal DeLancey asked.

"No, Your Ladyship, I am not a mage."

She was about to ask a follow up question, but Cardinal Vanida interrupted her. "Why would the mages trust you? Are mages not inherently untrustworthy about…what do they call us? *Normals?*"

Lex did *not* like where this was heading. DeLancey tried shushing Vanida, but he refused to give way. He demanded Lex answer before Lex finally said, "The mages knew me."

"How?" Vanida demanded. "How did the mages know you well enough to know they could trust you?"

"I was a part of the Contessa's *personal* security. I was tasked with protecting her, but I was also there during the riot. Along with Lieutenant…*Dodd*. We went everywhere with the Contessa. Under her orders, we were fair to the elemental mages. In fact, we arrested anyone who harassed them, all on the Contessa's order. To be blunt, I never gave the mages a reason not to trust me."

"Then you admit you were not doing your duty?" Vanida asked.

"I was following orders," Lex said flatly.

"You were not following the orders of the Lord God Almighty. François, it's clear that this Consort is nothing more than a mage lover who…"

Lex grabbed the gold necklaces that hung around Cardinal Vanida's neck and dragged him down to eye level. "Who the fuck do you think you are?"

"Let me go!" the cardinal squeaked.

"Lex!" Rainier said sharply.

"It is *your* fault the Contessa is dead. If you hadn't blocked the shipments of bread coming to the Abbey, we wouldn't have had a riot. Little Ferret wouldn't have ended up on the scaffold. Nineteen people wouldn't have died in the Borro riot. You fucking paper-pushing piece of…"

"That is enough!" Rainier roared. "Lex! This is a cardinal."

Lex pushed the Cardinal away, wincing from the sharp pain in their side as they did. "Piece of rotting shit."

Cardinal Vanida brushed down the front of his robes. When he spoke, his face was red with rage. "I demand this man…"

"Oh, shut up, Vanida. For the love of God, man!" François said. Then his tone turned dark. "Is it true? Did you block a shipment of bread?"

"I do not have to..."

"Did you block it?" It was the Holy Father's turn to roar with anger.

"Unlike the rest of you, I was doing what was right."

Rainier let out a shocked sound. "*Right?* Borro was overrun with refugees over the winter, and you were the reason we went hungry? How is that right?"

Cardinal Vanida puffed out his chest. "I will not compromise my beliefs for anyone."

Cardinal DeLancey tutted. "You need the hard conservatives to vote for your reform bill and they hate you. You only did this to warm them to you."

Cardinal Vanida sneered.

"When this crisis is over, you will stand before the censure board," the pope said, and there was a surprised gasp in the room.

"I beg your pardon?"

"Please see the healers to have your ears cleaned. Lieutenant Lex, please, ease yourself. What is done is done. You will only delay your recovery if you excite yourself. Be at peace."

Lex lowered their head in shame. Rainier exhaled, an annoyed sound, but carefully pushed against Lex's shoulders, easing them back into the pile of pillows. "Easy now, Lex. The Holy Father is right."

"I'm sorry, Captain," Lex managed to say, exhaustion, pain, and drugs all washing over their body in waves now.

"You should be…" Vanida began but was cut off by a smack across the forearm from Giso. "Ow."

"What the good father means is that we all understand you are under significant stress. All of us lash out when we are hurting, and you, my child, are hurting. It is time to lay down your burden." The pope smiled. "You did good in the eyes of the Lord God Almighty, and in my eyes, too. Now, you are ordered to rest and to heal."

"Yes, Your Radiance," Lex said meekly. All the fight was gone now. Just pain, weariness, and grief.

The pope put a hand on Lex's shoulder, a gentle touch like he was afraid to cause more pain. He closed his eyes and said, "Lord God Almighty, heal this brave protector."

Lex bit their trembling lowered lip until it hurt more than the sword wound.

Francois gave Lex a final, but supportive, smile, and then, in a harsher tone, said, "Everyone? In my chambers."

A cardinal Lex recognized, but didn't know the name, cleared his throat. "I wish to ask…"

"*Now.*"

Francois looked at Captain Rainier. "You, too. My chambers."

"I'd like a word in private with Lex, if you don't mind, Your Radiance."

Francois nodded and, when the door finally closed behind them, Rainier asked, "Did she try to use fire on him? Allegra, I mean."

Lex struggled to answer. Whatever the apothecary had put in the wine was kicking in full force now. "She was so weak that…honestly? Captain, if I hadn't known, I would have sworn she was pulling a trick for kids. Do you think they believed me?"

"I don't think it matters anymore. François will repeat whatever you say. What's more, if Cram and…Allegra miraculously make it back, you've already established that Cram was busy and she was nearly unconscious. If they happen to spill a different story, it's easily explained away. The Holy Father can work with that."

Lex nodded. Their eyes drooped, suddenly heavy.

"Get some sleep, Lex."

"Promise you'll wake me if…"

"I promise. If *anyone* else shows up that we know, no matter who it is, I'll either come myself or send someone. The Holy Father is right; you need to heal."

Lex closed their eyes. "I'm sorry I attacked him, sir."

Rainier squeezed Lex's shoulder. "He deserved it. Rest now."

Lex was asleep before Rainier was out of the room.

STANTON EASILY CAUGHT up to the cardinals and joined their somber procession to the Holy Father's chambers. It shouldn't have surprised him that they didn't speak of what had passed with Lex; they fundamentally believed they were the Lord God's rightful messengers and, therefore, their knowledge was not for the common people. Their burden was knowledge, or so he was always taught as a boy.

He formed his own opinions now that he was an adult. Knowledge was the true source of power in the world. A man could not attack if he did not have key information. These cardinals and bishops, and all of the clergy, pretended they traded worldly power and influence to giving their lives to the Almighty, but it was an illusion. These were the most powerful individuals in all of Serna, for it was their secrets that could tear down nations.

He'd been silently struggling with his faith before the attack. He'd always believed he was serving what was right and good in the world. Then, he met Allegra. Then, he'd seen the refugees, the riot, and then the burning of Borro. What was a struggle was now a wall of stress fractures. With all of that, however, he still believed. He still wanted to serve. So he would, and hope his love would come home. In time, he hoped he would be able to talk to a priest, maybe Father Michael, and learn how to mend his faith after all he'd seen over the winter months.

Stanton drew in such a deep breath that it caught Cardinal Giso's attention. The priest looked over his shoulder at Stanton, and a dawning realization crossed the man's face. He halted his pace just long enough to fall into step with Stanton, and then they continued for two corridors without a word uttered. It was Giso to break the silence.

"I have always respected Lieutenant Lex. I will send my personal apothecary over to check on him at regular intervals to ensure he receives the very best of care." Giso offered a wry smile. "And to ensure he is following *all* of the surgeon's orders."

Stanton gave the cardinal a weary smile. "Thank you, Your Grace. I appreciate it, and I'm sure Lex and his parents will, as well."

"You must miss her terribly," Giso said. A glint flickered in his eye. "I hope she returns safely."

Stanton did not know if the knowledge of his and Allegra's budding relationship had even reached Orsini's walls, though he supposed they knew everything here. Nevertheless, he didn't want to add to the gossip, not at a time like this. So, he simply said, "We still need her."

"I suspect some of us more than others," Giso said with a supportive warmth to his voice. "I shall pray for her."

"I would appreciate that, Your Grace," Stanton said.

They didn't speak again until inside the Holy Father's chambers. The papal residence took up a significant portion of the grand palace; it had to, to accommodate all his meetings and guests. They turned right, instead of the usual left for Stanton, and entered a room he'd only been in a few times. A long table dominated the room, surrounded by ornately embroidered chairs plated in gold filigree. Two massive chandeliers hung low from the ceiling, though the candles weren't lit since daylight streamed through the stained-glass windows. Sideboards made of imported wood lined one wall, flanked by silver tea-serving tables, set on wheels for immediate delivery to refresh a parched cardinal.

The resentment that bubbled inside Stanton caught him off guard. The rich ostentation of the room had triggered too many memories of starving children and half-frozen nursing mothers. This room alone could have bought enough food to fatten them all up, and yet here it sat, hidden away, protected from the dirty fingers of mages.

He finally saw it. Finally, he saw the world through Allegra's eyes. No wonder she was angry. No wonder she fought. For in this moment, it took all of his reserve not to rip the chandeliers from the ceiling and throw them out the windows.

This is what he had fought for: the preservation of wealth and power. He had not been fighting for the Almighty. He saw that now, in the flicker of sunlight bouncing off crystal.

"Captain? Is something wrong?" Giso asked quietly.

Stanton stared at the cardinal and saw him with new eyes. What was happening to him? Still, he shook off the internal crisis and said, "I am fine."

Giso motioned at a chair ahead, and Stanton took it. He sat down and tried to listen as the Holy Father launched into a series of half rants and frantic security questions. However, Stanton struggled to keep up, for his heart had been moved. He realized, with horror, that Walter Cram and Allegra had been right all along. These people were indeed the oppressors of mages. They did not speak for the Lord God Almighty, for surely, he would never want his people to suffer while others lived in such extreme comfort. Even his riches, even Allegra's riches, paled laughably in the face of even this room.

What was happening to him? Was this the result of grief?

"Captain, what are your thoughts?" the Holy Father asked.

That shook Stanton from his troubled thoughts, and he turned to address the gathered cardinals. There would be time for all that later. For now, he had a duty to protect the innocent people of Orsini. For that, he was certain, was the will of the Lord God Almighty. Until he figured out what was happening to him, he would always ask the question: what would the Lord God want him to do?

CHAPTER FOUR

ALLEGRA CROUCHED BEHIND the boulders and massive roots of upended spruce trees and waited for Walter to give the all-clear. The pounding of her heart made her vision blur. She tried to breathe deeply, taking her time, blowing out the air, but all that did was make her heart race more because she was reminding herself how scared she was. They'd seen Cartossian soldiers ahead. Some stayed on horseback while the others ransacked an abandoned farmstead.

Dodd whispered, "I think they're saying it's the third abandoned house. No way that's a coincidence. Looks like the captain took some of the farmers with him."

Allegra silently agreed. They'd seen large stocks of sheep, pigs, and cows in the distance being pushed away from the conflict. They'd stayed away, just in case. Even then, Dodd had commented the flocks seemed unusually large, given the farmstead sizes around the area. There were a lot of animals for just a handful of men to own, and now with the farmsteads abandoned themselves, it seemed reasonable to Allegra that these were combined herds for the sake of speed and safety in numbers.

Still, she couldn't see this as solid evidence Stanton specifically had made it out alive, though hope did surge despite her rational self's more conservative approach. "I can't see Father Michael or anyone else leaving people behind." She let the statement hang in the air, unable to finish her thoughts aloud.

Dodd shook his head and whispered, "Contessa, this is the Captain's work. Mark my words. He'd have sent the men into the mountains with the herds, and taken the women, children, and anyone too old to make the hike. He's done it before when there were raids in the east."

"I hope you're right," Allegra whispered.

A few minutes later, Walter left his own protective shelter behind an uprooted tree ahead to belly-crawl back to their boulder. "I don't see the main army anywhere, but they're definitely with Bonacieux."

"Could they just be bandits?" Dodd asked.

Walter shook his head. "They're wearing the full Cartossian uniform. No bandit is going to wear those neck stocks."

Dodd sighed. "I guess we have to wait until they go. So much for sleeping in there tonight. Damn. I think it's going to rain again, too."

"What's taking Bonacieux so long? This isn't like him. The army should have passed by now. Maybe we'll be lucky and they're dealing with demons."

"And if we're not lucky?" Dodd asked.

Walter shrugged. "Either he's waiting for reinforcements or he's burning his way straight to Orsini. I suppose it's possible he's lost control of his troops and they're just looting now, but..."

Dodd finished the sentence. "If that were the case, they'd have taken off those fucking stocks from their necks."

"They've got to be still under his thumb. I think he's waiting for more troops to cross the border before he attacks Orsini."

"You still believe he's going to the Cathedral?" Allegra asked.

"Cram, that's fucking madness. He's a murdering asshole, but he's not insane."

Walter snorted. "I have more experience with him. He *will* attack. Anything else will be weakness in his eyes. You'll see."

"He killed the queen!" Allegra protested. At Walter's shushing, she said in a much lower voice, "Set aside everything else you say, he murdered the queen. We can testify to that fact, and the cardinals *will* excommunicate him for that. When that happens, he can't rule Cartossa or anywhere else. He can't even hold a high post with that stain upon him."

Walter stretched his neck to one side until it cracked. Then he did the other side. Another loud crack.

"Can you please stop doing that?" Dodd begged.

Walter shrugged, and his shoulders cracked. "The damp makes my joints ache. Look, all Bonacieux has to do is say Portia was out of control and he had to stop her evil magic or else innocent lives blah blah no one cares. Cartossa will believe him. Almighty save us, but they might make him king for it. My guess is that's what he wants now that Portia is gone."

"He wouldn't dare! My cousin will..."

"Ally, she doesn't have a standing army, and that assumes she's still alive. We have no idea who survived the abbey, and those who survived don't know that we did. We don't even know where the other mages are who were up there with us." Walter cleared his throat. "Those that didn't die from the fall, anyway."

"Quiet! Do you hear that?" Dodd whispered. When they both nodded they hadn't, he belly-crawled toward Walter's previous upturned spruce tree, its roots spread wide enough to provide cover. He pulled out his spyglass to look through the roots.

Allegra hoped they wouldn't have to run. Walter had found her a tree branch that resembled a crutch, but it was awkward and had bruised her armpit, so she still struggled to walk with any speed. While the crutch was better than putting pressure on her ankle, which now buckled under the slightest pressure, it was not possible for her to outrun soldiers.

Dodd motioned for Walter to join him. Walter gave her a "stay put" gesture, which made her roll her eyes. It was painful simply sitting on the damp ground. Where in the name of God was she supposed to go?

A minute or so passed. Allegra's ears tweaked at a distant sound. Horses. A lot of horses. Her stomach clenched. Her hands found her crutch, and she wrapped cold fingers around it. She dragged herself along the ground toward the root stump ahead. "What is it?"

"I don't think those are Bonacieux's horses," Dodd whispered. Walter motioned for the spyglass, but Dodd shook his head. "Wait. The ones at the house are mounting. I think...yup, they're running away. Horses can't be theirs. Cram, look."

Walter lifted himself enough to peer through the crack in the tree roots with Dodd's spyglass. He was still for a painfully long moment, before laughing. He jumped to his feet and waved his arms. "Over here!"

"Cram! What in the Lord God's name are you doing?" Dodd exclaimed, tugging at Cram's trouser leg. "Sit your fucking mage ass down!"

"Over here!" Cram shouted. He pulled off his jacket and waved it in air. "Help! Help!"

"Walter!" Allegra gasped, also pulling on his other trouser leg.

"Help! We're over here! We have the Arbiter! Help!" Then, in a loud voice, not even bothering to whisper, he said, "It's the king's colors!"

A giggle escaped Allegra, and a massive grin spread across Dodd's face. "Are you sure?"

"I've ran from them enough times! I'm sure! Over here! Help!" Cram shouted again.

Using her crutch, Allegra managed to push herself to her feet. Dodd helped steady her as she hobbled around the boulders and roots to stand in plain sight. She staggered and tripped over the smaller rocks that littered the ground from a previous avalanche. Walter didn't help because he was too busy waving his jacket in the air.

Allegra could clearly see the horses now. The bulk of the cavalry—they were, indeed, in King's colors—chased the fleeing Cartossian soldiers, but easily a couple dozen riders headed straight for Allegra. The armor made it impossible for Allegra to identify any of these people. Amadore, for sure, and it looked like members of the Royal Hussars. Grey trousers, blue coats, black wool hats, except for the officers. Tall, black wool hats, heavy with gold braid. The leader had a long tail of horse hair...

She let out a gasp. "Good God Almighty."

That made Dodd unsheathe his sword and take a defensive stance in front of Allegra. "Contessa?"

"Dodd, put your sword down. They're not here to hurt us," Walter said, not even bothering to hide the relief and exuberance in his voice.

Walter stepped out in front of both of them. When the horses slowed and approached, Walter bowed deeply and said, "Your Royal Highness."

Allegra's heart pounded with excitement. There were about six different people the armored figured could be, and all of them would be a welcomed sight. She reached her hand out to Dodd, touching his sword arm. He lowered slowly, though Allegra could still feel the taut muscles through his jacket ready to strike.

"The Arbiter is safe, but injured," Walter said as he raised himself from his bow. "This is Lieutenant Dodd, of the Holy Father's Own Consorts." Walter licked his lips. "And, of course, we have met."

The leader jumped down off the horse and took off her helmet. She was a tall woman, even taller than Stanton. Her thick, black hair was braided away from her face. Her normally flawless dark skin had a swollen, dark spot near her jaw, and her cheeks were bright with color, no doubt from the exertion of riding. Her face broke into a smile, but she planted both of her fists on her hips.

"*Alleycat.*"

"Your Highness," Allegra said, struggling to curtsy. "It is so good to see you. I would curtsy, but I fear I won't be able to get back up if I do."

"Who is this?" Dodd asked. His sword was still out.

"Princess Imogen, allow me to introduce Lieutenant Dodd, who has been keeping me and Walter safe."

She gave Dodd a slight incline of the head, while Dodd struggled to sheathe his sword. Then he bowed and said, "Your Highness. I apologize for brandishing a weapon in your presence."

"Under the circumstances, it was justified. What are you doing here? I heard you were all dead. I can't believe my eyes! Lord God. It is so good to see you. Is it really you?"

Tears of joy welled up in Allegra's eyes at the sight of her old school fellow. "It's really me."

"Did any of the other mages make it out? We heard some of what happened from those who'd escaped into the mountains. Why aren't you with the convoy? They're probably at Orsini by now."

Allegra immediately turned somber. "We were separated when it was clear we couldn't kill the demon without collapsing the abbey. How did you end up here?"

She waved away something black buzzing around her face. "My brother sent us to bolster the border, but we were caught behind Bonacieux's army. We've been dodging his looters ever since, in hopes of taking their attention away from the convoy so they could escape."

Her brother being the king of Amadore. She was the youngest of the brood, and far enough down the line of succession that she had been permitted to follow her own passions: soldiering. Imogen was a fine officer; everyone said so. She held the rank of major, mostly because her brother refused her the rank of general and the risks that position would expose her to. However, from the tales Allegra had heard over the years, Imogen had seen plenty of conflict, and had put herself in harm's way many times. It made Allegra happy, even now, that her old friend got to live the life she'd always wanted. A gasp escape Allegra, as she struggled to keep her emotions in check. Walter put a hand on her back and rubbed for a moment, until the intimacy of the gesture became awkward. He pulled away just before she was about to ask him to stop. Old habits die hard, and she was not angry at him for his gesture; she knew he meant well.

Imogen glanced at Walter. Then, her eyes widened when she recognized him. She blinked and leaned forward. Then she looked at Allegra. "Is that Walter Cram?"

Allegra cleared her throat. Ginny knew *all* about Walter, including the very personal bits. "He is the reason anyone made it out of Borro alive."

"Walter Cram the demon lover? What are you doing back with this waste of mage skin?"

Walter shrugged. "You know me, Your Highness. Always helping the less fortunate."

"Shut up, Walter," Allegra whispered.

"I nearly caught you the last time," Imogen said.

Walter shrugged again. This time, one of his joints made a popping sound. "I'm under the Arbiter's kind protection at the moment."

"So I've heard," Imogen said, deadpan. "Otherwise, you'd be tied to my horse right about now."

Walter only smiled. "I have a piece of paper that says you can't arrest me."

"Paper can be lost," Imogen said.

Allegra sighed dramatically. "For once in your life, Walter, would it kill you to not anger someone? Never mind. Don't answer that. Your Highness, which way did you come? Through the pass?"

The princess nodded. "We encountered sheep herders who were bringing their flock through the pass. Dangerous time to have animals up there, but they told us they were hiding from the Cartossian army and that Borro Abbey was destroyed, and that you were dead. I took the men through to clear up the stragglers and looters, hoping the army moved on. He's still down there, though."

"Your Highness, may I ask you, do you know *why* he's not moving?" Walter asked.

"We were wondering the same thing," Imogen said. "I believe he's waiting for reinforcements from across the border. Blind luck for everyone at Borro, if that's true. Apparently, that gave Barrington a chance to get as many out as he could."

Allegra's eyes widened. "Did Stanton make out it? I mean, Captain Rainier?"

Imogen's mouth quirked upward, and Allegra's cheeks heated up from the knowing look. "Captain Stanton Rainier, as you call him, survived the fire and formed the convoy. I have no news beyond that, though, and I did not see him with my own eyes. However, I know he was alive three days ago because he was seen."

Allegra gasped and put her hand over her mouth. Tears streamed down her face as she giggled and sobbed into her hand. Three days ago. He was alive three days ago.

"Your Highness, might I ask," Dodd said, his words halting. "Do you know if a Lieutenant Lex made it out? He was one of the Consorts."

"I do not. Some did not make it to the convoy, and I know others were killed during the escape. I also heard there had been one gravely injured that had been with mages in the fight against the demon spawn. I have no news beyond that."

Walter reached around Allegra to slap Dodd on the back. "He made it out."

Imogen glanced between them before saying, in a gentler voice than she'd used to deliver the news, "If I have the correct person, the last word I had was it was unsure if he'd survive the journey. He had been stabbed and had an infection. I am sorry that I cannot offer better news."

Dodd closed his eyes and nodded. In a whisper, he managed to say, "Thank you, Your Highness."

"I would not give up all hope yet, however," she said. "After all, he was still alive when he passed through this area. I'd heard that from the farmers. If they got him to Orsini, he will most likely make it." When Dodd didn't reply, she said, "So, what happened exactly? No one seems to know, beyond the obvious."

Allegra quickly relayed the details to her old schoolmate, before her own magic manifested and forced her into a different school. They had remained writing pals through the years, though, and usually saw each other every couple of years at Borro or the Cathedral. Imogen did not know Allegra was an elemental, only that she was a mage, and so she left off the parts where she helped with the demon slaying.

"Bonacieux murdered Portia? Does he honestly think he can get away with that? God Almighty. My orders were to help with the border, so we've been staying back to ensure the farmers and refugees were safe. However, under these circumstances, I believe I should escort you to Orsini myself. So, allow me to formally extend my protection and escort you to the Cathedral. We travel light, but we have food and a couple of tents, when it is safe to use them."

"Thank you, Ginny," Allegra whispered, letting the intimate nickname escape her lips. Her eyes welled up with tears and her voice quavered. "I don't think I could have done this much longer."

Imogen smiled. "I shall keep you safe."

CHAPTER FIVE

STANTON KNOCKED ON the door with the back of his hand and waited for Lex's reply. He'd been with the cardinals all day. Two hours were wasted on blaming each other, followed by grand speeches that were more blame, just said in fancier language. Finally, they worked themselves into exhaustion and only the finest of meat pies, the whitest of breads, and the strongest of red wines could stop their tongues from wagging.

While the cardinals shoveled grand food into their mouths, Stanton made several suggestions regarding security measures. The other captains were called in, and together, they discussed the situation like gentlemen and ladies, and not like pampered cardinals who were there to line their own pockets.

The depth of his own anger surprised Stanton, and more so because he let it boil over on occasion. He'd even snapped at Cardinal Giso, who did nothing to deserve his wrath. Yet, Stanton watched so many of them take one or two bites off their plates, and then ask the servants for another bowl or plate of something else. That plate of perfectly acceptable food was whisked away. They even mocked him for finishing his plate of food before asking for another serving.

"There's plenty, Captain," Giso had said.

That upset Stanton far more than he'd expected. He snapped back, "I can clearly see that."

Worse, Stanton was famished. He'd not eaten properly in days. He had to repeatedly remind himself not to gorge his food.

Even still, he finished two full plates of food before his stomach stopped complaining. An hour later, while the others were daintily finishing off their dessert course, he asked for another plate of any of the supper dishes, but they'd all been hauled off out of sight.

He did not know what happened to the pope's scraps and it bothered him. Perhaps the servants would get to eat it. Maybe the poor were given it. Would they be brought over to the hundreds of hungry stragglers in the ballroom? Or would the highest of rank have already been escorted to the dining halls, while the poor sat there gnawing on stale bread.

It troubled him that these questions lingered, yes, but what ate at him more was that he didn't know the answers. Those were questions he would need to ask when the crisis was over.

He re-focused on the topics at hand: tactics, evacuations, safe zones, fortifications, weapon availability, food stores. He pushed open the door in front of him. And keeping his second-in-command alive. He'd lost too many already. Lex had made it this far. By the Lord God Almighty, he had better make it now.

"Hey, Captain. Here to rescue me?" Lex asked with only a hint of a slur to his words. His eyes didn't look quite so dark and sunken as they'd been earlier that day. He still looked too pale, though.

Stanton closed the door behind him and held up a bottle of wine. "A gift from the Holy Father. Don't worry. I cleared it with the surgeon."

"Any food?" Lex asked hopefully.

Stanton tried to put on a brave face, offering up a weak smile, but he was too tired to hide his exhaustion. He pulled out a napkin-wrapped bundle from his pocket. "I stole some tea cakes."

"Tea cakes and wine?" Lex chuckled. "Interesting combo, sir."

"Not all of us are lazing around in bed. Some of us have jobs to do."

That earned him a snort. Lex motioned for Stanton to pull up a chair, which he did. He put down the two glasses he'd been holding with his fingers, ditto the wine bottle in the crook of his elbow, and then the small bundle of cloth in the other. Lex reached in and pulled out a tea cake.

After taking one bite, he said, "Oh, wow. These are so much better than the crap they serve us."

"That's because I took those from the Holy Father's buffet table," Stanton said. When Lex started laughing, Stanton said, "There are perks with rank, Lex. One of them is stealing the good tea cakes."

Lex's laughter turned into a rasping cough. He held up a hand to say he was fine. Once he was done with the fit, he took a sip of the offered wine. "I can't wait to get out of this bed, sir. I feel so useless. As soon as I can stand up, I'm going to find Bonacieux and I'm going to wring his neck with my bare hands."

"Then I shall ask the surgeon to chain you to the bed," Stanton said. "We need you well, not dead."

Lex's expression turned dark. "He killed the queen. Right in front of me. I should have stopped him, but...It happened so fast. You have to believe me."

"I do," Stanton said. He meant it, too.

Lex took a long drink from the glass. "I knew he was up to no good, too. Like, in my gut I knew, but he'd not done anything. He was just talking to Queen Portia, so I waited. And he was going on and on and all the words sounded right, but my gut...ya know, sir? My gut said it was all wrong. Then he shoves this fucking needle right through her throat and...shit, he just kicked her into the portal like she was trash. She was trying to help, Captain. She was...helping...and...." Lex's voice cracked.

Stanton simply nodded, letting Lex take his time. The cardinals had forced the base story from Lex, but even then, it was facts and details. It wasn't how Lex felt. It wasn't his heart and soul. This was. Stanton knew he needed to get it off his chest, but he also knew Lex needed to do it at his own pace. He didn't need Stanton's well wishes.

"She was just trying to help, ya know? Like, everything they say about mages, but…she was helping. They all were. A bunch of them died helping, and then I come back here and they have the *nerve* to act like they were trash all over again. They died for us, and no one gives a good god damn fuck about them."

"We give a damn about them, and me and you will never forget them, or what they all sacrificed for us. When this is over, I think we need to look at mages very differently."

Lex took a methodical bite out of his tea cake. A moment later, he shrugged and said, "I hope so. I suppose it depends on how all this turns out. Either we're going to end up with a newfound appreciation for each other, or mages are going to be worse off than ever before."

"At least there aren't any open demon gates around here," Stanton said. He didn't know what else to say.

"Thank the Lord God Almighty," Lex said. "I have nightmares about that thing still."

Stanton gave Lex what he hoped was a supportive smile. "They should ease."

Lex didn't look up from his tea cake. "What if they don't?"

Stanton took a long drink of wine. He hated this question because he'd asked it once, too. "Then it's up to you to figure out how you live with that."

"Sir, I've never asked…about what happened, back then, but…"

Stanton rarely talked about it, and even rarer did he bring it up. He knew Lex needed him to, though, so he swallowed down his own nightmares and answered. "It wasn't until I was safe that I started having trouble. My mistake was that I kept it to myself for months and suffered needlessly. I drank too much to help me sleep. Sometimes, I lied to the surgeons and said my injuries bothered me so that they'd give me sleeping tea. Eventually, Father Rupert, as he was then, showed up one day and sat down across from my desk. He told me he'd been having nightmares and had been too afraid to tell Pero. He'd been sleeping on his settee. He'd told Pero it was because his hip hurt. Then one day, he decided to tell Pero about the nightmares, and doing so helped him not to feel so alone."

"What happened?"

Stanton snickered at the memory. "He got up and left."

"That's it?"

"That's it. He didn't ask me a damn thing. Just told me that story, knowing I needed to hear it. A few days later, I wrote my uncle. He'd seen a lot of war. He was a Colonel in the border wars. I told him he didn't need to write back. I said I had to tell someone who I didn't need to see every day how I was feeling."

"Did he write back?"

"Eventually. He said he struggled to talk about the war and my letter brought back his own demons. He knew it was important I talk, so he had to learn how to talk himself." Stanton laughed. "Look at us. A bunch of old men talking about our feelings." Stanton glanced at Lex. "Well, you're too skinny to be old. I think you've gotten thinner since you've arrived!"

"I thought I'd put on weight without Dodd..." Lex's lip quivered. "Shit."

"I hope he made it out."

Lex blew out a long breath, trying to steady his quivering jaw. "I miss him. Ya know, he would've sat here and forced me to tell him about the nightmares, and then he'd sit and...This is all bullshit."

"I know."

"I just want it to be how it was. I want him here and I want us doing our usual work. I don't want to be tied to this fucking bed anymore where I can't do a fucking thing to fix anything."

Stanton didn't know what else to say, so they silently ate their tea cakes and drank their wine. The first glasses went fast, but they both lingered on the second glass. Likewise, the tea cakes. Caraway. Allegra loved caraway tea cakes. Cook always sent up two just for Allegra whenever she sent up tea for their meetings.

"Chances are, she's with Dodd."

Stanton snorted. "Am I that obvious?"

"Pretty much."

"Lex," Stanton began, but shook his head. "Never mind."

"How did I end up downstairs when she was jumping?"

"I didn't want to ask because I didn't want you to think I was trying to blame you."

Lex shook his head. "No more than I blame myself. I was bleeding bad. Cram made one of the mages drag me downstairs while he held the demon off. He said they weren't strong enough to fight it, and he said for everyone to run. The mage—Lord, I don't even remember her name—got me down most of the stairs, but then a ceiling beam hit her. She went right through the floor. Fuck, it was all on fire. I didn't even stop to see if she was alive or if I could help her climb out. I just kept going. I'm such a coward."

"Oh, Lex," Stanton said.

"Don't use that tone on me!" Lex snapped.

"All right." Stanton licked his lips, waiting for Lex's breathing to settle back down. "Then, buck up."

"Excuse me?"

"I said buck up. If I can't be nice, then you must pull yourself together. Pick one."

"Fucking asshole," Lex muttered.

"I'm going to blame your injury for that, but you talk to me like that again, I'll put you on report." Stanton smiled to let Lex know he wasn't upset, but they both knew he would absolutely do it. "I must maintain discipline."

"I'm not digging through shit looking for your buttons. Could cause another infection. I'll get a surgeon's note."

"Want half of what's left?" Stanton asked, holding up the bottle.

Lex nodded, and Stanton portioned out the last of the wine between their glasses. "This is some bullshit, sir."

"Yes, it is."

"Is there anymore wine? I think I'd like to get roaring drunk, sir."

Stanton emptied his glass. "Let me make a trip to the carts first. I'll see if there's a pie."

"Gammon, sir."

"I know, Lex. I know. You want the gammon pie. If there isn't any?"

"Don't care after that. Meat. Fruit. Meat and fruit. Whatever."

"All right, then. I have a good bottle of port in my office drawer that I've been saving. Want me to break it out? My brother sent it to me for my birthday."

"Sure."

Stanton got up and moved toward the door. Lex said, "Stanton?"

He rarely used his name. "Yes, Lex?"

"Thanks."

Stanton nodded. "I'm still thinking about putting you on report. I'll go find you a pie."

Stanton turned the quick walk to his office into a ten-minute trip. He pushed the door open carefully and found Lex snoring. Stanton smiled; he'd figured he'd have fallen asleep after the wine. Stanton walked to the papal residence and knocked.

Francois opened the door. "Rainier! What's happened now?"

Stanton raised the bottle of port.

Francois's features relaxed and the weariness showed in his face. "Come in. I've just emptied my bottle of wine. I could use something stronger."

So, Stanton and Rupert shed their titles for the evening and quietly drank in remembrance of old friends, old battles, and new worries.

CHAPTER SIX

IF ALLEGRA'S ANKLE was sentient, it might have sighed in relief at being atop the sturdy back of a horse. Her bruised, swollen armpit rejoiced at being relieved of the task of holding her upright. Now, Walter sat behind her, holding her upright. Imogen made unhappy comments about their slow pace, as they were sticking to the beaten paths in the woods and brush as much as possible, but it was significantly faster than Allegra had been doing hobbling on her crutch.

The birds chirped happily, and the chickadees sang their *fee-bee* songs, with the occasional annoyed *dee-dee-dee* song. Squirrels chittered at them, upset that invaders disrupted their acorn hunting. Flies buzzed around the horses, and Allegra waved off a few clouds of tiny winged insects, keeping her mouth closed shut to avoid swallowing them.

Most likely, Stanton had survived. Every time she thought of that, her arms filled with goose bumps, as the shiver of hope spread through her. She tried to control her excitement and her worry, but the news that he'd gotten out of the abbey only heightened both.

By contrast, the news of a gravely injured Consort stirred the pit of her stomach. Dodd refused to speak of the injured Consort, but she knew what he was thinking that it was probably Lex. So, while she had something to hold on to, Dodd was emotionally preparing himself for the death of his best and closest friend.

The emotional whirlwind ripped at her. She was so tired and longed for a bed. She wanted them to go faster, but also knew the horses couldn't handle a hard pace for long, not without proper food and rest. Plus, it was too dangerous to use the highway below.

As the day went on, they stopped occasionally to eat meager supplies, adjust equipment and saddles, and tend to any injuries. However, as night approached, it was clear that the old wood cutter's path they'd been following was descending toward the main highway. They tried to veer off the path, but a boulder field blocked their route. Downward was the only option.

"What should we do?" Allegra asked Imogen as they stopped by a small stream of snow runoff.

Imogen was on her hands and knees washing her face in the freezing water. She called Walter and Dodd over before she answered the question. "Cram, are you able to protect the Contessa if we're attacked?"

Walter nodded.

"All right, good. Dodd, how experienced are you fighting mounted?"

Dodd made a so-so gesture. "I've trained, but I don't have much practical experience."

Imogen came to her feet and patted her face with a cloth, careful with the swollen bruises around her jaw. "Let's keep the three of you in position like before. If fighting breaks out, get her out of here. Head toward Orsini. Leave us behind. Understood?"

"Imogen, we can't…" Allegra began.

Walter cut her off. "We understand, Your Highness. We'll get her to Orsini."

Allegra whirled on Walter. "You don't get to decide that for me."

"You can't fight," Walter said, slowly, emphasizing much more than just her ankle and lack of sword training. "Dodd and I can get you out, if Her Highness gives us time."

"Cram's right," Dodd said.

Allegra scowled, but said nothing. She did not want to run away and leave her friend behind. But she also knew that there was nothing useful she could do. Even if she helped in a fight, experience had taught her she didn't have a clue what she was doing. She was just as likely to start a forest fire as she was to take care of Bonacieux's soldiers. Then, that would leave the awkward scenario of Imogen and her soldiers all knowing about her.

Allegra hated feeling trapped. Yet, she was. Again, and always.

The last streaks of sunlight were all that was left on the horizon when they saw the clump of buildings ahead. The little farm church, surrounded by a handful of cottages, was a welcome sight, though Imogen and her soldiers were cautious. They sent ahead a couple of scouts to check the place out. Several uneasy minutes later, the church's windows lit up and the sound of horse hooves approached.

Allegra had to be helped down off her horse, but she was so grateful at the sight of the two sisters who ran the church and their hospitality. They learned from the sisters that the farms had been evacuated a few days before, though they remained behind in case aid was needed. As the soldiers dismounted and began their individually assigned tasks, Allegra got her first bit of recent news.

"Yes, there was a captain from the Consorts. I'm terribly sorry, but I don't remember his name, Your Ladyship," the elder of the sisters said. "Margarite, do you remember?"

She shook her head. "Very handsome, though. Tall, dark complexion. He was with Father Michael. The bishop from Borro Abbey."

"That's Rainier," Cram said. He gave Allegra a tight smile. "Good."

Allegra's lip quivered, and she wasn't able to manage anything more than a sharp nod at the sisters. Two days ago, Stanton was still alive. The Lord God Almighty just had to see fit to let him live a little longer.

When Dodd didn't ask any questions, Walter asked, "Do you know if the injured Consort made it? The one that had been stabbed."

The sisters exchanged a look, and then younger one gave the more senior a pleading look. The older sister looked between Dodd and Cram. "Father Michael said the caravan had been attacked more than once. There were several injuries and I believe two Consorts perished in the assault. There was a gravely injured one. Lieutenant...oh, what was his name?"

"Lex," Dodd whispered.

"Yes, that was it. Lex! We gave Father Michael the last of our healing stones in hopes that the boy would make it to Orsini." The old lady looked at Dodd and said, "I am very sorry for the loss of your comrades, and I wish I had better news about your friend. But, if I am to be honest, I think his fate is in the Almighty's hands now. We will pray for him. And you."

Dodd paled, all trace of hope washed away. "Thank you, Sister. How can I help here?"

Sister Margarite nodded at her senior before saying to Dodd, "I could use help bringing in wood and lighting a few fires. It will be damp tonight."

"Might I have paper? I'd like to record what supplies we take for later reimbursement, which I insist," Allegra said.

The evening took a sober tone once the news of the Consorts' deaths spread through Imogen's soldiers. They still laughed and bickered outside, but they were careful with their laughter inside, knowing how important it was to allow their three guests to grieve.

Dodd kept busy helping Sister Margarite with the wood necessary to keep a couple of roaring fires going all night. Walter helped Imogen's soldiers raid the nearby cottages of their supplies, reporting back to Allegra everything they'd taken. She did not want these people to suffer for their hospitality.

Approx. twenty pounds of oats, taken from: Maria C, Maria A, and Francisco C.

Hay bundles taken from: Maria C (4), Maria A (3), Francisco C (9), Our Holy Faith (2), Riza (5), Oco (4).

½ sack of grain taken from Maria C.

2 sacks of potatoes taken from Oco

Apples taken from Maria C (30), Maria A (11), Francisco C (29), Our Holy Faith (40), Riza (12), Oco (38)

Maria C and Our Holy Faith – Entire greens garden

On went the list, detailing the pears eaten, the carrots plundered, and the cheese taken. When they were done, Allegra carefully copied over the list, handing the clerics their own copy. "In case anything happens to me, please use that to have the Cathedral compensate these people."

Both horses and humans had a decent supper. The soldiers organized themselves into shifts, with some keeping guard around the church itself, others scouting the area, and still others looking after the fires, tending to the horses, or helping pack food for the days ahead. There was a small kerfuffle about Allegra's sleeping arrangements, but those protests fell on stubborn ears.

"Sister Bianca, I understand your reluctance concerning an unmarried woman of my rank spending the night with two men under your roof. However, let me be very clear in as kind of a manner as I am able. These men are the *only* reason I remained alive throughout this ordeal. They will remain by my side until I am delivered safely to Orsini, and their duty to me discharged."

"What about your reputation, Your Ladyship? That one is a rebel," she whispered, as if it was a secret from Walter.

"Sister, my reputation is sound and will remain so. They will be sleeping in this room with me tonight. I will not yield."

Eventually, the sister relented, though she mumbled on about the reputation of her country sanctuary and how on earth would she explain this to the bishop. Allegra, Walter, and Dodd organized themselves in a small office, one of the few rooms with its own fireplace and chimney. Dodd helped Sister Margarite fetch blankets, and soon they were warm, nursing bowls of boiled potatoes.

"Your Ladyship, don't worry about Sister Bianca. It's been very stressful, what with the refugees and now this war. Please don't take what she says to heart. It's just her way."

"I won't," Allegra assured Sister Margarite.

The fireplace flickered merrily and soon chased away the lingering chill in Allegra's bones. Her clothes were a long way from dry, but even now, her woolen outer layers were closer to wet than water logged.

It took three bowls of potatoes and butter before Walter finally bothered to speak. He was propped up against the wall, seated on pillows and wrapped in a blanket. "As far as things go, this has been the best on-the-run place I've stayed at. Comfort-wise, of course. I've stayed in the cellars of some grand houses. The comforts were lacking."

"Now that you say that, I don't even know if my estate *has* a cellar," Allegra said between bites.

"All big houses have a cellar," Walter said. "I'm sure yours is lovely."

"Well, if you ever end up that way, please ask the butler if you can stay in mine."

Walter snorted. "Lord God Almighty, there is nothing quite like hot potatoes and butter when you've been cold and hungry."

"I'd rather a meat pie," Dodd said. Then, he whispered, "Gammon pie."

Walter gave Allegra a quizzical look, but she shook her head at him. "Lex is a fighter."

"What if he didn't make it? You heard them. How bad was he hurt if they're begging healing stones off some poor country church? And two Consorts are dead? No offense, Contessa, but if you weren't here? I'd have gone hunting for Bonacieux by now."

"Then it's best I am here," Allegra said sharply. When Dodd looked up at her, shamefaced, she moderated her tone. "We are all worried but running after Bonacieux with no help and no plan is suicide. You will be needed at the Cathedral. Either Lex is alive and will need you during his recovery, or…you will be needed in the aftermath. Either way, you are needed alive, and not dead trying to vent your anger."

Dodd didn't say anything to that. He just picked at his potatoes.

Walter sighed and said, "He got out of the building. Chances are, Rainier was panicking and wanted to make sure the bleeding stayed stopped. Lex *was* stabbed through the guts."

"Walter! You're not helping," Allegra snapped.

"Listen, both of you! Listen to my words. It can take days to die from a gut wound. Do you hear me? Days. If Lex has been wrapped in healing stones since the abbey, then he's still alive. A surgeon can clean him out and sew him up with healing thread. Then Orsini can wrap him up in enough healing blankets and whatever else they have hidden in their closets that he'll never get sick again. I know about this stuff more than either of you, and you have to trust me. He's sewed up in bed right now worrying sick about the two of you."

"Lex would never worry about me," Dodd said, sadness creeping into his voice. "He'd get the mission done."

"That's unfair," Allegra said. "Everyone says Lex is the worrier, not you. Lex is probably as afraid as you are about him. And here you are, alive and well. Lex will be overjoyed."

"Yeah."

"What's the matter with you?" Cram asked. "Lex is going to make it."

"Let it go, Cram."

Allegra shot Walter a look and he shrugged, turning back to his potatoes in silence. Walter was licking the butter residue off his bowl when a knock came at the door. Sister Margarite held a spoon and two of Imogen's officers held a steaming pot between them. "Mashed onions, turnips and carrots. It's not much, but it's hot."

"It is perfect, thank you," Allegra said.

Walter held out his bowl. "I love a good turnip. Might I have a big scoop of your turnips? They look delicious."

Sister Margarite blushed, prompting Allegra to roll her eyes at him. The sister took Walter's bowl and shoveled a ladle-full of orange mash on top of it. She did so for Allegra, too, and for Dodd.

"I'm going to sleep like a baby tonight," Walter announced. "This is better than anything I've eaten at Borro Abbey."

"It's because you're hungry, Cram."

"Yes, I know I'm hungry, and I'm saying it tastes better than anything I remember tasting."

Dodd didn't have a witty comeback. He just sullenly went back to picking at his potatoes that were now underneath mash.

Then, Allegra got it. She understood what Dodd was feeling because it was what she was feeling. He'd barely talked about Lex, had barely brought up his best friend's name this entire trip. Now that they were safe and warm, Dodd could worry. He could let down his guard and work through the realization of emotion.

"Oh… Dodd," Allegra said, pity in her voice.

Dodd looked at her sharply. He knew what that tone meant. "It's not what you think."

"What? What's going on?" Cram asked through a mouthful of mash.

"Dodd, listen to me. You have to try not to worry."

"Seriously, I missed something here. What's going on? Why is Ally giving me 'Walter shut up' eyes?"

"Maybe because the Contessa wants you to shut up."

"Walter!" Allegra said, in an exasperated whisper.

"It's fine, Contessa," Dodd said sourly. Then, into his bowl of vegetables, he said, "You know, this is the longest Lex and I haven't been together since we were young. It's weird. At least then, I knew he was fine and we'd tell each other all our stories when we got together again. But now, it's so strange, ya know? You're friends with someone your whole life and then something happens and you look at them completely different. Then you realize it's too late. Nothing more to say."

Silence weighed down on them. Allegra wanted to say something soothing, but she didn't know what to say. She had teased Lex a few times about being secretly in love with Dodd, but she'd only ever meant it as light-hearted ribbing. Stanton and Lex had assured her there was nothing there, so she felt justified in a little harmless levity. It was different, though. Dodd's bluster about buxom widows was a bit of a front, a ruse. He might not have even noticed or had pushed it down so far that he didn't recognize it.

He couldn't do that anymore, and Allegra grieved for his pain.

"If you like him, tell him. Life is too short for regrets." It surprised Allegra that it was Walter offering the words of support.

"Just like that, Cram? Hey Lex, listen, I know we've been friends since we were tots and all, but while we were apart I realized I kinda like you in that other way. Wanna court?" Dodd scoffed. "Fuck, it doesn't work that way. You know that."

Allegra opened her mouth to speak, but Walter cut her off. "Take the risk. Worse that happens will be you lose a friend, but at least, you'll know and be able to move on."

"That's all, huh? Lose a friend. Like there will ever be another friend like Lex. I'd rather be alone in my fucking bed the rest of my life than give Lex up. Don't you get it?"

Walter leaned forward, his words clipped with anger and pain. "I have been in love more than once. Let me tell you a secret. I have never regretted loving any of them. I've regretted the pain, and the words, and all of the names I've called them and they've called me. I do not regret *them*." He spat out that last word. He took a long breath, calmed his tone, and continued. "Do you know the only regrets I have? When I was too proud to give up Walter

Cram, Demon Lover, and never told them who and what I was. I watched them in secret, always looking out of the corner of my eye. Thinking. Wanting. Yearning. You know what happens, Dodd? That ache festered until I hated them. That's my only regret. Lex will take you, or he won't. But give him the fucking chance to decide."

"It won't be the same if I tell him."

"It's never going to be the same. Don't you see that? As soon as you look at Lex, your eyes will give you away. You know now how you truly feel and, even if you never say the words, you are going to feel it every time you look at him. Every time he laughs at another man's jokes, you will feel it. Every time Lex grins when a man flirts with him, you will feel it. Every time Lex sneaks back to the barracks in the middle of the night grinning, you. Will. Feel. It. It won't ever be the same now."

After a long pause, Dodd said, "Well. Shit. I thought I felt worse before. Fuck, Cram."

"I'm not even in love with Lex and I feel awful. Thanks, Walter."

"You're such a fucking asshole," Dodd said.

"Glad to be of service." A grin threatened Walter's grim expression. "Made you stop worrying about Lex being dead though, didn't I?"

"I hate you," Dodd said, throwing a pillow at Walter.

CHAPTER SEVEN

SHOUTING, STOMPING, AND pounding Allegra from a dead sleep. Disoriented, she struggled to bring her thoughts into focus. Dodd and Walter were already shoving feet into boots while Allegra blinked the sleep from her eyes. She managed to stand, with the help of her crutch, just as her door swung open.

Imogen's expression was grave. "We have to leave right now."

Dodd wrapped his sword belt around his waist. "What happened?"

Walter wrapped a blanket about Allegra's shoulders as Imogen spoke.

"Bonacieux is moving. His scouts are everywhere. We have to go now, or we'll never go."

"What about the sisters?" Allegra asked.

"We cannot leave them. He will kill them," Walter said in a harsh tone.

"Don't worry; they're coming with us. Can the three of you organize yourselves to get outside? We're leaving in five minutes."

Dodd and Walter exchanged a look before both nodding at Imogen.

"We'll be fine," Allegra said. "Get the sisters out."

Imogen gave Allegra's ankle a look and then nodded at the two men. "Five minutes, gentlemen. I need her on a horse and gone."

Dodd nodded. "We'll be out there."

Allegra had not bothered to undress, which had turned into a blessing. It would have taken her longer than five minutes to get back into her clothes. As it was, she feared it would take longer than five minutes to cross the church's floor.

As Dodd shoved his arms into his jacket, he said, "Cram, we need to carry her."

"Agreed," Walter said. "Allegra?"

Allegra swallowed her pride, but then nodded her consent. She put her arms around both men's necks and then gritted her teeth as they lifted her up by the backs of her thighs. Walter cursed at Dodd for being so short and Dodd told him to die in the abyss. She jostled back and forth a few times before they evened themselves out.

Allegra held tight as the men jogged her across the church floor. They were halfway to the front door when she remembered the crutch had been left behind, but she dismissed it from her thoughts. If they could not outrun Bonacieux on horseback, they would not be outrunning him on foot.

Outside, three horses waited for them. Thank the Almighty there was still supplies at the hamlet to feed and water the horses overnight, else the beasts might have been too exhausted for the task. For all of his protestations about aching joints, Walter smoothly vaulted up on his assigned horse. One of Imogen's soldiers helped Dodd lift her carefully up on her own. Finally, Dodd hoisted himself up.

The sisters pulled up alongside them, already on their own horses. Both had another horse tied behind them carrying a couple sacks each of what was probably food and fodder.

The sound of fighting grew closer. Allegra thought she heard metal against metal, as swords met in earnest. Imogen looked at Walter and shouted, "Get them out of here!"

"I can help!" Walter said as he pulled his horse closer to Imogen. "Highness, I will fight alongside you."

"Get your mage ass out of here!" Imogen slapped Allegra's horse and spooked it.

Allegra screamed as the horse charged away from her friend. She did not want to leave Ginny behind, yet the decision had been made for her. She worked to slow her horse, desperate to regain control. The sisters pulled next to her. Sister Bianca's face was grave, and Sister Margarite's face was visibly wet with tears, even in the moon's light.

Dodd caught up quickly and pulled alongside her flank. Her horse was slowing its pace now, the full gallop too much for the animal to sustain for any length of time. She kept looking over her shoulder for Walter. She heard the approach of hooves and he appeared from the shadows. Even in the partial light, Allegra could see his anger.

Over the sound of the horses, Walter shouted, "Let me set the pace. I know this part better than any of you. Dodd? In the rear, please. Keep an eye out as best you can."

Dodd looked at Allegra, who nodded her agreement. Dodd silently pulled his horse out of step with them, waited for them to pass, and rejoined. Allegra looked over her shoulder and saw him behind the spare horses. Then she saw the blaze in the distance, where the church had been.

She wept silent tears as Walter set their pace and led them away from the fight.

STREAKS OF DAWN were visible on the horizon when Walter finally called for rest at another abandoned cluster of farmsteads. Allegra was unable to control her shivering by this point; exhaustion, stress, and the cold night all conspired to make her miserable. Walter helped her down. Dodd helped Sister Bianca down, easing the older priest to her feet.

A moment later, Dodd successfully lit a torch. With the extra light guiding them, Sister Bianca helped Allegra inside to the stable—to rest in sight of everyone—while Sister Margarite was instructed to get the water trough pump going. Walter unpacked one bag each from the horses, setting it aside, before leading the horses to the small water trough. He took over at the pump and managed to splash out a small amount of water, which the horses greedily lapped up. Sister Margarite lectured him on the proper care of horses, and he nodded silently, not cutting her off.

That made Allegra smile, even though the stress. She always liked that about Walter. He had a way to make anyone feel like they were the only person in the room. When he wanted to, anyway. Often times, Walter wanted everyone in the room to only think of him, but likewise he could turn that around and make people feel special and heard. She thought maybe that was one of the reason she'd been in love with him that summer so long ago.

Dodd announced he'd found a partial sack of feed and asked Walter where to put it. He said there were a handful of apples still up in the loft, so he'd bring those down as soon as he found a bucket.

"Only use the one torch, if possible," Walter called out. "This is going to be a short rest break. As soon as there's light or any sign of scouts, we're going again."

"What about the horses?" Sister Bianca asked.

"Hopefully, we can give them a rest, then a meal, and then a quick rest again. It's at least an hour before dawn, and I think we can chance it a couple more hours after that. Once it's full light, though, we have to be moving."

"Sisters? Let Cram and I stay up and care for the horses. The three of you get some sleep, if you can," Dodd suggested.

"I will look for more food," Sister Bianca said, completely ignoring Dodd. "Sister Margarite? Come with me, if you please."

Allegra got the impression that Sister Margarite was going to follow regardless if she pleased or not.

Dodd tossed her an apple and offered her his signature goofy grin when she fumbled the fruit several times before finally gaining control of it. Walter came by with a wooden mug filled with water. She gulped at the water, washing down the apple bits stuck in the back of her throat.

"Is Imogen going to be okay?"

Walter took the mug and didn't answer. He met her gaze for a brief moment before turning to walk back to the horses. Her insides knotted and contorted from worry. Her fear said they should be back on the road, getting far from Bonacieux, but Walter had been right. If the horses didn't rest, they'd all be walking. So she tried to empty her mind of her worries. She was only partially successful.

Time passed around Allegra as she faded in and out. She'd wake to see the sky a little redder. The torch moved to a different location. Once, Dodd was snoring next to her. Another time, she blinked her eyes open and found Sister Bianca asleep where Dodd had seemingly been a moment before. She woke every time Walter worked the pump, slowly dispensing water to the horses.

"Who's there?" Allegra asked in her sleep-deprived haze.

"It's me, Ally. Go back to sleep."

"What are you doing?"

"I'm getting the horses a bit more hay. The sun is starting to come up, so we'll need to go soon. Try to sleep more."

"Any sign of Imogen?"

"Go back to sleep," was his reply.

When Allegra woke again, it was to the gentle touch of Sister Bianca. Allegra blinked several times before her brain kicked in. The sky was bright and sunny with the morning light. She bolted upright and demanded, "What's wrong?"

"We have to go, Your Ladyship."

"Of course."

Allegra wrapped an arm around the sister's waist and they carefully made their way out of the stables. Outside, Allegra recognized eight of Ginny's riders. Eight. Out of forty-odd men. Her stomach soured.

"Where is Imogen?" Allegra demanded. "Where is she?"

"Relax, Contessa. She's with Cram, back up the path. Come on. I'll give you a boost up," Dodd said, motioning at her horse from the evening before.

Once again, Allegra was up on the horse. She hoped the poor animal wasn't as tired and hungry as she was. The constant sleep interruptions made her woozy and had upset her stomach. She was about to say something to Dodd, but the earth shook under their feet. Her horse bucked. She hadn't been prepared for the fright and landed on the ground with a hard thud. She cried out as she smacked her ankle against the hard ground. Dodd quickly knelt by her side, checking to ensure she was unharmed. She managed to hold back a snide comment about her ankle and reminded herself that attacking him would not make her feel better. Sister Bianca and Sister Margarite worked to calm the horses through two more tremors.

"What is happening?"

"Her Highness asked Cram to buckle the highway in hopes of giving us more time. She said it went back against the general's men, and there were more on the way."

"Are these all that made it?" Allegra whispered the question.

Dodd pulled her to her feet. "No. There are more with her and Cram, plus some are staying behind to slow those who get through Cram's trap."

Trees groaned in the distance before disappearing completely from view.

"What is he doing?"

Dodd shook his head. "Like anyone knows what he's doing. Did you hurt yourself?"

Allegra shook her head. "Everything aches, but I'm fine."

Sister Bianca was soothing the horse. "Lieutenant, put the Arbiter on my horse. I'll take Rita. She'll behave for me. She's just scared."

Dodd did as the sister instructed, and Allegra finally got a proper look at the Amadore soldiers. They were in rough shape. Most were injured in some form. All were covered in the brown splatter of dried blood. She gulped, worried that they might not make the trip in this condition if attacked.

Allegra wanted to blame herself, and she did feel some guilt that these soldiers were here in the open because of her status. If she were just one of the sisters, or a farmer's wife, she'd be told to head out of sight until the conflict ended. Instead, they stayed because of her.

The guilt doubled when Imogen arrived a few minutes later, with Walter and the rest of her injured soldiers. At first glance, Allegra didn't recognize her. She wasn't wearing her helmet and one side of her face was wrapped in a blood-soaked cloth. "Good. You're all ready. Sisters, did you get food?"

Sister Margarite nodded. "One sack of apples, carrots, pears, that kind of thing. Sister Bianca has two sacks of feed. Same with Lieutenant Dodd."

Imogen nodded. "It's not much, but it'll have to do. Let's move out."

"What about your horses?" Sister Margarite asked. "They must be exhausted."

"We'll stop at the lake. For now, we must keep moving. There's not enough distance between us and the scouts, and I think the entire army is on the move now."

"Let's go," Allegra said weakly. Then they moved out and down the highway toward Orsini.

CHAPTER EIGHT

HOW SHE REMAINED upright for the next several hours remained a mystery to Allegra, but she had done it. Likewise, how the horses had kept going was nothing short of a miracle from Tasmin. Finally, mercifully, they stopped mid-afternoon when Imogen fell from her horse in exhaustion. After a several hour rest, they got back on their horses, but stopped again later that evening when one of the Amadore soldiers' wounds refused to cease bleeding.

It was the middle of the night when they came across another abandoned homestead cluster and Imogen called for a full night's rest there. Imogen wouldn't allow a fire, leaving them stuck with freezing well water and raw vegetables. They also found some soft apples in the loft, where the very last of the previous autumn's apples were holding on. They ate the best ones, with the horses clearing off whatever was left. Same with another bucketful of carrots. Allegra's hands were cramped from the cold, and she kept dropping her apples until, finally, she gave up and fell into the sleep of the truly exhausted.

Sister Margarite woke her and said, "Your Ladyship? Her Highness says it's time to go."

Allegra hauled herself from the floor of the dark room and stumbled outside into the bright morning light. Water dripped from every surface, and the ground squished under her feet. She'd not even heard the rain storm. Dodd was grinning and pointed into the distance. That's when she saw it: Orsini's spire.

They'd made it.

It wasn't until three hours later, when their horses' hooves hit the cobblestone path that Allegra wept. They were now less than two hours from the Cathedral. Safety was within reach. She just had to hang on.

At first, the merchants and travelers along the path didn't recognize them, or at least didn't care about the bloodied Amadore soldiers flanking three civilians in their midst. However, the closer they reached the gates, the more people stared slack-jawed at the battered group of soldiers and the half-dressed woman wrapped in a blanket.

"Walter!" shrieked a young boy's voice.

Allegra snapped her head around to see a very clean Little Ferret in a page's uniform, with a massive leather messenger's bag slung over one of his shoulders.

Little Ferret jumped up and down waving his arms. "Walter! They said you died!"

At that, people started taking notice of the bedraggled group. Some asked Little Ferret who the people were, and he happily shouted out, "It's the Arbiter and Lieutenant Dodd and Walter Cram!"

"Ah, shit," Dodd muttered. "Your Highness? We're going to be thronged if we don't keep moving."

"Understood," Imogen said. She ordered her men to keep moving.

"Ferret," Walter said in that warning tone generally reserved for parents.

Little Ferret flushed and he sheepishly ducked his head. Still, when he spoke, he shouted. "Sorry, Walter."

"Is that the Arbiter?" someone asked, pointing at her with shock written across their face.

It took most of Allegra's strength, but she raised one arm to wave at the crowd.

Cheers went up from the vendors and merchants along the path. Shouts of "Almighty be praised" were alongside the more heart wrenching, "Have you see my brother? My husband? My daughter?" And the more fearful shouts asking, "Is Cartossa invading us?"

"Let's keep moving," Imogen ordered. In a louder voice, for the benefit of the crowd, she said, "Clear a path. We must get inside!"

However, word was spreading faster than the horses moved. People gathered, forming a circle of shouting, weeping, begging individuals who pushed tighter against the moving horses. Dodd's horse panicked when someone stumbled and bumped against the animal's flank. Dodd managed to keep his spooked horse under control. However, one of the injured soldiers weren't as lucky and was bucked from his horse. He hit the cobblestones hard. He didn't move.

In one smooth gesture, all of Imogen's men unsheathed their swords at once and began shouting, "Get back!"

Allegra saw Little Ferret pushing against the crowd to escape. Moments later, he was running up the incline toward the first set of guard towers.

Though Allegra was exhausted, she pushed all of the energy she could into her voice. "Please! Get back! Her Highness needs to get her injured men inside. Look at her! She needs a healer and a surgeon herself! Let us through!"

That placated some of the crowd, but others simply fell to their knees pleading for news. Others pulled on her petticoat, hands begging for help. Still others, especially toward the back, angrily shouted and shook their fists, shouting about mages.

Two of Imogen's men climbed off their horses to help their fallen comrade. Allegra could clearly see the blood smear on the cobblestones, though the man did stir when they talked to him. Concussed, for sure, but at least he yet lived. Dodd positioned his horse in front of the soldiers, trying to shield them from hands as they eased their friend up on his horse. One got on behind him, taking the reins in one hand and wrapping the other around his friend's waist to keep him upright. Walter pressed his horse against hers, quietly soothing both animals by whispering in their ears and stroking their necks.

"Be calm! Please! You must be calm!" Allegra shouted again. "I don't know who survived the abbey, either. We have been through much and are injured. Please let us through!"

"Why is he here?" someone shouted at Walter and grabbed Allegra's ankle to get her attention.

Allegra screamed with pain. Without thinking, she kicked the man right in the face, and he stumbled backward into the crowd. Stars flashed across her vision and she buckled over. She would have vomited from the pain if there had been anything in her stomach. Even still, she gagged and heaved. She'd lost her shoe, too, and she knew it was going to swell uncontrollably now. She could almost feel it puffing out as she panted through the nausea, pain, and blurred vision.

In the distance, galloping hooves cut through the shouting. She dimly saw the colors of the Orsini guard through her pain, all of them running and riding to stop what was about to become a riot.

"Back!" the lead guard on horseback shouted. "Get back! All of you! Back!"

The guard began to swing their clubs. They hadn't unsheathed their swords, but memories of Borro Abbey and those who'd been killed flooded her, intermingling with the pain, and she cried out for everyone to stop.

Thankfully, no one had the stomach to fight the guards and the horsemen quickly surrounded their party, protecting them from the crowd. It still took several minutes to push the crowd back properly, but they eventually fell back along the sides of the road as the footed guards arrived, helping to push the crowds back even further.

Finally, the lead mounted guard approached them and asked, "Who am I addressing?"

"I am Princess Imogen of Amadore, sister of the King, Major of the Royal Dragoons, 1st Company."

"Your Highness. Welcome," the guard said, bowing. "I am Captain Brett Thomas of Orsini's Dragoons, 3rd Company. Forgive the question, Your Highness, but what are you doing here?"

"My orders were to assist the refugee effort out of Borro Abbey. However, we were trapped behind enemy lines since the

Abbey's destruction. We have been attempting to get the Arbiter to safety. I have lost most of my men. We are all in need of healers, and I have vital news about the war for Captain Stanton Rainier and the Holy Father."

Captain Brett looked beyond Imogen until his eyes met Allegra's. He squinted, as if he didn't believe his own eyes. "Your Ladyship? Is that really you?"

Allegra nodded weakly.

"Of course, it's her, Brett," Dodd snapped. "Stop lollygagging with your fucking mouth open. We need inside the walls. *Now.*"

Captain Brett blinked at Dodd before a wide smile stretched his face. "God Almighty. Dodd! I never thought I'd see your ugly face again, you son of a whoring witch! They said you were all dead."

Allegra ignored the vulgarity, mostly because she was too exhausted to argue with anyone.

"So, shall we be permitted to travel on?" Imogen asked, not bothering to hide the impatience in her voice.

"Let's get you inside. Back! I said, get back! Your Highness, Your Ladyship, Little Gopher is gone to get word to the Holy Father."

"Little Gopher?" Allegra asked.

"The little guy? You might not have seen him. Consorts brought him here a while ago. I think from Borro, actually, or somewhere near there. He's been running messages ever since for the Consorts and all the guards. Everyone calls him Little Gopher, because he's the smallest of the messengers, but he's a fast little guy. Back! Get your ass back!"

Dodd, Walter, and Allegra shared amused looks. It did her heart well to know the little fellow made it and was safe. And, more, his name was changed so that no one knew he was the little thief that started off the Borro riot. To their word, the Consorts kept Little Ferret safe.

Then tears trickled down her dirty cheeks as their horses slowly made their way up the inclined path. Soon, she was going to be safe, too.

TWO HUNDRED AND five people. That's how many Stanton had managed to get to the Cathedral. There was no official count, but Father Michael's people had estimated there were over seven hundred refugees still in the village of Borro at the time of the attack. At Borro Abbey itself, Father Michael said there were about two hundred people staying at the abbey itself. None of those numbers took into effect the camped soldiers.

Two hundred and five made it out.

As it was, they were lucky to have gotten out that many. Anyone from Borro was cut off by Bonacieux's army. They'd been forced to take the logging path down to the main highway, as opposed to going through Borro. How many people had he left to their deaths by taking that route?

Stanton silently prayed that the Lord God Almighty would forgive him and ease his guilt. He wished he could have saved them all, and would have if he could have. Unfortunately, the demons had other plans.

"This is the proposal for all military groups in Orsini to assist with guard detail in the main ballroom," Nathan said, sliding a piece of paper in front of him.

At least, he'd gotten some out. And he'd gotten all of Allegra's staff out, even if she didn't make it. She'd have been happy about that. Nathan. Serafina. Calm Seas. Kia. Nadira. They'd all made it out. She'd be happy about Father Michael, too. And all of the Consorts. Except Maxwell, Amis, Jehan. *Dodd.*

He signed the paper in front of him.

"This is for a curfew…" Nathan said.

"I don't support a curfew," Stanton interrupted. "However, the others do, so I won't argue the point. However, I will not sign."

"Understood, Captain," Nathan said, carefully removing the unsigned document from the desk.

And on it went. He agreed with the proposal to increase the guard presence and believed it might be an opportunity to increase training opportunities across the different guard and soldiers that existed inside Orsini's walls. He also agreed with the proposal to recall the small trained cavalry unit that was north of the city, tasked with hunting down runaway elemental mages. They should be recalled back home to do something useful.

Stanton paused at that thought. When did he develop such strong opinions against the hunting down of elemental mages? He'd always felt uneasy by it, but never held a strong opinion. He'd arrested a couple over the years himself, though mostly because they were actively breaking the law. He'd also arrested two mages a couple years prior for protesting. However, after spending all winter at Borro, he wasn't convinced anymore that mage protesters should be arrested. Things had changed. He had changed.

And he realized, at that moment, he was glad for it. He hoped everyone would soon change. It was time to reevaluate the words of the Guardians and move to a greater acceptance. Cartossa's unchecked aggression and obsession with persecuting mages had caused this entire crisis. Specifically, it was General Bonacieux's single-minded obsession with wiping out every single mage from his country that had caused this. When he'd driven most of them out, he came to Amadore to do the same. It was time the cardinal conclave did *something*.

Part of him wanted to blame Allegra—for no other reason than to be angry at her for dying on him and leaving him alone—but she was only a small piece of a larger, more intricate puzzle. She helped open his eyes, but he'd been the one to change his mind.

Looking back, it was Little Ferret's trial that had changed him. He walked through a door that permanently locked behind him. Every single word of Walter Cram had echoed in those moments. Every sermon, every protest, every argument between Pero and Francois at the dinner table. All of them had rushed back to him in that moment. He hadn't realized it at the time, but looking back, that was when he stopped caring about the word of the law.

"This is a proposal by Captain Brett, asking to put all elemental mages in Toll Gate Prison until the crisis is over," Nathan said.

"Absolutely not," Stanton snapped.

Nathan glanced at Serafina, who was seated at a tiny desk in the corner of his office scribbling in the account ledgers. "Of course, Captain. I will…I'll let Cardinal Giso know, since he expressed concern about the measure."

Then he realized something about himself. He wanted freedom for all. Mage. Elemental. Normal. Rich. Power. It did not matter. He was not neutral. He was a mage abolitionist.

In that moment, something else dawned upon him. He would refuse any order to arrest or harass a mage for no other reason than them being mages. Lord God Almighty forgive him, but he would refuse those orders.

"Captain? Is there a problem?" Serafina asked. "You look sickly all of the sudden. Do you need me to fetch a healer?"

"I apologize. My mind wandered. Nathan, I will not, under any circumstances, agree to the harassment of the mages we brought from Borro. I absolutely do not support the arrest of the elementals who were granted asylum by the Arbiter's office. She would not have supported that, if she were here." He gulped. "Now that she is not here, I believe it would be a grave miscarriage of this office to go against her wishes now."

"I understand, Captain," Nathan said. He shuffled a few pages out of his stack and handed them back to Serafina.

Serafina squared her shoulders and blew out a breath, like she was preparing herself for a battle. "Captain, I will *personally* deliver our notes and your comments to the Holy Father."

"I can do it myself, if you would prefer."

"No, Captain," Serafina said. "It is my job and I will do it."

"Captain," Nathan said, glancing at Serafina. "We also want your opinion on what to do with the Arbiter's debts."

"What debts?"

Serafina, taking her cue, said, "We've both kept comprehensive records of everything we've taken during our escape here. As well, Nathan took the account book during the evacuation."

Stanton turned to give Nathan a withering look. "Young man. When a building is on fire, you leave it. You do not risk your life to get the accounts ledger. Do you understand me?"

Nathan cleared his throat. "Um, yes, Captain."

Stanton sighed, though he was grateful for the distraction. "What about these debts? We'd taken supplies from many abandoned places. Others have since joined us here and won't be going home for some time."

"When we couldn't assign names, we both recorded the housing positions in the hamlets in hopes that we could identify the owners later. However, I am concerned that these people will not have houses to return to."

"If the rumors are true, Bonacieux will most likely torch all of the houses. There will be nothing left."

Stanton nodded his understanding. "Did you speak to Father Michael about this? He is the bishop for the area, after all. He may have a better idea than myself."

Serafina nodded. "He said to check with you, or perhaps the cardinal clerks to be sure, but speaking as the bishop, he felt the Arbiter's office should provide those who came with us at least a quarter of the payment we owe them. Then, we give them the remainder when they leave Orsini, or they decide not to go back. He felt it would do no good to make them rich now, only to not afford to feed their flock later."

Stanton shrugged. "I have no clue what is appropriate here. Did you ask the cardinal clerks for their opinion?"

Serafina glanced at Nathan.

Nathan cleared his throat and said, "I did earlier today?"

"And...?"

"They said the Arbiter's money wasn't for reimbursing rabble."

Stanton managed to catch the hot words that boiled up, but just barely. *Rabble.* Who did these pompous asses think they were? They did not have even the capability of compassion, let alone the common sense and dignity given to them by the Lord God to know how to use it.

"What do you think Allegra would have done?"

Serafina glanced at Nathan and said, quietly, "She would have said to the abyss with the clerks and ordered them to pay the accounts."

"Then to the abyss with the clerks. Pay the accounts," Stanton said.

"Um, I don't mean to be insensitive, but are we allowed to do that?" Nathan asked. "If she is…I mean, I don't want to say it, but…someone has to…"

Nathan's voice trailed off. No one wanted to say it. Stanton sure didn't, but he knew the words had to start coming out of his mouth eventually. "Until the Arbiter is declared dead, or is replaced and you are fired, I think we should continue to act in the service of the office. We were all appointed to it, so let's keep working for the office."

He didn't even know a damn thing about paperwork, but Serafina was in way over her head. So was Nathan. However, together, they weren't to be underestimated. Allegra had increasingly relied on them as the winter dragged on, and both young people had shown themselves adaptable and clever: qualities that always impressed him.

"I think the best course is for us to bring Father Michael into our confidence and carry on as if—"

The office door flung open and Father Michael stood there, out of breath, his face bright from running. "Rainier! Amadore troops are coming up the path! People are saying there is news about Allegra."

STANTON AND FATHER Michael stood next to each other, breathing heavily from their sprint through the administrative building to get outside. There was no mistaking Amadore's soldiers. Likewise, there was no mistaking the very tall soldier directly in front of him when she took off her helmet.

He tried to steady his breathing, but he couldn't wipe the surprise from his face. "Your Royal Highness."

Ginny smiled at Stanton before handing one of the Orsini guards her helmet. She dismounted and walked toward them. She looked terrible. One side of her face was a sheet of dried blood. Some of her hair was missing, and he thought that maybe part of her ear was, as well. She had a limp. Nevertheless, she walked toward him, the smooth movements of a soldier who feared no one. And one with a smirk on her face.

"Lord Barrington, I'd heard you lived. I am pleased to see it is true."

Stanton felt his face heat up. She always did this to him. "Your Highness, I am known as Captain Rainier here."

She grinned. "I know. That's why I said it, Your Grace."

Stanton laughed and they clapped each other on the back like the old friends they were. "Please don't take this the wrong way, but what in the name of the Almighty are you doing here?"

Ginny grinned at him. She turned and motioned to her men. "Delivering something you left behind."

He'd not noticed the crowd laughing and weeping behind her. It was difficult to see through the gathering, with the guards helping her injured men and women out of the circle of bystanders. But Stanton would never mistake that shock of red hair coming through the crowd.

"Hey, Captain. Got any pie? I'm starving."

Stanton gripped Dodd into a bear hug. "Almighty, I cannot believe you made it. Your mother is going to kill me! I have already told her you were missing!"

"You're crushing me, Captain," Dodd wheezed. When Stanton finally let go, giving Dodd a wide smile and a clap on the shoulder, Dodd said, "I brought you a couple of presents."

Stanton looked over Dodd's much shorter shoulder. His breath caught in his throat as his body forgot how to do the most basic of tasks. He blinked several times, unable to move. Were his eyes deceiving him?

"You said my job was to protect her, sir."

"I did, didn't I?" Stanton said, his voice cracking.

"Who am I to disobey an order?"

Behind him, he heard Father Michael say, "Come, my son. Lex has been waiting for you."

He wanted to tell Dodd how Lex was fairing, but he couldn't speak. Walter Cram was holding up a limping, struggling Allegra. She was wearing nothing but her undergarments, a jacket, and a blanket, but she was alive. She was alive in front of him. She was *alive*.

He just stared at her, as she slowly made her way through the crowd. Dimly, he was aware of their cheering and praises. Cram looked up and gave Stanton a knowing smile. He said something to Allegra, and she looked up sharply. Her face brightened, and she stumbled. Cram held her up.

That broke him from his trance. He rushed to her, pulling her close to his chest. Cram had to disentangle himself, but he did so in time to avoid being crushed into the embrace. "My love. Oh, my love."

Soft, gentle arms wrapped around him and she buried her face in his chest. She stank, and was dirty, and she was perfect.

"Oh, thank the Lord, you're safe. I was so worried." Stanton's voice cracked when he said, "I thought I'd lost you."

A strong hand rested on his shoulder briefly, and Stanton glanced to see it was Cram. Cram gave him a sharp nod.

"Lancaster."

Cram stopped at the use of his real name. He looked at Stanton cautiously.

"Thank you for bringing her back. I am in your debt."

Cram's confident, even arrogant, façade slipped. Now, Stanton could see the weary man who carried too many burdens. Cram bowed his head and let out a long sigh. Then, he patted Stanton's shoulder once more and jogged to catch up with Dodd and Father Michael.

"Walter saved our lives, as did Imogen. Please make her get help. She's terribly injured. And the horses. Someone needs to look after the horses. They have been going on almost no food or sleep. They're exhausted. And…"

Stanton covered her mouth with his. He didn't even care how she tasted, or the mud or the dirty or any of it. He didn't care about the crowd when they whooped and howled. He didn't care about any of it.

A giggle escaped her, and she pulled away. The crowd cheered louder, and her cheeks flushed dark. "I'm never going to hear the end of this now."

"Everyone knew," Stanton said, leaning his forehead against hers. "Father Michael is the biggest gossip in Serna."

"Did he…"

"Yes, he made it." Stanton pointed and said, "That's him, with Dodd and Cram."

"Lex?"

"He's not out of danger, but he's alive. Nadira, Serafina, Nathan, Calm Seas, Kia... They're all here."

Allegra broke into sobs and he held her tight, not bothering to hold back his own tears.

"Thank you, Lord. Thank you," she whispered over and over.

He was quieter with his praise, but praise he did all the same.

DODD FOLLOWED THE chattering footman, Father Michael, and Cram through the maze of corridors deep into the papal wing. He'd been inside the building plenty of times, but never past the closed inner doors. Dodd realized how filthy he was when the eyes of the others met him. He didn't care. He had to see Lex with his own two eyes. Then, and only then, could he know the world was going to be all right.

People stopped, whispering and pointing, at first. Then, louder did the greetings grow.

"Is that Lieutenant Dodd? That's Lieutenant Dodd!"

"Lieutenant Dodd! Lieutenant Dodd!"

"The Arbiter? Is she alive?"

"Praise the Almighty! Lieutenant Dodd!"

Dodd tried to smile, for words would not come from his lips. His worries had wrapped his guts into knots and were cutting off blood flow. He had to see Lex with his own eyes. He had to see him.

Cardinal DeLancey stepped in his path. In her frail voice, she asked, "Did you bring the Arbiter back to us?"

Dodd forced his feet to a stop. He bowed, his heart thudding the entire time. "She is in the courtyard, Your Grace."

DeLancey closed her eyes. "She lives?"

"She lives."

She blew out a breath and whispered a praise. Then she said, "Your friend has had the best possible care. We know what risks he took to fight the demon. We have not abandoned him."

Dodd sucked in a breath until it forced down the lump in his throat. Lex was alive. He needed to be calm. He needed to be reserved. Lex could not know what stirred inside him. All that mattered was that Lex was alive.

"Father Michael, who is this?" DeLancey asked.

"Walter Cram, Your Grace."

"The demon lover?"

It shocked Dodd to see Walter bow to the cardinal who'd just insulted him. But he did it. And when he spoke, his voice was measured and respectful.

"Yes, Your Grace. Father Michael takes me to the refugees. Thank you for treating them all, no matter who they were."

She lifted her chin. "All are equal in the eyes of the Lord God. So, all are equal in my eyes. Now, go. I have to see the Arbiter with my own eyes."

They turned two more corners before Father Michael departed with Cram. By now, the footman had to continue pushing through to form a path as word spread through the cathedral. The prodigal children had returned home. There was praise and rejoicing. However, he still needed to see Lex.

The servant stopped and motioned at a door. "He is in here. Sir, may I remind you that he is very weak. He might not wake. He struggles with dreams, you understand? The apothecary's attempts to medicate them away have been…not completely successful. You must prepare yourself, in case."

"I understand," Dodd whispered. Bonacieux should thank the Almighty that he wasn't here yet, else Dodd would have gone out there and killed him with his bare hands.

The servant nodded and knocked lightly. He pushed the door open and asked in a low voice, "Lieutenant? Are you awake?"

"Yes."

Dodd's heart thudded so hard his vision blurred for a moment. He nodded at the servant and stepped inside. Lex was propped up on pillows, wearing a white bed tunic. A pile of hand-stitched patchwork quilts surrounded his old friend. Across Lex's shoulders rested another quilt. A small fire crackled in the corner, and the window was open a crack. Only a sliver of light escaped into the room, from where the heavy curtains were parted a crack. Just the perfect mixture of fresh air, warmth, and light. And in the middle of it all was Lex's pale, drawn face.

Lex turned heavy-lidded eyes toward the door. "Dodd? Is that you?"

Tears welled up in Dodd's eyes, a mixture of relief, anger, worry, uncertainty, and something much deeper and worrisome. He smiled, though. He couldn't stop that no more than he could stop his tears. "It's me."

"You stink," Lex muttered.

"You look awful."

Lex faded out for a moment but opened his eyes again. "Did the Contessa make it?"

Dodd walked over and sat on the bed next to Lex. "Me, Cram, and the Contessa. She hurt her ankle, but other than that, we're fine."

"Cram is alive, too?"

"Yup. Not all prayers can be answered."

Lex chuckled, and it seemed to rouse him. He blinked a few times and said, "It's really you, isn't it?"

"Yes, it's me." Dodd's voice cracked. "It's me, Lex. We made it."

"I'm cold," Lex whispered as he closed his eyes.

The ends of the blanket around Lex's shoulders had slipped down his narrow shoulders, so Dodd pulled them back up, crossing the blanket across his friend's chest. Then he stirred the fire a little more, adding another piece of wood. He looked at the window and considered closing it, but thought better of it. The fresh air might have been necessary orders by a surgeon, and Dodd didn't want to do anything to upset the delicate balance of Lex's recovery.

He came back to sit on the edge of the bed. He cupped Lex's chin with his hand. Lex's cheekbones were always stark against his narrow face, but now they were sharp and painfully prominent. "Don't ever scare me like that again."

Lex opened his eyes and a wide smile beamed across his face. "Look at you, you big baby."

Lex reached out bony arms, disrupting the blanket Dodd had just carefully folded into place. Dodd accepted the hug, though, very careful not to crush Lex, even if he wanted to so badly. Small whimpering sounds came from Lex, and Dodd realized he was crying. Dodd's heart wept for him. How hard must it have been for Lex to worry while trying to stay alive.

"Why are you dead?"

"I'm not dead," Dodd said. "I'm very much alive."

The servant and Father Michael had given him the basic details of Lex's injuries. A deep sword wound, blood loss, a lingering infection, and general weakness. Add to that the hunger and dehydration from the journey, and the mental distress, and it shocked them all that Lex had even made it to Orsini. As Dodd thought those things, and the thought of how close he'd come to losing his best friend, all sense escaped him. He pulled out of the embrace, just enough to look into Lex's eyes. His eyes were glazed and wet, but there was still so much of Lex in them.

"I missed you so much," Dodd whispered.

"I love you, Dodd," Lex said, his words slurred.

"I love you, too. So much."

If someone had asked later, Dodd couldn't have said who moved first. He thought he'd been still the entire time, but cracked, dry lips crossed his. Just a brush. Just a hint. When he came to his senses, Lex's wide eyes were in front of him, much clearer than before. Had Dodd kissed him without even realizing? Had Lex done it? His mind was muddled. He was so exhausted, so weary, that maybe he'd fallen asleep and this was a dream.

"Dodd?" Lex asked, confused.

"Sorry about that," Dodd said reflexively, not sure what else to say. Had Lex really said those words?

"Dodd!" Lex let out a little shriek and wrapped his arms tight around Dodd.

Then realization struck when Lex said, "I thought I was dreaming. You're really here!"

Dodd's eyes welled up with tears and he buried his face against the shaggy curls that were starting to form around Lex's ears. Lex hated those "cursed curls" as he called them because they would tickle his ears. He'd need a barber soon. Maybe Dodd could sneak in a pair of scissors and just snip the ticklish ones away. A little comfort, a little display of affection…

Dodd gasped and held Lex tighter. Oh, Lord God, this was even worse than he'd thought. He was so certain he would be fine. He was never going to be fine again.

"You're hurting me," Lex said.

Dodd released Lex as fast as the words registered in his brain. "I'm sorry, Lex. I didn't mean to."

Lex's eyes glazed over again, but the smile was there. "Look at you! Are you crying?"

"Fucking loser," Dodd said, unsure what to say. But then, the curl taunted him, and he reached up and twisted it around his finger. He felt a smile tug at the corners of his mouth.

"Dodd?"

At Lex's confused tone, Dodd realized what the fuck he was doing, and pulled his hand back so hard that his shoulder popped. "You need a haircut."

Lex reached up to the curl that Dodd was about to toy with. "It tickles my ear, but the surgeon said I'm not allowed to have a haircut until I can get out of bed and walk over to that chair in the corner without any help."

Dodd looked at the chair on the other side of the room. It was a small room, but Lex looked so frail underneath all the blankets. It seemed like an impossible distance. "Without any help, huh?"

"The surgeon said she will tie me to the bed if I try before I'm ready," Lex said. A cough shook his body. "Mark my words, Dodd, as soon as I can get out of this fucking bed, I'm going to find Bonacieux and I'm going to make him wish he'd never been born."

"Amen," Dodd said soberly.

"I hate being stuck here," Lex said, the slur and weakness coming back into his voice.

While Dodd was relieved for any conversation that wasn't about the kiss, he was very confused. It was dawning on him that Lex was heavily drugged. Did Lex even mean the words? Did Lex mean the kiss? Should Dodd bring it up? Hearing the words, feeling Lex's lips brush his, though…Lord God, how was he supposed to go back to how it was before?

And yet, Dodd was also relieved for any conversation. "How long do they think before you'll be allowed to try to get out of bed?"

A disgusted sound escaped Lex, his voice growing stronger and alert. "Everyone has an opinion, even the damn pope. He visits me every day with a couple of cardinals. Some of them come visit me on their own. They *read* to me. Cardinal Giso came in and did services for me. Father Michael is here every free minute he gets. He said he'll get me a copy of the *Tattler Times* when I'm able to sit up in bed on my own."

"I thought they banned that again," Dodd said.

"They did," Lex said with a smirk. "But he knows which clerk is printing it."

Dodd snickered, but the mirth faded when Lex's head drooped. "Get some sleep, Lex."

"They drug my food," Lex whispered.

Dodd stroked the side of Lex's cheek gently. Lex leaned against his hand for a moment before drifting off to sleep. As Lex's shallow breaths steadied and came in a regular pattern, both sadness and anger sunk deep into Dodd's chest. Bonacieux was going to pay for this.

And Walter Cram could go to the damn abyss and may the demons eat him alive. He'd been right that night in the church. Knowing that Cram was right just made it all just that much worse.

CHAPTER NINE

THE CELEBRATION CROWD in the courtyard grew larger and larger, with shouts and cheers drowning out the cries for news about loved ones. Servants, stable boys, healers, and surgeons rushed about the courtyard. Allegra wished she had more news for those who asked, but there had been so much smoke, so much disorder, in the final moments when they jumped from the abbey.

Purple flashed in the distance and a group of cardinals came rushing down the marble stairs to greet her. Stanton helped her take painful steps toward the fast-approaching group. Rupert flung his arms around her, not even waiting for Stanton to pull himself from her.

"I have been so worried!" Rupert said, and tears flowed down his cheeks. "Lord God Almighty, you are here now. Your brother would have murdered me if I let something happen to you."

"My brother would have inherited my estates. He might have given you a cottage for it."

"Don't speak such nonsense," Rupert said, pretending to be offended, but laughing as he said it.

Rupert pulled out of the hug long enough to let Pero give her a tight embrace.

"Welcome. Welcome, all! Your Royal Highness! It is an honor," Rupert called out. "Welcome all!"

Imogen inclined her head and said, "Thank you. If I might be rude, Your Radiance, I must get my men to the healers."

"And yourself!" Rupert said. "Follow the guards, they'll show you. But you, too."

"It looks worse than it is," she said.

"Nevertheless. It is my wish that you are tended to."

She gritted her teeth, but she bowed. "Of course, Your Radiance."

"Where is Lieutenant Dodd?"

"Father Michael took him to see Lieutenant Lex."

"Good. Perhaps that will bolster the boy's will to fight. Welcome all! Welcome!" Rupert called out to Imogen's soldiers who marched behind a healer. Many of them were being fussed at by other medical helpers. "Good. Good."

"Do I know you, sir?"

Allegra turned to find Walter standing behind her. He ignored Rupert and said, "There's no sign of the others yet."

"Oh," Allegra said, deflated. She'd hoped Walter would have spotted someone.

"Is there a problem?" Rupert asked, in his tone that said he wanted to be included in the conversation.

Allegra cleared her throat to better address the gathering about her. She was not looking forward to this. "Cardinals, Holy Father, allow me to introduce to you Walter Cram. He's the elemental mage who defeated the demon at Borro, and who saved my life too many times to count."

Allegra could hear the whispers of the people around them. Cardinal Giso was behind the gathering, patiently waiting his turn. His facial expression turned pensive, waiting to see what happened.

But Rupert surprised them all, except her, by reaching out a hand. Walter took a beat to consider, but then he accepted and shook Rupert's hand. "It is good to meet you in the flesh, Mr. Cram. Our Lieutenant Lex told us already about your bravery."

Allegra noticed that Rupert's voice grew just a shade louder, catching the attention of the closest gathered.

"I know you and the Arbiter will need to be interrogated by the cardinals far too soon for your liking, but I must be the first to thank you. You did not have to stand for the faith or the people there, but you did. That is bravery, and something I believe the Lord God Almighty will reward." Then he turned to Allegra, and still in the slightly-too-loud voice, said, "And to you, Contessa, thank you. Lieutenant Lex told us how you fought the beast with nothing more than smoldering pieces of wood. How Bonacieux could ever confuse kindling for elemental magic, I have no idea, but I am grateful that all you sacrificed was your ankle."

Allegra let out a long breath. Lex had covered for her. Of course, he had. He had sworn to protect her, had he not? Lex seemed to her the type to never take a promise lightly. Rupert gave her a knowing look, one that screamed for her to remember the lie well. She would.

"I think Bonacieux just assumed because the rest of us were there, and we were all elementals. Except for the Arbiter and Lex, of course. So he assumed, incorrectly," Walter said.

"Indeed, he did." Rupert offered Walter his hand again. "I'm glad we could clear up this misunderstanding before anything unfortunate happened."

Walter had an excellent poker face, but his voice softened just slightly as he said, "Thank you, Your Radiance."

Rupert gave Walter a very small incline of the head. Then, in his jovial voice, he said, "Not at all! Not at all! You brought us back our Arbiter! I am heartened by the knowledge that the Arbiter has the trust of so many, and that they would risk their lives for her safe return."

"Some gave their lives, Your Radiance," Walter said.

Rupert turned somber and said, "I will ensure they are never forgotten."

Walter's voice cracked when he said, "Thank you."

Rupert surveyed the scene and said, "Now, we must get the Arbiter inside and cared for. There is much to discuss. Cardinal Giso?"

"Yes, Your Radiance?"

"Will you kindly put one of your people in charge of all of this?" Rupert made an all-encompassing gesture at the courtyard. "Who *are* all of these people anyway?"

Allegra explained in quick terms how Imogen's people found her, and how they picked up a couple of sisters along the way. Then, how the crowd gathered further down the path, and had followed them to the courtyard, needing the guard to assemble.

Rupert took it all in, nodding to himself as she spoke. "Right. Right. Giso? Could you?"

"I'll see to it myself. Will you call someone to fetch me when you gather the cardinals?" When Rupert nodded, Giso said to Allegra, "It is good to see you, my child."

Allegra gave him a stiff smile. She had not quite forgiven him for his snotty letters about her over the winter months. She turned to Rupert and said, "Did you add more steps to the staircase while I was away? I don't remember it ever being this steep."

"I'll carry you," Stanton offered.

"It's too far," Allegra insisted. Though, she looked at the incline and thought she wasn't going to make it up them on her own, unless it was on her hands and knees.

Walter cleared his throat. He'd done that a lot around Stanton at Borro, and had slipped back into the habit here, too. "Rainier, it'll take both of us. You'll break your neck carrying her by yourself."

"Thanks," Allegra said dryly.

"Walter Cram, are you hinting I am not strong enough to carry the Contessa?"

"No, I'm saying very loudly that the stairs are slick with rain water and you're going to slip and break your neck showing off," Walter said calmly.

Stanton muttered under his breath, "He really is the most irksome man in creation."

Allegra rolled her eyes, but also accepted their help. She needed it, and she was in too much pain to argue.

The crowd was thinner inside the papal palace, though it was still busier than usual with people coming to gawk at the Arbiter's arrival. Word spread quickly in a place like Orsini, where there was no true anonymity.

She wasn't able to answer the barrage of questions and let Rupert and the others handle answering. Walter and Stanton ignored them, focusing instead on the duty of carrying her swiftly through the crowded corridors, with the cardinals and bishops telling people to hold their questions. Wait. Wait. Just wait.

It hurt Allegra's soul, though, all the same. Some of the sisters broke into song, singing praises for her return. Others demanded to know what had happened. Fear was laced in so many voices, especially those who'd come from Borro or the abbey and had lived through the attack. After being hunted like prey, she needed calm and quiet. Yet, listening to the cardinals talk amongst themselves about their next meeting and what they needed her to answer, well, she knew calm was not in her immediate future.

Walter and Stanton passed her to two guards, to rest their arms. They walked with her, though, everyone hammering with endless questions. Thankfully, Rupert's cue about Lex's story gave them a chance to adjust their own tales just slightly enough to make passing comments without needing to come up with detailed stories. She knew they would all need those stories and would need to coordinate with Lex, but for now, the hint was just enough to get through the next fifteen minutes of getting through the corridors.

"Over here," Rupert said, pointing at a door. "Lex is just a couple of doors down. That will make it easier on my surgeon while we get your rooms organized. Captain, might I appoint you her personal protector while she is convalescing, so that I can continue my duties knowing she is safe?"

Stanton blushed, but he nodded and said, "I would be honored, Your Radiance."

"Good, good. Let's get you inside."

"Wait, where is Lex? I need to see him."

"Me, too," Walter said.

They carefully placed Allegra down in front of Lex's door and she tapped on it before entering. Allegra was shocked by the sight of Lex. She'd not realized how bad it had been. Lex was sleeping, however, seated upright and well wrapped in blankets. The air was fresh and warm, too, so the room smelled like the market outdoors and not of wood smoke and sweat.

Allegra smiled at the sight of Dodd asleep on the edge of Lex's pillow. His back was going to ache from being sprawled across the chair and the bed, but Allegra didn't want to wake him, either. She heard Walter let out a self-satisfied sigh, though, like the scene before them had always been inevitable.

Stanton also let out a sigh, but his was more annoyed than anything else. "I see Dodd ate Lex's food."

They closed the door, leaving the old friends to sleep undisturbed. Allegra asked, "Are they drugging Lex's food?"

Stanton nodded. He leaned in to speak in a low tone. "Lex has violent nightmares. He's torn his stitches out twice."

"I've heard him screaming in my rooms," Rupert said somberly. "The poor child gets into these vicious nightmares and just screams and screams until he exhausts himself. No one can wake him up. Pero tried one night. The servants all try. So they are drugging the wine and hoping time and healing helps."

"Lord," Allegra whispered.

"The healer asked the mages to work a slumber spell into the blanket that's across his pillow, and then the surgeon has been drugging his food. It's the only way he can sleep without hurting himself," Stanton said. "We've tried not to have him left alone, but sometimes he insists, and..." Stanton shrugged.

"Now that he's sleeping, it's been better," Rupert said. "He's been healing, too, and the worst of the infection is finally clearing up. He fought a real demon, and then a monster, and now he fights the ones in his mind. It is unfair."

"Your Radiance, may I stay with him? With respect, I know what he is going through better than anyone. I can help."

Rupert put his hand on Walter's shoulder. "I would appreciate any help. I'm rather fond of the boy."

"Can someone have a plate of food sent up to me, though?" Walter asked. "A very large plate, if possible."

Rupert motioned for the footman who lingered discreetly a few doors down to approach. He ordered a change of clothes, blankets, pillows, and a full meal for Walter. "Bring him a good bottle of wine from the cellar, too. Not the crap they serve the bishops, either. Tell them I want one of the good bottles."

The footman bowed and hurried off. When he was out of earshot, Rupert said, "The footmen are keeping an ear out for Lex. I have them instructed to get anything for him. Anything at all."

Allegra nodded. "Thank you. Has Nadira been allowed in here? I'd think she'd want to keep Lex company."

Stanton chuckled. "Nadira has been organizing Lex's recovery and seeing to the meals, the wine, the broth, all of it."

"Poor Lex," Allegra said. "She's going to browbeat Lex into healing."

"That was the goal," Stanton said. "You would have been so proud of Nadira. She kept us all from starving. She kept everyone as busy as possible, too, so that people didn't succumb to their despair."

Warmth rushed through Allegra, hearing them speak of her maidservant. She knew that Nadira was an employee, but Nadira was also not *only* her employee. Nadira had raised Allegra, and there was a bond between them that Allegra didn't have a word for, but it nevertheless existed. She was so proud of Nadira, and that pride only grew with each tale of her helpfulness and kindness.

"Let's get you to your room, my dear," Rupert said. "You need a bath, a meal, and a change of clothes. Well, more accurately, you need clothes."

"I gave some of it to a group of children." She blew out a breath. "Did they make it? I don't remember the sister's name with them, I'm sorry."

Stanton smiled at her. "A messenger came with news yesterday. A caravan picked up the sisters and the children, plus a handful of stragglers. They are taking the north road a little further before coming back down to drop off the children."

Allegra blew out a breath. "Oh, that is good to know. So, there's truly no word about any of the mages who'd helped us?"

Stanton shook his head. "I'm sorry, no. Honestly, they might be here, but I wouldn't know who they were, and I doubt they're going to announce themselves. For very obvious reasons."

"You wouldn't dare arrest them, would you?" Allegra demanded.

"I wouldn't, no. I am not the only one here with authority, however." His voice was gentle. He must have known she snapped out of pain and exhaustion, not out of malice.

"Let us deal with one crisis at a time," Rupert interjected. "Allegra, I need to assemble the senior Cardinals, and you need to speak to them. Is three hours' time sufficient for you to prepare yourself? We have much to discuss and it can't be delayed."

All Allegra wanted was to crawl into a hot bath and sleep until the water turned cold. Then, she wanted to crawl into an iron-warmed bed and sleep with her feet propped up on blanket-wrapped hot bricks.

"Three hours," Allegra said wearily. She wouldn't even have time for much of a nap. She considered asking one of the servants for her own drugged food to help with the ache in her ankle. Instead, she said, "Please look after Her Highness. They saved our lives. We would not have survived if not for them."

"She and her people will have the best possible care," Rupert assured her. "I will personally see to it. For now, please, go rest and eat."

Allegra nodded at the footmen and they lifted her back up and carried her to her room. She fell asleep on the way from Lex's room to her own.

RESOLUTION OF FAITH

BLESS ME, LORD God Almighty, for I am an instrument of your will. The armies of the abyss are upon us. The faithful must see the light. They must learn to put their trust in Your Ladyship.

Bless me, Lord God Almighty, for my sins are numerous.

Bless me, Lord God Almighty, for I must carry out your will, though I risk destroying the very thing I wish to preserve.

Bless me, Lord God Almighty, for I am but one man.

CHAPTER TEN

ALLEGRA BEGRUDGINGLY WOKE when she was placed upon her new bed. Stanton spent the next few minutes filling her in on the latest Cathedral goings on, all the while touching her as much as possible. She longed for rest and quiet with Stanton, but it was not meant to be for them yet. Still, they made the best of their time. A squeeze of a hand. A gentle brush of fingers across bare skin. A hug whenever tears threatened.

Allegra had no clean clothes to change into, nor water to wash, so she waited for the servants. The first item to arrive was a plate of cold goose and bread. The goose was overcooked and the bread undercooked, but she was too hungry to turn it down.

Maids came in and out with firewood, warm water, blankets, and linens. Footmen arrived with wine and brandy, gifts from clergy who'd heard of her safe arrival. The room's door did not lock, and she didn't know the servants bustling in and out. Her relationship with Stanton was obviously now common knowledge with their blatant display of affection in the courtyard, but she did not want to share her private moments of their reunion with strangers. They were cautious with their affection, even as all they wanted to do was indulge it.

Finally, the trail of servants died down, and the couple were left in relative privacy. Allegra wrapped her arms around Stanton, burying her face in his chest. She'd been so frightened the entire journey, and the emotions were finally boiling over now. The relief, the worry, the stress, the trauma, all of it.

Finally, she managed to speak, even if the words felt so insignificant. "I have been so worried."

He kissed the top of her head, not risking letting her go. "I thought I'd lost you."

They sat on the edge of the lumpy bed together, and enjoyed several minutes of quiet words, worries finally expressed, and the simple sweetness of their kisses and caresses. They did not linger, however. They both felt the press of time, the clock ticking in another room, where others gathered to plan her future. She was needed. She was still the Arbiter.

Eventually, they pulled apart to help her prepare for her meeting. Stanton helped her out of her petticoats, and they made several private jokes about the intimacy of undressing and his plans for her later. One of Stanton's teases caused heat to rise in her cheeks, both from the embarrassment of his words and the promise of what would come when time was less pressing and her ankle didn't ache.

She savored his words, allowing memories to fully form in her mind. Too much of her time with him was taken up with duty. They had not been given enough time to be *together* and she was determined to rectify that as soon as commitments permitted. Until then, she would steal these moments and lock them away.

Stanton used the sponge provided by the maid to wash the back of Allegra's neck and shoulders, ensuring he tested each clean spot with a kiss. For just those few moments of peace, Allegra was tempted to give in and forget her responsibilities. It would be too easy to dismiss the cardinals, to claim exhaustion and injury, and spend the remainder of the day in bed with the man of her heart.

The door flung open, causing Stanton to drop the sponge. A line of wet splashes made her dirty shift cling to her skin.

"It's true!"

Nadira was normally a woman of strong emotional control, so it broke Allegra to see the old woman break into tears. Allegra wrapped her arms around her servant since childhood; Nadira was her employee, yes, but she was also the woman she trusted with her life. Allegra couldn't keep her own tears in check, when Nadira's flowed.

"It is so good to know you are well," Allegra said. She pulled out of the embrace and said, "Stanton told me you were working with the injured."

Nadira pulled out a handkerchief from a hidden skirt pocket and dabbed her eyes. "I came as soon as that Little Gopher got me." She gave Stanton a stern look. "Did you explain to her about his name? We can't have any mistakes. Those snakes will come after him again."

Allegra assured her that she'd been instructed how the Consorts were hiding Little Ferret, and how they were calling him Little Gopher now, as he was the gopher for the Consorts and the various guards. "The Consorts will protect him, as will I. And, Walter."

"I heard that *thing* lived. Well. The Almighty makes his own choices as he sees fit, I suppose."

"He helped save my life, Nadira."

Nadira made an unimpressed sound. She'd never liked Walter. Before he became the great demon lover and rebel leader, Nadira had always called him a ragamuffin because he trimmed his hair in the latest fashions.

Nadira's expression darkened as she gave Allegra a stern once-over. "Your Ladyship, I am sorry to say that you are a mess. The servants here are useless. Did they bring you anything edible?"

"Cold goose, bread and jam," Allegra said.

"I wouldn't feed that goose to the pigs," Nadira scoffed. "I'll get a proper platter brought up. Your rags will need to be burned. I'll speak with Serafina. I'm sure she can find you a dress. It won't be pretty, but at least you'll be decent."

"Nadira," Allegra said in a calm voice, ignoring her servant's protestations about the shoddy service at the Cathedral. "Have you been treated well here?"

"I am your personal servant. No one would *dare* treat me poorly," Nadira said. "I have spent most of my time between Lieutenant Lex and Calm Seas."

Allegra sighed sadly at the mention of one of her personal servants from Borro. "How is she?"

"She's in the infirmary with severe burns. I must confess I charged some small expenses to your personal accounts to help her. Serafina said it would be fine, as did the Captain. I hope I did not cross a line."

"Not at all. You know me well enough to know I would have done the same if I were here. Will she recover?"

"They have an entire group of mage sisters and brothers doing nothing but weaving healing and restorative magic. That, with the surgeons and the physicians, plus the apothecary is mixing potions and laying on poultices. There is no better place to recover. There will be scars, but most aren't on her face."

"I should like to visit her soon. In fact, I would like to visit everyone. Can that be arranged?"

"I will speak with that Nathan boy of yours. He's a strange little thing, but between us, Your Ladyship? He can get anything done around here." Nadira leaned forward to whisper. "*Anything.* If someone said he were a mage and this was his gift, I would believe it. Well, Your Ladyship. Finish washing. Captain, I realize you are a man, but please try to assist Her Ladyship as best as you are capable."

"I will endeavor to do my best," Stanton said flatly, successfully managing to hide the smile Allegra knew he was tempted to show.

"I'll find you clothing and food worth eating." With that final command, Nadira squared her shoulders and marched out of the room, pointedly closing the door behind her.

Three more servants entered moments later, with more water and more wine. Allegra rushed them off to do their own duties. Then, she said, "I appreciate the sister who gave up her room for me, but I believe I will be sleeping in your bed tonight."

Stanton raised one eyebrow. "Are you propositioning me, Your Ladyship?"

"Absolutely," Allegra said, reaching up to kiss him. "But, first. I have to wash the grime out of my wrinkles."

"My love, you have no wrinkles."

The next hour or so was a blur of servants and employees. Serafina burst into the room when Stanton was helping her out of her dirty shift and Nathan burst in when she was wrapping a blanket about her naked, but clean self. Both chattered on endlessly and excitedly, until Allegra had to tell both to turn their backs because she was naked. Nathan, especially, seemed surprised to hear of her clothing state and stared at her until her cheeks flushed. Then, his cheeks flushed, and then he and Serafina both turned so that she could finish drying off while they chattered on.

The clothes Nadira had found were "woefully plain," as she called them, but as Allegra had no interest in going before the Cardinals naked except for a scratchy blanket, the basic wool dress and shoes were acceptable. She'd have gone in the plainest of sisters' habit styles if it meant having herself clothed.

Nadira had to tell Nathan twice more to turn around, as she helped her mistress into her clothes. Serafina didn't even draw breath the entire time Nadira helped dress Allegra. She only followed a quarter of what her assistant said, but she didn't ask questions. There would be time later for that. For now, she was just happy they were all together again. And Serafina seemed so delighted to share her paperwork burden with anyone, so Allegra let her ramble on.

Decently attired, if rather plain, Allegra sat down again on the edge of her bed with Stanton pressed close to her. Nadira brought her boiled ham and jam-filled tarts that caused her stomach to growl protestations that she was not eating fast enough. However, her stomach also protested that she was eating too fast and she gagged on a too-large bite of tart. Then, she gagged on the wine she'd tried to wash it all down with. After that, she took steadying breaths between each bite, willing herself to slow down. She was famished, though.

While she struggled with her appetite and upset stomach, Nathan and Serafina rapidly spilled all of the details of her accounts and their work, all interrupted with personal stories of their escape and trials since returning to the Cathedral without her. They frequently talked over each other, nodding at some stories or disagreeing over the minutia of others. Nadira and Stanton occasionally interjected their own version of events, offering up more factual and less emotional perspectives, but those were brushed aside by her excited, youthful assistants.

And all the while, she and Stanton didn't stop touching. Be it thigh against thigh, arm against arm, a hand brushing away hair from eyes, neither was interested in letting the other go just yet.

Too soon, though, the ominous knock came. Nadira opened the door to the stoic expressions of two footmen. Both were in the bright colors of the inner servants; those who worked directly for individual cardinals.

The elder of the two said, "Your Ladyship? The senior cardinals have gathered for a supper meeting, and they wish you to join them."

By now, Allegra's exhaustion was tugging at her. It had been a long day, and she'd not eaten nearly enough to stop the dizzy spells that occasionally washed over her. Even Nadira commented on how she'd noticeably lost weight from her journey and would need to fatten her back up.

Still, she regretted eating the tarts, for they had become a brick in her stomach that tortured her as muscles clenched. Allegra blew out a breath. In a whisper, she asked Stanton, "Is there anything else I need to know?"

"No."

She nodded and, with his help, stood up from the bed. She feared what might come despite Stanton's repeated assurances that Lex had already established the truth. The story was straightforward, as there was only the tiniest of white lies added into it. She had no issue lying to the cardinals to save her own skin. Her worries came from the fear of telling the *wrong* lie. However, Lex had thought of that, too, and already established the reason for any inconsistencies. She'd hit her head. She couldn't remember. The details were foggy. Nothing will make perfect sense or be totally clear.

Allegra was astounded by Lex's clear thinking. Despite being near death, Lex had maintained his wits well enough to devise a simplistic narrative that made just about anything plausible.

"Where should I go, when I'm done?"

"My office in the barracks. My room is on the other side. I just realized you've never been in there." Stanton smiled. "It's not as nice as my room at the abbey."

"I'm surprised you didn't rent one of the houses or upper apartments. Don't they pay you?"

Stanton shrugged. "I had no need to entertain, and since I had no ladies in my life, privacy wasn't a concern. The boys like having me nearby, and I like being around to harass them whenever they come in loud and drunk."

"Depending upon how this goes, I might, too, be loud and intoxicated," Allegra said with a chuckle. "I will endeavor to be silent."

"I was planning a celebratory glass of brandy myself," he said, eyeing the expensive bottle that the Bishop of Orsini had sent her. "With your permission, of course." With her nod of approval, he said, "Good! I'll wait for you, though. Don't worry about waking me. Serafina and I still have a lot of things to go over. I've been helping her with some of the administrative issues she's been having."

"Anything I need to fix in this meeting?"

He shook his head. "Mostly, it's her not knowing which wheel to grease."

"Ah, yes. That's why I am not letting anyone take Nathan away from me." She glanced at the door. "Time to face the demons."

He gave her arm one final squeeze and said, "Good luck."

Thankfully, one of the maids had procured Allegra a new crutch, and one that was both correct for her height and well padded. She was still slow, but at least she could make her way down the corridor under her own power.

She'd never spent much time here during her appointment to Arbiter; all of her time had been spent preparing her trip to Borro Abbey. Now, she had the opportunity to look, as she hobbled down the corridors. The walls' stonework was covered in rich tapestries like the rest of the palace, but that soon changed to gleaming wood. Gone were the tapestries in favour of paintings and curio boxes filled with various curiosities and historical delights. The floors here were still stone, but they were covered in rich carpets of dark blues. She hoped her ankle would heal soon enough that she could enjoy these items. Though, if Bonacieux arrived, she suspected she would be in the infirmary tending the healers and surgeons, since what use was a fine lady in a time of war?

She shook off her thoughts. She hadn't the time to prepare a speech or even presentation of thought. She'd not even gotten a chance to curl in bed with her lover. Instead, it was work. Get the story right. Make sure everyone was in their place in her mind. Refresh her memory over the events that were real and adjust her memories accordingly to fit the lie. It scared her that so many people were involved in this lie now. She knew Lex had to come up with a story about how she had fire in her hand, and she knew Bonacieux would instill a notion of doubt if they just flat out denied him.

But kindling?

It seemed a rather silly excuse.

Then again, perhaps that was the brilliance of it. Something as innocent as a burning stick, as opposed to the evil manifestation of the abyss. How easy to mix up the two in a fight.

"Is that the ballroom, where the Borro refugees are located?" Allegra asked her escort.

"Yes, Your Ladyship."

"I will take a moment to step in and say hello."

"The cardinals are waiting," he said.

"A few hours ago, they thought I was dead," she said, forcing a smile. She didn't care about making them wait. "It is important I speak with these people."

She'd not expected her hands to shake, but they did when she walked into the assembly of victims. The scene before her was too close to the refugee's arrival at Borro for her comfort. A stark reminder of how little rank or fortune meant when the world was ablaze. There, they'd been gathered into the ballroom. There were so few of them here now, though. Only half of the Abbey even made it out. There was almost no one from Borro itself, including the tent-dwelling refugees who'd survived the winter. None of the elemental mage dissidents.

She steadied her thoughts, pushing her grief as far back as possible. The children were safe. She'd made it back. Stanton's convoy had made it. There was no reason to believe those caught behind the army wouldn't have run for safety. For all they knew, Bonacieux might have left them alone, though it did not seem likely. All she could do was hope.

Though, as Allegra examined the room, she noticed some oddities. At Borro, the fires were roaring and there was always a line up for a hot beverage of some type, or for slices of bread with butter to hold off the hunger. Everyone's bedding was rough, and everyone was on equal footing.

Here, she could tell that the people had been separated by rank whenever possible. Some of the wealthier members were propped up on hay mattresses, though they did not look injured or frail. Whereas, on the opposite end, she could clearly see refugee mages who'd been living in tents at Borro Abbey were still wearing soot-stained rags and had the thinnest of blankets.

She took her time, leaning on the crutch provided to her, and slowly made her way around, starting at what was clearly the poor side of the ballroom's residents. She recognized some of the servants, as well as a few of the errand runners, and the like.

"Are you being well cared for?" Allegra asked a mage she recognized.

The mage nodded, her eyes downcast. When Allegra asked her what was wrong, she whispered, "We aren't allowed bread."

Allegra blinked. "What do you mean, *not allowed?*"

"We can only have two bowls of soup a day, and we're not allowed to have more or to have bread, even if we're hungry." She looked down at her hands. "I don't mean to be ungrateful, Your Ladyship. I just, well, the others are allowed bread and they get three meals, and we all were just as hungry as them trying to get here. Some of us are hurt, even, but the healing rooms are all full. So we gotta wait."

Allegra narrowed her eyes. She tried to tell herself that some of her anger was caused by her own exhaustion and hunger, but she also knew that this was wrong. "Who is getting better treatment?"

The mage motioned to the corner where Allegra immediately recognized several wealthy individuals who'd been at the abbey. None of them were mages.

"Is it just the servants, or are they separating the mages?"

She glanced up at the sisters gathered in the back of the room, and then back at Allegra. "Mages, Your Ladyship. The sister doesn't like us."

"Which one?"

"The brunette. Sister Ellouise."

Allegra nodded and said, "Thank you for letting me know. Rest now."

Allegra made her way over to the half dozen sisters gathered about the fireplace gossiping. They looked as though they were supposed to be distributing bread, but were too busy. None of them recognized her in her plain clothes.

"May I help you?" the brunette asked.

"Who is in charge here?"

"I am," the brunette said, her voice slightly more guarded.

"I would like to have bread for my friend over there."

Sister Ellouise sneered at Allegra. "You already had your soup for the night."

"I asked for bread."

"If you don't like the accommodations here, feel free to leave."

"Sister!" one of the others whispered, her eyes a little wide, staring at Allegra. "Sister!"

But Sister Ellouise shushed the subordinate. The sister behind her mouthed an apology to Allegra. "Was there anything else?"

"Why are the poor mages only being fed soup?"

"I beg your pardon?"

"Why are the poor mages only being fed soup?" Allegra asked, in exactly the same tone as the first time.

"I…" She cleared her throat. "I answer to the Almighty and not to you."

"On the contrary, you will be answering to me."

Sister Ellouise scoffed. "Who do you think you are?"

"I am Allegra, Contessa of Marsina, Arbiter of Justice, and I want to know why you are starving distressed mages on purpose."

Sister Ellouise's jaw slackened for a moment. In a much more uncertain tone, she said, "You're not the Arbiter. She's dead."

Behind her, one of the sisters whispered, "That's her. That's what I was trying to tell you."

"It can't be. She's dead. Everyone's said so."

"I am not dead," Allegra said. After spending too much time with Dodd, she nearly made an uncouth comment, but she managed her tongue. "So, I await your answer."

"To what?"

The sister behind Sister Ellouise shook her head and made an audible sigh.

Allegra gave Sister Ellouise a hard look. For the third time, and allowing a little irritation to slip into her voice, she asked, "Why are the poor mages only being fed soup?"

"We have limited food, and I was advised that this was an acceptable course of action. Considering, of course, the quality of people we have in this room."

"Quality of people," Allegra said. Her patience was growing shorter by the syllable.

Sister Ellouise didn't seem to notice. "For example, over there, we have a marquis and his family. They are all injured and the healers are refusing to let them go down to the rooms. They said some of the servants and the witches were hurt more. So now we're stuck with things like this here."

Things.

When Allegra got inside the cardinal dinner, she was going to find out who was in charge of this mess, and she was going to have choice words for that person. Depending upon who it was, her words might be very choice.

"Sister Ellouise, from this point forward, all of these people are to get equal meals until accommodations can be found for them."

"Your Ladyship, I don't believe you understand the situation fully," the sister said with a hint of a laugh in her voice. "Some of these people are witches."

Allegra tried to steady her anger as best as a weary, hungry person could. "And?"

"You don't actually expect me to feed witches?"

"Yes."

"To be completely blunt with you, I think—"

"At no point in this conversation did I ask your opinion, Sister. You will carry out my instructions or I will find someone who can do this very simple task."

"I will follow my conscience."

Allegra eyed the woman's white robes with a blue embroidered patch on the chest symbolizing outstretched arms. "Order of the Society of Charity, correct?"

She lifted her chin. "Yes."

"I will be speaking to the senior cardinals shortly and I will be passing along my report about your mistreatment of mages."

"I cannot be forced to act beyond my conscience."

"I care not about your conscience or your objections." Allegra turned to the other sisters. "I want the bread distributed immediately and do it fairly. It is cruel to continue starving poor people who just endured the most hideous of circumstances due to your own personal issues. And you all pretend to be sisters of the cloth. You should be ashamed of yourselves."

Allegra turned on her crutch and hobbled out of the room, her wrath boiling as she went.

IT TURNED OUT that the senior cardinal's meeting was only across the hall from the ballroom, so Allegra did not have to inflict much more strain on her bruised armpit. This was where the card tables would be set up during balls and events, where clergy, soldier, and law person alike would gamble far more than what the Lord would think was good sense. However, good sense, like common sense, wasn't inborn in this lot.

Most were seated at the card tables, designed to sit eight. Square tables were also set up about the room. Two sideboards were filled with various lidded dishes, the contents ready to prevent malnourishment in anyone of rank. This food should be sent immediately across the hallway, to help people who'd escaped a burning inferno.

Allegra had assumed, clearly incorrectly, that senior cardinals meant an inner circle of a dozen or so of the purple robes. Instead, basically everyone with more than a handful of years' seniority in the conclave was gathered here. As she understood it, the majority of the conclave was away at their estates, no doubt escaping the rising heat.

Allegra's insides knotted again when she noticed Vittorio and Vanida sneering at her. She knew them well enough to know they'd have arrived with suspicions and reprisals for her. They'd just continue, only now to her face. Hours ago, she was on a horse fleeing an army. Now, she was here dressed in a servant's church clothes, trying to convince them they were in danger...and not from her.

The footmen helped her to the chair Rupert motioned for her to sit in at the front of the gathering. It had a small side table next to it, as well as a footstool. They eased her into the chair and helped position the stool for her comfort. Another footman passed a plate of finger food to the assisting footman, who put it on her table. Then, a glass of wine. Finally, they bowed and left the chamber, shutting the doors behind them.

Allegra adjusted herself as best as she could into the chair, to maintain an air of respectability and authority. One of the benefits of her dresses was that she used them (and her corsets) to project a haughty importance. Here, in this chair and simple dress, she felt her exhaustion acutely. It was difficult to even sit up properly without a properly-fitted corset to hold her up. She found her shoulders kept drooping, desperate for rest.

"How are you feeling?" Rupert asked. Normally, she could adjust her mind to calling him Francois whenever he put on the formal robes, but today she could not. It required a level of concentration she simply did not possess in her state.

"The surgeon came by briefly. She recommended rest, elevation, and a twice-daily soak in cold water. I have planned a visit to the infirmary building tomorrow, along with the healers, to visit those from Borro Abbey, so I'm certain I will see more of her then."

"Your Ladyship, have the healers seen you yet?" Cardinal Astoria asked.

Allegra didn't think there was anything nefarious in the senior cardinal's question. She was a calculating woman, more interested in her own elevation and ambition than any one cause. She was on the original nomination ballot for Pope during the last round of voting, though Rupert took the lead eventually. Nevertheless, Allegra was cautious in her reply. "Not yet. Just the surgeon. I was told the apothecary will be by tomorrow."

"Why haven't they come to see you yet?" Cardinal Reinhold interrupted.

"No doubt they are very busy with Princess Imogen and her soldiers. They were in graver need of healers than I, with a mere swollen ankle."

Cardinal Astoria *hmm*ed. "I'm concerned about the bruising. I can see it through your stockings even from here. Your Ladyship, are you certain it isn't broken?"

Allegra spent several minutes explaining to about thirty elderly cardinals that her ankle was not broken. She had twisted it when she'd jumped from the canopy at Borro Abbey. She would recover with rest and several hot, good meals.

No, it was not broken.

Yes, she was certain.

No, she did not need another opinion.

No, the healers did not need to be spoken to.

Yes, she was in perfect health otherwise.

Finally, Rupert ended the interrogation by saying, "Then we appreciate you coming so swiftly, especially since you clearly need rest to recover from your ordeal in the woods."

Allegra caught herself before she snorted. Dodd and Walter had been horrible influences on her. She had to get her court face back on and her language back into prime shape to survive these politicking priests.

It was obvious to her that Rupert and Cardinal Astoria had planned the meeting to start like this. It was a primer for the rest of them, a reminder that Allegra had been through a lot. She might struggle answering questions, might not recall things, and might even hesitate. All could be explained away with exhaustion and hunger. No one was at their best when tired and without a full stomach, after all. Mistakes must be accommodated.

Lord God, he was good at this.

"Thank you for inviting me. I confess I am tired, but I felt compelled to address at least the senior cardinals to help prepare for Bonacieux's arrival." She smiled at the gathering. She knew it didn't touch her eyes. "And, obviously, whoever else wished to attend is very welcome."

A younger male cardinal raised his hand. She couldn't remember his name. Albert, maybe? "Your Ladyship, how do you know General Bonacieux is coming here?"

"He's been on Cathedral Way since the attack, slowly making his way here. He has had opportunity to cross back into Cartossa, but yet he remains on the Amadore side. Princess Imogen informed me he'd been waiting at the border, and that was consistent with our observations. However, something changed because he's moving once more. For the last day and a half, we were under constant attack by his scouts. It's clear to me he is coming here."

Murmurs went up before Cardinal DeLancey asked, "Forgive the question, but did you see it with your own eyes? I can't wrap my head around it. Honestly, Your Ladyship, and please forgive this, but I'd not have believed anyone else if it weren't Father Michael and Captain Rainier who'd told us. I'd have said they were imaging things. How did a demon come through at Borro?"

Allegra didn't answer immediately as her mind was flooded with recollections of horror. It was hideous and a scene that integrated into her worst nightmares. No longer did she dream about being dragged by the hair to be tossed into a dark, endless pit. Now, she dreamed of being thrown into the maw of that living nightmare.

"I saw it," she finally whispered. "Everything they told you is real."

Cardinal Giso said, "Your Ladyship, I thought you were a non-believer."

"Yes," Allegra said. "I have never hidden that fact."

"But you sit here in front of us and say you believe you saw a demon?"

"I do not believe I saw one. I know I saw one, with my very eyes."

Rupert turned and asked, "Is it possible, at all, that it could have been a trick of magic somehow? Or, had you hit your head before you saw what you think was a demon?"

She knew he was asking to prime her for the crowd, but his question irritated her all the same. She knew how to handle a crowd, and all his question did was plant into their minds that it was a trick and not real.

"I was called to Queen Portia's bedchamber and the portal had already opened. The demon was massive, even though only a small portion of it had come through. If it had managed to come through, it would have been at least as tall as Borro Abbey itself. We were lucky that as many of us survived as we did."

Cardinal Reinhold shook his head. "Your Ladyship, forgive what I am about to suggest. We have never seen a demon. Ever. Many people, even within this group, believe demons are a figurative story to help us understand mages, magic, and the Lord God Almighty's mercy. But you, as a non-believer, are saying that you saw one with your very eyes. Has this not changed your belief at all?"

"I hardly think the Arbiter's faith is..." Cardinal Giso began.

"I'll answer the question. It's a valid one, and I would be lying if I said I hadn't been thinking on it of late."

She looked down at her hands. The skin was cracked around her knuckles, and her fingernails were crusted in tiny scabs from hangnails and cuticles tearing and splitting. Two of her nails were torn unevenly, down past the quick, and ached every time she used those fingers. She had been through so much since taking the position of Arbiter, and she could not shake the feeling that so much was her own fault.

"I think I was wrong about a great many things, and I don't know what I believe anymore. I don't know if the Lord God Almighty is real or not. I saw a demon. I did not see him. Tasmin did not come through the demon portal at Borro, like the stories said she would. But, there is an abyss. I saw it with my own eyes. And we fought, and mages gave their lives to give the rest of the abbey a chance to flee. I know you are asking me questions because you want to know if I now believe the stories about demons and elemental mages. Well, Your Graces, nothing has changed on that score. I do not believe demons are a manifestation of our sins. I do not believe elemental mages corrupted themselves or their bloodlines with the seed of demons. I remain steadfast on those points."

"How can you sit there, after what you claim to have seen, and say that?" Cardinal Vittorio demanded.

"Very easily in fact. Frankly, Your Grace, you did not see elemental mages risk their lives to save us all. And allow me to be very clear. They saved us, Your Grace. Do not mistake it for anything else. We should all be dead, and are not because of the sacrifice of those you seek to oppress."

"Not us," Cardinal Vanida said. "We are safe here."

Allegra turned a sour expression to him. He had been the one who hampered resupplying at Borro Abbey. He'd been the one to stand in Nathan's way. He'd been the one to argue she should have been arrested after Little Ferret's brush with the noose. She hated him and found herself wishing for a portal to open. With luck, he'd be the first to go through it.

"You are not safe, Your Grace, and you would have died without the sacrifices of mages. Everyone breathing in this room right now should be dead, but you are not because people who many of you own like cattle risked their lives. And most of them died protecting not just the abbey, but the world around it. Do you have any comprehension what that kind of bravery looks like, Your Grace? They protected the very people who were fighting to have them shackled and sent to mines. Yet, they gave the ultimate sacrifice to save the world. No, they are not made of sin."

"They will not see the blessings of the Lord God Almighty, even with their—" Vanida began.

"I will not tolerate the disrespect of those mages in my presence," Allegra interrupted, her words clipped and angry. "They died so that I could live. I will not allow anyone to degrade their memory by speaking such hate against them. Furthermore..."

"This is not the time..."

"I will not be interrupted," Allegra yelled. Her voice echoed through the room. The shocked silence afterward pressed against her soul. She collected her temper as best as she could before she spoke. "Let me be blunt. The few elemental mages who arrived with Captain Rainier are under *my* protection. Furthermore, the elemental mages who fought at Borro Abbey will be receiving full pardons from my office. Furthermore...*Furthermore*...Cardinal Vanida, you cannot shout me down. Be silent and let me speak, Your Grace. I *will* be letting it known that I will be issuing letters of protection and pardon to any elemental mage that comes to any representative of the Arbiter's office."

"You ask too much, Your Ladyship!" Cardinal Reinhold exclaimed.

"I do not ask enough!" Allegra shouted. Tears welled in her eyes, but she refused to wipe them away. "These laws you enforce have brought us to this point. You are all to blame, with your hatred and your bigotry. The war is marching down the highway this very moment and there is *nothing* any of you can do to stop it. It will rip apart our walls and it will murder us in our beds. None of us are safe and you are all the reason why!"

Vanida puffed his chest out. "Holy Father, this is an outrage! I demand..."

"You demand? *You* demand?" Allegra said, her hands shaking now. She couldn't control her temper even if her life depended on it right now. She was exhausted, hungry, injured, and traumatized. And, what's more, she was angry. She was so goddamn angry. "Is that like the letter I received from you demanding I send back your starving, battered slaves?"

"We are not here to discuss—"

"We are here to discuss how you pretend to be a man of God Almighty, and yet force innocent people to farm your lands without proper compensation. How you force them..."

"Your Radiance, I will not stand for this. Those people were not slaves. They were paid."

"Two pennies a week, and they were not free to leave to find other employment. That is the definition of slave." Allegra leaned forward in her chair. "Be thankful, Your Grace, that Borro Abbey burned. For you were high on my list."

"Is that a threat?" Vanida asked.

"The Arbiter does not mean—" Rupert interjected.

"She absolutely does," Allegra said. "No more will I protect any of you. What's more, if you remove me from the office of Arbiter, you won't just have an army outside your door. You will have a riot inside your walls by the time I am done."

"How dare you threaten us!" Cardinal Vittorio said, mocking outrage in his voice.

"Am I the only person here who can see what is before us? Bonacieux is marching upon us. Now. This is not an imagination. He is coming. He will demand I be murdered."

"He wouldn't dare," Giso said, shock in his voice.

"Then you are a fool, Giso," Allegra said.

"I believe the Arbiter is exhausted from her journey, and we must make allowances..."

"Oh, shut up, Rupert. Enough of this posturing. You asked me to do a job. Allow me to report on what it has been like. I spent the winter with a refugee crisis on my hands, while some of you refused us bread."

Reinhold cleared his throat and said, "Lieutenant Lex informed us of the situation."

"Did any of you know that Cardinal Vanida interfered with my Arbiter accounts? My assistant, Nathan, is able to prove that he has been stealing from it all the while refusing to send me money."

"How dare—"

"Serafina, my secretary, has been going through the books again since her return to Orsini. She has proof that Cardinal Vanida also attempted to interfere with my personal accounts so that I could not personally buy bread for the mage refugees last winter. I had people starving to death, and was forced to write my own brother asking him for ready cash to buy barley and cabbages so that we wouldn't starve. Father Michael sold several gold relics just so that we wouldn't freeze to death. But all of you seem to be experts on the situation. So, please, tell me what we should have done differently?"

"You shouldn't have brought the likes of Walter Cram into the abbey," Vittorio said.

"So, you would have allowed the refugees to freeze to death?"

"They are a separate matter from Cram."

"No, they are the same, Your Grace. The refugees came because Walter Cram hadn't been arrested. They knew it was safe, as evidenced by the fact that Walter Cram hadn't been dragged off in irons. So, again, tell me how you would have fixed the situation."

"The mages were the ones that caused the demon portal to open," Vittorio said.

"Most likely," Allegra agreed.

"Well, there you go."

"So, you're saying that I am the reason that the demon portal opened?"

Vittorio cleared his throat. "I didn't say that."

"Then what are you saying? Please be clear, for I am exhausted."

"That clearly a mage did it. So, therefore, it wouldn't have happened if you hadn't let the mages in."

"So, we should ban all people from Orsini, since one of them might be a thief?"

"It isn't the same thing and you know it," Reinhold said.

"What I know is that you are all ignorant."

"Allegra!" Rupert said, shocked by her tone.

The room fell into awkward silence. She should not have said it, yet she didn't apologize for it was the truth. They were ignorant. The more Serafina went through the Arbiter accounts, the more the young secretary learned about a seedier side of Orsini. One where cardinals stole from the poor to purchase their own comforts, or to gain power and influence. When this crisis was over, she would absolutely call for an investigation into the corruption directed through the Arbiter's office from the financial clerks.

"Your Graces, before I came here, I stopped in the ballroom. The sisters there have separated the victims of Borro Abbey by rank and situation in life. Poor, refugee mages who risked their lives to get to Borro, who survived a riot, harassment, and then a dangerous journey to Orsini are now being starved because they are mages."

"That's a lie!" Rupert said.

"Perhaps you should speak to Sister Ellouise, as she said mages don't deserve bread. They are to receive two bowls of soup a day. No bread. Nothing else. That is charity of the Cathedral."

"I will investigate this. I promise," Rupert said.

"I have already instructed the other sisters to feed everyone equally until appropriate housing can be found for them."

"That isn't your job," Rupert said, in an annoyed tone.

She stared at him coldly. Who did he think he was to speak to her like that? He knew her far too well to know he was in the wrong, and what he should be doing is apologizing and not posturing for power. "I am the Arbiter of Justice. I arbitrated justice."

"I believe you are tired," Rupert said.

"Yes, Your Radiance. I am tired. I am tired of your hatred, and inaction, and your posturing. I am tired of you all."

"Then perhaps you aren't the person for the job anymore," Cardinal Vanida said.

A loud, indelicate bark of laughter escaped her. "Voting me out will not change the situation you find yourselves. So hold your vote if that makes you feel better, Your Grace. When Bonacieux shows up and claims I am an elemental, send the guards for me. And when you are convinced letting him hang me from the front gate will solve all your problems, know that there are hundreds of mages within your walls who will not let that happen to me. Do not declare war upon me, Your Grace, and think you have any chance of winning."

As Allegra pushed away her footstool, Rupert asked, "Where are you going?"

"I am exhausted."

"We have barely begun," Giso said. He sounded like he was stunned by the proceedings.

Allegra successfully got to her feet and leaned against her crutch. "What is there left to say?"

"Your Ladyship, let me help you," Cardinal Giso said, standing up.

"I do not require assistance," she said coldly. Let them see her limp out of there. Let them see her suffer. Let them feel how despicable they were.

She had made it only a couple of steps when she stopped. "Let me give you a piece of advice. If Bonacieux demands you declare me an elemental to hand me over for his justice and your peace, you had better pray the Lord God Almighty is real because he will be the only one who will stop the mages that will come for you. Because I sure as the unholy abyss won't tell them to stop."

She left them like that, in shocked and scandalized silence. She knew what was coming for her. They were fools if they thought she was going to meekly take whatever Bonacieux had in store for her.

RUPERT WATCHED HIS husband grow visibly angrier the more he relayed what happened at the meeting with Allegra. It had been a complete disaster. She had actually dared them to vote on her removal. They didn't, obviously, since he and Giso were able to calm down Vanida before he had a stroke. Even Vittorio was a decent voice for calm, and the man was an ass most days.

"So that's everything," Rupert said. He stretched his legs out in front of him. "Lord, I'm exhausted."

"I can't believe you're just sitting there, relaxing."

Rupert waved a dismissive hand. "Ah, I'll talk to Allegra in the morning. She needs to cool down and get a good night's sleep. I'll get her to apologize to the cardinals then."

"It's you who needs to apologize," Pero said, and it dawned on Rupert that his husband's anger was pointed at him, and not Allegra.

"What did *I* do?"

"You shouldn't have put her in that situation in the first place. She's hurt, for God's sake, and she'd been sleeping rough for a couple of weeks now. Then you put here there, in front of all of those power-hungry assholes—Oh, don't roll your eyes at me."

Rupert wanted nothing more than to go to bed and sleep off this day. All of this paranoia and fear-mongering was wearing him out. He needed a good night's rest so that he could be a face of calm reserve in the panic tomorrow, as the worry of General Bonacieux's actions spread through the populace. For now, sleep was his main concern. "Pero, let's just go to bed. I'm tired."

"Of course. You're too tired to argue with me, but she's not too tired to be put in front of the wolves."

"They aren't wolves."

"Vanida denied the refugees bread. I heard it from Serafina *and* Rainier. They're wolves in there."

Rupert yawned and was too tired to lift his hand to shield the wave of spittle that came with it. "Fine. They're wolves. And you know what? They are wolves she has to answer to if she wants to keep her power, and what did she do? She attacked them, threatened them, and then stormed out like she was having a tantrum like a child. You should have seen her! She was acting like she was about to hauled off to the gallows. She even threatened a mage riot if we dared remove her from power."

"What else should she do? Bonacieux thinks she is an elemental and he is coming here!"

"He isn't coming here," Rupert insisted. He sat up and said, "Pero, listen. I know that's what she thinks, but there is no way that General Bonacieux is going to risk dragging his army through Amadore to attack us. It won't happen. They're all scared."

"Princess Imogen thinks the same thing. As does the Grand Duchess."

"The Grand Duchess is just hoping someone will remember she isn't a has-been and give her power again. And Princess Imogen is hurt. Her judgement is flawed."

"This is incredible. It's going to happen, and when he shows up, he's going to demand you hand Allegra over. Then what? Huh?"

Rupert shook his head. "No one is going to demand anything. Pull yourself together. You're acting like an old woman."

"I can't believe you sat in there and let them get away with talking to her like that!"

"For the love of God Almighty, I'm not a dictator and I'm not her father. I can only do so much."

"I thought you were the fucking pope, or did they demote you when I wasn't looking?" Pero shouted.

Rupert pushed himself up from the chair. "Keep your voice down. The last thing we need is the servants talking."

"I don't care what the servants think about me, Roo. I don't care about them. I don't care about the gossip. I. Do. Not. Care." Pero raised his voice enough that he could be heard out in the public hallways. "This is my home and I'm going to shout if I want to."

"Everyone knows you don't care about the servants, but I care."

"Yes, everyone knows how much you care about what others think of you. That's why mages are still enslaved and you're wearing that fucking stole two decades before you should because of it."

"Oh, no you don't. We are not arguing about that tonight. I don't even know why we're arguing. I didn't do anything wrong today. Allegra was the one who lost her temper."

Pero rolled his eyes. "Stop being such a coward."

Anger surged through Rupert's body. "Don't you ever call me that again."

Pero crossed his arms. "You can't even stand up for your friend, and you think you're going to stand up for mages? You are a coward."

Rupert clenched his teeth, trying very hard not to shout at his husband. "I never said I was going to stand up for mages, Pero. That's always been your thing. Not mine. I am here to keep the peace."

Disgust filled Pero's expression. "Are you saying you aren't an abolitionist now?"

Rupert had no idea where this was coming from. "I've never said I was one. Those words have never come out of my mouth. You're the abolitionist. I'm here to make sure the world doesn't fall apart while you're off trying to break it."

Pero stared at him like he was looking at a stranger. "I can't believe this. Who are you?"

"I'm the person I've always been. You just won't accept that."

"Are you telling me you've been lying to me all these years?"

Rupert shook his head, scoffing as he did. He just wanted to get some sleep. Pero clearly needed to go have a piece of cake and a glass of wine because he was out of control. Was there something in the air? "Stop twisting my words."

"I don't need to. You're the one suddenly for oppressing the mages."

"For the love of God, shut the fuck up about mages! I don't give a horse's shit about them!" Rupert screamed.

Pero's smug smile crawled under Rupert's skin.

"There, are you happy now, you goddamn fucking asshole."

"Lower your voice, Roo. The servants might hear," Pero said in a sing-song tone, like he'd been doing this purposely to pick a fight.

"Get out of my sight. I can't stand to look at you right now."

"How mature. What will the servants think?"

Rupert got in Pero's face and shouted, "Get. Out."

Pero walked backwards, arms extended. "I'd rather be anywhere but here with *the* mage oppressor."

CHAPTER ELEVEN

THANKFULLY, THE DARKNESS made it possible for Allegra to escape without being seen. She hobbled down the stairs, and began the trek to the barracks and Stanton's embrace. She hadn't even been back in Orsini for a full day yet, and it was already falling apart. She'd always said this place was broken; now, she had proof. There was some comfort in the entire situation that it was not all in her head. Unfortunately, that would matter little when her head would be demanded upon the spike.

She wanted nothing more than to be alone with Stanton, but she also relished the chance to be alone with her own thoughts. So much had happened, and that fight with the cardinals had rubbed in how much she'd changed over the winter. They were all still acting like the crisis was building. They could not see that the crisis had exploded, and that things would only get predictably worse. Bonacieux was going to come. He was only slowed by Walter's destruction. A day, maybe two. Maybe a week. She had no idea what was going on in Bonacieux's mind, but she knew him well enough to know his hatred would not allow mages to stay unharassed.

She could not get that through the cardinals. They seemed to think Bonacieux would behave rationally. Some seemed genuinely shocked by his crimes. It did not shock her. It was consistent and a predictable outcome of the policies of the Cathedral. These people had created this mess. They were fooling themselves if they thought a few stern words would fix it now.

"How did it go?"

Allegra looked over her shoulder to see Walter smiling at her. He walked up to her and offered his arm. She took it, leaning heavily on him. "What are you doing lurking about in the dark?"

"I was with Lex. I heard you were still inside yelling, so I figured I'd wait around. So. How did it go?"

"Awful," Allegra said. She recounted the highlights of the argument with the cardinals. She admitted that she shouldn't have raised her voice at them, but she was also so tired. They insisted on seeing her, without giving her an opportunity to rest. They needled her, said horrible things, and then all of that was after she'd seen firsthand the mistreatment of the Borro mages. They deserved everything they'd been given.

"Huh," Walter said.

"That's it?"

He shrugged. "It's hard to know what else to say. You said it all."

A bitter sound escaped her. It wasn't quite a laugh, but it was close. If lives weren't on the line, it might have been funny. "They are ruining the world they claim to be protecting."

"I told you that years ago."

"I know."

"Yeah, I suppose you do."

They walked on in silence for a while. Most of the food carts had closed for the evening, with the late-night carts hours away from coming out to meet the needs of the gamblers and carousers. The courtyard was nearly abandoned, with some already having finished late night supper and nursing a glass of wine before bed and others preparing to hit the taverns and brothels. It was perhaps the quietest time of the day, here in the late evening.

She turned to Walter and asked, in a quiet voice, "Do you still hate me?"

Walter sighed wearily. "No. You?"

"No. It just seems so far away now, like none of it matters that much anymore. What was, was, and what is, well, is."

"I've tried to keep hating you, but I can't. I think the worst of it, though, is that I finally believe you made the right decision in not coming with me. I hate being wrong."

She smiled. "Yes, I do remember that about you."

"That life would have killed you, one way or another. You were meant for this. I see that now." He let out a little happy sound, like he was laughing at a personal joke. "It's so easy for someone like me to forget our cause also needs people like you."

"Walter, I think I just made it worst."

Walter scoffed. "You ruffled their furry stoles. They'll recover. Or not. Either way, the war or the rebellion is going to show up here."

"They gave me the impression that they did not believe us."

"Then they are in for a shock."

They walked in silence for a while until finally reaching the next set of stairs at the administrative building. If they expected her to go back and forth like this, then either a healer must find her something to speed along her ankle, or she would require relocation. This back and forth was torture.

"Pero always told me that they needed just a few more abolitionists in the senior cardinals, and then we'd get true change. I used to believe him." She gave Walter a sad look. "I don't anymore."

"Why not?"

"Once people taste power, they do not want to lose it. They keep moving their positions, calling for smooth transitions. Then, they slow down the progress to not upset the balance. I believe some of those people truly do think they are still doing good. However, I have changed my mind on it. If they are advocating for the enslavement of mages for another twenty or thirty years, just to allow for this supposed smooth transition, they are not on the same side as me. It is time I stop trying to appease them."

"Then you will lose your power, will you not?"

"Until a credible accusation of elemental magic is pointed against me, I will always have power in some form. If the Lord God Almighty does exist, then he is the one who gave me my power. It would be a sin for me not to exercise it for the betterment of society."

Walter let out a whistle. "I think Nadira is right."

"About what?"

"Your Ladyship, I am a bad influence on you."

They howled with laughter, and Allegra realized that Walter had once again become her friend. For that, she was grateful, for she knew she needed all of the friends she could find in the coming days.

ALLEGRA LET OUT a contented sigh as she sank into the copper bathtub and its hot water. She was in Stanton's bedroom, and was surprised by how small it was for someone of his rank and wealth. His bed was larger than typical of those elsewhere in the Cathedral she'd seen. Though, that was most likely due to his height and the dangers of exposed feet dangling over the bed's edge.

His tub was even better for his height, for him to sit comfortably. For her, though, she could almost completely stretch her legs out in front of her. She sunk down low, bending her knees to the side, until she was completely submerged in the water. She held her breath for a while, rejoicing in the water muffling the sounds beyond. It was good to just be alone with her thoughts.

Soon, though, her lungs burned, and she bobbed her head out of the water to take in a deep breath. She pushed the wet strands of hair from her eyes and blinked them open. Stanton was poking around the corner of the screen smiling at her.

"Sorry to interrupt your playtime," he said with a grin. "Did you want some food brought up? Martin said Mathieu got his cart set up early and he's making a fresh batch of buns, so the boys are thinking of clearing him out."

Allegra chuckled. "I would love a hot bun."

"Can I get you anything in the meantime? A glass of wine?"

"Just your company."

Stanton held up a finger and ducked back behind the screen. She smirked when she heard him bossing around the Consorts in the room beyond, telling them this and that, and repeating three times that he wanted the curry lamb buns if there were any.

Eventually, she heard the door close again and his heavy footfalls coming closer. Her stomach muscles clenched, though there was no real reason for it. Just the excitement and relief of being back in safety.

"How are you feeling?" Stanton asked as he pulled a chair closer to the edge of the tub.

She rolled her head over to look at him. It was so good to see him. "Too exhausted to sleep."

He nodded. "I get like that sometimes. You're dead tired, but your brain just won't stop planning everything you need to do. It's like it knows you're going to be useless for hours once you do crash, so it's trying to plan everything now."

"Something like that," Allegra said. "The healer dropped off a stocking I'm supposed to wear from now on."

"For your ankle?"

She nodded. "The surgeon insisted it wasn't broken, so the stocking should help speed up the healing process."

His tone gentled. "How are you? Really, I mean."

The room felt colder somehow. She curled her knees a little closer to her body and kept her shoulders under the water to suck in the last bit of warmth from the bath. "I'm afraid to sleep. I'm afraid what's going to happen tomorrow, and the next day, and the day after that. I'm terrified to think what will happen when Bonacieux gets here. I know the cardinals don't believe me, but he's coming. You believe me, right?"

Stanton nodded. "Absolutely. I think anyone from Borro knows the general is coming here next. The only question in my mind is *when*, not *if*."

She nodded. In a whisper, she said, "I worry what's going to happen to me."

Stanton gave her a pitiful look. He came to kneel next to her and touched her face. "They will have to come through me first."

"But what if..."

He cut her words off with a kiss. "They will have to come through me first."

"I don't want that to happen, either." She pressed her forehead against his. "I was so scared. I was sure you'd died, but Dodd and Walter insisted that you wouldn't haven't come after me if there were still people alive. They know you better than I."

"Don't say that," he said in a whisper. "They were thinking with their heads, and you were thinking with your heart. We all do it."

"Do you care that I'm staying here tonight?"

He pulled back a little, just enough to look into her eyes. "Why would you even ask that?"

Allegra glanced away, a little embarrassed. "Well, everyone's going to know now."

"Why would I care?" He leaned forward and asked, "Do *you* care?"

"Well, no. But, yes." An embarrassed giggle escaped her. "I'm used to people not knowing anything about me. Now, my entire life is a play being performed for people across Serna. Everyone seems to know everything about me now. I get a sick feeling in my stomach whenever I think about it."

"Love, they knew about us before there was even an us," Stanton said.

"That isn't comforting," she insisted. She flicked water at him. "I'm well aware of the gossips. I've lived such a quiet life for so long that I forgot what it felt like to be the subject of so much of it."

"After the display in the courtyard..."

Heat rose in her cheeks. "My emotions got the better of me."

"That just makes me love you more," he said. "Are you getting out of that bath anytime soon? We have curry lamb buns on the way."

"Let me soak until they get here?"

"All right. But if you turn into a prune, don't complain when I make you sleep on the settee."

WALTER STARED AT his door. Someone was knocking at it. He waited for the sound to stop, since he knew better than to open the door to strangers.

The person on the other side sighed loudly and said, "Cram? I can see the light under your door. Will you please open up?"

Walter was surprised to hear Father Michael's voice on the other side. He got up to open his door, cautiously opening it. He kept his foot wedged so that it couldn't be forced wider. "What's the matter?"

"I need somewhere discreet to spend the night."

"Why?"

"Can I come in please? It's freezing out here. Don't they have fires in this building?"

Walter opened his door and said, "No, I'm in the servant area. You'd know that if you weren't over with the bishops. What are you doing here? It's the middle of the night."

Father Michael sighed. "Pero needed somewhere to stay, and the room I was put into isn't big enough for two grown men who aren't sharing a bedroom."

Walter looked about his tiny room. "And you thought I'd have a bigger room?"

"I thought you wouldn't have as many neighbors gossiping about you if I stayed here, as opposed to spending the night in a room with the pope's husband."

Walter offered Father Michael a glass of wine. He nodded. "Don't they have, like, a million rooms?"

"Apparently, Francois kicked Pero out."

"My God, really? You can stay if you tell me more."

ALLEGRA STAYED IN her bathtub until her fingertips wrinkled and the water chilled. She wrapped herself in Stanton's dressing gown and curled up on her side of the bed with the steaming mug of tea Stanton had prepared for her. They chatted and kissed and embraced, until finally the food arrived. It took several minutes to organize the food, and she listened through the opened door with a smile on her face. She was exhausted, yes, but there was something invigorating hearing the sounds of laughter and joy over something as simple as food. Dodd was the loudest, declaring he wanted two of everything, protesting that he nearly starved to death in the service of the Arbiter...and he also promised Lex to bring him some food.

Eventually, Stanton wrestled some food from the clearly starving Consorts and came back into the room with a tray of tarts, buns, and rolls. He put the tray down in the middle of the bed and crawled in beside her. "No curry lamb."

She picked up a jam tart and made a contented sound. "Food."

"When we made it back, I must've eaten a week's worth in a day. I was famished, and I'd not been walking the entire time." He kissed his cheek. "I'll make Martin go out for more if you're still hungry."

She tried to smile through her chewing. Instead, she made a mess of the tart's crust and sent crumbles all down her front. "Sorry."

He responded by trying to nibble the crumbs off the front of the dressing gown, tickling her sides to make her drop more crumbs.

"Stanton!" she cried out with something between a laugh and a cough, as a few crumbs caught in her throat. She continued the cough-laugh until he finally relented and let her sip at her tea.

"I missed you," he said.

She let out a final cough and said, "I can't believe I'm here."

She noticed the tears glisten in his eyes. "I love you."

She leaned her head against his shoulder. A wave of exhaustion fell over her. She managed to whisper, "I love you, too."

She fell asleep seconds later, still holding a tart in her hand.

CHAPTER TWELVE

THE CONTESSA READ her letters aloud while Lex slipped in and out of consciousness. She had read four nearly identical letters all accusing her of causing the refugee crisis, and four nearly identical letters all accusing her of being the spawn from the abyss itself. Two of the letters were from nobodies, so she said she'd put those aside for Serafina to file. Three of the letters were from prominent members of society who were upset that she didn't arrest any of their slaves in Borro to ship them back to work. And the rest were from clergy members.

"I think I shall work some of these letters into future speeches when I am required to quote the hate spewed in my direction," the Contessa murmured.

"That sounds like a good plan," Lex whispered.

"Lex! How long were you awake?"

"Since Father Malcolm's letter about how he wanted you to come speak at services."

That made the Contessa chuckle. "Why didn't you say something?"

"Thirsty," Lex said. "My mouth feels like it was stuffed with cotton."

"Would you like some water?"

Lex eyed the crystal gobbet. "Can I have something without drugs in it? Please?"

"You can have some of my tea."

She put her papers aside, assuming she'd have to help Lex sit up. However, Lex lifted a hand to stop her and did it without help. Lex winced and groaned, but they didn't faint and that was frankly a positive at this stage.

"Look at you!" the Contessa said, her face beaming with pride.

"The surgeon says not to push myself, but I'm sick of being in this bed. I can't handle much more, Your Ladyship." Lex accepted the tea. "Thank you. Can you convince them to stop drugging me? Please. I'm so sick of waking up and feeling like shit."

"They worry about your nightmares."

Lex rolled their eyes. It hurt. "Look, I can't control them."

"We know," she said gently. "Everyone wants to make sure you sleep well. One of the healer apprentices told me that they are concerned you might develop some anxiety about falling asleep, and that would be bad for recovery. So the powder helps overcome that until you are able to do so yourself."

"Fine. Can I have half a dose? It's just too much. I'm sleeping all the time."

"What else would you be doing, other than sleeping?"

"Anything! Getting out of this fucking bed."

"Can you get out of bed?" she asked quietly.

"No," Lex said bitterly. "But that's not the point. I'm never going to get out of bed if I'm always asleep."

The Contessa sighed. "Sleep is important."

"I will get plenty of sleep when I'm dead, Contessa."

"As I understand it, you came too close to death for my liking."

"You sound like my mother."

"In this case, you need to listen to your mother."

"This is a damned conspiracy."

They hated the Contessa's pitying expression. Lex didn't mean to take their frustrations out on her. They just didn't want to be stuck in bed anymore. Lex was desperate to do something, anything, that wasn't being drugged into blackness.

"Contessa, listen. I want to learn how to sleep without the drugs. Don't you understand? I can't do that if I'm constantly out of my mind."

She nodded and offered a smile, supportive smile. "I understand. How about I call the servant for some food. They won't drug it, if I say it is for me."

"Are you sure? From what Dodd and Cram's been telling me, you might need your own taste tester."

The Contessa laughed at that. "Yes, I do believe I am starting to irritate people."

"Starting?" Lex grinned. "I'd like a pie."

"What kind?"

"Gammon, if they got it. Anything else after that."

"All right. I will order a pie *if* you help me write insulting, but not vulgar, replies to some of these letters."

"Insulting is one of my best traits."

DODD POUNDED ON Walter's bedroom door.

"Yeah, yeah," Walter called out. "Keep your trousers on. I'm coming."

Dodd knocked hard.

Walter winced at the sunlight when he swung open the door. "There had better be demons, Dodd. Oh, sweet God, I'm hungover."

"I wanted to see if you'd want to come hat shopping me with," Dodd said. He looked over Walter's shoulder and said, "Father Michael?"

"Good morning, my child," Father Michael said in tone that suggested this was not the first time he'd been found in some strange mage's bed first thing in the morning.

Walter sighed.

Dodd cocked an eyebrow. "Well, I see you're too busy to come shopping with me."

"Oh, shut up." Walter winced, and rubbed his head. "Why did you think I'd want to come shopping? *In the morning.* Oh, shit, my head hurts."

"You aren't as young as you used to be, Walter Cram, demon lover. You can't drink like a young man anymore."

"Oh, shut up," Walter said. "Seriously, though. Why are you here?"

Dodd tsked. "Maybe because your drunk self said last night, oh hey, Dodd, take me with you when you go shopping for Lex's new hat because I'd like to get new shoes."

"Did I say that?"

"Yes," Dodd said. "Cram, man, you're too old to keep up with the twenty-somethings. You gotta pace yourself."

"I told him that," Father Michael called out. "He rejected the wisdom of age."

"You're not that much older than I am," Walter snapped back.

"Yet, I am wiser, for I did not drink another bottle of wine last night."

"You drank *another* bottle of wine? Oh, Cram," Dodd said with extreme disapproval in his voice. "You're too old for that shit."

"Oh, for the love of God, shut the fuck up, Dodd."

Dodd grinned at him. "Come on, put your boots on and let's go find you some clothes that don't smell like someone died in a brewery."

Walter rolled his eyes, but let Dodd into the cramped confines of the bedroom. Father Michael was still sprawled across the sofa, his legs dangling over the edge.

Father Michael let out a roaring yawn. "I suppose I should make some kind of excuse for why I am here, lest you think ill of our dear demon lover here."

"Not you, too," Walter said. The priest's yawn was contagious and his own stretched his face. "Father Michael's room was unavailable last night."

"Pero got kicked out. I heard."

"How?" Walter exclaimed. "It happened like, a few hours ago."

"Yeah," Dodd said, as if it had happened weeks prior. "I know everything. Father Michael? Did you want to come with us?"

"No, I will join the old men in the dining hall."

"You're like what? Five years older than me? I'm not buying this old man crap," Walter said.

"I know how old Father Michael is," Dodd said.

"How?" Walter and Father Michael both asked.

Dodd grinned. "I told you, I know everything."

"I hate you," Walter said with a scowl.

Dodd and Walter bickered for twenty straight minutes as they walked from the servant quarters, across the courtyard, and to the food carts to get bacon rashers on cabbage leaves, crumpets, and pickled oysters before heading down to the merchant district with its proper stores.

"I can't remember the last time I was in a store without the intention to steal," Walter said. "This will be a new experience."

"Do you need money? I can lend you some."

Walter snorted. "No need, Dodd. I'll just steal whatever I want."

Dodd knew Walter was just bullshitting him, but that was what made Walter fucking Cram so fucking annoying.

"How are you not dead yet?" Dodd asked.

"The Lord God Almighty appreciates a charming man."

Dodd made a disgusted sound.

The first shop bluntly refused to sell Dodd anything because the shopkeeper recognized Walter. In fact, he told Dodd to leave and never come back with that *thing*. Dodd told the shopkeeper to die in the abyss before storming out. That happened at two more stores before Walter finally said, "Now I remember why I started stealing."

"What a bunch of pompous assholes," Dodd said. "Well, fine. They don't want my money? Then they won't ever get it again. And I'll make sure the Contessa knows all about this. Mark my words, she'll have it all over Orsini by tomorrow morning. Ain't no one coming in here after today except assholes."

"You don't have to put a show on for me," Walter said. "I appreciate what you're trying to do here, but it's not necessary. I'm used to this."

"Yeah? Well, I'm fucking not having it. Come on, let's head down to the shops the dancers use. They'll sell me a hat."

Off they went, bickering their way to the back alleys, where the tourists and visitors weren't welcome to ramble. Walter hadn't been to Orsini in years, and he'd never been to this part of the Cathedral. Where it was less piety and more party. The streets were incredibly narrow here and mostly potholes and mud. Dodd always preferred this part of Orsini, where it stopped being popes and cardinals, and became honest folks making honest livings.

"How are things with Lex?" Walter asked.

"I wish you'd just drop dead," Dodd said. He regretted asking Cram along already and they hadn't even bought one hat yet.

"Ah. You looked at him and immediately knew it had changed."

"I would have been fine if you didn't put it into my damn head."

"It was already there and you know it."

Dodd had no interest whatsoever in talking about him and Lex, and how he'd basically fucked up the only true relationship he'd ever had with another human being and it was all Cram's fault. So, instead he decided a little pay back was in order.

"So you and Father Michael, huh? I didn't know you were into men."

"Depends upon the man," Cram said. He shrugged. "Not really into priests as a general rule."

"I'm hurt, Cram."

Confusion spread across his face. "Why?"

"Am I not your type?" Dodd said, deadpan.

Cram broke into genuine laughter. "Not even in the slightest, my friend. Besides, your heart is already taken. Alas, for me."

Dodd stopped in front of a shabby brick building. There were clearly people living in the rooms above, but the street level portion had a big painted sign that said, "Mandy's Departments."

"Is that like a euphemism?" Walter asked.

"Nah. Mandy holds the permits for all of the taverns in Orsini. She set this up so all of her dancers could find clothes, since none of the cobblestreet merchants will sell to them. Can't have the riff-raff in the front stores where the cardinals might be embarrassed."

"You don't think they'll have that problem with me?"

"Mandy's a mage, so, no, she won't give a shit, Cram. You might even get a discount. Ooo, if you do, pass it along to me. I plan to get matching hats for me and Lex."

Dodd was happy to discover that he got his own discount—for being the brave Consort who brought the Arbiter back home to safety—and that he found the perfect hat for him and Lex.

Cram found shoes, which was good because Dodd couldn't stand listening to him whine about his blisters anymore.

STANTON BUSIED HIMSELF with his paperwork in an attempt to alleviate his frustrations. All the paperwork did, however, was make him more frustrated. In front of him was a denial for a modest increase in salary for his Consorts. He'd only asked for an extra silver a month for everyone, with four silver a month for Dodd and Lex. Basically, it was an extra day's pay for everyone a month. Nothing extravagant, Stanton thought. It was less than what any one cardinal spent in wine in a day, and he'd been sure they would approve the increase as a statement of faith and appreciation for the work all of the Consorts had done in the winter crisis. But the accounting clerks denied the request.

Captain, we understand the difficult circumstances your men faced in the egress to the Cathedral. However, as they are entitled to free room and board, including unlimited access to the administrative common dining halls, an increase in salary is excessive and beyond the scope of the Holy Father's edicts to control spending. Therefore, we must all tighten our belts, as it were, and suffer in the name of the Lord God Almighty.

Stanton could not remember the last time he'd seen any of the senior members of the Cathedral's upper ranks tighten their belts. He'd eaten at enough cardinal tables to know they would never die of starvation. They did not even drink common wine. Francois only served imported wine that cost more per bottle than the annual pay increase for Lex and Dodd combined. There were so many silver spoons in the Papal Residence that a few of them could be melted down to cover the costs and no one would ever notice their absence.

A knock interrupted his thoughts and he called out for the person to enter. Stanton was relieved to see Father Michael's smiling face. "Good morning, Father. What can I do for you?"

"I came to check on our dear Arbiter."

"She's with Lex," Stanton said. "She has been instructed to keep off her ankle for the next couple of days. So, to make the healer's job easier, she's doing some of her paperwork while Lex recovers. You're welcome to go visit her, though. I'm sure Lex would also appreciate the company."

Father Michael smiled at that. "I had hoped she would have rested a little longer, considering she only arrived yesterday."

"Father, come now. You know her better than that."

"True, my son. True." His face grew pensive. "How are you?"

Stanton let out a weary sigh.

"Ah. Shall I take a seat while you tell me what happened?"

Stanton told him about the denial of the pay increase, which Father Michael listened with a disapproving expression. "I know that I can pay the boys out of my own pocket. And I plan to do so, but that's not the point here. It would have been a statement from the Cathedral itself, saying that they recognized the work the Consorts did during the crisis and the escape here. Let's not forget that we lost some of our own."

"I have not forgotten," Father Michael said.

"I know, Father. I apologize. I did not mean you. I am so frustrated by the attitudes of the people here. We were out there, trying desperately to do the Lord's work as best as we could, and the people who sacrifice the most aren't even allowed a modest financial gain to show they are appreciated." Stanton scoffed. "But, Lord forbid the papal table be anything less than magnificent. As if they'd even notice a handful of silver coins missing."

Father Michael was silent for several beats before he asked, "Captain, may I make an observation?"

"Of course, Father," Stanton said. He braced himself for the soothing words of it being all the Lord's will, that they could not know the pressures of the cardinals, and all that.

However, that wasn't Father Michael's tactic.

"It seems to me that you are experiencing a crisis of the soul. Oh, don't worry. You wouldn't be the first. It happens to us all."

The words stung a little, but only because he knew they were true. "I'm sure it's never happened to you, Father."

"On the contrary. I lost my faith once. I looked about me and wondered why I dedicated my life to supporting people who were not following the same vows I had taken." Father Michael's expression grew grave. "I watched those mages come to Borro Abbey and I felt my faith drain from my soul."

"You didn't say anything."

"Of course not. I am the Bishop of Borro. There is, after all, a certain expectation of the faithful when one hears the word *bishop*. However, I would be lying to you right now if I said there weren't days when I spoke about the Lord God's healing hand and His plan for us that..." He trailed off. "It all sounded so hollow to me because I had lost my own faith, and yet I was expected to prop up the souls of others. For a time, I believe I experienced hatred toward certain members of the clergy, especially when we struggled to find grain."

"Did you find it again?"

"Yes," Father Michael said simply. "And you will find yours, too, Captain."

Stanton frowned down at his hands. They still bore the scabs from the fight out of Borro Abbey. "How did you find yours after everything we saw?"

Father Michael let out a contented sigh. "Truthfully? I had to decide what I truly believed, and why I was put on this earth. When I took my vows, I vowed to give my life to bringing peace and togetherness to all those I encounter. At times, my superiors have asked me to make choices that violated that vow. I decided the best thing I could do to serve the Almighty was to honor the vow I made to Him, no matter what my superiors may wish."

"Just like that, huh?" Stanton said with a little smirk.

"Well, I will confess this is an ongoing action." Father Michael smiled, and it lit up his eyes. "But, I felt my faith return. Slowly, at first, but it is returning. I hope it will continue to come back until I am filled with all of the grace and goodness of the Lord God Almighty. Every action I take now, I ask my conscience if it will bring people together. If it will not, I will not do whatever that is, even if it is in violation of my superiors. Because, I made a vow to the Almighty first. So you, Captain, will have to decide for yourself, too. Why did you come to the Cathedral to work? Why have you stayed? What about your faith always made you go on? Then, once you answer those questions for yourself, you can decide what to do."

Stanton drew in a breath before he whispered the words that pressed on his soul. "Father? I don't know if I can arrest another elemental mage, for just being a mage."

Father Michael let out a sigh. "Oh, my son. You are far from the only one having that particular crisis at the moment. Myself? I worry that I might be throwing myself upon the sword if I were to see it happen in front of me. Yet, there were times in my past where I would have turned away from it. But not now. Too much happened to us over the winter, I think. Those of us who survived will ever be changed."

"Is that a good thing?"

"Change is just change. It's neither good nor bad," Father Michael said. Then, he smiled and said, "Besides, I think the Almighty appreciates it when we question our faith at times. It's how we grow, is it not? Come! The paperwork will wait another day. Let us go get some grilled kippers and then visit Lex and Her Ladyship."

"We better bring Lex a penny pie," Stanton said.

"I will purchase him a two-penny pie," Father Michael said. "Sometimes, the best way to fuel the soul is to eat well."

CHAPTER THIRTEEN

ALLEGRA WOKE WITH the birds. Stanton was still asleep next to her, and she could hear the muffled snores of the Consorts from the next-door barracks. The healing stocking had continued its job and her ankle ached a lot less. Beyond the bedroom walls, she could hear the faint sounds of the morning bustle. The smells from the food carts increased with every passing minute, until her stomach finally protested with gurgling pangs.

She carefully rolled out of bed, not wanting to wake Stanton. She pulled on her servant's dress from the day before, shoved her feet into shoes, and wrapped herself in Stanton's heavy cloak. She took a moment to inhale how it smelled like him, and how much she'd missed it. And, a little heat formed on her cheeks as she thought of how great he'd smelled in bed last night when they finally got to *properly* celebrate surviving Borro's fire.

"Where are you going?" Stanton asked sleepily. He let out a yawn.

"Sorry, I tried not to wake you." She limped over to his side of the bed and sat on the edge. "My ankle feels a lot better today."

"Good to hear," he said. He reached up to touch her face. "Come back to bed."

She leaned against his hand with a soft moan. "The baking bread keeps waking me up and my stomach won't stop growling."

"It takes some time to get used to the smell." He gave her a wicked grin. "You were too coy before to end up in my bed the last time we were in Orsini together."

"That's because I was a proper lady and immune to your charms."

"And now?"

Allegra gave him a wide grin. "As I am still richer than you, I'm still a proper lady in the world's eye."

"You are so much trouble," Stanton said. "Give me a minute to put some clothes on, and I'll come with you."

Allegra openly watched a naked Stanton get out of bed and enjoyed the flutter in her heart at the sight. He caught her watching and gave a little flex of his muscles, and she laughed at the expression on his face as he did it.

He'd been right about one thing.

As he shared the intimacy of dressing in front of her, Allegra realized she was perfectly fine with the world seeing a tiny glimpse of her life, and the kind man who'd captured her heart.

WALTER STAYED IN bed until he couldn't listen to the bishop's snoring anymore. Father Michael snored and farted his way through the night. Walter tried everything to get the man to shut up, including throwing an apple at him. The apple hit him square in the chest, and all Father Michael did was choke mid-snore, roll over on the small sofa, and go right back to snoring.

After years on the run, Walter had shared sleeping accommodations with hundreds of people, maybe even thousands. He'd spent nights in abandoned mines, caves, basements, pantries...If he could sit, he could sleep. And he could honestly say that Father Michael was the loudest sleeper he'd ever shared a space with.

Walter crawled out of bed and picked up the basic clothing left in the middle of the night by a servant. His old clothes were still on the floor. He took that to be a hint that the laundry wouldn't be accepting his rags. He doubted the wool would ever lose its hint of mildew scent anyway.

Father Michael let out another ear-spitting roar before gasping, coughing, and then settling back into a low rumble.

Truthfully, Walter was a little relieved to have the bishop in his bedchamber, even if it meant he'd never get another good night's sleep again. The priest offered Walter protection. Not that Father Michael could physically do much, but rather he had the authority of his rank. Orsini was not safe for someone like Walter, and he only came because of Allegra's assurances.

He'd lost the paper Allegra had given him, declaring him a free man. He doubted the paper mattered now anyway, since he'd arrived with her. She had given her tacit approval of his freedom just by having him next to her. Still, he should get her to write him another.

Of course, Walter thought grimly, that all assumed they didn't defrock Allegra of her powers.

There had already been the massive argument with the cardinals, where she'd told them off. Walter thought they deserved it. Lord, he thought she'd gone easy on them. Others disagreed, and now the Cathedral was basically abuzz with arguments ripping apart friendships. Lord, Father Michael was on his sofa snoring himself into the abyss because of just one of those arguments.

And while Walter always appreciated juicy gossip, a pit formed in his stomach whenever he considered the situation. The moderate Holy Father and his abolitionist husband had fractured. It was possible that they could be reconciled, though every day Father Michael was here, it was another day that Pero was not in his marital bed.

And, to Walter, every day Pero choose to not be with the pope, was another day Allegra was in danger. The servants all talked about how the pope kicked Pero out because of slave and mage rights. That meant Allegra's oldest and dearest friend was not the champion of mage rights like he pretended. Walter always said that, but Allegra never wanted to believe that about her dearest friend.

Now, they were all in danger. Walter could feel it breathing down his neck.

Walter shook Father Michael. It took several heavy shakes before he stirred. "I'm going out. Take the bed."

"Are you sure?" Father Michael slurred.

"I'm sure. Go on."

"Thanks," Father Michael said. He stumbled from the sofa and collapsed on the bed He was snoring as soon as he pulled the blankets over himself.

Walter frowned at the pang of jealousy that swept over him. He hadn't slept that soundly since he discovered he could shake the ground underneath his feet.

DODD LAY IN his bed and pretended not to hear the Contessa and the captain giggle their way out of the barracks. He didn't know why it bothered him so much. Before the demon, he'd been a huge supporter of those two crazy kids getting together. Now, it just irritated him.

He sighed. It was unfair for him to think that way because the Contessa absolutely deserved someone kind in her life, and the captain was a lot nicer with her around. His mood was, as ever, all Walter fucking Cram's fault. If Cram had kept his damned mouth shut, he'd have never given Dodd the idea to say something to Lex. Then, Dodd would have just kept it all close to his chest and never breathed a word.

Instead, they kissed. And, what's worst, is that they kissed when Lex was drugged out of his skull and seemed to either have no memory of it or had just decided to pretend it hadn't happened. Neither suited Dodd, since he wanted to know what Lex was thinking about the entire thing. But he couldn't ask, because then he'd have to ask…

Dodd sighed again. This was bullshit. He stared at the two hats on the small nightstand next to his bed. Both were brown leather, nicely broken in but not shabby-looking. A red feather was held into place by a fashionable belt of black leather and a silver buckle. One side of the brim was rolled up, positioned into place with hidden wire. It was perfect, and he was too afraid to give it to Lex.

He was going to get something to eat from the carts before all of the good pies were gone.

HER ARM SUPPORTED by Stanton, Allegra maneuvered the slick stairs down to the courtyard. Her ankle was more of an ache this morning, as opposed to an unrelenting throb, though it was still unsteady. She took her time down the stairs, mindful of her footing.

"It's busy for the crack of dawn," Allegra mused.

"That's right, you haven't ever spent much time here. It's always like this. The food carts start setting up around three or four, just after the bakers get the ovens going. Some of them only open at night, even," Stanton said. At her quizzical look, he said, "Where else will all of the late-night gamblers get food? The kitchens only serve at certain times, and they don't serve everyone."

"I didn't know that," Allegra said. "I thought the kitchens served everyone in Orsini."

"They like to pretend they do, but no. They only serve the clergy or anyone working for them."

"But I've been fed here. Oh. I hadn't thought beyond my own circumstances."

"They feed all of the nobles, but the regular folk who come through here? No. They're all on their own."

Allegra noticed the bitterness in Stanton's voice, but she didn't push. She had her own wave of bitterness washing over her in any case. She'd been at Orsini enough over the years, especially after becoming the Contessa of Marsina. She'd never stopped to ask if her servants were fed, and no one had told her. Had Nadira just looked after it all for her? Nadira was the only person allowed to charge against Allegra's personal accounts at Orsini; had she been the one to ensure everyone ate?

"What's wrong?" Stanton asked.

"It occurs to me that I don't know if my servants have even been fed here," Allegra said. "I shall be speaking to Nadira at the first opportunity."

"Knowing Nadira, she probably looked after it all so not to bother you."

"Still."

Allegra looked about the courtyard. Several dirty workers were lined up at one cart, waiting for their turn to drink from the cups provided. From here, she could only make out the word hot. The rest of the painted words were too faded for her to read. Likewise, two more carts were lined up alongside, also with their own customers drinking from cups and mugs. As they got closer, she could read the signs. Hot Chocolate. Hot Wine. Hot Coffee. Hot Tea. A metal barrel stove burned behind the carts, its tall stack carrying pumping wood smoke into the air. On the barrel were several kettles.

"Where are they getting the water?" Allegra asked, pointing at the stalls.

"There are pumps and wells everywhere. There's also the river just outside the walls. You can get at it from the north gates. Sometimes, it's faster for the kids to cart it in from there than wait in line for the pump. Then, they sell to the costermongers, and on the cycle goes."

"Huh," Allegra said.

Stanton gave her a quizzical look. "What's going on in that brain of yours?"

"I had never considered there were two economies working in Orsini, side by side. It's as if there are two different towns all living in the same space."

Stanton looked about the courtyard. A few robed priests walked by carrying sticks with strips of meat on them. "The clergy all use the carts, too."

"But the workers don't get to eat inside, do they?"

"No. I suppose not."

They had stopped walking and were now looking out over the stalls, carts, and wagons that were preparing for the day's trade. She asked the question that crossed her mind. "How many of these carts are owned by the clergy?"

Stanton made an annoyed sound. "You've been hanging around Cram for way too long."

"I *am* a bad influence, Captain."

Allegra turned around to see a scruffy Walter and a scruffier Dodd. "What are you doing up at this hour?"

Dodd rolled his eyes. "You two woke me up."

Walter made nearly the same expression. "Father Michael snores."

"I heard Father Michael has been permanently sleeping in your room, Cram," Stanton said in a gossipy tone.

Allegra let out a little gasp. "Walter! He's a priest!"

"It's innocent!"

"Nothing you do is innocent," Dodd said darkly.

Walter glared at him. "Father Michael needed somewhere to stay, so I let him stay. I had no idea the man snored."

"Are Pero and Rupert still fighting?" Allegra asked.

"My God," Stanton said. "What are they fighting over?"

"Allegra," Walter said with a grin on his face.

She gave him a dirty look which she had hoped would have scared him into silence. Alas.

"Either way, those two need to make up soon because I can't live under these conditions," Walter said. "I've slept better in cellars."

Allegra didn't like that Pero and Rupert were fighting. There was the obvious aspect, of course: they were her dear friends. However, perhaps more pointedly, if the rumors were true, then they were fighting because Rupert had declared himself no longer an abolitionist. With his attitude toward her during the cardinal dinner, she worried that this was a lot bigger than a squabbling couple.

Silence fell on the small band of friends. At least, Allegra saw them all as friends. True, Dodd and Stanton couldn't stand Walter, but that was part of Walter's charm. Finally, she said, "We should get some food. I'm getting a chill."

Walter and Dodd happily lined up for the hot wine. Allegra took one look at the communal grey cups and had a gut feeling they had been white an hour earlier, so she decided a hot beverage coated in soot wasn't for her.

The next circle of carts was around a metal-lined fire pit. The grate over the top of the fire was knee-height, and had five pots sitting on it, with various kettles and covered pots all around the outside, pressed against the metal. She decided on a potato and an egg, and Stanton paid the penny and a half for them, since she had no ready money on her. Both hot items were handed to her in raw cabbage leaves, and she used the overlong arms of Stanton's coat to make a mitt in her left hand. She balanced the cooking cabbage leaves there and picked at her steaming boiled potato.

"I need a hat," Dodd announced. "Someone remind me today that I need a hat."

"You need a hat," Walter, Stanton, and Allegra all replied.

Dodd sighed dramatically. "Lex and I both lost our good hats to the demons, and I think we both deserve a new hat."

"I'm sure Lex would appreciate it," Allegra said.

"What's wrong with the hats we bought yesterday?" Walter asked.

"They're awfully nice," Dodd said. "I'm not sure Lex is ready for that much plumage, man."

"I'm certain Lex can handle your plumage," Walter said in a caustic tone.

Dodd punched Walter unnecessarily hard in the bicep.

"What's that all about?" Stanton asked, looking at Allegra.

She answered by rolling her eyes. She knew Dodd would not want her to tell Stanton. She also knew that Dodd knew she would absolutely be telling Stanton at the first opportunity.

On the morning went, with them buying odds and ends of hot food as the stalls set up for the day's trade. More sleepy-eyed people filtered into the courtyard market-area, as merchants prepared for a day's trading or workers got out of bed to begin their own day.

Allegra eventually finished her egg and potato, once they'd both cooled enough. She tossed the soggy, half-steamed cabbage leaves into the appropriate pig food barrel, and then grabbed a cooled slice of pound cake, opting to pay the extra quarter-penny for a smear of mixed berry jam and butter.

Allegra found herself thinking about how easily she was slipping into life at Orsini. Perhaps they were wrong about

Bonacieux. Perhaps he wasn't coming, and they had all just worked themselves up. Walter was trying to talk Dodd into giving Lex the hat. Stanton planned a day of relaxation and eating his body weight in strawberries, as the first full crop from the hothouses were rumored to arrive that afternoon. Allegra decided to join him, and to the abyss with paperwork.

Unfortunately, the dream of relaxation ended when mounted guards came charging through the gates, closely followed by carts, wagons, and people simply running with children in their arms. For though she couldn't make out most of what was being said, she clearly heard one word: army. Her heart sank.

Bonacieux was here.

CHAPTER FOURTEEN

STANTON CAUGHT SIGHT of the Holy Father and waved to get his attention. The Holy Father raised his hand in recognition and the papal entourage briskly walked across the courtyard toward Stanton.

Allegra stood next to Stanton and was busy answering questions by evacuating civilians in terse and simple terms.

We don't know yet. Keep moving inside.

Move further into the courtyard so those behind you can also come inside. Keep moving, please.

Yes, I am alive. Please keep moving.

I do not know. Please, keep moving. We must get everyone inside the walls.

As needed, Stanton issued orders and directions to the militia guards who'd arrived with the civilians. Most of the people pouring in appeared to be the merchants that lined the cobblestone road into Orsini. They lacked either the coin or will to pay the weekly rent fees the stalls cost.

"What about the beggars, Captain?" Captain Brett called out.

Stanton glanced behind his mounted peer to see a trail of disabled and infirm. Some walked by their own power, while others were carried, assisted, or dragged upon litters. Likewise, those, too, were unable to procure the weekly begging rights from the Office of Issues—either because some clerk did not approve the seal, or because the person did not raise enough funds to pay for the fees.

Stanton reflected upon Father Michael's words: why was he here at the Cathedral? He had joined the guard, then later the militia, and then finally the Consorts all to help. He looked at Captain Brett and said, "Get them inside the papal ballroom."

"These people?"

"Yes, *these people!*" Stanton snapped.

Captain Brett gave him a disapproving look, but didn't argue. *Captain Stanton Rainier*, of the Holy Father's Own Consorts, Duke of Barrington, and Savior of the King of Amadore, was a reputation that Stanton struggled with. However, in rare moments like this, it was rather handy.

A gaggle of hangers-on formed around himself and Allegra. Some argued with each other, some screamed their disproval, others laughed at the idea of being bullied by the likes of Cartossa's general.

"Please! You are slowing the flow! You must continue inward," Allegra urged.

Stanton called out to more of the arriving militia guards to help with the crowd. A couple of the younger Consorts arrived with Martin, and together they helped encourage the crowd to keep moving. Though, the clergy struggled with the idea that the rules also applied to them.

"Cardinal Ragno, please! Keep moving!" Stanton urged a young priest, one of the newly-appointed to the conclave over the winter.

"As cardinal, it is my job to—"

"Your Grace, move inside. *Please*," Stanton instructed.

"I will not, Captain. It is my duty to…"

"To get out of the way," Stanton finished for him. "*Please.*"

Thankfully, more guards were arriving by the minute now. They quickly formed a corridor straight from the papal palace itself down to the main gates, where desperate people still poured through.

Stanton issued instructions to the guards who began forming a new corridor to his left. That would allow the new arrivals a path and would helpfully push as many people toward the north gate. The last thing anyone needed was a mob forming next to the main gates where Bonacieux would be arriving soon.

Movement above him caught his eye. The Arrows of Faith had arrived. The Cathedral's company of archers were no slouches and absolutely were not for show. Most of them had served elsewhere in their youth before dedicating their lives to the protection of Orsini. They were all highly skilled and highly experienced. The battlements quickly lined with archers, and page boys ran behind them distributing gear.

A wave of relief washed over Stanton. While he couldn't see inside, he knew the towers and the gatehouse were also filled with archers, poised and ready for any and all trouble Cartossa had come to offer.

Martin called out to him. "Captain! Her Highness is on the way. I can see her through the crowd. She's struggling to get through."

Stanton gave Martin a tight nod. "You? And you? Go with Martin and escort Her Highness through the crowd."

Before breaking with the guards to escort the princess, Martin said, "Walter Cram is coming through, too. Over that way."

That did not offer as much comfort as Imogen's approach. Still, he instructed another two guards to fetch the troublemaker.

As the Holy Father's procession grew closer, more of the Consorts fell in line to the sides, pushing the crowd back to ensure Francois could get through unmolested. Worriedly, Stanton looked around when he lost sight of Allegra. His heart slowed its painful pounding when he saw her, back turned to him, still calmly instructing the frightened people to keep moving no matter what.

"Send word to the all the kitchens. I want enough food to feed everyone a hot dinner tonight. It can be as simple as soup and bread but tell them the Arbiter said we're feeding everyone one meal today. Get Cardinal Vittorio's secretary to arrange servants to help with the meal preparation and serving."

That brought a flicker of a smile to his face. Cardinal Vittorio's office was in charge of the Cathedral kitchens. He was going to have a meltdown when he found out she had issued orders above him in his own domain.

Stanton noted Lex was conspicuously missing and he wondered what extreme measures had been taken to tie Lex to his bed with Bonacieux on approach. Perhaps, they might have used actual rope, since Lex wasn't known for following surgeon orders in the best of times. The elderly members of the clergy were also missing, as he'd personally sent Nathan and two guards to escort them to the papal chapel. It was a safe enough location in case of an attack.

Francois finally arrived at his side. "Good morning, Captain. Contessa."

They both inclined their heads. Allegra looked rather foolish in his oversized coat, but her peasant's dress underneath didn't offer any better authority. She wrapped his belt about her waist as best as she could, and he'd noticed she'd rolled up the overly long sleeves so that her hands seemed child-sized poking out of the thick leather cuff.

"Is it true?"

Stanton nodded. "He's allowing the people to enter the courtyard, but his army is directly behind them and pushing forward."

"Are we certain it's him?" Francois asked.

Stanton nodded again. "It's him."

"How do we know?" Francois asked.

Stanton tried not to let his irritation come through his voice. "He was recognized."

"By whom?"

Stanton gritted his teeth, but managed to say, "By Borro residents."

That placated the Holy Father for only a moment, before he began asking a barrage of questions that Stanton had no way of answering.

Finally, it was Allegra who said, "Rupert, enough! We don't know."

Francois bristled and said, in a harsh voice, "Don't call me that when we're out here."

Allegra raised an eyebrow, and Stanton had only ever seen that look a handful of times. Cram had called it her warning brow; when you saw it, you should immediately apologize for whatever you'd just done.

"Sorry. Sorry," the Holy Father said. "Sorry."

THE NIGHTMARE WE KNOW

Stanton turned to glance at Cram, who was busy failing to hide a smirk. Though, his mirth quickly vanished at the sight of the Cartossian uniforms behind the final stragglers. He ordered the portcullis lowered and locked. The outer gates hadn't been moved in years and had vines tangled around them. Stanton observed that those might need digging out in a few days, assuming Bonacieux was polite enough to allow that. At least the interior gates were clear of vines and debris and looked in good working order. Those could remain open. For now.

The crowd grew restless as the Cartossian soldiers approached the portcullis and said General Bonacieux wished to speak with the Holy Father. Francois nodded in agreement to the proposal. In the sweet time that it took Bonacieux to arrive, Imogen finally made it through the crowd.

"Captain," she said.

"Your Highness," he said in reply. "Good to have you here."

"I wouldn't miss telling this asshole to get off my brother's land for anything."

"We are not here to pick a fight, my child," Francois said.

Imogen made a displeased sound but did not offer up a reply.

And what a sight offered Bonacieux riding sedately up the cobblestone path. His uniform was spotless, quite the feat for a man who'd burned down an abbey, killed innocent people, and then lollygagged across Amadore like this was just another summer chapel picnic for the kids. He was flanked by about a dozen of his own soldiers, who were shoddier than him. There were also three others with him, sporting scarlet cloaks. Stanton didn't recognize their uniforms at all, and it wasn't until they were much closer that Stanton finally recognized their branded foreheads.

"What's he doing with mages?" Stanton asked in a whisper.

"He hates mages," Allegra answered. "This makes no sense."

"Oh, fuck," Cram said.

"What is it?" the Holy Father demanded.

"Is this a trap?" Instinctively, Stanton's hand went to the hilt of the sword that hung from his hip.

"I never believed this was true, though. Lord God, what has he done?"

Stanton really hated it when Cram muttered to himself. "What?"

"Hush," Allegra said as Bonacieux came into hearing range.

Bonacieux was still seated on his horse. Stanton got the impression he enjoyed looking down at people whenever possible. "You see, Barrington, I'm not the only one with mages on his staff."

There was no grin or taunt. Just a simple fact of a man determined he was right. Stanton knew never to trust men like this. He didn't answer or acknowledge the general's words, for there would be no point.

"Your Radiance, may we talk in private? I wish to have an audience with the Cardinals," Bonacieux said, as if it was the most reasonable request in the world.

Cram snorted and shook his head but said nothing.

"General, why are you here?" Francois asked. His voice was decently calm, but Stanton knew the man well enough to know he was somewhere between worried and angry.

An expression of genuine confusion etched Bonacieux's face. "I'm here to assist you, Your Radiance."

"With what?" Francois asked.

Again, the same expression of confusion. "Why, with your mage problem."

"Ah," Francois said. His voice soured. "Is your plan to murder more members of Serna's nobility here after accepting my hospitality? Princess Imogen is here. I understand you failed to kill her earlier this week. Are you here to finish the job?"

Bonacieux's face reddened with fury. He turned his glare to Allegra and did not bother to hide his disgust. "I see your witch bitch told you her lies."

Stanton held his breath after Bonacieux's insult, counting to ten and then counting backwards. He did not want to give this murderer the benefit of seeing him twitch.

The Holy Father tried to keep the same reserve, though his tone betrayed him. "Do not use that insult in my presence."

Bonacieux only glared at Allegra harder.

Stanton wondered what Bonacieux even wanted here. Surely, any sensible man with his experience would know that burning the abbey down, murdering a queen, and then showing up at the Cathedral in force was *not* the actions of a man seeking a diplomatic end to a crisis. This was a man who planned to burn and butcher his way through the world until he got what he wanted, or was turned into a martyr.

Stanton gave a side-eyed glance at Walter Cram, demon lover. A sinking, somewhat horrible feeling filled Stanton when he realized that Cram had always been telling the truth and nothing but the cold, hard truth. There were men of power hunting mages, and the Cathedral and the faith were allowing it. No, the faith *supported* it.

A cold chill gripped Stanton. This was not going to end well.

Francois drew in a deep breath and broke the silence. "General, several eye-witnesses have told me you attacked my own Consorts, burned Borro Abbey to the ground, and murdered Queen Portia. Is this true?"

"She was an elemental mage, and a blight in the eyes of the Almighty."

"Good God, man. She was only a child."

"She was a mage," Bonacieux said in that calm voice only the truly righteous could manage.

"You murdered a queen!" Cram exclaimed. "Right in front of us."

"Do not speak to me, mage." Bonacieux scoffed. "Francois, I can't believe you are standing here with this filth."

"Do not call me by name," Francois snapped. "I should have you arrested for regicide. You are not above the law of the Cathedral."

"Don't try to be holy with me, Father. You stand here with elemental mages."

Stanton cleared his throat. He always felt dirty whenever he had to defend Cram. "Walter Cram is here because the Arbiter—"

"I don't mean the demon whore, Barrington. Everyone knows about him. Though, I was so close to catching him at Lady Acardi's house last year. I should have burned it down sooner, but I have always been too merciful toward sinners." Bonacieux turned to

Allegra, even as he spoke to Francois. "No, Father, I am referring to the other whore in your midst."

Allegra's jeer was forced, but she didn't lash out. She put on a great act of not caring, as Bonacieux detailed her supposed use of magic against him, but Stanton knew she was terrified. Dodd had told him Allegra had purposely not even wanted to come back to the Cathedral, for fear Bonacieux's words would be believed.

Thank the Lord God Almighty for getting Lex out of that building because he was probably the only person in that room who would have been believed without reproach or question.

"General, as I see it, you aren't nearly as averse to mages as you were over the winter months yourself," Stanton said. "It's rather hypocritical of you to complain about ours now."

Bonacieux glanced around at his silent mages before turning hate-filled eyes back at Stanton. "Be thankful for the spring storm that delayed their arrival. Otherwise, we would have caught your little mage bitch, and we'd have well broken her, too."

Stanton's fingers twisted, but he kept them away from his sword. He even pushed away the image of decapitating Bonacieux right then and there. Soon enough, this butcher would pay. Stanton could afford to wait.

"Of course," Bonacieux said, happy that he'd boiled Stanton's blood, "my plan had always been to turn the demon whore into one. What a prized possession he would have made."

"Mr. Cram, what is he going on about?" the Holy Father demanded.

"They are mages who have accepted their curse and the sins of their fathers." Bonacieux spread one of his hands out, motioning to the army behind him. "They work to bring justice to an unjust world."

"Your Radiance, they are mages that he has tortured into submission." The earth underneath Cram's feet rumbled.

"Cram…" Stanton reached out and grabbed the mage's forearm. He squeezed. "Calm yourself."

The earth did not settle. "He tortures mages until they work for him."

"Be calm," Stanton said. Then, in the gentlest voice he could muster for someone like Cram, he said, "This is what he wants from you. Don't give it to him."

Cram's anger was still palpable, but at least the ground no longer groaned under it, and Stanton let go of him.

"Now, I offer you the same choice, demon whore. I demand that the Cathedral hand over the Arbiter, Walter Cram, and every other mage in this place."

"Or what?" Francois asked.

"I will turn Orsini into ash."

Stanton scoffed. He didn't mean for the sound to escape him, but it did. "You dare threaten the Holy Father? Are you mad?"

"General, what happened to the population of Borro and the refugees?" Allegra asked.

"I do not speak to witch bitches."

"Then speak to me," Francois said. "What happened to the people of Borro and the refugees that didn't make it here?"

"Cleansed," Bonacieux said.

"You monster," Allegra whispered.

Dead. They were all dead. A coldness seeped into Stanton's bones. Thank the Almighty for the iron between them, or he might have rushed the murdering bastard right then and there.

"I give you until tomorrow to argue with your mages. Matilda, give the Holy Father an example of my dedication to cleansing the world."

A young woman, with glazed eyes, lifted a hand and a spear of blue-white flame shot from her hand. It hit a tree, and it exploded from the boiling heat. Splinters shot through the air. She slumped on her horse.

"I have one hundred fifty such mages," Bonacieux said. "Think on that."

Bonacieux turned his horse around and trotted away, with his mages in tow.

THEY REMAINED A united front until General Bonacieux trotted off with his entourage away from the closed portcullis. Allegra was in the process of forming the words to demand his arrest, when Rupert of all people said, "I hope you're pleased with yourself."

His words caught Allegra off her guard and she stumbled her reply. She finally asked, "What does that mean?"

He leaned forward, trying to avoid the crowd listening in. "Perhaps if you'd taken a softer tone with the cardinals, we would be able to get a general vote to protect you."

Allegra was certain she had not heard his words right. "What?"

"The conclave might vote to hand you and Cram over to save themselves."

"They wouldn't dare!" Stanton said, raising his voice.

"Keep your voice down," Rupert said. He smiled for the crowd, and said, "I might not have a choice, Captain."

"You always have a choice," Walter said. "Let's be clear here, no one is handing me anywhere without a fight."

"Cram, this isn't helpful," Stanton said.

"Neither is threatening my life," Walter said. He pointed at Allegra. "Or hers. Or any other mage within sight of me."

"Control yourself," Rupert ordered Walter.

"I don't take orders from you," Walter snapped.

That's when the words sunk into Allegra's brain. He was talking about handing her over to be murdered, if she was lucky, and tortured, if she wasn't. Her stomach flip-flopped as the reality of Rupert's words crashed against her. Her hands began to shake. Surely, she'd heard him wrong.

"I can't have heard you correctly. Are you saying you are going to hold a *vote* to decide if I am to be murdered?"

Rupert leaned toward her so that he could keep smiling for the crowd's benefit, but said very clearly, "You were the one who mouthed off at the cardinals. That attitude will make you no friends in this kind of place."

"No one is taking Allegra anywhere," Walter said.

"I agree," Stanton said. "We can't barter our safety with human lives. The very idea is disgusting and, no, I am sorry, I will *not* obey any order whatsoever that involves me handing over any mage. I don't care who the mage is. I will not do that."

"You will do as you are ordered," Rupert yelled. That caused concerned faces from the crowd nearest to them. "Let us move inside, where we can talk about this privately like civilized individuals."

"Civilized? You're the one suggesting handing us over!" Walter sneered. "Maybe I should just kill you now and save myself the trouble later."

"I do not respond well to threats," Rupert said. "If you continue, I will order Rainier to arrest you."

Allegra looked at Stanton, whose only response was to look away from Rupert. That gave her a little courage. "You really are going senile if you think I will accept lectures from the people who tried to starve us this winter."

"You never listen to reason."

"And you never listen to reality! I issued the pardons. I issued the letters of travel. I bought the bread. I kept us from descending into civil war over the winter. The Cathedral did *nothing* except stand in my way. I kept all those people alive. Their allegiance is to *me.*"

"We are upsetting the crowd," Rupert finally said. "Let us move inside."

"Imagine how upset they will be when you hand over her." Walter tried to keep his voice low, but there was no controlling the anger in his voice.

"What has happened to you? All of you? Allegra, I have told you this over and over, and time again. I've said the same things to Pero. We cannot change the world overnight. That is not how it works. If you do not play the political game, then you risk losing everything you are fighting for."

"Rupert…"

"Stop calling me that. I am not Rupert to you right now."

Allegra stared at her old friend. He'd never spoken to her like that before. He'd always said he'd stand by her, protect her, and shield her to the fullest extent of his authority and power. He knew being taken was her greatest fear. He knew all of that.

Yet, here he stood, ready to bow to a bunch of frightened priests. They would vote to rid themselves of her, for no other reason than vindictive pettiness over her challenge to their authority.

"Don't give me that look," Rupert said in a patronizing voice. "All I've done is try to protect you."

Anger boiled in her belly. "Fine. We should not be arguing in public. Let us argue inside."

She turned on her heel and walked toward the main entrance, flanked by Walter and Stanton on either side. Rupert tried to step ahead of them, but neither man allowed him through, always stepping closer to the restless crowd. Shouts, jeers, and insults flew at Walter. Likewise, plenty hurled their insults and anger at Rupert, for not protecting mages. Others cried out for answers and how the Cathedral was going to protect them.

And none flew at her.

Instead, her name was on the cries for Rupert and the cardinals to protect her. If they handed her over, who else would they have murdered for peace? Who would protect them if she were dead?

Rupert might be His Radiance, but she was the personal savior of many of the crowd, and he'd forgotten that.

Rupert called out to Allegra from behind, trying desperately to get her attention. She ignored him, leaving him to walk in her shadow. Leaving him unprotected against the pressing, panicking crowd. Leaving him to not have a buffer on his sides for the taunts and insults.

Allegra's ankle throbbed mightily, but she refused any assistance. She winced with each step, but she set the pace.

The crowd wasn't much better inside, as it was full of noisy clergy who wanted to know what was going on. They demanded all of their attention, shouting so loud that Allegra's ears rang. She flinched against Stanton when a high-pitched woman shrieked in her ear.

"Be calm!" Rupert said, gesturing up and down with his hands. "You must be calm."

They ducked inside the first available room. Allegra spotted Father Michael and motioned for him to join them. Rupert tried to say no, but she simply spoke over him. She was too angry to even give way to his smallest wishes. Father Michael would have plenty to say about this plan to hand her over. There was already talk for a special meeting to elevate him to the conclave. Even the staunchest of pro-slavers couldn't find dirt to sully his name. Allegra felt this was a perfect opportunity for him to see what he'd be joining.

Once inside with the door locked, they took a moment to catch their breath. Father Michael spoke first.

"Is it true? I heard General Bonacieux is here. They're saying he wants the Contessa."

Allegra sat down in a nearby chair. She neatly crossed her ankles. She folded her hands in her lap. She waited.

Rupert crossed his arms across his chest and turned his back on her. Stanton stood with a brooding expression, one that said he was not impressed. Walter was flushed and ready to explode.

"Well?" Father Michael demanded. "Walter, what is happening?"

"Walter, is it?" Rupert shot back. "It's bad enough you're putting my husband up and making us the talk of Orsini. Now, you're whoring around with this thing, too?"

"I am not a thing," Walter said, hatred oozing from his words.

"One miserable winter together and you all behave like this?" Rupert shouted.

She sat back and let the four men argue. Her ankle appreciated the break, and the throbbing subsided to a dull roar. She suspected the stocking was running out of healing potential, considering how much she'd been on her feet already today and it was still morning. The healers were not going to be pleased with her, but she had a job to do.

A shiver went through her. At least, until she was shackled and handed over to the monsters.

"I will protect her," Stanton's deep voice, lowered by the evident rage in his heart, cut through the chatter.

"What do you think I've been doing all this time? I'm trying to protect her, too!" Rupert shouted at Stanton. "I've known her a lot longer than you."

A bitter sound that wasn't quite a laugh escaped Allegra. She turned to the man who had renamed himself Francois and realized, sadly, that he was no longer her friend. They knew each other, they had history together, but the Rupert she cherished was long gone. Destroyed by the toxicity of politics and compromise. "Your Radiance, you are protecting your position and nothing more."

"How can you say that to me? I have done everything possible to protect you. You are the one who stormed into dinner with the senior cardinals and picked a fight. It was not I who did that. It was *you*."

Allegra scoffed. That wasn't how it happened, and he knew it. They'd been the ones to insist on her not even having time to rest or recover. Then, they incited her temper, and *then* they all acted like she was the outrageous one.

"So, you believe Vanida was right to starve children?"

Francois rolled his eyes at her. "I never said that. You should have written to me, privately, and told me what was happening."

"I did," she said, at the same time that all three other men said, "She did."

"I received no such letter," Francois said.

"I wrote to you," Father Michael said. "You said you would consider my letter. Your Radiance."

"I have no memory of this."

Allegra knew him well enough to know he was lying.

"Regardless of who wrote what, it has no bearing on our situation. I can veto the Cardinal vote, but I can't veto everything, or they will come after my head next. And then what will become of you?"

Allegra snorted, a very unladylike sound. "All Bonacieux has to do is call *you* an elemental mage, and then he will rip down those gates and arrest you. And none of your precious cardinals will stop him."

"Don't be absurd. No one would dare touch me, let alone some butcher's son from the south."

"She's not exaggerating, Father," Stanton said. "It's what Bonacieux does."

"The Captain's right," Walter said.

"Your Radiance, please," Father Michael urged. "You cannot allow voting on handing over anyone to those monsters. For they are monsters."

Francois shook his head. "I believe you are all tired. I appreciate your counsel, but I must follow the rules of my station."

"He's a murderer, *Francois*," Allegra said, hotly emphasizing his chosen name.

"Murderer or not, I might be stuck giving you to him, all because of your mouth."

"Over my dead body," Walter growled.

Stanton stepped next to her. "And mine."

"Gentlemen, I realize you all care about her, but let us be very clear. I am in charge, and you will do as I say."

"Not bloody likely," Walter said. "I don't take orders from mage oppressors."

"You know what, *Walter*? I remember when you left her because you wanted to go off and be the hero. Did she tell you I was the one who had to comfort her after you abandoned her?"

And the four men began arguing all over again. She let them go on for a bit before she said, loudly, "Let *me* be clear. If you try to hand me over, there will be nothing left to this place but soot and ash."

They turned to stare at her in varied degrees of surprise. She hadn't even meant it like that. Though, she'd probably end up doing her own rain of fire.

"Do you honestly believe elemental mages here at Orsini will let Cartossian soldiers have me? You weren't at Little Ferret's execution, *Your Radiance*. The Consorts will protect me with their lives, and the mages *will* protect them. You can condemn me to my death all you want, but you will not get to see my neck stretched."

"Keep your voice down," Francois snapped. "People are listening at the door."

"I will not keep my voice down. If I am arrested, there will be nothing left to Orsini."

"You are drunk on your own power," Francois said, his voice dripping with disgust. "I did not recommend you to the position to turn into an arrogant…What has happened to you? To all of you?"

"We have been forged in the fire of war," Father Michael said. "Holy Father, we have been through much. No one can unsee what we have seen."

"This isn't the time…"

Father Michael cut him off. "On the contrary, Your Radiance, this is the time. The mages *will* keep her safe. The Consorts *will* protect her. Everyone at Borro saw Walter Cram risk his life to protect the Consorts. Then, what did she do? She protected Walter, after he unleashed so much elemental magic he collapsed from exhaustion. Then, she protected his friends and associates. She rewarded the mages who stood by her. They will never forget that, Your Radiance. If the conclave cannot understand loyalty on that scale, then none of you have any business serving the Lord God Almighty."

Francois scoffed. "Are you offering me counsel, *bishop*?"

"Yes, I am, for you are not above correction," Father Michael said. "I counsel patience, tolerance, and perhaps taking the word of those of us bearing Bonacieux's scars upon our bodies and our minds. Now, if you will excuse me, this fighting keeps me from my duties. Mistress Nadira has ordered me to find lanolin for the poorer burn patients, who are being ignored due to their rank. Some of us priests still remember our oaths, and I have wasted enough of my time speaking to dead hearts when my help is still desperately required. Arbiter, when I am needed, you may call upon me to stand by your side."

Allegra gave him a small smile. Father Michael made a point of shaking Stanton and Walter's hands, and ignored Francois. Then he pushed open the door, pushing past the people gathered outside the door. A couple of cardinals and bishops sneered at him, but most just continued bombarding him with questions.

"Out of the way!" he bellowed at them. The door then closed, leaving Allegra with the three men.

"This is what I mean," Francois said. "I am still in charge here. It is not you."

Allegra stood, and the action made her ankle ache, though not nearly as much as her heart did. She was worried, but for now, the hurt from Francois's betrayal was all that she could consider. Panic-driven thoughts could wait.

"Your Radiance. I'm sorry to have found the edge of our friendship, and that you have decided to cross that line. I will always regret this moment having had to happen. Please inform me of the conclave's decision. Good bye."

She walked out, Stanton and Walter at her heels, leaving Francois to spew and sputter behind them.

CHAPTER FIFTEEN

DODD SOON REGRETTED telling Lex anything about the altercation between Bonacieux and the Contessa. Everyone was under the strictest of orders not to let Lex get out of the bed. Even Nadira came by the Consorts' barracks and gave them all the biggest lecture of their adult lives. Yet, as Lex struggled getting his legs out from underneath the heavy patchwork blanket covering him, Dodd knew the only weapon he could use was guilt and common sense, and maybe a side of mashed guilt.

"Lex, your guts are still being held together by thread!"

"If they think I'm going to lay here in this Abyss-forsaken bed while they hand her over, you have another thing coming to you, Dodd. I'm not going to let them do it."

"The cardinals haven't even decided what they're going to do. No way are they going to hand her over. You have to be calm."

"Calm? Calm? You want me to be calm?" Lex's voice grew in pitch each time he said the word "calm."

"I think you need to think this through."

"I'm not going to let those assholes turn her over to that fucking butcher! They are going to have to come through me. Do you hear me? They are going to come through me."

Dodd withheld the comment that a determined bee could take out Lex and felt very proud for showing such restraint. Instead, he concentrated on common sense and guilt. The two tactics best used on Lex. Normally. "Lex, you can't help her if you are bleeding to death."

"You think I'm joking?"

"I didn't say that. All I'm saying is no one is going to let her be handed off to that bastard. So, relax."

Lex gave up struggling with the blanket. He hung his legs over the edge of the bed, blanket still tangled in his limbs. "Relax? That's your brilliant solution? Just sit here and trust the pompous pile of...of...popery?"

Dodd rolled his eyes at the sad alliteration. Clearly, the pain powders were still in Lex's broth. "Lex, *Lex*. Enough. Have some of your broth and—"

"I'm tired of the fucking broth." Lex sighed. "I want my wits, and I can't if I keep drinking that shit. I know it's drugged. I can't get better if all I do is sleep."

Dodd rested his hands on his thighs and said nothing. If their circumstances were reversed, he'd be saying the same things. But, then Lex would also be the one here, trying to stop Dodd from bleeding to death getting out of bed. He was failing at the guilt tactics. He was finding it rather difficult to guilt someone who was laid up with a sword gash. He should have brought the hat.

Dodd made a disgusted sound.

"What?"

"It's just bullshit and all. You know how it is around here. Look, the Contessa is in Rainier's room anyway. They'll have to come through everyone to get her, and I don't see a single guard in this entire place willing to face that any day of the week. It's not worth worrying about."

"Has anyone told Cram yet?"

"He was there," Dodd said.

Lex let out his own annoyed sound. "Great. The demon lover gets to go to things that I should be at."

"Don't be like that."

"I'll be however I want to be, Dodd, and you'll learn to like it."

"You just need to heal, that's all. Then you can kick Cram to the back ranks where he belongs. You gotta rest. That's what's important now. We can handle the rest."

"What has gotten into you?" Lex asked with a disgusted tone. "What did I do?"

"There's an army outside our gates, they're demanding the Contessa, and you're in here mooning over me like my guts were going to spill all over the floor." Lex flicked his hand, like he would have clipped Dodd's ear if it had been closer. "Use that brain of yours. My guts are going to end up on the floor anyway if Bonacieux attacks. Here you are, moaning and whining like you're the one laid up."

Anger boiled in Dodd. He wasn't used to feeling this way with Lex, and he didn't know how to deal with it. Normally, Lex might get on his nerves, or they might bicker because they were spending too much time together. But they never really fought. Except now. Now, Dodd wanted to pick a fight.

"Well?" Lex demanded. "What is it?"

"I don't get you. I'm trying to be a good friend and you're shitting all over me."

"What are you talking about?"

"I've been bringing you news, keeping you updated, and I've been bringing the wine up that isn't drugged, and finding you meat pies, and I stole the last jar of the cherry preserves from the kitchens, because you said you wanted some." Dodd sucked in a breath. "I'm trying to be a good friend here, but you're determined to get yourself killed. There's the door, Lex. Have at it. Try not to bleed on the tapestries. They're ancient."

Dodd pushed himself up from the edge of the bed, shaking his head. He wanted to say so much more, but there was no point arguing. Besides, Lex really did need to rest and recover. The healers and surgeons could only do so much. Lex's body still had a job to do.

"What is your problem?" Lex asked after him. "You've been weird as shit since you got back."

Dodd turned around, not even bothering to hide the incredulous expression he knew was on his face. "Are you fucking kidding me?"

"What?" Lex asked, in a genuinely perplexed tone.

"We fucking kissed, Lex! We need to address that eventually."

Lex mouthed several silent words before managing to force out, "What? We what? When? What?"

"I don't have the time to play stupid games with you." Dodd looked at Lex's face and knew Lex had no idea what he was talking about. "You don't remember, do you?"

Lex let out a long breath. "Lord God Almighty."

"You don't remember?"

"No, I do. I thought it was a fever dream. I keep getting them. It's why they drug the broth. For a few days there, the servants had to tell me what was real and not. Oh, Lord. Did I kiss you first?"

Dodd didn't say anything. He didn't know what to do. All this time, he'd been thinking and planning several steps ahead, because he'd assumed Lex had kissed him. Lex thought he was dreaming.

"This is why I don't want the damned broth. Yuck. God Almighty, that was a close one." Lex broke out laughing, a sound that stabbed Dodd's heart. "We nearly fucked that one up."

Damn Walter Cram. He was right.

Dodd looked away, unable to meet Lex's eyes. In that moment, there in Lex's recovery room, Dodd knew their friendship had ended. Oh, they would go on pretending and playing at it, but it was over now. It was never going to be the same, no matter what. No matter what Lex felt. No matter what Dodd said. Cram was right all along. He might as well have told Lex from the very beginning because there was no hiding this now.

"Dodd?" Lex almost never used that soft, gentle voice. In the dark, sometimes Dodd imagined that would be the voice Lex would use to confess his own longings. Now, it was just a dagger in the kidneys. "I didn't know. God, I'm so sorry. I didn't mean to laugh at you."

Dodd sucked in a breath through his teeth and then blew it out, controlled and steady. That managed to suppress the lump forming in his throat. He shook his head, unable to form words to say to his oldest friend.

He left Lex sitting there, on the side of the bed. No doubt confused. But Dodd couldn't deal with this. He couldn't even look back over his shoulder, let alone form the words necessary.

God damn fucking Cram was right.

CHAPTER SIXTEEN

WALTER GLANCED BOTH ways before walking down the muddy back alley that snaked between the cathedral proper and the wall fortification buildings. Too many people recognized him, and he wasn't keen walking alone in such a sparsely habited part of Orsini, but he had somewhere else to be, and wanted to be discreet in his arrival.

Thunder rolled overhead. He sighed and hugged himself to keep in the warmth. His only comfort in all of this was that the army was outside in this misery, and Orsini was closed to them. There would be no trade for them, no fresh food, no fresh supplies. Bonacieux would have to attack immediately, or he'd have to retreat until he'd better established his supply line.

A dark voice told Walter that it could be possible that the cathedral might hand him and Allegra over anyway, and in that case, there would be a bloody war on their hands. A very messy, very bloody war. The rain and a lack of hay would be the least of anyone's worries by the time he was done with this place.

He found the small entrance and weaved his way down the staircase and into the basement pantry. There was Dodd and a very pale, very shaky Lex.

"What is he doing here?" Walter demanded.

"He wouldn't listen," Dodd said, exasperated.

Lex gave him a hard look, which would have made more impression if the kid wasn't leaning against the table panting. "My job, Cram."

"All right, let's see it."

Walter silently followed the two, well, they weren't his friends, but two people who he trusted decently enough. Dodd had been the one to send word, along with a sketched map telling him where to go.

"What is this place?"

"The brothel used to be down here, but it kept flooding. So, they're around back now," Dodd said. "Mostly, they just use this for storing shit that won't spoil if it gets wet."

"Is it normally unlocked?" Walter asked.

Dodd shrugged. "No idea. We didn't want to poke around until you'd seen it."

Dodd passed his lantern to Walter. "It's there on the floor. We sent word as soon as we got the message."

"Who told you?" Walter asked.

Dodd and Lex exchanged a look, before Lex said, "We can't say who exactly, but we trust her completely."

"Why can't you say?" Walter asked.

They exchanged a look again. "She's an elemental mage, Cram. She was afraid..." Lex's voice trailed off. He shrugged and said, "She was afraid. She sent me the message, and I got Dodd because I needed help getting out of bed."

There was a strange trust between elemental mages. They weren't afraid to update each other, to keep the secret communications open between them. Even he, the unofficial leader of the mage rebellion, had no concept of how many mages existed. Nor did he know how many elementals existed.

It was a stunning statement of trust to have an elemental mage trust not just a normal, not just a soldier, but two of the pope's own guard. While he knew Allegra's words were true, he had not considered the depth of that truth. Mages trusted her, her staff, and all those who protected her. If she were anyone else, he'd fear anyone having that kind of power.

"Is she certain this is new?"

Dodd nodded grimly. He stared at the demon mark, burned into the wooden floor. "She said it wasn't here this morning when she fetched the candles. She came back for more and there it was."

Walter moved the lantern around and his heart sank. Make that marks, plural. They were all small, none bigger than the palm of his hand. The problem was that there were dozens, covering the ceiling, the wall, and even some of the furniture.

"Lord God Almighty," Walter whispered, carefully examining the floor around him. He managed to breathe when he saw they were concentrated in this area, as opposed to the entrance to the door. He could have set them off. He tried to calm the panicky voice in his head and focus on breathing.

"We didn't tell anyone else yet," Lex said. "In case that matters."

"What should we do?" Dodd asked.

Honestly, Walter had no clue what to do. At the Abbey, he worked to carefully disarm the portals. He quietly organized some of his most trusted supporters to assist him and they cleared out dozens of the things. However, there were more portal markings in this confined space than he'd discovered in all of Borro Abbey.

"Someone from Borro must be doing this," Walter whispered.

"How can you be sure?" Dodd asked.

"Seems a bit too much of a coincidence for them to show up there, and now here after the evacuation. God Almighty, they're going to burn us all at the stake if this gets out."

"Can you take it apart?" Lex asked.

Walter stared at the marks, trying to figure out how to do it both discreetly and without burning down the entire town. He'd need a helper in case anything got past him. He'd also need to collapse this section into the earth if he couldn't stop the portals from ripping into each other, thereby allowing a monster to come through.

"No. This is going to require significant coordination."

"Who can help with this?"

"I don't know if we even have time." Walter blew out a breath. "For all I know, they're out there trying to hand Allegra over to that son of a bitch."

"Not without a fight," Dodd said.

"Amen," Lex said.

Walter positioned the lantern toward the panting and sweating Lex. "Are you bleeding to death over there?"

"Fuck off, Cram."

"Good to see you improving. Okay. First, that mage who got you? Was she at Borro Abbey at any time while we were there?" Dodd and Lex shared a look before both shaking their heads. "That's good. Then we can eliminate her trying to trick me into starting a damned war. Okay. Okay. Who got who?"

"She came to me. Um, Dodd and I had just been talking, so I got her to get him before he left the building." Lex shrugged awkwardly. "It takes me fucking forever to get out of bed still."

"Why you?" Walter asked. He held up a hand. "I don't mean anything by it. I am trying to wrap my head around the events. This is going to be delicate work, and I can't move around here the way I did at the Abbey."

Lex tried to shrug, but it brought on a wince. "I guess word got out I'm not tight with the cardinals right now."

"What did you do?" Dodd asked.

"Didn't you hear? Lex rolled his eyes when Dodd shook his head. "I grabbed one of the cardinals by his collar and threatened him."

Walter snorted. "I wish I could have seen that."

"Since then, a lot of people have been visiting me. Some, I know are mages and some..." Lex shrugged. More wincing. "Either folks think I'm a mage or, at least, I'm a mage sympathizer. So here I am, *sympathizing.*"

Walter motioned for them to follow him out of the room, carefully. He examined the floor and every step he took was cautiously investigated. He instructed them not to touch anything.

Once they reached the door, Dodd asked, "Can any mage make these marks? Like, could you?"

"No, I can't."

A year ago, Walter would have taken that as a threat. In fact, from most people he would still take that as a warning to run, but he knew it wasn't like that with these two.

"This is what I know. Any elemental can close them, and I've heard that any mage with training can, too. This is well beyond that. I've only met one person who could do this, and she was out of her mind in pain when it happened. She didn't even know she was a mage. Since then, I've been trying to find information on the mages who can do this, but..."

"What have you learned?" Lex asked.

"Not much." Walter shook his head. This was more than just a mess. This was so much worse. "I've read that it's one of the elemental powers that mages can have, but I haven't met anyone else who's confessed that they could do this. Truth be told, I'm not sure I'd tell anyone if I could. Consider that I can only destroy a couple of buildings before I pass out. This? We're talking destroying the world. It's a whole other level. What a terrifying power to possess."

"What about the rest of us over here, Cram? We're the ones who can't even fight this."

Walter looked at Dodd and finally realized what it must be like for normals. A normal was no match for an elemental. For a moment, he had a sinking feeling that he understood why mages were oppressed and, just for that flicker, he felt dirty for even thinking it.

"I think it's time we all stopped fighting each other and worked together," Walter said quietly.

"I saw you open up the side of a mountain to swallow the abbey," Dodd said. "What good is the likes of me to you?"

"For one thing, you can stop someone from stabbing me in the back while I open up that hole," Walter said simply. "This is my world, too. It might be shit, but I do everything I do so that I will die having made Serna just a touch better."

The ability to form these portals could allow scholars to study the origins of the abyss, if that's where demons came from. They could even send expeditions to see if time operated the same there as here. If it didn't, perhaps they could find Tasmin and the others, and bring them back into the world. Imagine what possibilities could happen if they could harness their fear and direct it toward the pursuit of knowledge.

Sadly, people weren't that smart.

"More than ever, we need to protect the mages. We cannot let word get out of this, or there will be harsh recriminations. And, well, I'll be honest with you: I don't think any mages will stand for arrests now. Not after what's happened."

Dodd shook his head. "Cram, come on. We're not talking about a mage who is going about their business. Someone is doing this on purpose to hurt us. They have to be stopped."

"Agreed, but," Walter drew in a breath, "we don't actually know if it's one person or a group. We don't even know if this is a conscious choice. For all we know, these appear after the unsuspecting mage leaves an area, and are not even aware they are the cause of all that's happened."

"That's worse than someone doing it on purpose," Lex muttered.

"I have to agree, but we do need to consider that. Either way, I think the safest course is to notify Rainier and get his advice. I'd ask Father Michael, too."

"You know that neither of them really like you, right?" Lex asked.

"I mean, just because you're shacking up with Father Michael doesn't mean he's ever liked you," Dodd added.

"I'm not shacking up with him. But," Walter sighed. He didn't like trusting people, but he had to start somewhere. "Father Michael and I go way back. He's hidden me from the law a few times. No one know that, not even Allegra. So, keep it under your hats."

Dodd gave Walter a dirty look when Walter smirked. "Cram, look, what do you need from us? We'll have to tell the captain and the Contessa, but we can wait for that until after the conclave figure out where their asses are. This…though. I don't know, man. I don't think it can wait."

"I agree," Dodd said. "We need to fix this. Now."

Walter looked back at where the war to end all wars might begin. A war that would be so devastating, so complete, that there would be no one left to fight by the time it was over. "We need discreet guards in here, to restrict movement. Come up with a reason."

"Flooding," Dodd and Lex both said.

"It's not raining very hard," Walter countered.

Both Consorts shrugged and, in unison, said, "Flooding."

"Fine, flooding. How are we going to get mages in here to fix this? I can't do this all myself. I will need help."

"If a Consort is escorting the mage, no one will question it," Dodd said.

Lex nodded. "Get the ones from Borro, though. They'll understand this better than the Cathedral crowd."

Dodd made some protests, but eventually said, "I suppose. I've not been back long enough to know who is going to be on our side no matter what."

"You don't trust all the Consorts?" Walter asked. That gave him a rather comfortable feeling, which then brought on its own discomfort.

"Everyone from Borro knows the deal. The ones who spent the winter here, well, they might still be thinking handing a mage over to the authorities is the right thing," Dodd said.

Walter stared at Dodd. "Aren't the two of you the authorities?"

"Do you want our help or not?" Dodd asked.

"Fine," Walter said.

"Cram? Did these marks show up in Borro Abbey before or after the refugees?" Lex asked. He was sweating and wincing a lot more.

"Both," Walter said. "Which means, it's either a Consort, one of the clergy, or the servants. Well, also any of the public who came there, either to stay or from the town to deliver goods."

"That's got to be hundreds of people."

"Yeah," Walter said. "Plus, no one is going to believe me when I say it was pre-arrival. They're going to be convinced it was one of the new mages. I wouldn't be surprised if they think there's a giant conspiracy of mages doing this."

Lex groaned and wrapped his arms around his middle.

"You going to make it?"

"It's starting to really hurt now."

"The barracks are closer. Let's get you there," Dodd said. He hesitated and asked, "Can I put my arm around you? To help you, I mean?"

"Oh, fuck off, Dodd, and put your arm around my waist or I swear I'll stab you," Lex said as he staggered next to Dodd, leaning into him.

A wistful smile formed on Walter's face. At least something was going to turn out all right in the end.

Assuming they all lived.

IT TOOK FOREVER to get through the formalities of an emergency vote. With Cardinal Devonshire away, the bureaucracy tripled. The cruel irony of the situation that an emergency vote required nearly two hours of debate and posturing before they could begin discussing the reason for the emergency session. Thank the Almighty Bonacieux had given them enough time to get through the ceremonies or they'd have been overrun by Cartossian soldiers before they'd gotten through the prayers and blessings.

"Now to the reason we are here," Rupert said. He'd never felt as old as he did now upon the stage. "We are here to discuss the demands by General Bonacieux to hand over the Arbiter, Allegra, Contessa of Marsina, and Walter Cram, self-professed elemental mage and rumored head of the mage rebellion. I am opening the floor for comments for one hour and then we will vote." He said that last sentence and flipped over the hourglass with the blue sand.

To the surprise of no one, the complaints began, as opposed to debate. "This is a grave decision. It cannot be made in less than a week."

"We must have time to pray upon this."

"I need to hear all of the facts before I can make a decision."

When Rupert's patience wore thin, he said, "This decision has to be made quickly. We also need time to prepare our soldiers and defenses. We cannot do that if we spend the entire day bickering about protocol."

"If we hand her over, will we need to worry about our defenses?" Cardinal Vanida shouted out. That was bad enough, except that he followed it up with a laugh, as if they were discussing a practical joke and not the sanctioned murder of a high-ranking lady of wealth and consequence.

Rupert needed Cardinal Devonshire to get back into Orsini and soon because he needed her to censure Vanida. As head of the committee, she was the only one who had that authority, and the sooner she was back here, the sooner these disruptions would be out of his hair. He'd sent servants to fetch her, but she was a three-day return journey from her great-granddaughter's estate. She would miss the vote and Lord God Almighty help him if they handed over living people as appeasement items. She might censure them all to the stables, and she had that authority.

"According to all reports, there is nothing to suggest that he will respect or abide by any agreement with this conclave. Handing over anyone will just as likely embolden him to make new claims, as opposed to appease him and his wishes."

"We cannot handle an attack!"

"We're a fortress, you coward."

"We'd be under siege until Amadore came."

"That could be months!"

"Stiffen that lip of yours!"

"How long would a siege last?"

"Months!"

"We can't endure a fight that long."

"We are priests, not fighters."

"Speak for yourself! I fought in the border wars before I joined the cloth."

"You joined because you lost an arm in it. How good can you be?"

"Are you questioning my honor?"

"I am questioning your competence!"

"Enough!" Rupert roared over the arguing cardinals. The speaking stones echoed his words throughout the chamber. "Lord God, what is wrong with all of you? Are we frightened children under our beds? We live within a fortress. We have soldiers and guards, plus archers, and the Consorts. We have the head of the mage rebellion here and he is on our side. We have a war hero and the King of Amadore's own sister, who is an experienced soldier. We must look at this rationally."

The complaints simmered down, with only the mutterings causing a buzz in the air. But as they didn't use their speaking stones, they weren't interrupting him. "Now, Captain Rainier assures me that—"

Vittorio slammed his hand on his stone. "Rainier is sleeping with the Arbiter. How are we supposed to trust him?"

"Are you questioning Captain Rainier's integrity?"

"Who said they're together? I've not heard anything about this."

"He's always been a mage lover!"

Rupert sighed and pressed his speaking stone again. "First, there is no formal declaration that Captain Rainier and Contessa of Marsina are courting. Let us set aside gossip and concentrate on facts. Princess Imogen and Captain Rainier have both expressed concern about our water supply and sanitation needs in the event of a siege. As Princess Imogen has been through two, albeit short-lived, sieges, Captain Rainier has recommended we implement her suggestions in case we are attacked."

"What about Amadore?" Giso asked.

"Her Royal Highness also feels that we won't have a long siege by nature of who we are. Let us not forget that we are Orsini. We are where Tasmin and the guardians walked through a demon portal to save the world. We are where the light of the Lord God Almighty shines the brightest. Nations will not stand by and watch some nobody and his renegade army attack us. She suspects the longest we'll have to endure is until late summer."

That sent the cardinals into another tizzy about how they were all going to die in their beds. He glanced at the hourglass and feared it would take an hour just to answer questions and soothe their fears. He didn't know if his patience would last that long. He'd barely slept the night before. He wasn't in the frame of mind to handle these scared children voting to hand over his friend.

"Is it true that the Arbiter threatened you in the courtyard today?"

"We had a disagreement."

"What did she say?"

Since he could not say she'd ended their friendship, he said, "She warned me, and rightfully so, that the elemental mages might not allow us to simply hand her over."

"Are you saying they will protect her?"

"Was she threatening you?"

"That is a threat!"

"Your Graces, you must all understand. The Arbiter has fought for mage rights all of her adult life. Now, in her current position, she has continued that dedication by offering safety and protection to any who come to her. She has become a hero to mages, especially after her actions at Borro Abbey. People do not always respond well when their heroes are strung up from the church gates."

That sent the conclave into a panic.

"Your Radiance, what do you think General Bonacieux will do to her?"

"Kill her," Rupert said simply. "He will murder her as likely as he murdered Queen Portia."

"Do we even believe that report?" Vanida demanded.

"You certainly did before he surrounded us," Rupert shot back, not bothering to hide his annoyance at the gall of the question.

Vittorio pressed his speaking stone and Rupert sighed. "Your Radiance, this question will be distasteful for some, but I feel we need to be clear amongst ourselves. If we do nothing, our courtyard will become a slaughter ground. And, if we hand her and the mage leader over, we will have to live with their deaths upon our hands, but only theirs and no one else's. Is this not correct?"

"I did not give my life to this order only to hand innocent people to the wolves!" Cardinal Reinhold shouted so loud that Rupert could hear him without his speaking stone.

"You do that every time we refuse to pass a mage liberation bill!" Giso shouted back. He slammed his hand down on his speaking stone and said, "This is the result of our inaction!"

"We are not here to discuss the mage issue," Rupert interjected firmly.

"I disagree, Your Radiance. This is a mage issue," Giso insisted. "We have a mage killer outside our gates demanding we hand over our mages. How is this not a mage issue?"

"The issue at hand is if we are going to give two living, breathing people over to a known murderer," Rupert said.

"How will handing her over even help us?"

"He'll go away!"

"Are you a mage who can see the future?"

"He gave his word!"

"What is the word of a murderer?"

"All the more reason to give him what he wants!"

Cardinal DeLancey pressed her speaking stone. In her raspy voice, she said, very calmly, "This man threatens war upon us. Why should we give him anything?"

"Perhaps we can convince her to go willingly."

Rupert scoffed. He pressed on his speaking stone, still laughing, and said, "You expect the Contessa of Marsina to give herself up? I believe you've had enough wine this morning, Your Grace."

"For the greater good."

"For your robes to sleep soundly at night, you mean," Giso shot back.

"I cannot believe what I am hearing," Rupert said. "General Bonacieux murdered Queen Portia, and some of you are suggesting that we reward him by handing over our Arbiter. We should be arresting him."

"We can't defend ourselves if we are in the eternal embrace of our Lord God!"

Rupert let them argue until the sand ran out. By that point, the arguments were circular and getting them nowhere. Tempers were climbing, and no decisions had been made.

"Let us vote on the least controversial point first. Should General Bonacieux be censured? The details of which will be determined later, once Cardinal Devonshire arrives and is informed of the situation."

The vote easily passed to censure General Bonacieux. While Cardinal Devonshire would get the final word, they did do a second vote to decide upon a recommendation. The majority voted for full excommunication, barring him from Orsini's protection, arbitration, and even the front doors. A few hecklers pointed out that someone like the general might not ask before he stepped foot on the cobblestone courtyard, but Rupert firmly believed it was necessary to make a point. That killing a queen was not acceptable and that the Cathedral would not tolerate such distasteful actions.

"We must now vote on the matter at hand. Do we give the Arbiter and Walter Cram to General Bonacieux as he demands?"

"Point of order. I believe we should separate these two and vote individually," Reinhold suggested.

"I disagree. The demand was for both. Therefore, we must vote on the entirety of the demand," Rupert said. He'd hoped that, in the end, none of them would have the stomach to hand someone of Allegra's rank and power over to be tortured until her mind was forever changed. Or to be hanged right outside their doors.

Rupert called for an individual vote. The conservative side of the chamber was mostly full, though they were split between the yeas and the nays. The moderates, likewise, split, slightly favouring the yeas. The floor dropped out of his stomach. There weren't enough on the abolition side to take it, as most of them were out of town. The yeas took it with twenty votes.

"I exercise conclave law. Senior cardinals. Your vote is all that will be counted."

Several minutes were wasted with cardinals arguing the point back and forth. Finally, he called an end to the bickering and asked for the senior cardinals to vote. There were sixty senior members normally. Unfortunately, only forty-two were present. The vote was at twenty against, twenty-one for handing her over.

"I abstain," Reinhold said.

"Your Grace, you cannot abstain," Rupert said.

"Point of order, he can," the Speaker of the Chamber said.

"Your Grace," Rupert pleaded. "If you don't vote, you are still voting with your silence."

"I will not participate in this grievous miscarriage of conclave law."

"It isn't grievous! I am following the authority of the conclave and my position."

"I disagree and will not participate in the vote. Please log me as abstained."

"Then it's passed," Vanida said. "We hand her over and get back to our work."

"I hereby exercise my veto as Holy Father. We will *not* be handing anyone over to the likes of General Bonacieux."

Rupert's heart pounded in his chest as they shouted at him and each other, and mostly Reinhold who utterly deserved it.

He'd never used his papal authority before, but he wasn't going to hand Allegra over to a monster. And, if he was going to be very honest with himself, it was to protect him as much as her. She wouldn't go down without a fight. They would have to drag her, kicking and screaming, from the barracks, after they had murdered the entire Consorts and Almighty only knew how many mages between the Consorts and the door. Then, Allegra would kill herself and take as many with her as she could. She'd often said that's what she'd do. She had prepared herself for it. She'd prepared him for it.

And he would lose all confidence of the conclave if his best friend and his appointee to Arbiter turned out to be an elemental mage.

"Then I propose a new vote," Vanida said. "By conclave law, you cannot veto this one."

Rupert glanced at the Speaker of the Chamber who inclined his head. This was a disaster. "I still determine if the question is valid."

"I say we vote to remove the Arbiter from her position and appoint someone new," Vanida said.

"That will solve nothing," Rupert said. "That is the same as handing her over to Bonacieux. You think by taking away her power, she will disappear. Have you forgotten what happened at Borro?"

"How can we when an army is camped beyond our walls?"

The Speaker of the Chamber cleared his throat. "The question is valid. It can be voted on. However, you must put forward a name before I allow the chamber to continue."

Rupert shook his head. "This is wrong, my friends."

"You forced our hand!"

"You are a coward!"

"Come over here and say that!"

The Speaker of the Chamber broke the bickering. "The ruling has been made. You can vote on removing the Arbiter, but only after the chamber decides upon a new candidate. The Holy Father is permitted to recommend names, but he is excluded from the vote except in the case of a tie. He is then allowed to cast the tiebreaker. Otherwise, the Holy Father must remain silent and seated for the vote."

Rupert shook his head and walked back to his chair. He collapsed into it as the chamber erupted in argument. They were going to ruin everything he'd worked so hard to put into place. If they handed over Allegra, he would never forgive himself. He'd never be able to live with that shame. Pero would never come back. He would not be able to fairly rule any of these monsters after that. He would lose every morsel of power he'd scraped and clawed for, all because these people were cowards.

ALLEGRA SAT IN a comfy chair inside the Consorts' barracks and waited. Walter had dropped off Lex and Dodd, and then left with a few Consorts who'd been in Borro to help with a *situation*. Thinking about who from Borro Abbey could have been creating demon marks soured her stomach, and she fought back the constant belching that bubbled up.

That would have been enough stress without the waiting for the cardinals. The Cathedral-assigned Consorts were understandably very confused. First, the idea of Walter being free was a difficult concept for a few of them. Second, that several of the Borro contingent left with Walter to help with his *situation*. Third, that Dodd, Lex, Stanton, and Martin had pulled their chairs so that they were not-so-casually between the door and Allegra.

She understood their confusion. An elemental mage did not just get help from the pope's own personal guards. It also seemed rather suspicious that the same guard were preparing to violate any and all papal orders not meeting their approval. From the outside, this must all seem very strange.

However, that was life. She did not trust the Orsini Consorts as much as the Borro ones, though they seemed to adapt quickly once Dodd and Stanton were clear that anyone coming to take her away would be coming through their swords. Lex also added his threats; however, he was paler than spring lilies and was half propped up between two chairs and covered in blankets.

The gossip out of the conclave had not been inspiring. Plenty of rumors of shouting filtered down to her. Father Michael walked the distance back and forth constantly, bringing any and all news that he could. They all knew the math was not on her side. A third of the cardinals were missing, and many of those were abolitionists or, at least, her supporters.

"They won't actually vote to hand her over, right?" asked one of the Consorts. He was sitting on his bed and had been rather silent through all of the comings and goings. Allegra didn't know him; he'd stayed behind.

Nathan looked down at his papers. "Serafina and I counted that a senior cardinal vote only would net a tie, unless someone abstained or swung their vote. That would mean the Holy Father would break it. However, if they do an open vote, I doubt she will get enough. Too many of the abolitionists left for the countryside."

"They wouldn't dare, though," Martin said. "Right, Captain?"

Stanton shrugged. "A year ago, I'd say they would never be so inhumane. I don't know what my mind's opinion is anymore."

"They will vote against me," Allegra said. "Some of the antis will vote no, because they know that means their own necks will eventually end up in the noose alongside mine." Her voice was small, even to her own ears. "Many more will vote yes out of fear, though. I believe my days are numbered."

"They will have to come through me first," Stanton snarled.

"And me," Martin said.

"All of us," Rahna said. "We're here to defend you, even if that means defending you from the people who gave us the order."

Allegra tried to smile, but her heart wasn't in it. "What if you get new orders?"

"I don't follow orders against the word of Tasmin," Rahna said sourly.

"Nor I," Martin said.

"Anyone who isn't prepared to die today, leave now," Dodd said. He looked over his shoulder and said, "I mean it. The only way they take her is if we're dead. Am I clear?" There were hesitant nods, but they picked up momentum. "Don't think I won't fight any of you if I have to. I gave a promise. I will keep it."

The room fell into silence. Stanton looked back at her often, offering her a supportive smile. She tried to return it as much as she could, even as her own hands trembled. This was going to be her end, then. Minutes, hours, tomorrow. She did not know the time, but she knew it was fast approaching.

The worst of it was that they were voting to rid themselves of the mage that was, even now, risking his life to protect this God-forsaken place. All of her life she had a mixture of awe and loathing of this place. Now, here at the end, she only felt disappointed in them for living down to her expectations. She did not want this ending for herself. She had never wanted any of this. They had thrust the Arbiter's office upon her. They had sent the disputes to her. They had created the laws that imprisoned mages.

She stood, not having even formed her plan. She simply knew she was not going to die in this room. "All my life, I have feared this moment. I have worry about upsetting some petty noble and being turned over to the mines. I had never thought there would be actual cardinals vote to do it. I refuse to sit here and wait for them to end my life. Nor will I sit here and wait for them to end all of yours. If they wish to murder me, if that is their bold statement of strength, then let them do it in front of everyone. I am tired of being afraid of bullies."

"What are you talking about?" Stanton demanded.

"I wish to make my stand in the courtyard."

"No," said nearly everyone in the room.

Dodd added his own, "No, Contessa. Let them drag you out of here over our dead bodies. Make them pay for every inch."

Stanton said, "That is the only way they will get to you. Over my dead body."

"I do not wish to be dragged over your corpses," Allegra said somberly. "I cannot risk your lives to protect mine."

"That's our job," Lex said.

"And my pleasure," Stanton said. "Allegra, I will give my life to protect you. Always and forever."

"And then you will die, and they will spin whatever story they wish to," Allegra said. Her jaw trembled, but she managed to push past the lump in her throat. "Because that is what they will do."

"I did not crawl from that fucking room in Borro just to sit here and watch them take you," Lex said. His brow glistened from the sheen of sweat, and his hands shook, but his voice was strong. "I am not going to lay about while they threaten you. I won't even for Walter fucking Cram. He saved my life. I sure as shit won't sit here and watch them kill mages so they can sleep in their cozy fucking beds. I will burn this place to the goddamn fucking ground if I have to."

"Amen," Dodd said.

"I will light the matches," Stanton said.

"Um…" One of the Consorts in the back said, raising his hand. "Um, this isn't what I signed up for."

"Then get out now," Lex snarled. Lex pushed himself to his feet, though he held the edge of the chair the entire time. "I was there when Bonacieux killed Queen Portia. I heard him threaten the Contessa. None of the rest of you did. So, if you think I'm going to stay in bed while the blowhards in skirts think about handing her over, you don't know me very well. And if you think I will let you stab me in the back, then you don't deserve to be here."

"Then, let us make our statement in front of everyone. Let them come at us where they cannot hide our bodies. Where they cannot hide our murders. And them face the Lord God Almighty knowing what they did to us."

Stanton stood. "Okay. Should we get Cram?"

"Assuming they haven't arrested him yet," Martin said.

Allegra shook her head. "No. If they'd arrested Walter, we'd know already."

"Maybe they're keeping messengers from us," Rahna said.

Allegra tried to chuckle, but it came out too bitter for mirth. "No, Rahna. If they've arrested Walter, this building wouldn't be standing. Trust me when I say that we'd all be running *toward* Bonacieux if anyone was so foolish as to arrest Walter today."

"Contessa, that is not comforting," Dodd said. He stood and took the couple steps over to Lex. "All right. So, we're going to the courtyard. Are we just going to stand there then?"

CHAPTER SEVENTEEN

NADIRA FOUND ALLEGRA a dress, all right. It was an old-style Southumberland wedding gown, made of red silk and gold embroidery. She looked in the chipped mirror and gasped. Her skin was a perfect match for the dress's rich tones and fitted her almost perfectly. The hips were a touch too big for her, as was the bodice, but Nadira solved the second issue with a few quick stitches of red-dyed thread. The hem was a full finger length too short for her, which made it look a little comical; like she was a child playing dress up, though her figure said she was no child. She smiled. It was a strange choice, and yet, it was perfect.

Father Michael had returned with news: the cardinals were still in the chamber and were still arguing loudly enough that shouting could be heard through the bolted door and down the corridor. Rumor was, however, that it was not going to go well for the Arbiter. Father Michael said he did not know what to do. When Allegra told him the plan, he gasped, giggled, and then said, "It is not the death I imagined, but at least it will be a death I chose. Lieutenant Lex, would you like me to carry a chair for you?"

Allegra walked out of the barracks and headed toward the courtyard, her head held high. She knew what she was about to do. Serafina and Nathan hurried behind her, where Allegra knew they carried a stack of papers. Dodd, Lex, and Stanton all joined her, though she noticed Lex walked with Father Michael this time, as opposed to his usual place beside Dodd. Lex was shaky and pale, and the sheen of sweat on his forehead couldn't be good, but he insisted on coming with them. Behind them, the remainder of the Consorts not with Walter followed, and many carried writing desks, writing equipment, and chairs.

Allegra was seated first; a desk was set in front of her. While the others were organized, Little Gopher was sent to fetch Walter. Dust clouds and pebbles followed the boy as he sprinted across the courtyard's cobblestones, and Allegra couldn't help but notice how shabby the grounds were this afternoon. No one had bothered to do garbage collection.

One of the younger Consorts Allegra didn't know placed teacups on everyone's desks, and Nadira followed behind with a cast iron kettle, pouring hot tea into each dainty teacup. The exaggerated show began drawing a crowd. Why was the Arbiter sitting here, of all places, with all of her Consorts? Why was she being served tea? Wasn't there a vote happening right now to determine her future? Wasn't there an army within a stone's throw ready to charge through at her?

Nadira ordered the teacup Consort to fetch more hot water, and the young man obeyed. Nathan and Serafina organized the papers on their desks, all weighed down by a cloth and a stone on top. Each of them had their own assistant now—hired while Allegra was away and by Stanton's recommendation—and each stood poised at the edge of the desks. Then, both of her secretaries sat down at their desks. Then, Stanton took his seat at his own desk to her right.

Father Michael and Lex were positioned behind them, to observe the gate and any movement behind them. Father Michael stood; Lex was forced to sit.

There, they waited. Serafina and Nathan began writing furiously, with their assistants setting up a new stack of papers under another cloth and stone. Then, Little Gopher came into view, sprinting the way young children seem to do everything. Beatrix and Walter came into view a moment later.

Walter looked exhausted, but he managed to say, "Are you mad?"

"Will you help?"

"Will I help free the mages of this land? Oh, gee, I wonder," Walter said sourly.

"How is our little situation?" she asked.

He glanced back at the building. "Nearly finished. We accidentally opened one, but we dealt with it. I got the trickiest of the marks, and now the others are cleaning up. This is a good distraction anyway, in case they let a couple more snakes through. Are you sure about this?"

Allegra gave him one nod of her head. "I won't go without a fight."

Walter smiled. "Spoken like a true mage. I'll see what I can do."

Walter disappeared into the growing crowd. With Dodd's help, she stepped up on a chair, to gain a vantage over the crowd.

"I am the Arbiter of Justice. Right now, the Cardinals are voting to hand me over to General Bonacieux, Butcher of Fort Bonnet, the destroyer of Borro Abbey, and the murderer of Queen Portia. The Cardinals did not see what those of us from Borro Abbey saw this past winter. We lived together, mage, elemental, clergy, clerk, and farmer. We proved it is possible to set aside the animosity caused by centuries of Cathedral teachings that has led us to hate one another."

Some began to yell out taunts, with others shouting them down.

Allegra raised her voice. "The time to be cautious is over. Rebellion is now a truth. Civil war, strife, and invasion are realities that we have been facing for months. It is time to stop pretending we are safe. We. Are. Not."

"It's the mages that caused this!" called out someone in the crowd, which brought both cheers and jeers.

"Is it a mage army outside our gates now, or is it a man so filled with hatred that he would rather murder a young queen who was trying to save his life?"

"It was a mage that killed her!"

"I was there!" Allegra shouted. "With my own eyes, I saw it. I swear that truth to you by the bodies of my dead parents. I saw him murder her. And now, the Cardinals plan to hand me over to that man. A man who has threatened me, time and again. Who threatened my people, the Consorts, and the elementals under my protection. I am about to lose my power and my life. However, I also know that the edicts of an Arbiter are difficult to overcome. Therefore, as my last act upon this earth, I offer writs of freedom to any who ask!"

The crowd stared at her in absolute shock. There were gasps, but no taunts now. Just the shockwave of silence over the magnitude of what she was offering.

"My clerks are here. I will sign and stamp each and every letter of safe conduct and freedom. It will be virtually impossible to overturn it. You will be free."

Stanton scraped his chair against the cobblestone and stood upon his chair. "As the Duke of Barrington and Captain of the Holy Father's own Consorts, I will provide the witness and seal of my rank to each letter," Stanton said. "Today, you can be free."

He gave Allegra a tight nod. She beamed at him and realized she would marry him in this moment if he asked. She knew he was less sure this was the best path, but he was angry. Angry at Francois. Angry at the cardinals. Angry at all of them for even considering she was a game piece at the negotiation table. He was a man of honor, down to his soul. Orders, rank, uniform. That only went skin-deep. What was true honor and true duty was his word and his faith. She loved him all the more for it.

It was Walter's turn now. He stood upon a chair off to the side. There were significantly more jeers now. "It is time we stop being afraid. I am Walter Cram. I am an elemental mage and I have the letter of freedom from the Arbiter of the Cathedral! They cannot take that away from me now! It is a crime to take this paper from me. It is a crime to rip it up! It is now a crime to arrest me for nothing more than being a mage. I am free to walk down the streets of Orsini with my head high! I am free! For the first time in my life, I am truly free. Step out of the crowd and join me. Let us be free!"

Two mages stepped out of the crowd. Allegra recognized them immediately because she had provided them their own letters at Borro. She and Walter, and perhaps everyone else, knew the letters were only as good as the law enforcers who saw them. They could be stolen, ignored, destroyed. However, Allegra knew there was safety in numbers. There was clearly no way the Cardinals would ever move to being anything else but cowards, so she would use the last moments of power to make a difference.

She could not come out to these people. In doing so, she would lose her power. All of her edicts and letters and kindness would be put in jeopardy. So, she would deny herself the freedom she wanted so desperately for herself. When they came for her, she would let them take her and she would not use her elemental fire.

After all, she was creating her own personal army of mages here in this courtyard. They would do the burning for her.

A LOT HAD changed in the last year for Stanton Rainier. First, he'd fallen in love with a beautiful, intelligent, powerful woman. Second, when he discovered this amazing creature was an elemental mage, he didn't arrest her. Instead, he accepted her just as the Lord God Almighty created her and vowed her his protection. Third, he'd come to realize mages deserved the same freedoms and rights as anyone else. With that realization, he chafed at the uniform that represented those oppressions, all the while knowing that the uniform itself was how he could best protect those very mages, and the woman he loved.

Today was a very different matter. He had accepted that he had more than mere abolitionist leanings. He had accepted that he would not obey any order to arrest a mage without cause. He had accepted he would give his life to defend Allegra in her duties.

He had just never, ever, *ever* imagined he would be sitting in the middle of Orsini's courtyard witnessing with his official seal documents freeing individual elemental mages and slaves.

Yet, here he was, wearing his ring of Dukedom on his pinkie, a ring he rarely ever wore as part of his daily job, and pressing it into wax on letters hastily written by Serafina, Nathan, and three of the younger Consorts. If the Lord God could actually see the future and the choices a person made, he must have laughed every time a younger Stanton had insisted that mages needed their bonds to protect them from themselves.

The first three individuals who parted through the crowd were already pardoned by the Arbiter's office. It seemed pre-arranged by Cram, albeit hastily. Stanton could imagine why, though. Not even Walter Cram's insistence that it was safe was enough for a terrified slave or elemental mage to come forward and confess to their situation. It was simply too much of a risk.

But Malcolm of Westumberland came through the line and got his second letter of pardon and freedom. Some in the crowd jeered, hissed, and shouted obscenities, but others gasped, cheered, and whooped. He'd heard this Malcolm could turn the water in one's glass into a solid ice chunk, though he'd never seen it. It surprised Stanton to find himself planning career prospects for a man who could create on-demand ice in the middle of summer, as opposed to a feeling of fear and outrage. He *had* changed.

Stanton nodded briskly at the man and handed him back his stamped and signed letter. Malcolm read it, then jumped up on the chair Cram had used. He waved the document in the air. "I have been enslaved since I was eleven. Now, I am free! The Arbiter made me free!"

Chills went through Stanton's body. He glanced over at Allegra and recognized with a start the look on her face: power. All of this time, Allegra has been terrified. She had feared them coming for her. She had feared coming to Orsini, she'd told him. But now? Now that they threatened to take away her power? She realized how much power she actually held.

It made her intoxicatingly attractive and dangerous.

Another man stepped through the crowd and asked, "Is this really real? Can you do this?"

Allegra didn't smile. Instead, her voice was hard and determined. "I am the Arbiter of Justice, and this is an act of justice."

The man's jaw quivered for a moment, but he nodded sharply and said to Allegra, "I am Cardinal Vanida's personal valet and he has owned me since I was a child. I am not a mage, though."

"It doesn't matter," Allegra said. "I can issue your freedom, if that is what you want."

"My name is Thomas of Almsberg," he said to Nathan. "I would like to be a free man."

Nathan wrote Thomas's name and then passed the document to Serafina. She delivered it to Allegra, who signed her name. She melted the wax stick with her candle, dripping the wax in a little puddle. She pressed her ring into it. She blew on her ink and then passed the document to Serafina. It was his turn now. He signed his name in a clear script, above where Serafina and Nathan had earlier printed his and Allegra's names on dozens of pages while they had set up. He repeated her gesture with the wax and his ring.

Serafina accepted the document and passed the letter to Thomas. "You are now a free man."

He hesitated before taking it. "I can't read what it says."

"It says by the power of the Cathedral's Arbiter of Justice, you are hereby a freeman," Serafina said.

"Just like that?" Thomas asked.

"Just like that," Allegra said. "Serafina?"

"Of course." Serafina put her hand into her pouch and pulled out a gold sovereign. Two Consorts were gone to fetch more from the treasury, because he was certain plenty more would want their own coin. "This is to help you with your new life."

He accepted the coin as if he'd been handed a baby. Then he held up the letter and applause slowly grew in the crowd until it drowned out the mockers. "I am free!"

Stanton observed the crowd. The available Consorts formed a ring of protection. The militia and the guards did not join in, but they hovered nearby, ready in case they were needed. His scabbard rested comfortably on his hip, and his chair was far enough back that he could stand without impediment. He could even kick the desk if necessary.

And, God Almighty forgive him for even thinking it, but Walter Cram was there to open a crater around them if necessary.

Then, the next person stepped out of the crowd and said, very quietly, "I am an elemental mage. I would like to stop running now."

Allegra smiled at her. "Come and be free."

Stanton blew out a long, steady breath. He knew the glistening tears in Allegra's eyes were not just for these mages she was about to free. Those tears were for her, too, for to keep these people free, she would ever remain in bondage.

His heart broke for her sacrifice, both all of the ones she'd made until now, and the ultimate one they still might make today.

WALTER GAPED AT the line forming in front of Allegra's impromptu freedom party. He struggled to keep his emotions under control, but this was something he never believed he'd live to see. In his wildest dreams, he always hoped the Lord God would pull back the curtain, to let the dead look upon the living to see what their life's work had wrought. He always imagined he would die in flames, as the world exploded around him.

Walter Cram, demon lover, versus the world.

A tinge of jealousy laced all of his thoughts. He was self-aware enough to recognize the feelings for what they were: the green of envy that Allegra had done what he could not. That she had stayed hidden, even now in this moment, and that she could wield such shocking power. He'd always hoped he would be the hero. If not hero, then martyr was always a good one to ensure history never forgot one's name.

Yet, as he watched the crowd cheer louder and louder as writs of freedom were written, he decided he didn't give a damn about any of it. Sure, he wished it were his name they shouted, but at least they were shouting freedom.

"What's this?"

Walter glanced to his side to see Luchas and Rizardo standing next to him. "Is it done?"

Luchas nodded, not taking his eye off the growing, cheering crowd. "We checked all through the area, too. We got them all."

"Good," Walter said.

"So, what is all this?" Luchas asked.

"The Arbiter is giving writs of freedom to elemental mages and freeing anyone who is currently a slave."

"You're shitting me," Rizardo said. "Aren't they voting to hand her over?"

Walter nodded, and couldn't help but smile. "Yes. And she chose this as her final action. I am damn proud of her."

"Too bad you fucked things up with her," Luchas said. "You could've been a count."

"She wouldn't have married me. She's happier with him than she would've ever been with me." He grew a little wistful and said, "I have never seen power used like this before. It is beautiful."

"It is," Luchas said. "Should I go line up?"

Walter snorted. "Aren't you wanted for murdering a magistrate's wife?"

Luchas shrugged. "She deserved it."

Walter watched a teenage girl wave her letter in the air. "Anyone who denies these people freedom deserves it."

"Are you going to fight or run?" Rizardo asked. There was no judgement in his voice.

Normally, Walter would have ran. Knowing when to run had kept him alive all these years. He was good at fighting, and he was better at running, so he knew Rizardo meant no harm by his question. He did have to make a decision, though, and soon. The cardinals would not debate forever. Soon, they would let their fear and personal agendas sentence an innocent woman to the gallows. Selfishly, he knew he was also a part of that trade, but he lived his life being one wrong move away from the noose about his throat. This was no different than any other situation he'd been in. In fact, this wasn't even all that dire. He could just walk out the north gate. Just go. And the next time he returned to this place, he would collapse it into the ground for murdering his friend.

"I'm staying," Walter said. For better or for worse, Allegra's fate and his were intertwined. He would not abandon her. What's more, he was tired of getting along with these oppressors. Nothing cleansed like a hall burning. "I've always wanted to see this place collapse."

His companions discreetly left his side. He watched Allegra and Rainier sign document after document. Father Michael joined them and began writing the letters to save Nathan time. As the minutes passed, two more priests showed up and they, too, began helping write the freedom-granting documents.

Walter watched the crowd, and noticed his own people slowly infiltrating the front ranks around Allegra and the consorts. Several others found their way near him. Every new letter, he moved just a little closer toward the Consorts. They would need to close ranks and act quickly.

Allegra managed to sign and seal one hundred and seventy-one letters of freedom before the Holy Father and two senior cardinals came with an entire army of soldiers.

CHAPTER EIGHTEEN

ALLEGRA'S HAND CRAMPED around her quill. She had to physically push her fingers apart to stop the pulsing pain that turned her hand into a claw. Serafina helped her melt her wax, and Allegra pushed her ring finger into the red puddle. Her hand cramped again and she forced herself to stay steady until Serafina could get the page from underneath her hand. Serafina glanced at her hand, but went back to blowing on the ink to dry it. They all knew the clock was ticking louder and louder now.

Her joints audibly popped when she pulled each individual finger back away from her palm. The relief was immediate in some of the joints. For others, the muscles just convulsed more. She was exhausted, physically and mentally. She could not keep this up much longer. The cardinals were taking too long to make up their mind to kill her.

Her breath came fast as she thought about her death, of fighting and seeing all of these people killed in front of her. All to get to her. To see Stanton stand in front of her and fall. Her eyes welled with tears and she went back to the new document in front of her, signing and sealing, and focusing on that and that alone. Everything else had to wait. She had to do this.

She heard death before she saw it. Behind the crowd was a commotion, a growing sound of protests, shouts, and orders. Once she heard, "By the Holy Father's name," she began signing faster.

"They're coming," she said. She tried not to sound alarmed, but it was impossible to not show her fear. "Keep going."

Walter moved next to Nathan, and she knew her time was nearly up. Tears dripped down her face, and she had to pull back, lest risk the paper being smeared with her tears. Serafina had handed out gold coins like they were candy. She was now reduced to pressing several silver sovereigns into each hand. It wasn't much money—not nearly enough to truly reestablish one's life—but she could only work with the tools at their disposal. Withdrawing money from the vault would have taken too long; and could have tipped off what she was planning.

The crowd finally parted in front of her, and Francois, in all of his papal glory demanded, "What is going on here?"

Allegra didn't answer. The queue was growing frantic. They were so close to their own freedom. They didn't want to run now. They wanted their papers, too.

"Keep signing!" she ordered.

"Bishop Michael! Step aside," Cardinal Vanida ordered.

Father Michael kept writing, his head down, his quill going. Stanton's chair scraped across the cobblestones next to her. He stood and drew his sword. Once his sword was across his desk, he went back to writing, all the while standing and ready for an attack. The Consorts tucked closer, and hands all went to their sides.

"I demand you answer me and tell me what this is," Francois said.

Allegra didn't answer him. She dripped the wax on the letter and pressed her ring into the hot wax until it set around her insignia. Then she passed the letter to Stanton. Only then did she stand, her skirts pushing the chair across the cobblestones. She could feel the chair tipping ever so slightly against her, but she was not going to reach around to pick it up. Someone must have, though, because it reappeared a moment later just off to the side of her vision. Allegra folded her hands in front of her and said, "My duty as Arbiter."

"What are you doing?" Cardinal Giso asked.

"Using my authority, I am granting freedom to any slave or elemental mage who requests it."

Francois' Francois's eyes grew wide. His voice turned angrier than she'd ever heard it, and he roared, "You're doing what?"

She remained silent, though she defiantly held her chin high.

"None of this means anything," Cardinal Vanida said. "We will just pass a law overturning it."

Nathan cleared his throat. "Actually, that is incorrect."

"What do you know of papal law, boy?" Francois asked.

Nathan picked up his little notebook that he carried everywhere with him. "Over the winter, Her Ladyship asked me to investigate the extent of the power of her office. I looked into it fully, and it appears that it requires a conclave vote to overturn an Arbiter's ruling." He smiled. "A vote on each individual ruling. You would have to bring every single person she has ever freed before the conclave and then vote."

"That's a lie," Vanida said.

"No, it isn't," Nathan said. "I can have my assistant forward you the necessary documents."

Vanida looked at Francois said, "This is meaningless. We'll pass a ruling to change it."

"*Actually*," Nathan said, "the only way to change the office of the Arbiter is for a unanimous agreement between the ten longest tenured cardinals, and the Holy Father." Nathan looked at Cardinal Giso and said, "Unanimous."

Allegra wasn't able to smile, but she was proud of Nathan. He'd researched the laws of her office *thoroughly* and that is how she knew, with certainly, that as long as Giso lived and served the chamber, she would never have her edicts overturned.

"Witch bitch," Vanida snarled when he realized what she'd done.

Allegra turned to Vanida and said, in a cold voice, "I recommend you begin your search for a new valet. Yours has been freed."

Francois slapped her. *Francois* slapped her. Her eyes stung with tears. Then, her heart roared with fear as swords left their scabbards all around her.

Walter and Stanton stepped in front of her. Stanton's sword in his hand and Walter's hands outstretched and ready to call forth earthquakes.

"Gentlemen?" Francois said in a warning voice. "Allegra, I need you to come with us to discuss..."

"She is going nowhere, priest," Walter said.

Francois looked at Stanton. "I order you to step aside, Captain."

"No."

"Are you refusing an order?" Francois asked, shock in his voice.

"Yes."

"Captain Rainier, of the Holy Father's Own Consorts, are you refusing an order from me?" François roared.

Stanton pulled his shoulders back and raised his chin. "My orders were to protect her from all harm. Including from you, Your Radiance."

"Shut your mouth. Guards, arrest all of them!" Cardinal Vanida said. "Get that bitch and that thing out of here!"

"Wait just a moment!" Giso shouted, raising his hands. "You cannot arrest her. Or any of them! Stop!"

Allegra wished she could do a heroic stance, but her hands were shaking too much for that. She wanted to ask how the vote went, but the words wouldn't come.

"She is a heretic and she must be punished!" Vanida said. He tried pushing Walter out of the way, and the ground trembled under their feet.

"Get your hands off me," Walter said in a dangerous tone.

"Captain! Get your witch bitch under control!" Vanida shouted.

Normally, the insult rankled her, but not this time. This time, she knew she'd won. She was moments away from losing power, if not her life. She knew that, from all of their expressions. They'd come to rid themselves of a very particular pain. However, she had used her power right to the final second going against what these people wanted. Now, if they stripped her of her power here, in the courtyard of freedom...Allegra blinked.

She had not lost yet.

"How dare you use such an insult? Here, in the Courtyard of Freedom?"

"The what?" Cardinal Vanida demanded.

"What are you talking about?" Giso asked, who appeared desperate to stop a slaughter.

"From today forward, you will find this will be known as the Courtyard of Freedom, where one-hundred seventy people were freed from the bonds of the Cathedral's evil. From today, people will remember what happened on these cobblestones. No matter what happened inside the conclave. No matter what you and your soldiers came here to do. I want everyone to remember that this was where we began freeing the innocent. This is where it began. When mages in the future look back, I want them to think, yes, the Courtyard of Freedom."

"You can't do this!" Vanida shouted.

Francois gave him a harsh look. "Shut up. Your Ladyship, we have grave news from the conclave's vote. We would like to discuss it in private. Please come with us."

"You will say what you need to say in front of these people."

"I'm not playing games," Francois said. "Come with me."

"No," Allegra said louder for the benefit of the crowd. "I will not come with you. If you must speak, do it here for everyone to hear."

Francois licked his lips. He glanced at the crowd and said, "Then you give me no choice. Allegra, Contessa of Marsina, you are hereby stripped of your powers of Arbiter of Justice, effective immediately. Financial support and military protection is rescinded."

Allegra gulped when the words were finally spoken. So, this was how they would get her. They'd remove her supports, and then they'd leave it to Bonacieux to find her in his own way. She'd wished Giso or even Vanida had said the words. Hearing them from Francois was a cut to her soul. He'd been her friend her entire life. He'd kept all of her secrets. And now, he was throwing her out, without protection and without power.

She could not see how her friendship with Rupert could ever be repaired now. A small part of her hoped, right to the end, that he would find a way to rescue her from this abyss she was falling into. Now, she had to wonder if he'd even fought for her or if the only sides were his side and everyone else.

The crowd grew restless, as Francois's words filtered through. Finally, she understood Walter. She understood the allure of power that leading a rebellion brought him. She finally understood why he left her for this, for this feeling could be very addictive. It stirred something inside her that she didn't even know was there outside of the occasional daydream: the lust for power.

In the growing clamor of the crowd, inside the protective circle of drawn swords, Allegra realized in that moment how much power she truly possessed. As a mage. As a Contessa. As Arbiter. Even in taking away her power, Francois showed how much power she possessed.

She raised her hands to show she wanted to speak. There was shushing and shouts for silence and, after about half a minute, the crowd settled with only occasional yelled taunts—following by more shushing.

"So, I use my office to free people, and you take away my power," Allegra said.

Francois gave her a dirty look, one that said he knew exactly what she was doing and he hated her for it. "I will not discuss private business in the middle of the street."

"I will not go anywhere with you, if you are planning to hand me over to Bonacieux to be murdered." She stretched out her hands, showing she was unarmed. "You could just do it here in front of everyone."

"Over my dead body!" someone shouted in the background.

"And mine!"

"Mine, too!"

"Aye!"

Francois raised his hands to quiet the crowd, but the uproar was deafening. Angry fists were shaking in the air as they chanted, "And mine!" over and over.

Chills spread through Allegra's body. She had always said mages protected each other, but she had feared them, too. Associating with them could have compromised her position and her identity. She never wanted people to know who and what she was. But these mages did not care. They accepted her. They didn't even know her. They didn't know how much of a coward she'd been throughout her life, and she honestly believed they didn't care. For who better to understand the plight of a mage than another mage?

She had used her power and authority to elevate her own kind. She could have trampled them under her feet, but what did she do in her last hour of power? She granted freedom. How else could they react?

She had not done it to gain power. She granted freedoms because she believed it was the right thing to do. And though she was about to be punished for it—perhaps even with her own life— she'd changed close to two hundred lives this day. Those she did not free would never blame her. They would always blame the Cathedral and the cardinals for interrupting her. She would never be the monster in this.

In following her heart, in defying authority, she had created more power for herself than she ever could have schemed.

Allegra raised her hands to placate the crowd. It took them longer to simmer down this time, for the threat of harm was now upon the air. "Holy Father, I will come with you—"

The crowd angrily protested. They chanted and sneered, and all of their ire was turned on Francois and the cardinals now. They were not going to allow her to be dragged off like a common criminal now. She was theirs.

"Only to talk," Allegra shouted. She had to repeat it twice before the crowd was willing to let her leave their sight. "Only to talk, I promise. Your Radiance, you cannot just remove me as Arbiter. There are invoices and bills owing by the Arbiter's office that need to be paid. We have to discuss succession, transfer of staff, and all of the administrative duties that come with the position. I suspect it will take at least a month for that to happen."

"It'll take as little time as I say it will take," Francois said.

She ignored him, and instead stabbed at the heart of the matter. "But allow me to be very clear. I will not willingly be turned over to General Bonacieux. Even if I wished to, which I don't, my will is no longer the only vote. All of you get a vote."

"What the conclave decides is what is the law," Cardinal Vanida said.

"No, it isn't," Allegra said. In a lower voice, meant for only their ears, she said, "Welcome to civil war, Your Grace. It has finally shown up at your door. I recommend you pick the winning side before it's too late."

CHAPTER NINETEEN

THE GROUP RUSHED through the corridors of the palace, back to the papal residence and through to Francois's private dining area. Francois ordered everyone to remain outside in the hall. Stanton refused to leave her side, and Rupert did not seem in the mood to argue.

With Stanton refusing to leave, likewise Lex and Dodd were constant shadows, even as sweat beaded on Lex's forehead. Allegra pushed her concerns for Lex as far out of her mind as she could to keep her focus and wits about her.

At first, Walter insisted on staying with her, but she asked him to stay outside the door with Rahna and Martin. She was not confident of her safety, even in this most sacred place, and she wanted to know the door was safe to open. He understood and stayed outside.

Giso and Vanida came into the dining room, along with another dozen or so senior cardinals. Vanida tried to banish Father Michael from their presence the moment he walked into the room. Allegra insisted he be allowed to remain.

"You don't give orders here, little girl," Vanida said.

"Watch your tone, Van," Giso warned.

"Father Michael?" said a feminine voice. It was Imogen, who'd appeared in the doorway. "Perhaps me and you could check on the newly-minted freemen in the courtyard. I am concerned they will need guidance."

Father Michael glanced at Allegra, asking her permission. She inclined her head. He gave her a supportive smile, though it faded the moment he looked at Rupert. After giving the Holy Father a scowl that would warrant a demotion in any other time, Father Michael left the room with Imogen. They pointedly closed the door behind them.

"What have you done?"

Cold shivers cut through Allegra's body. Rupert—no, he said he wasn't Rupert to her anymore. *Francois* had been uncharacteristically silent the entire walk back to the dining room. She knew his temper was boiling and was about to unleash at any moment. She would only have one chance to get out of him what had happened in the conclave before he erupted.

"Are you handing me over? Yes or no."

"Of course not," Francois said. "What do you think we are?"

Giso cleared his throat, and Francois shot him a deadly glare. That silenced the cardinal, though he gave her a sideway glance before lowering his head.

Allegra eyed them and said, "What happened, Your Grace?"

"It doesn't matter," Francois said. "What matters is that your days as Arbiter are numbered and it's all your fault."

Allegra ignored his digs at her. She turned back to Giso. "What happened?"

Giso flicked a surly glare at Francois before answering. "The conclave voted to hand you over. That was vetoed by your supposed friend here."

"Careful," Francois growled.

"Your absolutely dedicated friend and supporter, Rupert, Francois, pope, Holy Father."

Giso could be an irritating, even demanding man, but he was never rude. He rarely lost his temper, not in the true meaning of the phrase. What Allegra saw now was open contempt. She wondered what in the abyss had happened in the conclave to bring this out in Giso's normally good-humored disposition.

"We do not have time for this nonsense," Francois said.

Giso carried on speaking to Allegra, speaking over Francois's interruptions. "Then, the senior cardinals voted to hand you over, and Cardinal Reinhold here could have stopped the entire thing, but he decided to abstain. Because he's a coward."

"I am not a coward!" Reinhold declared. "I acted according to my conscience."

"Yes, a conscience that said sending a woman to her death was the best course of action," Giso shot back. "I hope you work on how to explain that one to the Almighty when you meet him."

"Our votes didn't matter because *he* vetoed them!" Vanida pointed an accusatory finger at Rupert.

From there, the conversation devolved into a several minutes' yelling match between the cardinals and the pope. Allegra allowed them to vent their spleens at each other. The rush of anxiety released from her and left her an exhausted heap. She quietly asked Dodd to pour her a glass of wine. She gulped the glass. Her eyes watered from the burn that spread through her throat and sinus.

Francois whirled on her. "This is all your doing! What were you thinking? I had to use my veto to stop them from handing you over to that...that...madman, and what are you doing? Handing out letters of freedom in the courtyard? What were you thinking? How dare you embarrass me like that? Answer me, dammit!"

Allegra looked up at her old friend and realized, with a large amount of sadness and resignation, that their friendship would not survive this moment. Even worse, she doubted Pero and Rupert's marriage would survive this, either. Nothing was going to be the same now. They could strip her of her titles, her power, her authority. They could give it all back. They could give her more power. Less power. It mattered little now. There was no forgiving and forgetting something like this. She knew in her heart that all that would remain now would be sad regret that it happened.

She didn't answer him. Instead, she motioned for Dodd to pour her another glass of wine, pointing at the exquisitely-carved crystal decanter shaped like ivy vines. "That one. It's the Holy Father's personal favorite."

Francois's face turned scarlet. "Is that all you have to say for yourself? Are you going to do anything other than get drunk in my dining room? Why won't you answer my questions?"

She sipped at her wine this time, but it still burned harsher than any cheap wine she'd ever tasted.

"Say something!"

"I think your wine has gone off," Allegra said.

"What did you say?" Francois demanded.

"I said, I think your wine has gone off."

"Answer my questions. Now."

"No. I don't answer to you."

"The abyss you don't! I helped make you! Allegra, answer my damn questions!"

Allegra scoffed. She didn't want another glass of wine—her head was already swimming—but she motioned for a third just to anger Francois.

"My name is Contessa of Marsina. You will address me as Your Ladyship."

"This isn't a game, Allegra."

"Your Radiance, you will address me properly."

"Oh, grow up."

Allegra slammed her glass down on the side table so hard it made the bottles of liquor rattle. "You made your choice. You chose to throw away our friendship."

"Oh, be reasonable!" Francois threw his hands in the air. "This is childish."

"Who voted to hand me over to Bonacieux?"

"Your Ladyship..." Giso said, warning in his voice.

"Who?" Allegra screamed. She was shocked by the anger in her voice. Some of it was the liquor. Most of it was not.

"I did," Cardinal Vanida said, proudly raising his chin.

"Thank you for proving to me that you really have always been the monster I thought you were." She turned to Cardinal Giso. "What about you? Did you turn on me?"

"Of course not. I'm not a coward," Giso said. "We have had our disagreements, but I would never turn anyone over just to sleep well at night. I wouldn't even turn Vittorio over, and I can't stand him."

"Don't you start," Vittorio said.

"I know you voted to get rid of me," Allegra said. Her words slurred. She'd drank the wine faster than she was used, but it was strange for it to hit her so hard. "You were always a sniveling, crawling, little...little..."

She blinked to refocus her eyes. Her thoughts became a jumble of words and she could not sort through them. She thought back to when she'd last eaten. It had been hours since her last proper meal, but Nadira had wrangled the kitchen maids into providing a steady supply of hot tea and coffee, along with various cakes and biscuits. Allegra had nibbled regularly in the last several hours.

"Your Ladyship, are you well?" Cardinal Giso asked, reaching a hand toward her.

"Allegra? What's wrong?" Stanton asked.

The room lost their distinctiveness. Sharp edges turned hazy. "I... feel a slight dizziness."

"Maybe if you didn't drink three glasses of wine like a glutton," Vanida said.

"Shut up, Vanida," Vittorio said. "Your Radiance, I think there's something wrong with the Arbiter."

Francois was staring out his window and not looking at them. "She drank too much on an empty stomach."

She felt Dodd's hand press against her back. "Contessa? Do you want some fresh air?"

Allegra licked her lips. "I... I think there is something wrong with...I think someone..." Her eyes rolled back into her head without her permission. She lost a few seconds of consciousness before hauling herself back to semi-awareness. There was so much shouting around her now. "The wine. It's the wine."

She couldn't fight the next wave of blackness.

***

"Is she going to be fine or not?" Stanton demanded of the medical people in the Holy Father's bedroom.

They had carried Allegra to Francois's bed, as it was the closest. Walter, Giso, and Rahna had rushed off in different directions to find any and all medical guild members to help with the crisis. Now, six apothecaries, three surgeons, and four healers were gathered about the bed all muttering amongst themselves in grave, hushed tones.

"I believe we have identified the problem," one of the apothecaries said. She was the eldest of those gathered, assuming wrinkles and grey hair were an indicator of such things. "I don't believe this was meant to kill anyone. Typically, we administer this as a medication for severe headaches. However, it's not supposed to be mixed with alcohol under any circumstances. I believe what we are seeing here is the result of consuming a large quantity of the drug with a large quantity of wine."

It took Stanton a moment to realize his question had not been answered. "But will she recover?"

"We believe so. We need to dilute both the alcohol and the drug. We are discussing that now." She looked at the others, who nodded. "I believe thin broth, spooned every hour, as well as a rag soaked in water, dripped slowly into her mouth. Hopefully, that will progress her situation faster."

"And if that doesn't work?" Stanton asked.

"We will try all that we can, Captain. I promise you," the apothecary said. "Your Radiance, I do not recommend moving her until she awakes. We must press you to allow her to remain."

"Yes, of course," Francois said. He sounded exhausted. "I shall stay in one of the guest rooms."

"She needs a constant guard," Imogen said. "Your Radiance, how many guest rooms are in your residence?"

"Twenty-seven," Francois said matter-of-factly.

Stanton managed to hold in the shock that the Holy Father had *twenty-seven* bedrooms set aside for his personal use inside the palace. He considered all of the cardinals, the bishops, the everyday clergy. Then, all of the support staff, the servants, the clerks. And here was the man who was supposed to represent a simple life in exchange for helping others with *twenty-seven* unused bedrooms.

"Captain, I believe we should move Consorts and members of the militia directly into the guest rooms here. With your permission, of course, Your Radiance," Imogen said, inclining her head.

"Of course, he gives his permission," Cardinal Giso helpfully added to the situation.

Francois's expression didn't change. "Yes. Go ahead."

"Beatrix and Rahna? You are to guard inside the Contessa's room. You don't leave for anyone. Not healers, servants, the Holy Father, no one. Do you understand?"

Both women nodded.

"Dodd? I want a constant watch on her. Can you arrange that?"

"Of course, Captain," Dodd said. He frowned down at her. "Is there anything else we can do?"

"Yes, there is," Francois interrupted. "I want you and Lieutenant Lex to find out what happened here. Was this an attempt on her life or was it mine? Was this a mage thing? Did Walter Cram do this?"

"No, Priest, it wasn't me," Walter called out from an adjacent room.

Imogen helpfully shut the door. "We must not forget that this could be the work of Bonacieux."

"Your Highness, how are your men? Have most recovered?" Giso asked. When she replied they were mostly back to health, he said, "Then I recommend we use Her Highness's soldiers as guards. The Arbiter's staff is also under threat. I believe Nathan and that...girl of hers. I forget her name."

"Serafina," Stanton said.

"Yes, her. I believe they should be protected, in case this is a coordinated assault," Giso said. "This is not the time to take risks."

"And Nadira," Stanton said. "We need to make sure she's safe. And Calm Seas, too. She's still recovering. Your Radiance. If I can be so bold as to suggest..."

"Yes, of course," Francois said, still quiet. Then, he asked in the silence, "Are we certain she will recover?"

"Let us pray for her," Giso said. He clapped Stanton on the shoulder. "But, first, I think we need to pay that butcher at our walls a visit."

STANTON GRITTED HIS teeth as he walked behind the Holy Father, Princess Imogen, and several of the cardinals. He was still the captain of the Holy Father's Own Consorts, but right now, he wanted to be somewhere, anywhere, other than guarding this man who had betrayed Allegra.

And he saw Francois's actions as a betrayal, no matter how the man tried to twist it to be Allegra's fault. Though the betrayal was directly at Allegra, Stanton took it personally. He no longer trusted the Holy Father, a sentiment he never thought he'd experience in his entire life. If she died, he would never forgive him.

Stanton inhaled sharply. There was every indication she would recover, and this is where he needed to be. What's more, this is where she would want him to be.

He was not happy about the conclave's decision with regards with Allegra. First, he needed Giso to explain to him their decision chain three times before he got what they were doing. First, they decided to replace her with Grand Duchess Katherine, who wasn't even at the Cathedral. She had arrived with the convoy, but she'd continued north to a relative's estate. It was only another half of a day's journey beyond the walls and, in her words, she did not wish to be a burden upon the Cathedral.

By deciding upon her, the conclave then voted to remove Allegra as Arbiter. However, apparently no one remembered there was a dead queen in Cartossa and an empty throne.

So then they voted to appoint the Grand Duchess Cartossa's regent, so that government could continue.

But then they realized she would not be able to accept the position of Arbiter if she was also about to become the regent of a nation about to descend into civil war. So *then* they decided that they would just wait for Cardinal Devonshire to return to Orsini. They had dispatched a notice to her as soon as Allegra had arrived, but it could be a couple more days before she arrived.

All that just to teach Allegra a lesson. Stanton knew Cardinal Devonshire well enough to know the old lady would demand they reinstate Allegra. Then, the cardinals would enact their true might by taking away many of the powers of her office.

Of course, that was all before she decided to free nearly two hundred slaves and elemental mages, and before she was poisoned.

What Stanton wouldn't give to be able to listen in on Cardinal Devonshire's verbal whipping she was going to give the conclave upon her return.

They waited at the portcullis for some of the Cartossian lackies to fetch the general. It was Francois that broke the silence first.

"When this business is concluded, I will pray for Allegra's speedy recovery."

"Why?" Cram demanded. "You didn't care enough to protect her from politics. Why would we care about your prayers now?"

Francois's expression darkened. "How dare you speak to me like that?"

"I shall speak to you however I please."

"I will have you arrested if you continue in this manner," Francois said.

"Holy Father?" Stanton said, keeping his voice neutral. "I don't believe this is the time or place to threaten the leader and representative of the mage rebellion."

Francois scoffed, and he put as much mocking disdain into it as he could. "Walter is nothing more than an arrogant wastrel who self-appointed himself into the role."

"Nevertheless, into the role he now is," Stanton said.

"Besides, Priest, you and your kind are the reason there is an army outside these gates ready to murder us. Allegra was the first Arbiter to do anything with the position."

"And she started a war with it."

Cram asked Stanton, "Which one is he again?"

"Cardinal Vittorio," Stanton replied.

"Ah, right." Cram turned to Vittorio and said, "I was there the night your chalet burned to the ground."

Stanton was shocked that Vittorio kept his voice as calm as he did. "You were the filth that burned down my house?"

"I watched as the slaves I freed from your fields burned it all to the ground."

"I have six more such houses. It was only a temporary setback," Vittorio said.

"It amazes me how people who vow poverty amass so much wealth," Cram said. "And thank you for the tip about your houses. When this business is done, I will ask the clerks for a map."

"Cram..." Stanton said, pushing warning into his voice.

"Captain, I demand you order Captain Rainier to arrest..."

"Oh, shut up, Vittorio," Her Highness said.

"Don't dare speak to me like that, little girl."

Her Highness looked over her shoulder and gave the cardinal a withering smile. "Don't make me tell Mother on you."

Vittorio fell uncharacteristically silent. Cram tapped his elbow against Stanton's arm to catch his attention, offering up a questioning look. Stanton shook his head, unsure what it meant at first, until the family connection came to memory. Vittorio was Imogen's uncle, on her mother's side, if he recalled. Her mother was a terrifying woman who made the Grand Duchess Katherine seem weak-kneed and compliant.

"Related," Stanton mouthed to Cram, eliciting an eye roll from the mage.

Bonacieux took his time coming to the gate. Cram and the others bickered back and forth, with the Holy Father telling them to shut up more than once. However, when Bonacieux came into view, they all quieted and presented a united front.

"What have you decided?" the general asked without preamble.

"Did you poison the Arbiter?" Francois demanded.

Bonacieux looked surprised, but then a grin tugged at his mouth. "No. If I poison her, I can't hang her from that tree over there."

"Did you arrange it?" Francois asked.

"No."

Francois seemed to consider it for a moment before saying, "General Bonacieux, the conclave has voted. You are a rogue and in violation of the peace agreements Orsini has signed with Cartossa. You murdered Queen Portia without a proper trial or investigation."

"I saw her demonic form with my own eyes, Father," Bonacieux said with a scoff.

"You will disband your marauders and return to Cartossa. There, you will await Grand Duchess Katherine, who is, according to our records, the eldest of those with a claim to the throne you so thoughtlessly left vacant. Then, you will assist the Grand Duchess until the succession can be determined. By order of the Holy Assembly, you will comply."

"That bitch won't live to make it to Cartossa."

"Are you refusing the will of the Almighty?" Francois demanded.

"I don't recognize your authority. I don't recognize the authority of any of you. You aren't in charge of Cartossa. I am now."

"Considering that you are here and not at the capital says otherwise to me," Imogen said. "Seems to me you have a decision on your hands, General. Either die here once word gets out that you have gone rogue, or head back to Cartossa and face the civil war there that will happen when Grand Duchess Katherine arrives to dispute your claim to the throne."

"No one will follow her."

Imogen snorted, and somehow, she made it sound insulting. "They don't need to follow her. She will be there to ensure they don't have to follow you."

"I don't recognize your authority. Any of you. I am following the will of the Almighty. This is his will."

"This is your own blind ambition."

"We shall see, priest."

"Holy Father or Your Radiance. You will adhere to proper protocol if you expect to ever set foot inside our walls."

"A few ladders should fix that."

"General," Imogen said, interrupting all of them before they could respond to Bonacieux's threats. "I was sent to assist with the refugee situation and to report back to the king. My last letter to him states that a marauding Cartossian army was headed to Orsini under your flag. Tell me, do you think the king of Amadore will accept your invasion of his territory?"

"Orsini isn't in his territory."

"What about my Consorts you killed? What about the people at Borro you butchered?" Stanton asked.

"It's not my fault you are fucking a witch lover," Bonacieux said.

Stanton narrowed his eyes but made no other response. That's what a man like him would want, and Stanton wouldn't give him the satisfaction.

"I only wish I'd been the one to poison her, Captain. That way, I could tell you I did it, and dare you to come out here and face me."

"Get off our land, General. I pray you do so before Amadore's troops arrive," Francois said. "We won't be handing anyone over to you. Not now. Not ever. We have the Lord God Almighty on our side. You have some tortured mages and a bunch of murderers. We will triumph in the name of our Lord God."

"We'll see about that, Father."

Francois nodded at the soldiers who pulled down a wooden barrier from above. It cut off Bonacieux's view inside the portcullis.

Francois said, "What do we do?"

Walter spoke first. "We need to treat the stream water to the north as poison from this point forward. It can be used for fires, washing, and the like. It cannot be trusted for consumption by anyone from this point. That includes the animals."

Francois glared at Cram but said nothing.

"What about the underground wells?" Imogen asked.

"I had Nathan look into it," Stanton said. "Looks like anything on the west side of the palace is safe. Those are the deep wells. Anything on the north or east side, though, is touch and go."

"What about south?" Cram asked.

"Those wells are all dry," Stanton said.

"I have heard stories about the general poisoning water supplies," Imogen said quietly.

Cram was looking about the courtyard. The militia had kept the crowd back, but they needed to take the conversation inside and into privacy soon. "It's more than rumors, Your Highness."

"Should I send Consorts to look out for scouts?"

Cram shook his head. "It's too risky. We need to start stockpiling water *now*. There is no telling if he has people inside to get at the wells. The alchemists can keep testing it."

"Can they do that?" Francois asked. "Test the water, I mean."

"Yes," Cram said, not bothering with the honorific that Francois has insisted for Bonacieux.

"Might I make a suggestion?" Cardinal Giso asked. After a pause, he said, "I believe we should send messengers out. The word needs to be spread that we are under attack, and that Grand Duchess Katherine's life is in danger. And we also need to find her because she was sent a letter telling her to come to the Cathedral posthaste."

"I don't wish to break up this display of might," Cardinal Reinhold said, "but I must point out that General Bonacieux has not moved against us. He has done nothing."

"Nothing?" Stanton heard himself shout before his brain could stop him. "He murdered the queen. He burned Borro Abbey and murdered the entire village and all of the refugees who could not flee with us or on their own. He showed up here with his army and demanded we hand people over for him to publicly execute, and for him to torture Walter Cram. He has done plenty already."

"I merely am trying to remain a neutral party," Reinhold said.

"It's your fault we ended up in this mess," Giso said.

"Gentlemen, I do not wish to bicker in the courtyard. Your Highness, were you telling the truth about your letter?"

"Yes," Imogen said. "Though, I admit I didn't know it was a proper army or that it was Cartossian. I might have exaggerated those points to the General."

"Then we need to get another letter out," Francois said. "Mr. Cram. Since you have extensive experience running from the authorities, would you kindly work with Captain Brett on how best to get the messengers to the capital, the Grand Duchess, to Cardinal Devonshire, and basically anywhere else you think will help."

"Yes. Your Radiance," Cram said inclining his head. "Your Highness? I recommend we send several small parties of couriers. That way, if one dies, the rest will keep going. Each can have the same letters. The goal is to get to the king, but also we need to make sure the Grand Duchess is safe. Do you agree?"

"Agreed," Imogen said. "Rainier? What do you think?"

Stanton nodded. "This is necessary, and we should do it within the hour."

"I agree," Giso said.

"Well, I do not!" Cardinal Vittorio said. "This is happening too quickly. The conclave needs to..."

"There isn't time," Stanton said. "I'm sorry, Your Grace. I know this is how you are used to doing things, but there is no time for your meetings. We have to do it now, before Bonacieux attacks us."

"Then we should all leave," Cardinal Reinhold said.

"We're not going anywhere," Francois said. "This is our home."

"Then, Your Radiance? We need to protect it," Stanton said.

"Yes. You're correct, of course. Let us move this inside, though. We are drawing a crowd," Francois said.

Stanton nodded and they walked together toward the palace. Priests. Soldiers. Mages. Stanton thought bitterly that whoever created the demon portal in Borro Abbey had ended up bringing everyone together, even if their plan had most likely been to rip the world apart.

CHAPTER TWENTY

LEX INSISTED IT was time to move back to the barracks. Everyone was too busy stressing about the possible siege to argue effectively against a very determined Lex. Dodd tried, but even his attempts were pathetically half-hearted.

It annoyed Lex that they needed support to walk about still, though the healing thread in the stitches were finally doing their job. Ditto the bandages Lex was forced to wear wrapped about their torso. They still got tired quickly, though, and the wound oozed whenever Lex overdid it. However, the surgeon said if Lex was strong enough to complain, then Lex was strong enough to decide where to lay their head at night.

Lex leaned heavily against Dodd as they took the stairs slowly up to the barracks. Several people greeted them and gave their well wishes for their swift recovery. That made Lex feel pretty good. They recognized some of the people from Borro Abbey. Some were elemental mages, even. Lex never gave a good goddamn about that stuff before, and the last year had only reaffirmed that belief.

Dodd eased Lex down on their bed. Then, he took up position on his own bed across from Lex. "I don't think I've ever been here with the place empty."

"It smells a lot better," Lex said. "Hey, is that a new hat?"

Dodd made several embarrassed sounds before saying, "Yeah. Cram and I went hat shopping for you."

"You went hat shopping...with Cram?"

"He needed new shoes, okay? It's not a big deal or anything."

Dodd's entire attitude about the hat was clearly a giant sign made in gold leaf that screamed it was absolutely a big fucking deal.

"Why didn't you give it to me? I could have used a new hat while I slept my entire life away."

"I was saving it for when this mess was over."

"We might all be dead then."

Lex was certain Dodd muttered, "If we're lucky," under his breath, but as he made no effort to clear up whatever was eating him alive, they left it alone. The two friends sat in uncomfortable silence. It used to be so much better, back when they were just friends and not this weird bullshit whatever it was. They were about to all die! Well, some of them were going not. Not Lex, obviously. They knew the Lord God didn't let them live all this time only to kill them during a fight with some annoying asshole.

"Listen, Lex. I think we gotta talk."

"You talking is what got us here," Lex countered.

"Ignoring what happened isn't helping, either."

Lex eased their legs up on the bed to rest on the pillows. It wasn't as hard as trying to bend over to pick something off the floor, but it was nearly as bad. Lex would never take stretching for granted ever again. Once against the pillows, Lex let out a moan of relief. They had successfully managed one of the most basic body movements to be declared human.

"Dodd, listen to me. I'm trying to ignore it, okay? Fucking let me ignore it in peace."

"I just feel bad for whole kiss thing," Dodd said with a dramatic sigh. "Like, I didn't realize you were in a...drug haze."

"Gee, thanks, Dodd. You make it sound like I'm some kind of addict. Everything I ate and drank was laced with the powder. I can't help it that I don't remember."

"I'm not mad that you don't remember. I'm mad that I didn't even notice."

Lex tried to roll over, but they'd have to be on their injured side. The stab of pain let Lex know that this was an advanced position, well beyond their current abilities. Instead, Lex turned their head to look awkwardly at Dodd over the nightstand table.

"I'm not mad or anything. Shit happens, and it was an accident. For all I know, I did it first."

"I don't actually remember who started it."

"There you go," Lex said. They did not want to have this conversation, but Dodd clearly needed to have it. Plus, Lex's guts were hurting again and they just wanted some sleep. But Dodd was the sensitive one of the two of them. "Just let it go."

"Yeah, you're right," Dodd said. His shoulders slumped. "I suppose there's too much going on anyway right now for us to worry about this shit."

"Exactly my thoughts," Lex said. "So…when am I getting my new hat?"

Dodd glanced at the hat and back at Lex. A goofy grin spread across his face. "When you can roll over on your side to tell me off."

"Asshole." Lex frowned. "Imagine me throwing a pillow at you. I don't think I can reach behind my head."

Dodd helpfully picked up his own pillow and smacked himself in the face with it. Oddly, that helped Lex's mood.

STANTON GATHERED IN Francois's dining room with various members of the Cathedral and Orsini hierarchy as they worked out a plan of action. The apothecary reported that Allegra had already begun stirring in her sleep, which was taken as a strong sign that she might wake by the morning. Stanton longed to sit with her, but there was too much at stake. Soon, though. He would give her all his time.

As the afternoon faded into evening, food came and went. Servants brought hot beverages. Cardinal DeLancey was given her own special cup of hot broth, which she insisted helped her aching joints. She had missed the conversation at the main gates because she simply could not keep up with the physical pace, but she had plenty of thoughts to offer once seated.

Stanton nodded off a few times during the long-winded speeches. Cardinal Giso helpfully elbowed him awake before he could embarrass himself. He, then, returned the gesture for Giso as needed.

Around nine that evening, a messenger came. Francois read it and blinked several times.

"I can't believe it. The archers are reporting that General Bonacieux has taken half of his men and left." Francois looked up from the letter. "Why would he leave? And, why would he leave some of his men behind?"

"Perhaps he is going after the Grand Duchess," Stanton said. That brought frowns and looks of disappointment. "I remember things she said about him, back when I worked with her. She hated him. She always said he was a power-hungry misogynist."

"I've heard her say that, too," DeLancey said.

Stanton inclined his head to the elderly cardinal. "It is possible that the idea of her being regent has spurred him to chase her. He did threaten her life, after all."

"Is there anything we can do?" Giso asked.

"Our entire purpose here is to remain neutral," Vittorio said. "If we send any more soldiers to help her, we are not neutral anymore. We become legitimate targets."

"Your Grace, we already are legitimate targets," Stanton said, and he didn't bother to hide the weariness in his voice. "We'll have to keep the main gates closed still. We can't have people wandering in and out. It won't be safe for anyone. With that said, I'm not certain what additional aid we can offer her. Do we even know where on the road she is currently?"

"No, and I believe she will not inform us," Francois said. "Katherine is a smart woman. She will have easily foreseen this. The only hope is that she had left the estate and was nearly here when the messengers found her."

"Then why hasn't the messenger returned?" Vittorio asked.

"It's possible they are escorting her or joined her retinue until they could get her past Bonacieux's men," Stanton said. "If they ditched her carriage and went on horseback, it's possible they could get across the border without Bonacieux being able to catch her. Where's the nearest royal estate?"

Francois shrugged and looked around the room.

"I think it's only a few hours ride once through you cross the border east of the River Three," Imogen said. "I've not been there in years, but I vaguely recall it being a short carriage ride once past the bridge."

"So what you say is that the only assistance we can provide is prayer," Cardinal DeLancey said.

"Yes, Your Grace," Stanton said.

The old woman nodded sadly. "Then it would be more efficient for us to finish this meeting and save the prayers for later?"

It was past midnight before Stanton was finally released from Cathedral obligations. With Francois's permission, he spent the night sharing the comfortable papal bed with Allegra, who moaned and kicked most of the night as she fought the poison in her body.

"Fight it, my love," he whispered into her ear. "We still need you, and my life would be empty without you. Fight it."

DODD WAITED UNTIL Lex's mouth was full of pork and pasty until he said, "We gotta talk."

All Lex could do was make grunting, disapproving sounds, interspersed with moans of delight about the mouthful of flaky pastry and slow-roasted pork.

"I want to be clear that I didn't know you were stoned, and that I shouldn't have kissed you. Or you kissed me. Or whatever happened, I shouldn't have done it," Dodd said.

Lex struggled to chew through his food, and made more grunting, disapproving sounds. Also, hand gestures signaling Dodd to stop speaking.

Dodd continued in case his nerve failed. "The thing is, all I care about is us being friends. That's the most important shit here. I'm sorry I've been weird and shit, and I'm sorry we've been arguing. So, fine, you don't like me that way. That's fine. I just want us to go back to being awesome and finding out who poisoned the pope's wine."

Lex audibly gulped down his food. It must've hurt because he made a pained face and his voice was strained. "Dodd, I want you to listen to my words. I don't want to talk about this. Stop talking about it."

"Why not?"

"You keep saying you want us to go back to how we were. I can't do that if we keep talking about how you fucking kissed me."

"You said you didn't remember."

"I was lying!" Lex cried out in exasperation.

Dodd stared at Lex and was very confused. He sifted through his memories and remained so. "I have no idea what's going on anymore."

"That's because you kissed me and messed everything up, like you always do. Impulse control, Dodd! Learn it. For all of our sakes!"

"Me? I'm not the one with a stick so far up my ass it pokes into my brain."

"That isn't even…that's…you are so frustrating!"

Dodd tried very hard not to laugh. He really did. He loved it when Lex got flustered because it meant he'd won the argument. The pork pie smelled really good, too, so Dodd reached over to break off a piece.

Lex twisted, moving the pie out of reach. "Oh, no you don't. You don't get to take my food."

"Since when?"

"Since now, Dodd. Since now."

Dodd put on the sulkiest face he could manage. He sighed heavily. He let out a little huff. His stomach gurgled.

"Oh, come on! No one can make their stomach growl on command." Lex glared at Dodd. "How are we supposed to work together like this?"

They were silent for a few beats before Dodd said, "We have to be able to work together."

"I'm trying, Dodd. I. Am. Trying. My guts aren't even all back in place yet. I can't deal with this, too."

Dodd was silent.

"Oh, don't give me the silent treatment."

"I was letting you speak."

"Whatever. You're sulking."

"I wasn't sulking! You are always complaining about how much I want to talk about things. So, I decided, oh, hey Dodd, how about you be quiet and let Lex talk for a change. I bet he'd like that."

"You are such an ass."

"I'm hungry."

"Oh, for the love of…fine. Have some of the fucking pie."

"I don't want it now," Dodd lied.

"I will shove this pie down your throat," Lex said.

Dodd and Lex looked at each other and they broke into something between giggles and laughter. It was impossible to be mad at Lex.

"So…should we split up and, I dunno, you look for demon portals coming out of Cram's ass, and I talk to the pope about how he ended up poisoning the Contessa."

"Go away. Run away. That's what you do best." Dodd said it in an easy tone, without much heat. He'd expected this from Lex. At least he'd gotten some pie out of it.

Lex grabbed the pie back from him. "What does that mean?"

Dodd leaned over and took a bite out of the pie. "It's no secret you've always been afraid to feel anything for anyone. This is what you do."

"That's unfair and you know it."

"Look, all I know is that you're trying to avoid your best friend in the entire world because you're uncomfortable talking about your feelings."

"Are you a fucking priest all of a sudden?" Lex pushed his face into Dodd's personal space. "Keep this up and you don't be my friend for much longer. You don't know anything about me."

Dodd laughed. He couldn't help it. "Really? I don't know anything about you, huh? I know you hate your laundry smelling like lavender. I know you hate it when your hair grows just long enough to tickle the tops of your ears." He ran the back of his hand across Lex's ear, where the hair was just growing to rub the tip of it. "I know you love being called sir by the merchants. I know you're ticklish on the small of your back. I know your feet get cold easily, and you wear stockings to bed all year round because of it.

I know you always get extra food on your plate so that I can share it. I know you don't like lamb, but you always get it because I like it. I'm not asking you to love me or sleep with me or fucking marry me. Just don't lie."

Lex blinked back the tears in his eyes. "I don't love you."

"No, of course not."

"I don't, Dodd."

"I know," Dodd said quietly. He was trying to twirl the little tuft of hair away from Lex's ears now. "You need a haircut."

"It's a really hard time right now," Lex said, not even noticing the jab about his hair.

Dodd gave his dearest friend in the world a soft smile. "I know. And your guts are still hanging out. I'm surprised I can't see them hanging down to the ground."

"It's more than that. You can't just show up and fling this on me. It isn't fair, Dodd. And you have to stop flirting with me. It's weird."

"Fine," Dodd said, pulling his hand back. With the other, he stole the pie. "Investigate attempted murder. Quietly keep checking around for demons. Avoid flirting. I got this. Well, go on then. Shoo. I have a pie to finish."

Dodd watched Lex hobble away and was both fascinated and creeped out by the thoughts that crossed his mind. Lex looked over his shoulder and said, "Are you done watching my ass yet? Did you want to see where I got stabbed in the guts, too?"

"Actually, yeah!" Dodd said enthusiastically. "Is the scar going to be sweet?"

"It's going to be so amazing!" Lex said. "I'm tempted to ask Rainier if our uniforms can be cut-off tunics because this scar is too good to hide."

"I need to see this immediately." Dodd rushed after Lex. "I didn't think it was polite to ask, ya know. I didn't know the rules for when it was fine to see one's mangled guts."

"Give me that," Lex said, stealing half the collapsing pie. Lex shoved way too much into his mouth and coughed, spewing some of it on to Dodd's uniform.

"Hey! Learn to chew!"

Lex laughed and punched Dodd hard in the bicep. And just like that, the chasm between them didn't seem so far apart.

ALLEGRA STRUGGLED TO open her eyes, but they eventually obeyed her. She had to blink several more times to get them to focus. Then, several more heart beats passed before she realized she had no idea where she was. She searched her memories for any clue but found nothing useful. The last she remembered was drinking Francois's good wine while he yelled at her.

She tried to sit up, but her head throbbed. She winced but pushed herself upright. Had she gotten drunk? She didn't remember it at all, and she wasn't the sort that suffered blackouts from intoxication. She typically remembered every single embarrassing thing she did under the influence of a bottle of good wine.

"Oh! She's awake! She's awake!"

Allegra winced as Serafina's too-loud shrill stabbed through her ears and into her brain. "What happened?"

It sounded as though the entire Cathedral rushed across the floor to push into the strange bedroom. She winced more.

"Finally!" Stanton said, sitting down on the bed. He kissed the back of her hand. "Welcome back to the land of the awake."

She looked about the room. There were two small, portable desks set up in it. Three cots off to the side. "What happened? And, where am I?"

"You need to drink this first," Stanton said, passing her a glass.

She accepted the glass of cloudy water and sipped. She gagged on the bitter drink and tried to pass it back to him, but he instructed her she needed to drink as much as she could.

"That was no hangover medicine," she said between gags.

"No, it isn't," Stanton said. He did give her a pleased smile when she handed him back the empty glass, however. "You were poisoned."

Allegra's heart pounded painfully in her chest. "Poisoned?"

"We don't know who the target was, but someone poisoned the Holy Father's wine." He kissed her hand again. "But you thankfully collapsed in a room full of people. Once the apothecary figured out what you'd consumed, it was only a matter of treating you and waiting for you to wake. The Holy Father let you stay in his bedroom and we've all been here working and helping in the meantime, to be certain you were safe."

"Good Lord. How long was I out?"

"Over a day," Stanton said.

She stared at him in shock. Then, she reflected on the painful fullness of her bladder. Then, she sniffed delicately to see if she had lost control of her bladder during this over-a-day period, but all she could smell was an unfamiliar lavender oil soap, so she tried not to dwell on possible humiliations.

"Is anyone else hurt?"

"No. Word spread quickly. The alchemists have been working on testing drinks, but it appears it was only in this room."

"That's terrifying," Allegra said. "Um, might I have some privacy?"

"Of course," Stanton said. He ordered everyone out of the room and left her to take care of her neglected bodily functions. Her guts ached and her head pounded, but her ankle felt nearly completely healed.

She puttered about the room until she found a dressing gown. She wrapped herself in it and shambled out of the bedroom. She knew the room beyond well; it was Rupert's most private living area. Very few people had ever seen this room. Today, it was filled with people milling about. She pulled the gown tighter.

"Good morning everyone," she said.

Happy faces and congratulations on her health came in reply.

"How do you fare, Your Ladyship?" DeLancey asked her.

"Dizzy with a terrible headache. Though, I am pleased to announce that my ankle is on the mend."

"Excellent. Are you ready to work?"

Stanton stepped beside her. "Your Grace! She's only just risen from bed."

"No, it's fine. I should work." Allegra blinked. "Do I even have a job anymore?"

"About that…" Stanton said. "A lot has happened in the last day."

Allegra eased herself into one of Francois's cozy armchairs while she listened to the updates. Bonacieux had left with his cavalry and some of his mages, but his infantry remained. They did not have an official count, but Captain Brett's men estimated there were about a thousand strong outside the main gates. Because of this, the portcullis was ordered to remain down and locked, with the inner gates closed and bolted. The exterior gates were considered too far gone to be of use.

She sipped salted beef marrow broth as they told her of the conflicting reports about Grand Duchess Katherine's escape to Cartossa. Their best guess was that she'd either made it across the border near the River Three, or she had headed west and was hoping to sneak down to the capital that way. Everyone took it as a positive sign, however, that Bonacieux had not returned.

"Oh, and since Grand Duchess Katherine sent word that she declined the office of Arbiter—this was before she discovered she was appointed Regent of Cartossa—the Holy Father has temporarily appointed you back to the role of Arbiter until after Cardinal Devonshire returns to the Cathedral and can reconvene an assembly to decide," Giso said. With rather a gloating smirk, by Allegra's estimation.

"I'm Arbiter again?" Allegra said. "I was certain you were all telling me the opposite while I was being poisoned."

"I see your acerbic wit hasn't suffered damage."

Allegra sighed at the sight of Francois entering the room. "Hello."

"How are you feeling?" he asked in a cold voice.

"Improved enough to work," Allegra said simply. "Though, I admit I was looking forward to sleeping and perhaps reading a good book."

Giso let out a snort. "Alas, Your Ladyship, there is no rest for the wicked."

Allegra smiled and tried to keep the sadness out of it. Giso did not know she was an elemental. She wondered what he would say, if he discovered the truth. A frown tugged at Allegra's heart. She knew what they'd all say.

"Where is Nadira?"

Everyone looked at each other, all hoping the other would break some kind of bad news. Finally, Stanton said, "She is with Calm Seas in the isolation infirmary."

"Why? What happened?" Allegra demanded.

"The child took a very bad turn last night," Giso said softly. "An infectious fever has broken out. Nadira apparently survived the fever in her youth, so the surgeon says she cannot get it again. She, and a few others like her, are helping tend to the ill, while the surgeons control the fever."

"Oh no. Will Calm Seas make it?"

Stanton and Giso shared a look. It was DeLancey who answered. "There is concern about lasting damage. I have seen this fever's work before."

"Is there anything I can do?" Allegra asked.

"Stay as far away from there as possible," DeLancey said firmly, but her voice wasn't unkind. "I give you my word, Your Ladyship. The Guild of Healers, the Mercy of Tasmin, *and* the Brotherhood of Peace are all helping. We cannot have a widespread outbreak right now. Stay here where the fever has not spread."

"And, of course, we are all praying," Francois said.

"And are we feeding them?" Stanton blurted.

Allegra looked at him sharply. He bowed his head, clearly embarrassed. She knew of his struggles since returning to the Cathedral. Still, with the glare Francois was giving him, she shook her sleep-addled brain into action.

"The captain is referring to…" Allegra raked through her memories. "The concerns that were raised to my office…that…visiting servants weren't being fed from the Cathedral dining halls, so obviously I would be very concerned to discover that Calm Seas was being deprived in any fashion."

Francois's glare could have peeled ribbons of steel off a sword's blade. "We are feeding the sick."

"Miracles abound." And she hoped she said it with the same glare he'd given her. "Where is Dodd and Lex? And Walter?"

WALTER STARED AT the garbage barrel, shaking his head. "Why are we staring at this?"

Dodd was eating strawberries from a small cloth sack. "Little Gopher told me that he'd overheard the cleaners say all of the rats around this barrel were dead this morning."

"And...?"

"We found a glass vial that we sent to an alchemist we trust," Lex said between bites of strawberry tea cakes that he was pulling out of his own small cloth sack.

"And...?"

"Apparently, it's the same stuff that poisoned the Contessa."

"And...?" Why would they call him here for this? He was worried about Allegra, sure, but the apothecary said she'd taken a positive turn over the night. All that was left was waiting.

"Well, I don't know about you, but Lex and I thought it might be nice to point out the demon mark on the ground here, right by the side of the building where all of the rats died of the same poison used on the Contessa."

Walter snapped his neck to look at Dodd, who pointed at the ground. Sure enough, a tiny black demon mark was on the ground. If he'd walked over to look inside the barrel, he'd have set the damn thing off. He looked about their location wildly. People milled around them, busy about their lives, none knowing what danger was right upon their doorsteps.

"What's around this area?" Walter asked.

"The posh servant entrance is over there," Dodd said, pointing with a plump berry in his hand.

Walter snatched the berry and shoved it whole into his mouth. "What else?"

"Hey! These cost me a fortune," Dodd said. "I had to buy Lex's, too, ya know."

"I forgot my purse," Lex said.

"Likely story," Dodd said sourly. "The servant dining hall is around back. Um...a couple of apothecary shops. A surgeon.

Clothing, hats, shoes. Oh, the bakery. That's for the people who can't eat in the dining hall."

"This section is basically what? A small village of servants?"

"I suppose," Lex said. "I mean, it's more the servants of the important people, as opposed to just the ordinary folks who work at Orsini. The shops are set up for them. Well, I guess anyone visiting the isolation clinic or the hospice would come this way, too. That's way further down, but this is the only way there."

"Ah," Walter said, nodding. "That makes more sense."

"Why?" Dodd asked.

"I think our poisoner is our elemental. And, I think they might be a servant."

"What makes you say that?" Lex asked.

Walter shrugged. "How else could they get into the pope's actual living space and yet they are hanging around down in this section?"

Dodd and Lex shrugged in unison, but didn't argue.

"I'm not saying we should rule anyone out, but this is suspicious," Walter said. He blew out a breath. "How in the abyss am I supposed to deal with this while there are people everywhere?"

"That's why we called the demon lover extraordinaire. You're the expert," Dodd said.

Lex helpfully rolled his eyes for Walter's benefit. Then took another bite of cake.

"All right. If you two can, I don't know, distract people or something, I'll see what I can do." Walter eyed them. "Or you can just stand there, eating."

"If anyone asks, we'll say you dropped a gold sovereign," Dodd said.

"Good one," Lex said.

"Thanks, Lex."

Walter sighed audibly. He got on his hands and knees, wincing as he sank into what he prayed was only mud. It pained him, but he needed to tell Rainier what was going on. And then the pope was going to find out. And then the mages might actually want the abyss to swallow the world whole when that happened.

COMMITMENT OF THE HEART

THANK YOU, LORD God Almighty, for showing me the path through the wilderness. I am your ever-humble servant, unsure of which way is the path to righteousness. I only wish my every action to elevate your grace.

The plans have been laid with Your guiding hand. The unjust will not prevail. Though the lives of the innocent will be lost, they will go to Your embrace. I shall live with their lives upon my soul and I shall endeavor to be the champion of their sacrifice today.

May Your plan unfold through my hands, oh Lord God Almighty. Let their sacrifices not be in vain.

CHAPTER TWENTY-ONE

THE NEXT TWO days were relatively quiet, and Allegra had enough time to recuperate at her own pace. She still worked far more than Stanton felt was necessary, but she had to keep busy. Someone had tried to poison someone. She wasn't certain if she was the intended target. She wasn't even sure if there was an intended target. That was a terrifying revelation, and she struggled to adjust her mind to that uncertainty.

Dodd and Lex had been working to trace the bottle of poison they'd found. They'd narrowed the search down to a couple of possible merchants who both used that particular glassware in their custom items. However, they couldn't remember anything out of the ordinary, as they sold it for headaches. It was normal to sell dozens of bottles a day, and they often sold large quantities to the various healing guilds. The best they could do was identify some of their regulars, which turned out to be a very long list of everyone from the very important and untouchable all the way down to several street cleaners.

Walter was convinced it was a servant, but Allegra wasn't nearly as certain. Nevertheless, she asked Dodd and Lex to look at the servants who purchased the medicine/poison to see if they found leads or even anything remotely suspicious.

She still thought it was Bonacieux's doing. The General did not follow the rules. Even if she didn't believe Walter's stories, she'd seen what Bonacieux had done to the Abbey. The Consorts had all seen what Bonacieux and his men had done, and she was certain no one could exaggerate that many tales and still maintain a common thread of truth. No, they had to be true. They were all true.

He wanted her dead, and she'd nearly died. She thought it was him. After all, he had mages with him. He could have sent them to make the demon portals in Borro even before his own arrival.

Her muscles tightened at the thought of her cousin racing through the woods in hopes of avoiding Bonacieux's troops. She did not have a positive relationship with Katherine, true, but she sure didn't want her cousin murdered, either. Cartossa was amid a civil war; or, rather, they would be once Katherine resurfaced. There had been stray rumors and reports, but confirmed news was scarce. Bonacieux's leftovers had allowed clergy and messengers through to the main gates, but most people were either detained or detoured toward the north entrance. Everything, from news to trade goods, moved at a painfully slow pace now.

It was a total mess. Allegra felt it was all well beyond her abilities. She was not equipped for this level of political maneuvering. She knew how to play an earl against a duke in a land dispute, yes. This was the movement of nations now, not minor lords squabbling over slaves and land.

Stanton walked into her temporary office, which was a different room from all of the other temporary offices she'd been assigned since becoming Arbiter. This one was shabby, but it was two doors down from Stanton and the Consorts. Safety was more important than furnishings.

Stanton produced a wrapped cloth from his pocket and handed it to her. "This is from Lex."

Allegra unwrapped the present and smiled at the two slices of pound cake. "Doesn't Lex need to keep up his strength?"

"I think Lex needs to figure out whatever in God's name is going on with him and Dodd."

"Blame Walter."

"Lord Almighty, what did he do now?" Stanton asked. He collapsed into one of the chairs across from her desk.

She explained.

She explained that Dodd was having conflicting thoughts about his feelings for Lex during the journey, and how Walter encouraged him to tell Lex, since it was all going to change now anyway.

Stanton shook his head. "Why does Cram have to stick his oar into everything? Can't he just steer his own boat and leave everyone else's alone?"

"It's the leader in him."

"Martyr, you mean. That's a man trying desperately to be strung up for his cause."

Allegra didn't like that, but she also couldn't deny it. "Perhaps. How was gate duty?"

Stanton picked off a corner of her cake when she offered him a slice. He popped the piece in his mouth. "Desperate. We let in anyone who could be vouched for, but then that left about fifty folks outside. We found relatives to vouch for another dozen or so, but the rest are going to have to wait."

"Do you have that authority, Captain?" Allegra asked in a playful voice.

"Apparently," Stanton said, and she could hear the eye roll in his voice. "I keep trying to put other people in charge, but they won't stop asking for my opinion. So, Her Highness finally told me it was time to step up."

"That's Ginny."

"She's far more experienced than I am."

"You know Orsini better than her."

Stanton sighed. "That's what she said."

"She's a smart woman."

"So are you," Stanton said.

He stood to walk around the desk. He sat on the edge facing her and reached down to plant a soft kiss on her mouth. "You need to stop worrying me."

Allegra looked about her desk. The work could wait. "Did you want to head to bed early?"

"Oh, if you're tired, just go on in."

"I'm not tired, Your Grace," Allegra said with a wicked grin. "I was thinking a little privacy might help alleviate your fears and worries."

"I am always open to a little privacy. Lead the way, Your Ladyship."

STANTON BOLTED UPRIGHT. The cathedral bells clanged with no melody or purpose beyond alerting the residents of something. As his sleep-addled brain struggled to catch up with his senses, Stanton could hear shouting in the corridor. Then, the pounding at his door.

"Captain! Contessa!" Someone called out.

Stanton shook Allegra, who slept the sleep of the truly exhausted. He grabbed his trousers from the floor and shoved them on before everyone stormed in with him still naked.

"Captain!" Martin shouted. "Are you here? Contessa?"

"In here!" Stanton yelled. He forcefully shook Allegra, when his gentle touch clearly wasn't enough. "Allegra!"

She groaned and blinked her eyes before bolting upright herself. In a gasping, near panicked voice, she asked, "What is it?"

Stanton pulled a tunic over his head as Dodd and Martin came into view around the paper screen room divider. "What's happened?"

Dodd spoke, out of breath. "Several demon portals just opened on both sides of the main gate."

Allegra pulled the blankets closer to her throat. "Bonacieux's men?"

"Looks like it was meant for them, but the portals are opening on our side now. It's those damned little flying bastards, but Cram said we're going to have the big ones if we don't get everything closed. Lex and Beatrix are organizing soldiers around the mages because people are losing their fucking minds out there. Rahna and Gopher are off trying to find more of Cram's mages, and Father Michael was trying to do crowd control when we left him."

Stanton tossed Allegra her dress while he listened to Dodd's report. The others turned their backs and continued talking while she dressed.

"Father Michael was the one who alerted us. He was up looking for breakfast and saw one of the little bastards come flying out of nowhere. None of the Orsini crew knew what the fuck it was and they all thought it was some weird bat, but then Father Michael apparently was shouting for mages to come help him, and then you can imagine how fast that all went to shit," Dodd said.

"Where is Princess Imogen?" Allegra asked. She emerged from the bed dressed now and was pulling stockings on.

"I sent Her Highness to fortify the north gate because I had no idea what was going on up there. Father Michael is going to stay with the archers and any militia until someone can get Captain Brett and Lieutenant Emsley."

Stanton shoved his feet into his boots. "Excellent work. How long has this been going on?"

Martin shrugged. "It can't be more than twenty minutes. Some of us were already up, getting ready to hit the early morning carts like we always do. Cram was heading down himself when the alarm went up. We've been moving as fast as we could."

Dodd nodded. "It was a good time to get hit, honestly. Some of us were already awake, but it wasn't too crowded out there. As far as I understand from Cram, the portals hadn't started merging yet. The archers are trying to deal with the little fuckers. And then we just hope the mages can fix this shit. Fuck, I never thought those words would come out of my mouth."

Stanton tightened his sword belt. "Excellent work. Let's get down there and help the mages. Allegra, I need you to get the clergy and anyone who can't fight to safety. I recommend start pushing them toward the ballroom and anywhere else with locking doors and no windows."

She gave him a displeased look, but then she nodded in agreement. She wasn't a fighter. She was, however, calm in a crisis and that would be needed.

"Get the elderly, the children, and the untrained to safety. But be safe yourself, too?" Stanton gave her a soft smile. "Promise me."

She returned his smile with one that reminded him of how perfect she looked the previous night on top of him. She reached out and touched his face. "Be safe, all right?"

"Always," he said. He kissed her fingers, taking one final look at her. Then he released her. "Let's go."

Stanton tugged his jacket on while Dodd and Martin updated him on everything they knew, no matter how small or unimportant. The corridors were filling up with screaming people now, with some running away from the main doors and others running toward them. Stanton didn't stop to do crowd control, trusting that Allegra would take on that role to her fullest ability. He worried for her, especially so soon after they were united, but he buried that fear as deep as possible.

When they cleared the bottlenecked doorway, the fear rose in Stanton again. The courtyard was already aflame. There were very few civilians left in the main area, either because they were dead on the ground or smartly fleeing for their lives. The small bat-like demons were swooping down at the heads of mages and the archers. Precision arrows followed the demons, slicing through their airborne bodies. Some, one arrow was enough to stop their flight. For others, it served as a mere irritant.

"Oh shit," Dodd whispered. "What the fuck happened?"

Demons the size and shape of goats ran across the courtyard, fighting with each other and soldiers alike. Some resembled winged lizards and dove toward Stanton. They all ducked, with the screams of the gawkers behind him running away now.

"Get inside!" Stanton bellowed. He pushed two gawkers out of the way to pull one of the doors closed. Dodd grabbed the other and did the same.

Stanton unsheathed his sword. "Dodd, do you know for certain if the demons can be killed with swords or arrows?"

"The little ones, yes. Almost anything will kill them," Dodd said. "The bigger ones? You gotta cut their heads off, crush their skulls, that kind of thing. The fucking massive guys? Let the mages deal with them."

Stanton looked around at the chaos. There were no massive demons yet, no massive dark holes of shrieking creatures. Yet. "What about the big ones? Like, the one at Borro?"

"Only magic can take them out. Cram says it's easier to collapse the portal in on them and drop a mountain of rock than to kill them."

Stanton's stomach dropped. "Let's hope that doesn't happen. Show me where Cram is fighting. We need to help him and the mages. Let's move."

ALLEGRA TUGGED ON one of Stanton's greatcoats and tied it about her waist with a belt. She tugged up enough above the belt so that it didn't skim the ground. She took three deep breaths and then stepped out of the protection of the barracks and into the administrative wing's chaos.

"Get to the upper ballroom!" Allegra called out. She grabbed a militia guard who was trying to get through the crowd and said, "You! These people need to be away from windows and open doors. Help move them toward safety. No windows. No open doors. Do you hear me?"

A door opened and out stepped a young woman in her nightgown, with a blanket thrown around her shoulders. She refused to move from outside her door. Sister Margarite demanded, "What is going on?"

"Do you hear me?" Allegra asked the guard.

He nodded. Then, in a bellowing voice far louder than she could have ever managed, he shouted, "If your room has a window, head toward the kitchens, the dining halls, or the small ballroom two floors up. If your room has a window..."

And through the crowd he walked, pushing against the crowd, and calling out to people he knew to help push people to safety.

"Sister Margarite! Go!" Allegra called out.

"What is happening?" she demanded.

A panicking servant bumped against Allegra, shoving her against the wall. "Sister Margarite! We are under attack. I am trying to get the clergy and the children to the ballroom. Captain Rainier says it is the safest room. We must go."

"Is General Bonacieux attacking us?"

All the clergy were like this, as she tried herding them to safety. It was irritating Allegra. "I don't know. Please. I need you to hurry."

"Arbiter, shouldn't we be out there mediating this dispute?" Cardinal Rigi asked. He was one of the younger cardinals…and was coming out of Sister Margarite's bedchamber.

"No, Your Grace. You need to get to the ballroom. Your Grace! What are you doing? Get back here! Rigi! Rigi! Get back here!"

Cardinal Rigi called over his shoulder, "I'm going out to help!"

"You will do nothing of the kind!" Allegra shouted. She ran after him and grabbed his arm. "Get back here, Your Grace!"

"Unhand me! I am trained…"

"You aren't trained in this! I need you to get to the ballroom. It has no windows, and there are a hundred locked doors between there and the main doors. I need to get this building secure, and I can't do that if you are wandering about!"

Glass shattered inside Sister Margarite's bedchamber and what was background noise became an audible shriek.

"Run!" Allegra shouted. She pushed Sister Margarite toward the main double doors further down the corridor. "Run!"

A demon crashed through Sister Margarite's opened door and took the entire doorframe with it. Cardinal Rigi stared at it in shocked horror. The demon panicked inside the cramped confines of the corridor. It saw the frozen Rigi and let out its shriek. Allegra knew that was the sound of attack.

Sister Margarite yelled for Rigi to follow her, but he was frozen. She screamed even as she grabbed a fallen servant and helped them to their feet.

Allegra crashed against the cardinal with all of her weight, knocking both of them to the floor. The carpet stopped them from sliding but didn't absorb any of the fall's force. Allegra winced when her hip hit the floor.

"Sister Margarite! Run!" Allegra shouted. "Keep running!"

Rigi regained his senses and backpedaled on his bottom, crawling backwards in a frenzied panic. The demon was struggling with its wide wingspan inside the cramped corridor and kept smashing against furniture, as well as the broken doorframe tangled on the floor.

Allegra got to her feet first and grabbed Rigi. "For the love of God, run, Your Grace! Run!"

She hauled Rigi to his feet and they ran in the opposite direction of Sister Margarite, who was still weeping and screaming at the other door. "Sister Margarite! Lock the door!"

"Rigi!" Sister Margarite sobbed out.

Then Allegra heard the door slam behind them. Allegra desperately tried doors until she found one that was unlocked. They both rushed through, and discovered it didn't have a lock, and it had two tiny, sparrow-sized demons trapped inside the room. The demons were as terrified of them as the humans were of them, and Allegra managed to shoo them like birds toward the smashed window.

Once they were outside, Allegra leaned against the door, panting.

"Your Grace, are you hurt?"

Cardinal Rigi stared wide-eyed at Allegra. "You may call me Rigi, Your Excellency. Thank you for saving my life. Are those demons?"

"Yes. We can't stay here. They'll keep coming through the windows. The little ones will only bite us, but the bigger ones can easily rip us apart. We need to get back inside the palace and start pushing people to safety there. We'll have to rely on Sister Margarite now to save people in this building."

"The…um…um…" Rigi began to shake.

"Rigi!" Allegra said. She walked over to him and grabbed his forearms. "Rigi! Listen to me. Margarite is safe behind the big oak door. She got it closed. So now we need to get you back to her. How do we do that?"

"Um…where are we?"

"Mothers of Mercy wing," Allegra said.

"Right. The barracks are around the corner. Um…across the alley is therefore the…um…oh! It is the entrance to the undercroft. The isolation infirmary is down there for now. Then, on the other side, we can go back up through the servant passages there and we should be able to get back that way inside."

Allegra nodded. "Good. Okay, look. Help me drag the mattress over here." At his confused look, she said, "You don't have shoes on. There is glass everywhere."

"Oh. I don't."

Together, they dragged the mattress to the window and carefully crawled outside. Allegra gasped when she saw the billowing puffs of smoke rising.

"What is that?" Rigi whispered.

"That would be Walter and the mages, blasting portals shut."

"They would do that for us? After everything we've done to them."

"Come on, Rigi. Let's get out of here."

RUPERT STOOD NEAR the ballroom entrance and hurried people toward safety. "Hurry! Get inside! Come! Come!"

"What is that noise?" someone asked.

"Never mind the sound, just come!" Rupert snapped.

Rupert's heart let out a stutter of hard thuds when Pero and Father Michael arrived carrying Cardinal DeLancey between them.

Rupert rushed over and said, "Lacey? Are you injured?"

She gave Pero a withering look, but she did offer Rupert a wry smile. "Your husband lost his temper with my speed."

"I apologize, Your Grace," Pero said. "But time is of the essence."

They helped her down, steadying her on her feet. Rupert motioned her toward the ballroom door, where countless people were huddled together to wait out the fight beyond the doors.

"Are all the doors secure?" Father Michael asked. "We learned in Borro that the smaller demons can't break through solid wood."

Rupert pointed at the open one they'd just come through. "Just that one left. Come inside. We'll secure it all and wait."

"No," Pero said. "We still have another corridor to check on this floor."

Father Michael nodded. "And the entire north wing upstairs yet to go."

Pero grunted in agreement. "I don't think we can get them all down here. What about getting them to the library?"

"No!" Rupert interjected. "No, you're staying."

"Your Radiance, we need to get to those people."

"You have to come in here! I demand you come in here!" Rupert said, letting the panic in his voice come through. "Pero...Father Michael, I will send someone else with you."

"I'm going," Pero said. "Lock the doors behind us. We'll head for the archives. There's no windows in there, right?"

Father Michael considered for a moment. "I don't believe there are."

"The library has upper windows. The archives do not," DeLancey said.

Pero nodded. "We'll move them into there. Hopefully, the roof doesn't collapse."

"No!" Rupert argued. "You're not going anywhere."

He gave his husband a panicked look. They had been fighting even since the vote about Allegra and the mages. He'd always worried the mage cause would be the wedge that would come between them, but he also did not want to lose Pero in this fight. Pero's soldier days were long behind him. He gave it up to become a cardinal's husband. He couldn't just...

"What if I lose you?" Rupert whispered.

"I'll be fine," Pero said. He gave Rupert's arm a squeeze.

"Famous last words," Rupert muttered darkly.

"Rupert, love, I'll be fine."

Father Michael reached out and touched Pero's arm. "Pero, we have to go."

"What about us?" Rupert whispered. "If whatever breaks through, we're all going to die."

"If they break through," Pero said, "people are already dead."

"Your Radiance, please. Let us go," Father Michael pleaded. "The longer we stand here, the longer you are keeping us from rescuing the children in the upper nursery. Is that what you want?"

The bishop's words were a slap across the face. His anger rose, the sting of his ego wanting to lash out. His common sense quickly took ahold of his mouth, however, and shame filled him.

"How dare you...Right. Of course. I will stay out here, as long as possible, to help any stragglers," Rupert said.

"If you hear the shrieks coming closer, bar the door," Father Michael instructed.

Rupert nodded. "Good luck."

"Same to you," Father Michael said as he and Rupert's love rushed off for the stairs.

CHAPTER TWENTY-TWO

LEX AND DODD, along with four other Consorts, pushed their way through the fleeing crowds to get to Princess Imogen at the north gate. The smoke made it impossible to see clearly what was happening around them. They could hear the screams of terrified people, and the demon shrieks shook Lex's core. Lex knew they were all pushing past the terrified memories of those sounds, and all were focused on getting the job done. It was hard, though.

Princess Imogen was on horseback, along with two of her own officers, trying to push the panicked crowd back. The crowd pushed and screamed, and the Princess was weaving her increasingly panicking horse back and forth in hopes to both control the crowd and settle her steed. The other officers were doing the same.

Lex and Dodd shared a look, both pointed, and then they both sprinted for the wall. Demons shrieked in the background, sending a wave of desperation through the crowd. Some tried scaling the walls, but the archers had pulled up the ladders, and it was impossible for them to climb. Arrows whizzed through the air as archers tried to take down a winged thing that was diving at both them and now the crowd.

Lex's guts stabbed with pain, but they pushed the sensation as far to the back of the mind as possible. Stopping to rest was the same as stopping to let that beast in the sky eat them.

"Get back!" Her Highness shouted over the crowd.

Lex could now see a handful of various Orsini uniforms all at the gates themselves, trying to pull them back out of the way and allow people to escape. Then Lex got a sick feeling. There were also people on the other side of the gates—most likely, also being attacked by demons—who'd want inside the walls.

"Your Highness!" Lex shouted over the cries of desperation. They waved their hands in the air to get her attention.

She pointed at Lex and pulled her horse around. Her horse clearly knew how to handle a crowd, because it didn't buck, but the animal had an expression of terror on its face. Lex heard the portcullis as it pulled up, even though the wooden gates were only open a hair.

"It's chaos here! We have to get these people inside! There's too many demons!"

Lex looked around for the Consorts, but most were fighting against the smaller demons. "Did a portal open on this side?"

"I don't think so," Her Highness shouted back. "These are from the main gates."

"We'll deal with this. You have to help protect the mages. They are closing the portals, but they're being attacked."

A volley of arrows hit the diving demon, who then crashed into the gate. Wood splintered. Several people screamed in pain. Lex dropped to the ground, as did nearly all those around them. The princess raised her hand to protect her face, but they were too far back for the splinters to do damage against her and her horse's armor.

Lex hissed as Beatrix hauled them to their feet. Then it was only the princess's horse that stopped them from being trampled to death. The archers had taken down the demon all right: right into the portcullis. The metal was warped and there was no way to pull it up. That assumed anyone would even want to walk over the creature's corpse.

"Oh, shit," Lex whispered.

"Where is the Arbiter?"

"Last I heard, she's getting people to safety."

Her Highness nodded. "Can you try to get these people inside? Even some of them. They can't be out here."

Lex gritted their teeth against the pain and nodded. "Go!"

The princess made a hand signal and her officers turned. It was then that Lex saw several of what they'd assumed were just the rabble turn and push against the crowd. They must've come out without their uniforms on. Just hauled from bed, like Lex. Though, at least Lex had managed to get their boots and trousers on, along with their jacket and sword. Though, the sleep tunic was still dangling around Lex's mid-thighs.

Beatrix began shouting at the crowd, "Run! Get to the laundry! Run!"

Lex whirled to see four demons flying toward them.

WALTER'S VOICE WAS cracking from all the shouting he'd been doing. There was a steady stream of newly-arriving elementals now. Some had already formed an arc and positioned themselves toward the open demon portals.

Correction: the constantly opening demon portals, Walter thought grimly as yet another pothole exploded up through the cobblestones.

Lord God, they were popping open now like dried corn kernels thrown on hot rocks. Most were still small—some were only the size of his hand—but they were spreading fast. Eventually, they'd merge and rip bigger and bigger holes.

"Flanks! Keep the bat demons from getting past us!" Walter shouted.

One of the mages took one look at the demon portals and ran screaming. However, one of the larger bats attacked her and knocked her over.

"Steady!" Walter shouted. Pain rose in his throat. Nevertheless, he kept shouting and screaming for the mages to hear him over the mayhem. "Steady everyone! Flanks, get those demons! Everyone else, concentrate on the portals themselves. Push the demons back into them. Attack anything you see coming out of it. I'm going to close the portals."

He dropped to the ground and began the tedious, agonizing crawl toward the first open portal. It was him and him alone who could do this part. He couldn't find anyone else. Allegra could have helped, but he had no idea where she was—and that assumed she'd even risk her identity in such an open place.

A tornado of flame blasted to his left, beyond the walls. It slammed against the portcullis before whirling back into the smoke and mist. Walter stared at the sparks cracking through the smoke and felt nothing. In his mind, those mages died the moment Bonacieux tortured them into submission. He hoped their deaths would be fiery and dramatic.

And if the Lord God Almighty actually gave a care for mages, he'd give them the strength to kill every single murderer in that army before they died. There were worst things than dying in a blaze of glory.

Elemental fire blasted the creatures of the abyss above his head into smoldering ash. Fog and steam formed, as inexperienced and panicked mages cast elemental water crashing against fire. Elemental wind blew the smoke into his eyes, causing them to water. The ground trembled off and on, and Walter feared these idiots were going to kill him long before he even reached the first portal.

He pulled his tunic up over his nose and used the neck strings to tie it tightly in place. Then, he began the slow, methodical crawl forward through the smoke. Even flat against the ground, it was impossible to see more than a couple arm-lengths in the distance. However, he could hear the demon shrieks and they were getting closer. There was something up ahead.

Tiny dragonfly demons soared straight for his face and he ducked his head down into the crook of his elbow to avoid them bashing against his eyes. Needles jabbed into the back of Walter's bare neck, and he screamed from the pain of demon teeth sinking into his skin. He managed to see the hand-sized portal in front of him now, belching out dozens of the little assholes.

He tried ignoring the ones chewing through his clothing, trusting that one of the mages with elemental wind would figure out how to get them off him without sending him across the courtyard. The portal was so close. Just a bit more and…

A black cloud of dragonflies raced out of the portal and straight for his outstretched arm, biting and clawing through his linen sleeve. Walter cried out in alarm all the while dragging himself across the ground, one hand at a time. He had to reach that first portal, for no other reason than to stop the swarm.

More of the needled teeth sank into the delicate flesh on the side of his neck, his throat, and his cheeks. He could not risk stopping even for just a beat to brush them off. Every moment's delay meant more of these creatures entering reality. So, he pushed past the pain and reached out his arm as far as he could. His fingers skimmed the edge and he held his hand straight and steady, even as he cried out from the pain of the bites. He managed to get out the words necessary for him to push his power into the fissure between realities. The ground trembled and dipped inward, but the portal closed.

Unable to hold together his concentration any longer, Walter screamed from the agony of the bites. He rolled around on the ground hoping desperately to crush the dragonfly demons or to even simply dislodge them from his flesh. Blasts of fire and wind hit him repeatedly in the chest, and then Walter rolled along the ground against his will. His eyes watered from the smoky air forced against him. His brain screamed that something was wrong with his arm. He glanced and saw his clothes were on fire. He rolled around more on the ground, still trying to dislodge the miniature demons *and* put out the fire before he became a living torch.

A booming voice shouted over the cacophony: "Don't kill him!"

Strong, dark hands slapped his body far harder than was strictly necessary. Walter's eyes filled with tears from the burning, the bites, and the smoke. Finally, a familiar face appeared in front of him. "Is the plan to crawl away from the battle?"

Walter laughed, collapsing against the ground, still trying to steady his breathing from having the air knocked out of his lungs. "Rainier! What are you doing down here with the mages?"

"I heard you screaming," Rainier said. He was on his hands and knees, with cloth wrapped about his nose and mouth. "You're bleeding, but it doesn't look serious."

Walter nodded. "I need to touch the portals to close them, but there's too much magic flying around. And then those little bastards are vomiting out everywhere."

"Do you need me to keep them off you?"

"A sword is useless against these little ones, and that's all that's down here."

Rainier held up a large rock. "That's why I have this."

Walter managed to give the captain a speculative glance. "Can I trust you not to use that on the back of my skull?"

Walter had meant it as a joke, but Rainier appeared genuinely wounded by the quip. "You can trust me, Cram."

"I know, Captain." Those three words held a lot of weight for Walter. Those were words he never thought he'd utter to a non-mage, and yet, he trusted Stanton Rainier with his life. "I can see the edge of the next one. Can you keep them off me while I crawl toward that one?"

Rainier showed Walter his rock. "Lead the way."

Together, mage and normal crawled their way across the heavily-pebbled courtyard toward the next portal.

CHAPTER TWENTY-THREE

HORROR FILLED ALLEGRA when she stepped outside into the alley. Choking black smoke curled in the air from where she knew the main gate existed, though it was impossible to see that far. She could see flashes of flame even through the clouds and hoped this wasn't about to become a repeat of Borro Abbey.

"Merciful God," Rigi whispered.

Allegra squinted upward in the direction Rigi was looking. It was two winged demons. She sighed. "Hopefully, no one uses fire on those two."

"Why?" Rigi asked.

"Apparently, some of them can swallow fire and belch it back out."

Rigi's eyes went a little wide.

"I saw it happen," Allegra said. In truth, she'd been the one to cause it to happen, after their escape from Borro. It was also possible that Dodd and Walter might never let her live it down. "Come on. Hopefully, everyone downstairs is already gone."

Allegra had to swat away a swarm of dragonfly demons, and she stomped on the ones she'd stunned mid-flight. The door was unlocked and they pushed it open. Rigi held the door for her and then slammed across the heavy plank that was built into the wall.

At Allegra's silent question, he said, "This place was once a fortress. A few of the archivists spend their lives ensuring as much of the original architecture remains sound and working to honor the Guardians and their fight against the demons."

"It's good to know someone's on our side," Allegra muttered.

Allegra was dismayed by the sight of so many of the ill still being inside the infirmary. The nurses and healers were moving the injured and sick, but they were going too slowly. She stopped one of the mothers and asked, "Do any of the windows have shutters?"

She shook her head. "One of the...things broke the window. We were going to stay until it got in."

Rigi hurried down to the other end of the room, to where the stairs were located. As he did that, Allegra began shouting for everyone who could walk to start making their way to the back of the room. Rigi rejoined her and said the upper doors were unlocked, and they could get into the servant's chapel storage rooms from there. Those had no windows, he said, and it didn't matter if they couldn't get further, since they could lock themselves in if needs be.

"Your Ladyship, have you had the fever before?" Rigi asked.

"Apparently, yes. I was an infant. I asked my maid, who had been working with them. You?"

He shook his head. "Well, these people need our help."

"They do," Allegra said.

She had told anyone and everyone to close the doors behind them, and now she was trapped on the other side. There were still thousands of people stranded, though. This was as far as her help could go now.

She could not save everyone, so she had to keep her mind on whoever was nearby. "Hurry! We need everyone up the stairs and into the storage room."

"What if it's locked beyond?" one of the nurses asked.

"We will still be safer than here, where there are windows."

"We have to get away from the windows!" Rigi called out. "Please, we must hurry!"

Behind her, another windowpane shattered and more of the choking black smoke billowed into the sick room. Clutching terror pressed against her throat, as her mind tried to relive the events at Borro. She tried not to focus on it, because these people needed her calm. She would have to deal with these new nightmares and the smell of smoke in her sleeping moments eventually; for now, she had to get these people to safety.

"Your Ladyship!" Rigi called out. "I will get the mobile to the room, then I will come back to help with the bedridden."

She nodded. Eight of the stronger-looking caregivers had picked up one unconscious man by the mattress and hurried toward the staircase. They placed the mattress just off to the side of the staircase entrance, and then hurried back to the next closest patient.

Rigi reappeared and shouted out, "When you go in, take the left door. Do you hear me? Go left. Then, go down the corridor, all the way down to the end. Everything else is locked. All the way down! Go all the way down! Keep going!"

Dark shadows blotted out the limited light that was coming through the windows and the smoke. At the sight of the terrifying outlines, someone wailed, "Oh, Lord God Almighty, save us!"

"Why don't we break down one of the doors?" someone else demanded. "It would be closer for us to run, right?"

"There are demons inside the cathedral!" Allegra shouted in reply. "Go down the long corridor! Don't try to pry open anything that is locked. Just keep going!"

"Oh, Lord God!"

Patients coughed and gagged as the most mobile disappeared up the narrow stairway. Rigi urged them forward, repeating over and over how to get as deep into the building as possible. He'd seen a demon rip through a doorframe. One bolted door was not a guarantee of safety. She hoped several would be.

Though, a grim thought crossed her mind that everyone could just burn this building down around her, too.

"Go!" Rigi urged. "Keep going! Yes! Yes, that's it! Through that door! Go through the door and wait for us on the other side!"

Allegra glanced at the broken window behind her. It was difficult to see through the growing blanket of smoke, but she was certain the air was filled with flying demons now.

Massive swarms of what appeared to be tiny birds, or maybe even dragonflies, danced in the smoky sky. It was difficult for her to look away, as it was terrifying, but also beautiful. There was a closeness between the demons' behavior and that of the real world that stirred Allegra. Were the words true? Was the demon abyss where the sins of men manifested into living form? Were these beings created by the world, by their greed and sin and hatred? Was this their true punishment? To give birth to an entire existence of evil?

She pulled her eyes and thoughts away. Most of the patients who'd been able to walk on their own were now in the corridor. The sisters, brothers, nurses, and healers all began carrying the severely ill, a painstaking process, and would require several more minutes while they prayed the demons did not come through the open window.

Half of the bedridden were removed when the demons finally found them. Three flying beasts smashed through the window, ripping out the window frame as they plunged into the open room of easy prey. Shrieks of both human and demon filled the room as people pushed toward the too small entrance.

Allegra ducked the extended claws of the shrieking, near-panicked demons who were now as trapped as the people were. Bedridden patients screamed in terror. Rigi and two of the brothers were crawling on their stomachs, trying to reach the next closest patient.

Allegra was crouched next to a bed with a wide-eyed patient and realized it was Calm Seas. She was struggling to get out of her bed. Three sisters were crawling along the floor to reach her, all the while the demons were diving at them. If she used her fire, she would be exposing herself to these people. First, there was no certainty she'd even be able to effectively control her fire. She might burn them all alive by accident. And, second, there was the sinking realization that she would end this fight swinging from the front gates. And if those gates weren't standing? Well, they could always tie her to those fallen gates and burn her alive there. The best kind of mage was a dead mage. That's what Vanida and those like him would say. Allegra gulped and winced as the demons shrieked overhead. She didn't know what to do. That was until one of the demons made the decision for her.

One of the demons caught sight of Calm Seas in her bed, and began a dive toward her, talons extended. Calm Seas screamed and wrapped her arms protectively around her head. Allegra jumped to her feet, grabbed a glass bottle from Calm Seas' nightside table, and swung it at the demon. She struck its wing and it tumbled to the floor. Allegra slammed the bottle against the demon's head again and again, until the bottle smashed against the floor.

Only then did she realize she had smashed in the demon's skull. And that two more windows were missing, where the remaining two wings demons had clearly escaped. Allegra looked up at the shocked faces around her. She realized she was splattered in demon guts and gore.

Through gasping breaths, she managed to say, "I told you to get out of here."

They managed to make it as far as the confessional altar room before all the doors beyond were sealed. Allegra looked at the door behind them and fought the urge to rush back down in case more needed to get to safety. However, she wasn't sure she could even make the run back outside without passing out from the smoke.

Cardinal Rigi stood next to her. He took a deep breath and said, "You stopped me from rushing into needless danger. Shall I return that favor?"

She looked back over her shoulder at the patients. They all needed tending. She sighed heavily, and said, "Will you assist me in raiding the parish supply closet before we close this door as well?"

"Of course, Your Ladyship," Rigi said.

"Call me Contessa," Allegra said. "That's what my friends call me."

STANTON CRUSHED THE head of a smallish demon with his rock. He was panting hard. The heat from the streams of fire above him made the air thick and difficult to breathe. Thankfully, there wasn't much in the way of smoke so close to the ground, but down here he had to dodge the ditches and craters Cram made as he closed each portal. It was a painstaking task, and Stanton was singed, sore, and sweating.

The screams from Bonacieux's men cut through his soul, but there was nothing they could do. Cram was right; they had to close the smaller portals or risk ripping a massive hole that would make

Borro Abbey's demon attack look like an infestation of ants. He struggled to see through the smoke and steam around them. At times it was difficult to even see the demons until they latched on to himself or Cram.

Someone dropped to the ground on Stanton's right. "Captain."

"Brother Malcolm?"

He nodded. "Is there any chance I can pretend I'm helping kill the demons down here?"

Stanton wasn't sure what he meant, until he saw the priest slam his flame-engulfed hand against a portal the size of a jam jar. The father said several lines of scripture and the stones around the portal cracked and exploded from the heat. "Didn't you attack Cram with a knife last winter for being a mage?"

"Self-loathing is a problem of mine. As is the drink to cope with the self-loathing."

"Ah," Stanton said. "Are you sure?"

"I'm not going to cower when I know how to do this," Brother Malcolm said. "Can I have your word that you will ask the Arbiter for protection?"

"You don't need hers," Cram said. "You have mine. Welcome to the fight, Brother."

Stanton reached out a hand and offered it to the priest. They shook and Stanton said, "If no one else sees, then I didn't, either. And, if they do see, well, then I'm going to say you saved our lives."

"With my help, Rainier," Cram said.

"Yeah, yeah. Are you done resting yet? I can see another one up ahead."

Then, with that, the three men crawled through smoke, wind, steam, and flame to kill demons and stop the end of days.

AS HARD AS Lex had tried, it was clear to Dodd that his old friend couldn't fight. Lex had fallen several times now, and Dodd was certain he could see bloodstains under Lex's jacket. Their job was to try to get as many people to safety. Demons didn't give a dog's ass about gates and walls, and many of the people who'd fled to escape, thinking Bonacieux's men would come rushing through the other side, were now all climbing over themselves trying to squeeze through the damaged portcullis' bottom to get back to safety.

Dodd dodged the gnarled talons of a small demon and used a broken piece of ladder to bash it mid-flight. He crushed its neck in one smooth motion with his boot and kicked the limp body out of the way. He made a decision.

"Lex? Get some of these people out of here. Beatrix? As people are pulled back through the portcullis, get them inside. Break the windows, beat down doors, I don't care. Get them inside the buildings and then barricade yourselves in when it's full. The rest of you? Keep digging under to make more room. Once Lex and Beatrix stop coming back, two more of you will grab the next lot. Hugo? Help me kill these fuckers."

"I'm not going anywhere," Lex said, ending with a hiss of pain.

"You're bleeding and you're no good to us here. See if you can get some people into the back storage. I bet no one has locked those." Lex was about to argue, when Dodd said, "That's an order. I want these people out of harm's way. Go. Now."

"Who the fuck do you think you are?" Lex demanded. He ducked the swooping attack of a bird-sized demon. "Little asshole has been dive bombing me for five minutes now."

"I know how to fight these things better than all of you, and I'm not injured. Get these people safe. Argue with me later, but you know I'm right."

"We're not done with this, Dodd," Lex said, and he made it a threat.

"I know." He used his foot to crack another rung off the ladder and tossed it to Lex.

Then he used the remainder to crack a bird demon in the head. It fell to the ground, still wriggling. Dodd crushed its skull with the end of the post. "Get these people out of here."

"Beatrix! Rahna! You! You! You!" Lex pointed to militia guards. "Break these people into groups and let's find somewhere safe to stuff them. Let's move!"

Dodd watched Lex limp away, holding his injured side, and Dodd now clearly saw the blood-soaked hem of Lex's tunic that had come out of his trousers. He wanted to feel guilt for having given Lex the newbie job, but Lex was too injured to fight.

Liability. That's what Captain Rainier would have called Lex.

Dodd ducked his head from a trio of tiny bat-sized demons, whirled, and took two out with his make-shift bat. The third escaped, soaring back toward the cloud of smoke and fog by the main gate.

"You heard Lex! Head toward the back alley! Leave the carts! Leave everything! Just go!"

Dodd watched a little boy struggle to pick up his frightened dog, but the dog was nearly as big as the boy. He was going to shout for someone to get the boy out of there, but Lex grabbed the dog, wobbled, and then started running in the direction of the storage cellars.

Dodd gulped, and called out for the remaining Consorts to form an arc of protection around the diggers at the gate. "We defend them until everyone's inside. Then, we join the main fight. Remember, their necks! You have to break their necks or crush their skulls. Nothing else kills them. No mercy!"

CHAPTER TWENTY-FOUR

STANTON DIDN'T DARE take off his jacket, even though he was faint from the heat and smoke. He was also dragging Cram, who'd fainted twice from either exhaustion or the thick air. Cram's nose was bleeding and he struggled to keep his eyes open. But Stanton would move him to another portal, place Cram's hand on it, and the damn demon lover would push a little bit more of himself into the hole that led to the other realm. Then, they'd do it all over again.

There was a lot of shouting and fighting around them. He had no idea how many mages, Consorts, militia, archers, or anyone else were left standing. He just knew his task, right now, was to drag Cram along the ground.

"There's a big one, Cram. Just up ahead," Stanton shouted in Cram's ear.

Cram managed to open his eyes a crack. "How big?"

"As long as a man, but only an arm's length wide. It's like a long fissure in the ground."

"Fuck," Cram said. He licked his cracked and bleeding lips. "I think...I think that's all I'll have left in me. I can't...think..."

"Come on," Stanton said. He hooked his arms around Cram and began hauling him across the shattered remains of the courtyard's brick and stonework. "Come on. One more and I'll let you sleep for two minutes."

The tale-tell shriek of a demon broke the air around them, gaining distance on them. Stanton pushed Cram flat against the ground. Cram was too exhausted to protest. Brother Malcolm appeared in the fog and took out the demon with a broken wagon wheel spoke. He dropped to his knees next to them. One side of his face was a sheet of blood.

"Something's wrong. The bastard's men aren't attacking or helping or doing anything. They should be in here by now."

"Isn't the portcullis still down?" Stanton asked.

Brother Malcolm shook his head. "I'm fairly certain I just saw one of the big eagle demons fly by with it."

"Merciful Lord," Stanton muttered. "Protect us for a bit longer? I have to get Cram to this next portal."

Brother Malcolm nodded. He pulled his jacket sleeves back over his hands, pivoted, and crawled off, disappearing into the smoke and fog.

Stanton was exhausted, but he managed to drag Cram the next few lengths to the long fissure. Cram passed out twice during the spell or whatever he did, and Stanton had to rouse him. Each time was more difficult than the last. Though the ground rumbled, Cram didn't make a dent or a collapse this time. Just the faintest crackle of magic. With that final working, Cram collapsed where the demon portal lay just moments before.

There was no rousing Cram now, the exhaustion and smoke finally having done him in. Stanton was nearly as bad, if he were honest with himself. Standing would mean putting himself into the thick again, and he wasn't certain he had the endurance to withstand even one lungful of the soup above. At the same time, he couldn't leave Cram here.

Weariness overtook Stanton. He laid his head on Cram's back. Something in his head said he should move, but his body wouldn't listen to the voice. He closed his eyes. He was so thirsty. He would just take a break. Just a moment. He wouldn't fall…

"Captain! Are you alive?"

Stanton snapped his open. His lungs let out a raspy cough when he tried to speak. It took him a moment to realize Father Michael was shaking him.

"What are you doing here?"

"Moving the unconscious mages out of harm's way while the archers take out what's left. They're dropping like flies now."

"The mages?"

"The demons."

"Can you help me pull Cram toward the big one?" Stanton asked.

"What big one? The fissures are all closed."

"What? How long was I out?"

Father Michael shrugged. "No idea. The fight's mostly over now. Put this over your mouth."

Stanton accepted the offered prayer stole and wrapped it several times around his face and mouth, until breathing was difficult, but at least the air was more filtered. He accepted another piece of the bishop's ceremonial habit and did the same for Cram.

"Stay here, Captain. We'll be right back to get you."

"We?"

Stanton blinked and realized Pero was standing there. How long had he been out?

Father Michael and Pero picked up Cram by the armpits. Stanton passed out before he could look about him.

CHAPTER TWENTY-FIVE

THE AFTERMATH WAS hard on Allegra's soul. It was dusk when the pounding upon the doors began, and the shouting that the demons were all dead. There were worries about Cardinal Rigi's health, after being exposed to the fever, so she alone left with the militia who'd found her.

She had to step over bodies of animals, people, and demons alike. It would take days just to bury all of the corpses, let alone clean up the disaster that was the Cathedral. Allegra staggered through the dissipating fog and haze. Imogen was the first person she recognized. She was coordinating the newly-arriving guards who'd been locked inside the buildings when the attack happened.

"Allegra, it is good to see you alive," Imogen said.

They embraced, and laughed about the mess they were both in. Allegra's was too high-pitched, too nervous, but she did not know what else to do beyond weep. When she asked about Stanton and Walter, Imogen said she thought they were by the palace stairs. A weight lifted from Allegra's shoulders.

Eventually, she found her way to the palace stairs. Father Michael saw her first and waved her over. Stanton was seated on one of the bottom steps, his legs spread out in front of him. Walter was unconscious next to him. She rushed over and dropped to her knees.

"It is good to see you, my love." He pulled her close and tears welled up in both of their eyes. "What happened? Look at you."

Allegra grimaced. "A demon attacked the isolation infirmary. Cardinal Rigi and I got everyone to safety."

"How did you end up over there?"

Allegra smiled weakly. "A very long story. Is Walter…"

"Exhausted. I can't even count how many portals he collapsed." Stanton coughed as his voice cracked. "The smoke was horrible. I'm so relieved you are safe."

"Brother Malcolm, what are you doing here? Are you hurt?" Allegra exclaimed, seeing the priest laying on the ground near Walter's feet. He was completely covered in soot and was wheezing.

Brother Malcolm tried to speak, but all he could manage was a coughing fit.

Stanton answered. "The good brother here helped me drag Cram's sorry ass to the portals."

"Didn't Brother Malcolm attack Walter with a knife?"

"Everyone makes mistakes when they're drunk, Allegra."

That's when she noticed Stanton's gaze. She glanced at Brother Malcolm, whose eyes were pleading with Stanton. She knew that look well.

"Thank you, Brother, for helping, especially given your views on mages. We all have to come together sooner or later. I am glad you could when we needed you the most." He tried to speak, but he continued into coughing fits. "There's no need to speak. Rest your lungs, now. I'm certain we'll be seeing the surgeons and healers soon enough."

"Did you see any of the Consorts?" Stanton asked through his own coughs. His eyes were heavy, like he struggled to stay awake. He looked exhausted.

She wanted to stay with him, to wrap her arms around him and never let go. But she looked about them and asked, "Do you want me to go look?"

She glanced back at him. He was asleep. She told Father Michael she was going to look for the Consorts. She staggered to her feet, squared her shoulders, and walked toward what used to be the main gate. She stopped in front of the pile of collapsed bodies. She knew they were the mages who'd come to the Cathedral's aid. Some were clearly dead. Horrible wounds. Puddles of bloods. She tried not to look, but it was impossible. Death was everywhere. She shook a couple without obvious injuries. Some groaned, others didn't stir. She rested a hand on the shoulder of a weeping mage, wrapped about the body of another mangled mage. They had to find how these portals were being caused, or this would only keep happening.

The question pressed on her mind the more devastation she saw. Why would anyone do this to them? The Cathedral wasn't perfect, but this was not the answer.

Then, Allegra saw why it was done. There was a gathering by the hole where the main gates once existed. She made her way there, and found Dodd and Lex, along with many somber-looking Consorts.

"Dodd, Lex, Martin! It's good to see you all. What are you doing..." Her words died.

Bonacieux's men were destroyed. Killed did not come close to the carnage beyond. Parts of bodies were scattered everywhere. The earth was scorched, and she realized a portal had swallowed many of them whole. Around them, were the bodies of Bonacieux's mages. The stench was appalling.

A familiar hand pressed against Allegra's back and she saw that Dodd stood there. "It looks like Bonacieux's mages didn't know what to do. They were trying to kill the demons, not close the portals."

"How did they close the portals then?" Allegra asked.

"Cram's mages."

Allegra didn't want to look where Dodd pointed, but she did. There was a small pile of bodies next to the opening where the gates once were. "Are they all dead?"

"Everyone beyond the main gates are dead." Dodd audibly swallowed. "There were too many demons coming out of that thing. They must've known they had to close it."

"And that they'd die," Allegra whispered.

"Yeah," Dodd said. "Contessa?"

"Hmm?"

"I just want to say that I'm never going to obey any order that says I have to arrest a mage just because they're a mage. Not after this."

She looked at him. "What makes you say that now?"

Dodd didn't stop looking ahead at the dead mages. "Because they're going to make us find out who did it. And it's got to be one of us. From Borro, I mean. And they're going to round up every single damn mage. I'm not going to do it. Not after this. I'll arrest whoever did this, but…"

Dodd's voice cracked. Allegra touched his arm and his jaw trembled.

"We need to stop whoever is doing this," Dodd whispered. "This isn't right."

"No, it isn't. My God! Lex!" Allegra exclaimed.

Allegra and Dodd both turned to see a bloody Lex staggering toward them. When Lex got closer, and could see Dodd's half-angry, half-terrified expression, Lex scowled.

"Relax. A lot of the blood isn't even mine," Lex said defensively. "And the rest is when I tripped. I think I tore some of my stitches."

"The surgeon won't be pleased," Allegra said.

"Well, at least I'm alive for the surgeon to bitch me out," Lex said. "Is the captain…?"

"He's fine. He's with Walter."

"Is Cram all right?" Dodd asked.

Allegra nodded. "He passed out. A lot of mages did, apparently."

"They're not all dead?" Dodd asked.

Allegra smiled and motioned at the palace stairs. "A lot are asleep over there. It was a long fight. Thank you."

"For what?" Lex asked.

"For…everything." Allegra's lip quivered. "Just…everything."

Lex pattered her shoulder awkwardly. He was the worst at giving support. Dodd did the same. Seriously, they were both terrible. "Contessa, we'll get to the bottom of this. Won't we, Dodd?"

"There's a lot less dead than there would have been," Dodd said. "You did good work, too, Contessa. And you, too, Lex."

"Yeah, well, you can go fuck yourself. I'll never forgive you for pretending you could pull rank on me."

"In a crisis…" Dodd began.

"Enough fighting, you two," Allegra said. "Lex, will you sit down and rest if I tell you to?"

"Yes, Your Ladyship," Lex said with a weary smile. "I would really like it if you ordered me to sit down."

IT WAS NEARLY midnight before Allegra finally relented to protestations that she sleep. There was so much clean up to do. So much destruction. Finally, it was Rupert who ordered everyone not assigned an official security role to go to bed. Allegra lingered, until Cardinal DeLancey yelled at Stanton to get his woman to bed. Allegra was unsure her face would ever stop burning after that.

As she walked through the damaged hallways, her steps grew slow and heavy. She was exhausted. She was terrified to sleep. She feared tomorrow.

Locking up the cathedral had prevented damage to the inner rooms, which meant that there were safe places to move everyone whose homes were currently under rubble. Anywhere with a window was unlivable, filled with dead demons and their sulphur-stinking shit and piss everywhere. It was going to take weeks to clear this place up, and months to finish repairs.

"I'm so tired," Allegra whispered to Stanton.

He pulled her close as they walked through the devastation. One of the guards, a blurry-eyed kid who was minutes away from falling asleep standing up, helped Stanton push the door open. The frame itself was bent. On the other side, though, it was like nothing had happened. Candles illuminated the corridor. Not a speck of demon blood. Not a picture frame so much as askew on the walls.

"It's bizarre how normal it looks in here," Stanton said. "You did good work getting this place locked up. I'm proud of you."

Allegra gave him a tired smile. "I heard you saved Walter's life. Thank you."

"Well, no one else was going to help him, and we needed those demon holes closed." Stanton let out his own sigh. "Don't tell him I said this, but I think I'm starting to like the bastard."

"It's part of his charm, making you wish you could wring his neck and also want to have him over for cards. And then wring his neck when he wins. He makes everyone feel like that."

"Oh, good. I thought it was just me."

"Stanton, I was in love with him once upon a time, and I wanted to wring his neck."

They stepped over the sleeping forms on the barrack floor. The demons had not gotten in here, and so the Consorts, servants, a few mages, and even a couple of priests were asleep. A number of the consort bunkbeds had been pushed tight against one another to form one giant bed, and it was packed with sleeping bodies. The floor was an obstacle course of bodies.

The door to Stanton's bedroom was open, and the slumbering bodies continued. Nadira and Serafina were asleep atop a pile of clothes, along with a number of female servants who tended the barracks. Nathan and several male servants were likewise on the other side of the room, only they were on top of linens.

Stanton placed his candle down on the nightstand. He didn't bother to light the lamp. There was a clean linen shift in her drawer and she pulled it over her head, instantly feeling better to have the mess away from her. She longed for a bath and a scrub brush, but she'd settle for a clean shift and a clean bed.

They both slipped into bed, and she snuggled in close for both his warmth and his comfort.

"Stanton?"

"Yes?"

"What happens next?"

He was quiet for some time before answering. "Clean and repair, obviously. Secure food, water. Then, we'll have to fix the gates and our defenses. Bonacieux is not going to be pleased when he hears his men are dead at the hand of demons."

"I don't understand who would do this," Allegra said. "Dodd was talking about it to me just a couple days ago, but I've been thinking about this for a while. It has to be someone we know."

She felt his shrug. "I asked Cram a couple days ago about it. He said he'd happily turn over the person, if he knew who it was. But he doesn't."

"Could it be Walter?" Allegra hated herself for asking, but she had to ask. "Could he also know how to open them and be doing this to...I don't even know."

Stanton blew out a breath. "Do you think it's him?"

"No, but it has to be someone."

"Yeah. It has to be someone, doesn't it?"

CHAPTER TWENTY-SIX

THE FIRST TIME Allegra had walked these sacred halls, they weren't covered in soot and mud. This part of the Cathedral suffered the least casualties, where the doors were first locked and those first protected from the demons. The palace kitchens weren't damaged, either, and were the only ones running at full capacity. Even now, the faint scent of roasting meat drifted through the air. There was still soot, though.

The soot clung to everything, as people struggled to shutter windows. Others had no such mechanism and the soot poured in through broken windows. Sometimes, demons poured in, too. But while the small demons could not get under the cracks and crannies of doorframes, the smoke and soot did. It had been four days since the attack, and four days of scrubbing, mourning, burying, and repairing. Eventually, the servants would get to the soot.

The last time Allegra walked down these corridors, she was forced to wait outside the massive doors, alone, until permission was granted. That time was past now. There was no time for the ceremony of old men and women stuck in the privilege of pomp. The senior cardinals who'd been recalled back home to deal with the previous Bonacieux crisis had finally arrived and there was no time to waste now. Cardinal Devonshire made that completely clear once her carriage was finally able to get into Orsini.

So now, she walked in silence through the filthy corridors with the Holy Father by her side. There was too much to discuss now; small talk was simply too superficial to even attempt. She and

Francois had not made up since their original fight. She did not know if she would ever completely forgive him. He had put his own power ahead of her very life, and it had been a betrayal that cut deeply. When faced with her own personal drawn line, he lashed out and struck her. He had shown he would choose the duty of Francois over the commitments and relationships of Rupert.

Perhaps she could have eventually forgiven all of that, or at least allowed it to settle into the back of her mind. However, Pero had shared his own tales. He could not even stand the sight of his own husband, who'd boldly declared that he was not an abolitionist after all. He'd insisted to Pero that he'd never been one, but she and Pero both remembered a younger, less powerful Rupert who had been a strong voice in the plight of mages. Power, it seemed, was stronger than his commitment to the cause.

She'd talked to Stanton about it the previous night. About how much the Holy Father had hurt her soul. He understood all too well. He and Francois has been friends, even if they kept the bonds of rank very rigid between them. That friendship was over now in Stanton's eyes. Francois had threatened to remove Stanton from the Consorts, and it was only the urgings of Cardinal DeLancey and, shockingly, Cardinal Vittorio who had managed to convince him that a personal vendetta was beneath the position of Holy Father. And, besides, Cardinal DeLancey argued, he was threatening Captain Rainier's lover. Of course, the captain reacted poorly.

Rupert took a long breath and said, "Pero said last night that he will leave me for good if I do not support full emancipation."

It took Allegra a moment to register that he'd spoken to her. She did not look at him when she asked, "What did you say?"

"I called him many words I regretted in this morning's light."

"There is a lot of that happening."

Then the silence overtook them again, and they continued their march toward the conclave, where Cardinal Devonshire had demanded a new session be called to address the situation of both the Arbiter and the current crisis.

She had to pause for a moment to remember that she'd been made temporary Arbiter again, before the demon battle. It was becoming difficult to keep up with the conclave's changeable demands upon her. And yet, here she was again, heading into the den of snakes to learn if she were to remain Arbiter, if someone else was replacing her, or if…after the vote to hand her over to Bonacieux to be killed, she didn't even know what new and torturous thing they would support with their votes.

She had already decided the night before, however: either she would be reinstated permanently as Arbiter, with all of the power she had previously had, or she would leave for her estate and establish a refuge there for any mages who'd want to come.

She'd told Stanton in bed the night before. At first, he brushed it off as exhaustion, but she very soon convinced him of her seriousness. He had been quiet for a while before saying he'd rather go back to Marsina with her, than remain at the Cathedral alone.

Somewhere in all of this, she stopped worrying about being dragged off to her death because she knew it would come. She'd always thought she'd be terrified of this moment. And, when she dwelled on the notion of her death, she became physically ill and struggled to breathe. However, she also found a courage within her that she did not realize existed. She'd always told herself she'd turned down Walter's offer all those years ago because she was scared. And, there was truth to that. But, there was more to it now, she could see.

She had found a strength within her. She had proven to herself that fear was no longer an excuse. She was terrified to her core even now, as she walked silently down the long hallway to the cardinal's conclave. But, from that fear, she harnessed a strength that she'd never been taught to access. It wasn't magic. It wasn't spiritual. It was the simple, unshakable knowledge that her fear was no longer an acceptable reason to do nothing. The fear of reprisal. The anxiety of mistakes. The terror of destruction. These were no longer good enough reasons for her. She was convinced her time was borrowed from the Almighty now, and she would use it to the full extent of her personal power.

The conclave doors came into view. Francois stopped walking, and reached out to touch her arm. She stopped to look at him.

"Will you ever forgive me?"

Allegra had to look away because she needed her wits about her when she walked inside those doors. Looking into Rupert's pleading eyes would not help her. "I don't know if I can or even if I want to."

"I am sorry."

"I believe you believe that," Allegra said. "Though, I don't know if I believe that you had done everything you could to protect me."

"I am trying, Allegra."

"*That* I believe. I guess we'll soon figure out if any of it was enough or just all in vain."

"I will use all of my power to protect you."

"That's my worry, Father."

"That I will use it?"

A weary sigh escaped her. Being angry at Rupert was exhausting. She reached out for his hand. He took it. "Perhaps I am worried your power isn't as great as you think it is."

He squeezed her hand before releasing it. "Then I guess we shall both see soon enough."

They walked into the sacred room of power. The last time Allegra stood on this dais, she was dressed like the woman she was: rich, powerful, arrogant, influential. Now, she wore a dirty peasant's dress, with a ridiculous hemline well above her ankles. She wore old work boots, from one of the stable boys who'd outgrown them. However, she was alive, which was more than what could be said for her dress's previous owner. It would be her job now to remember those who died in the previous days, and those who still lay dying from their wounds.

So much had taken place since her arrival in Orsini that it felt like a memory more than reality as she made the short journey from the door, across the floor, up the short few steps, and on to the dais. It was almost an insult that they were gathered here again, when the maids were scrubbing the floors, the footmen were repairing the windows, and the soldiers were burying the dead.

Still, it surprised her to see how full the conclave was this time around. She saw Cardinal Devonshire, who had called the meeting. She doubted anyone else could have swayed Francois to put everyone through this ordeal all over again.

She looked down at them, and finally put into words the *something* that had been stirring inside her for days: impotent rage. For a terrifying moment, as she looked down upon the faces of power, she truly understood Walter's unquenchable thirst for justice at any cost.

She did not have notes this time; there had been no time. Instead, she pressed the speaking stone before her, a magical artifice so advanced that the world beyond these walls never even considered something so strange and amazing. This kind of merger of magic and development could rapidly change the course of Serna, and yet it was kept from the people whose taxes and tithes paid for its creation. Still worse, the people who made that decision to keep this ability from the world sat in front of her, restless for her to begin.

She did not speak. She stared down at them, not even bothering to smooth her face to hide her anger, her disgust, and her heartbreaking grief at what they'd all just endured. The audience coughed and shuffled as she looked down at them in judgmental silence. She heard the doors latch shut, and it dawned on her that the last year of her life had been a series of doors locking behind her.

"I am angry," Allegra said finally. A weight pressed on her chest with the acknowledgement of those words. "I am so angry."

The chamber echoed the rustling of fabric, of wooden seats creaking as bodies shifted uncomfortably. But silence continued.

"I am angry at all of you."

Silence.

"I warned you all what would happen, and you refused to heed my words because they were *my* words. Now look at us. Look at our home. Think upon the dead we have had to step over, and recall their faces. You caused this.

"From the beginning, I have said we would end up here. Yet, you refused to heed my words. None of you came to Borro to see the refugee crisis for yourselves, or you would have known this day was destined for us.

"Over the course of the past year, I have learned most of you do not like that word. Refugee. A person seeking refuge in a world of turmoil. It must harken too close to the scripture. *Open your kitchens to the weary, for they seek the refuge of the Almighty through you.*

"But you did not wish to because it sullied the glory of this place. So the Lord God Almighty decided, in His wisdom, to force you to open your kitchens for this is only the beginning. I see some of you snickering."

She pointed to a group of cardinals with sneers on their faces as they tapped each other to point and whisper about her. Her gesture caused craned necks through the assembly to catch a glimpse of who had disrespected her speech.

"I don't care what you think of me. I believe the Lord God, if he's real, would be proud of what we stood for in Borro. Mages. Refugees. Citizens. Residents. Vagrants. Clergy. Soldiers. We made our stand together against hate, against hunger, and against a demon itself. And when Orsini had its chance, it did nothing until it was too late and scores of innocent people died because of your inaction. Their deaths are upon your souls."

"This is an outrage!" Vanida shouted into his own stone.

Anger like Allegra so rarely felt spewed from her mouth. It was doubtful she even needed the speaking stone to be heard by all. "Hold your tongue, Cardinal! We are here because of you!"

Gasps and tuts filled the room. Vanida pretended the shock of disrespect was going to send him into an apoplexy. She even heard Rupert gasp behind her.

"Ah. You are all shocked by my disrespect. How dare I disrespect His Grace, the slave-owning Cardinal Vanida, who purposely starved refugees. Don't speak, Your Grace. You may suffer a fit. How many of you disregarded my warnings and instead attempted to strip me of my power in order to keep men enslaved."

"No one cares!" Vanida shouted.

"Order!" the Speaker of the Chamber shouted back. "Cardinal Vanida. You will refrain from this disrespectful behavior, or I will have your speaking stone removed."

"To answer the cardinal's question, I care. The Earl of Southampton—that would be father of Lieutenant Dodd of the Consorts—and the Marquis of High River—the father of Lieutenant Lex of the Consorts—cared enough to help Borro Abbey feed the refugees. What did Orsini do when those escaping

Borro Abbey needed help? They segregated and starved mages. This, the house of the Lord God Almighty, could not even muster the spiritual fortitude to serve people bread with their soup.

"Then, you become possessed by your own power. There is no other way to put it. You became possessed and voted to hand *me* to the very man who caused the deaths of hundreds of us. And you wonder why some unbalanced mage opened up a demon rift in hopes you would all fall into it."

"Your Ladyship, please, get to the point of this lecture," Cardinal Vittorio said into his own speaking stone.

Allegra knew she was rambling a little, but she was angry. She was mourning. She was scared senseless. But, mostly, she was angry.

"The point, Your Grace, is simple. You caused this. And you, Cardinal Giso. And you, Cardinal Reinhold. And you, Cardinal Vanida. I can go on, too, listing what each of you did to cause the soot that is even on the frescos of this room. How each of you contributed to the devastation that has been heaped upon us.

"I believe I'm supposed to be here today to plead with you to once against grant me the position of Arbiter of Justice. I am supposed to grovel before you. You. The people who voted to hand me over to General Bonacieux, who is slaughtering his way through Cartossa. But, somehow, all of you thought handing *me* over to him, to be murder on your front steps, would have improved your lot. Somehow, the man who slaughtered the bulk of Borro and its refugees would have his thirst for power over mages quenched by getting to murder *me*. And you wish me to grovel."

"Know your place!" someone shouted. They didn't use a speaking stone, so she couldn't quite hear who it was, beyond it was a man toward the back. Heads turned to see who had spoken.

"All right, Your Grace. Let us discuss my place. I am a mage. This is no secret. However, until the demon at Borro, how many of you knew Queen Portia was a mage? None of you. I did not even know. Setting aside that she was an elemental mage, she did not even admit to being a mage. That is the place mages live. Endless, intense fear of a world that will reject us, enslave us, torture us, steal from us, and, too often, kill us.

"Queen Portia knew what would happen to her when Cartossa discovered she was an elemental mage. Yet, she stood there with the other mages and fought. Her reward was not understanding. It was a dagger through the throat. And, then, all of you tried to do the same thing to me. So, yes, Your Graces, I absolutely do know my place."

"You brought that demon lover here!" Vanida shouted.

"Then let us discuss Walter Cram, Your Grace. He has been chased across Serna for years. There is a death bounty on his head. He has had buildings burned down around him, with servants and children inside, just in the hope of rooting him out. He told what General Bonacieux would do when he arrived, but you all scoffed at it. Even you, Holy Father. You said I was tired and needed rest, because I was letting my emotions get the best of me."

She glared at them, and let a snarl come into her voice. "Now will you listen to me?"

Shocked silence filled the chamber before Vanida shouted, "You are a witch!"

Allegra's heart pounded so hard that she raised her voice just to hear herself over the thud-thud-thud. "You are a murderer!" Tears burned her eyes. "Everyone here murdered those people! You are the reason people died here this week! It was you! You are the cause of all of this! You shall answer for it!"

Vanida grabbed his speaking stone off his desk. "Get that witch bitch off that stage!"

Cardinal Giso wrestled the device from Vanida's hands, all the while Vanida chanted, "Witch bitch! Witch bitch!"

In her blinding rage, Allegra threw her head back and laughed. In the back of her mind, she knew she could stop talking. She knew she probably should. She knew she had already gone too far. She'd made her point so cruelly, so brutally, that no one would support her now.

So, she said the first thing that came to her mind.

"All of your slaves will be freed the moment I leave this room."

Shocked silence filled the room. Even Giso paused in his wrestling match with Vanida to slack-jaw stare at her. She'd not actually planned for those words to come out of her mouth, but they sounded right.

"Your Graces, there is a war spreading across this land. Your slaves will be freeing themselves one way or another. So I will be walking out that door, and I will be issuing an edict that no cardinal can own another human being. Even if you decide to burn me at the stake in the middle of the damned courtyard, I will still have done it. And you can vote to undo it, and you can enjoy the riot that my ashes will create."

"You cannot," Rupert whispered behind her. She turned to see his face shared the same shocked expression as the others. He pressed his hand against his speaking stone and said, "Your Ladyship, you cannot threaten this assembly without consequences."

"What threat? I will be freeing people, as part of my office. We will need all of the support we can get to survive what is about to come for us."

"What have you done? You'll ruin me," Vanida said in a gasping, strangled voice. He sat back down in his chair and held his hand to his chest.

A coldness spread across Allegra's body, and she said in a voice that she did not even recognize as her own, "Good."

HAVING KNOWN ALLEGRA for the majority of his life, it shouldn't have surprised him at all that she would choose this very moment to do the one thing that would shock all of the cardinals into silence: freeing their slaves.

Personally, Rupert felt it was distasteful for those of the faith to own human beings, be they mage or otherwise. Those were his personal feelings, of course, and he would have never allowed them to seep into his duty as Holy Father. That was how he become the spokesman of the Lord God Almighty. He had sat on the fence of compromise for so long that he had dents in his flesh.

The chamber was out of control now. Not even the Speaker of the Chamber could silence them. Rupert remained seated, watching decades of frustrations and grudges unfold because one mage dared to challenge their authority. That's all it was at the core of the argument. Allegra had backtalked them, shaming them with her words. They weren't used to such behavior. They didn't know how to cope with that, so they lashed out.

He could have stood to attempt to bring order, but he chose to remain in his seat, upon the fence of compromise. Since the destruction of Borro Abbey, Rupert had been faced with the ugliness of himself and those he called friends and colleagues. It was not news to him that the clergy was filled with ambitious, political people, who'd crawl over their dead grandmothers if it meant a drop more of power in their grasp. It just had never occurred to him that *he* was also one of those people.

Worse, he'd never thought of them as cowards. Yet, that is what they were. Himself, included. He was not brave. Pero had called him a coward and the reason it stung him like poison was because *he was a coward.* He was not the brave protector of mages. Or of the poor, the needy, the downtrodden. He had sacrificed his own beliefs for power.

The truth always finds a way, as Tasmin once said. True to her holy words, truth found a way here today, too. It found it into his soul, and the into the souls of many of the cardinals gathered here.

Giso was shouting at Vittorio now, calling him a slave-loving coward. Those two had hated each other since before Rupert joined seminary school in Orsini. They had gotten into an argument during class once, when they were lecturing on interpretations on the words of the Guardians. Tasmin was always a favorite of the people, with her sword aloft. Kasta was held in a romantic light; a man and his entire generation sacrificing themselves to the demons so that others could live.

But it was Lonstein that Rupert had always identified with. Wrestling the demon who had attacked his children. Who had maneuvered the creature back toward the rift and then sacrificed himself as he fought the demon into the abyss itself.

Rupert has always seen himself in that role. However, as he looked about the chaos that descended upon the assembly, he knew he was no Lonstein.

"I will not yield!" Giso was screaming now. The old priest's dedication and passion for mage rights and, indeed, the rights of all human beings no matter who or what they were, had not faded with time. If anything, age had made him bolder. Power had made him stronger. He used his passion and his power like a cudgel now, standing against the conservative block that shouting at him to sit down.

Allegra stood silent at the podium. What more was there for her to say? She had unleashed her volley into the conclave and by the Lord God Almighty, it had hit the mark. Allegra had always said there was no neutral ground in this matter. He hadn't believed her. Now, though, he realized it wasn't that he didn't believe, but rather he didn't *want* to believe her.

He had laid his hopes upon the moderates and that they would, in time, become a valid faction of their own. Now, as they fractured to choose the only two sides that really mattered, he realized that moderation in this was just another word for power over people. Their vows were people over power, but very few in this room had kept to that vow. They truly had the stain of blood upon their souls. May the Lord God Almighty forgive them, for the innocent might not.

Cardinal Angelo, the youngest in the chamber and the newest elected to the order, shoved Giso. Giso's hip contacted the pointed edge of a desk, and he crumpled to the floor in a heap of limbs, fur, purple, and curses of pain. Unsurprisingly, that did nothing to quell the crowd's anger. The shouting grew louder, more intense, and more divided.

Rupert stood. He did not know how to end this brawl, but it had to end. Physical violence was unacceptable in this sacred space of the Almighty. He was thinking of his words, of what to say to stop the lunacy, when Cardinal Devonshire decided it was time to end the madness.

ALLEGRA HAD BEEN staring at the growing scene and felt both helpless and rather responsible for it. When Giso was attacked by that young cardinal she didn't even recognize, she was in the middle of forming the word, "Stop!" when Cardinal Devonshire grabbed one of the speaking stones in her gnarled hand and threw it to the floor with all of her strength. The shattering stone reverberated through the chamber.

Allegra collapsed forward against her podium, and she grabbed on for support. The sound was a physical force against her body and her mind. Even after the reverberations faded, her ears rang and water dripped from her eyes and nose. A headache like she'd never experienced formed and began pressing against her skull.

When Allegra finally managed to focus her vision, she saw that nearly everyone else was collapsed to the floor or against their desks. Some were helping each other to their feet now. In fact, the only people still standing with perfect poise were those who were hard of hearing, or partially deaf. Even they had grimaces upon their faces, as the sound had been something to feel as well as hear.

In that stunned wake of the speaking stone's destruction, Cardinal Devonshire grabbed a stone from a nearby desk and shouted into it, "Enough!"

There were meek protestations, as people were still regaining their wits, but she only spoke louder. "I said enough! How dare you disrespect the house of the Lord God Almighty in such a display of wanton violence? How dare you raise your hand to Cardinal Giso! How dare any of you call yourselves followers of the Lord God when you would debase yourselves in such a manner!"

Allegra stared at the old woman, whose face was red with fury. Cardinal Devonshire had never really been on anyone's side. She was the eldest cardinal by at least a decade, and she had no tolerance for nonsense.

"I have been a member of this holy order for longer than any of you, including the Holy Father. I have never seen such an offensive display of cowardice in my life. Is this what we have become?"

The protestations were a bit louder now, but that only served to fuel the old woman's fire. "You do not get to speak, Cardinal Reinhold, for you could not even raise yourself to vote against handing an innocent woman over to a murderer. Oh, I have been well informed of this conclave's activities over the last several days, and I have never been so disgusted in my life."

Allegra had not expected *that*. She kept quiet, though. She had already caused enough of a ruckus. Perhaps her mother was right all along; silence was indeed a virtue.

"You are pampered children who have grown too used to our fine wine and good food, that we cannot even look into the face of our decisions. The demons that ripped through our holy place and killed so many of us is the face of our decisions. Look it in the eye and know that our self-righteousness, arrogance, and cowardice caused the demons that attacked us!"

Allegra heard a man's voice, but she couldn't make it out. However, Devonshire made it obvious when she sternly said, "Vanida! Be silent. As head of the censure board, I hereby censure you now to be removed from the conclave for a period to be yet determined. The charge is the disrespect of this chamber, fraud, and the purposeful starvation of the innocent."

Allegra stared as Vanida was dragged—screaming and near-frothing—from his seat. He fought the guards the entire way, collapsing to the ground like a toddler amid a tantrum. The guards that protected the doors, however, grabbed him by the ankles and dragged him across the floor. Throughout it all, he spewed a flurry of insults and curses.

Allegra watched the scene with a stern expression, though she smiled on the inside. Cardinal Devonshire had turned down the papal robes three times in her life, and until this moment, Allegra had never completely understood exactly why. It was clear now. As the senior-most cardinal, she could wield her own form of power very differently than if she were the Holy Mother. Cardinal Devonshire was the head of the censure board and could kick a cardinal out of the conclave. She had the power to call the conclave to assemble, to dissolve it for the summer months, whatever she wanted. No one else held that power, not even Rupert. From committees outside of the pope's control to the respect of her age and decades of service, she was the one who truly held the power.

Allegra was in awe of this powerful woman who so rarely used her power openly.

"There has been a rot festering inside this chamber. Factions have taken over, where power, and not mercy, is what guides our decisions. We are now in a time of war, and this is no time for inaction, for confusion, and for factions. Yet, it is clear to me that this chamber is unable to meet the necessary conditions to survive the coming days. Therefore, as head of the censure board, and the head of the Etiquette Board of Cardinals, I dismiss all but the senior cardinals from this conclave. Your reinstatement will be determined when the threat has passed."

Allegra blinked. She looked back at Rupert. He was as surprised as anyone else. He was leaning forward in his chair, jaw dropped.

Allegra cleared her throat and said, "I apologize, Your Grace. Is that...is this possible?"

Devonshire gave her a stern look, but the look she gave Rupert could have turned sand to glass. Her words were for him, as well. "If *you* had done your duty when first appointed to your office and read the tenants of your position as I instructed, you would have known to write to me and demand I enact war measures the moment Captain Rainier appeared within our walls. We are a Cathedral, Your Radiance, but we are also a small city state. And Orsini, as a city state, has allowances for times of war."

Allegra looked back at Rupert again, who was now rising from the chair. He walked over to the podium, and Allegra stepped aside to allow him to speak. "Your Grace, are you certain this is the course of action you wish to take?"

The factions broke into bickering and shouting again. Devonshire let them go on for a moment before she said, "With the exception of Cardinal Vanida, I hereby create the Orsini Assembly."

Allegra glanced at Rupert since she had no idea what that was, but Rupert clearly was just as confused. "Your Grace, did you just make that up?"

"No, Your Radiance, I did not," Cardinal Devonshire said in a caustic tone. "Again, if you had bothered to read the material that I outlined when you were first elevated to your office, you would already know all this."

It took all of Allegra's court training to not burst out into laughter at the cardinal's rebuke.

"I cannot allow a conclave to guide us during a time of war that voted to hand over the Arbiter to a murderer, simply so you could all sleep comfortable at night. Orsini must speak with one voice from now on, and it is clear this assembly is not capable of that."

The quarreling took a more self-righteous tone, with some arguing they were always on the side of the Arbiter, with others justifying their actions. Again, Devonshire let them go on for only a handful of seconds before she spoke. They stopped immediately; no one wanted another speaking stone assault. "The Orsini Assembly is to have the Holy Father, ten senior cardinals, the colonel of the militia, and the constable of Orsini."

Cardinal Devonshire outlined the ten senior cardinals. Herself, Giso, Vittorio, DeLancey, Reinhold, and a handful others that were across the political factions. "Your Radiance, you will need to choose a colonel of the militia, since we do not have one currently. We also need to choose a constable of Orsini."

"What about the Arbiter's position?" Rupert asked, glancing at Allegra. "Forgive me, Your Grace, but the Contessa basically caused all this."

Allegra gave Rupert a dirty look. When she looked back at Cardinal Devonshire, the old lady was giving him a very similar look. "We failed the Arbiter and her office, and by doing so, we failed the people she was appointed to protect. This war was not her doing. We *did* help create it, however, and we must bear that responsibility upon our heads and hearts. Your Radiance, I recommend that we set aside the office of Arbiter now, until this crisis ends, and instead combine it with the office of Constable of Orsini."

"That's only a ceremonial position," Rupert said. "How will that help?"

"The Constable of Orsini is allowed, by *Orsini* law, to sit on the Orsini Assembly and vote." Cardinal Devonshire looked at Allegra and said, "The Arbiter has been right about one thing. We *must* set aside our political factions to work together to turn the Cathedral into a place of refuge, for those already inside our walls and for those who are fleeing toward our walls. We will not escape this war by hiding. And may we seek the Lord God Almighty's grace that our folly will not damn us to the abyss."

Rupert glanced at Allegra. Her shoulders slumped. She was never going to get away from Orsini politics now.

CHAPTER TWENTY-SEVEN

ALLEGRA SAT AT her new desk, inside the new suite of rooms she'd been assigned. Similar to her Borro Abbey rooms, these began with a spacious office as the entrance. Visitors would have to walk past her guards, her administrative staff, and her maids to get to the drawing room beyond. From there, she had a smaller, more intimate drawing room, and finally a well-appointed bedchamber that made up for any lack in size with a massive bed and a breathtaking view of the north gate.

She pulled up her shirt sleeve and continued writing, ignoring the gathering around her office. They seemed patient enough, and she had to ensure she'd written down everything. The first time she was made Arbiter, they'd given her a dirty office with broken furniture. Now that she was made Constable of Justice—just more words to say arbiter, but it conveniently side-stepped concave law—she was given a spotless, gleaming office.

Well, she noted, spotless before Stanton tracked mud across the carpets.

"Stanton, Nadira will have your head if she discovers it was you who tracked mud in on her carpets."

"I will bring her strawberries from the hothouse as soon as they are ripe," Stanton said.

"Bring some for Calm Seas and Kia, too. They are going to be beating those carpets," Allegra said with a little smile. She kept writing.

"Nearly finished with the notes." Serafina was there, of course, as was Nathan, but they were about to have their own tasks. No longer would they have time to manage her day-to-day life. She would need *another* secretary for that. Nathan was already tasked with finding her someone that was both competent and an ally to their cause.

Allegra pulled up her suspender that had slipped down her shoulder again. She was tempted to just pull her arms out of the damn things, but then she'd be chained to her desk. The trousers she'd borrowed were too big for her in the waist. It was suspenders or pantlessness and while one of those would be good for Stanton's morale, it wouldn't be good for hers.

Finally, Allegra put her pen down. "Serafina, do you know when I'll have clothes?"

Serafina shook her head. "I'm sorry, Your Ladyship, no. Cardinal DeLancey put Nadira in charge of fabric distribution this morning. I thought you knew."

Allegra nodded the affirmative. She had had a visit from her servant, asking if she could take on the role. Nadira insisted she would be there to help Allegra at any time of the day or night, but Allegra waved off her concerns. Nadira said she wished to help Cardinal DeLancey and Allegra happily approved the scheme.

Nadira was now in charge of the cloth purchasers, who were sent out to find materials for clothing, bandages, blankets, and all of the other necessaries of life at Orsini. It wasn't safe for people to travel now, but they had to get supplies in. Nadira had a keen eye for cost and large-scale needs. Then, once she'd drawn up the list, armed and guarded merchants would head north of the walls and buy what they could.

"I'm mostly concerned people will struggle with the Constable of Orsini wearing men's trousers and a too-large tunic."

"I think it's very fashionable," Serafina said. "Perhaps you will start a trend."

"I doubt anyone would be interested in women walking around in clothes that are about to fall off them." Allegra looked at the expressions of the people in front of her. "Forget I said that. Well, let's get to business. First, Your Highness. I would prefer if you stayed in Orsini to help us, but I will understand if you need to return home."

Imogen's face had mostly healed from the original attack by Bonacieux's forces. She'd come out the demon attack nearly unscathed. Allegra was grateful for that. "The Holy Father asked me personally to stay as head of Orsini's militia. In good conscience, I cannot refuse an order from the second only from the Almighty. Messengers have been sent to my brother requesting his formal permission. Therefore, until I am dismissed or receive new orders to return home, I shall remain."

"I'm glad for that. I want you to organize with Walter. I want experienced elemental mages in every shift and at every guard posting. Is that understood?"

Imogen straightened her back for a moment, and Allegra thought she was going to argue. However, she bowed her head and said, "Yes, Your Ladyship. Mr. Cram, after this meeting, I would like to discuss possible ways to train willing mages. Elemental or otherwise."

Walter's mouth gaped open. "You want to what?"

"Did I say something amiss?" Imogen asked. "Mage and elemental are the correct terms, yes? I will adjust my phrasing accordingly, if they are not."

"No," Walter said, his words still filled with confusion. "I apologize, Your Highness. I am struggling to cope with all of this acceptance and cooperation."

"Struggle faster," Allegra snapped. That drew looks from the gathering. She drew in a breath to bring her tone under control. "From this point forward, anyone connected to this office must present a united face to the people. We do not have the luxury for division and infighting. There is now, officially, a civil war in Cartossa. We are going to be overrun with people fleeing the conflict. Also, I suspect we have not seen the last of General Bonacieux, especially when he hears about his troops being eaten alive by demons."

"They weren't eaten," Walter said, annoyed.

"When has Bonacieux ever cared about facts?" Allegra asked him. When Walter didn't reply, she continued. "I assume many of the elemental mages will need training of some form. I remember

Queen Portia struggled greatly controlling her magic during the battle. I recommend taking willing mages beyond the gates and away from anything flammable. However, you need militia in case of any trouble. Imogen, can you arrange that?"

"Yes. I recommend easing into that, as I'm concerned…" Her voice trailed off at Allegra's hard look. "I will speak to the militia and I will make it clear that their job is to ensure we have mages trained and ready to fight alongside us."

Allegra gave a sharp nod of approval. She looked down at her notes. "Right. From this point forward, Walter goes nowhere without two Consorts. Stanton?"

Stanton looked down at his notes. He made a few faces before looking back up. "Currently, some of the Consorts are helping with guard duty. We can add guarding Cram to the list, but that will mean double shifts for everyone."

"I need the Consorts sharp. I wish to move them to protective assignments. Me, the Holy Father, Imogen, Cram, Serafina, Nathan, Father Michael, you."

"I *am* a Consort," Stanton laughed.

"It is well known now that we are together. They will try to get to me through you."

"I won't let them," Stanton said.

Imogen let out an annoyed sound. "The guards are for *her* peace of mind, not yours. *Your Grace.*"

Stanton rolled his eyes. "Fine."

Allegra couldn't contain her smirk. Imogen loved to pull out titles and rank whenever possible on Stanton to make her point, and she was a master of it.

"Your Highness, how are your own men doing?"

"My men are healing well, and I think getting them out of the surgeon's house and into the field just beyond the courtyard will boost their morale. With your permission, I'd like to begin drilling them today."

"May I send some of my green Consorts to train with them? I don't always have tasks for them, and my experienced boys don't have time to train them," Stanton said. To Allegra, he said, "since they'll be busy guarding me."

"The more the merrier," Imogen said with a smirk.

Walter let out a dramatic sigh. "I suppose I will speak with some of the mages. I know some were soldiers. They might want to come help. I guess it doesn't hurt to ask them."

"Good. We need to work together to get through this," Allegra said. "The last news we've received out of Cartossa wasn't encouraging. Grand Duchess Katherine is under siege at a border palace, but she remains alive and is rallying troops to her side. Bonacieux is murdering anyone and everyone with the whiff of magic about them. Now with Borro and the abbey completely gone, there is nowhere left along this side of the border that can handle the number of people who will be fleeing the war. I have spoken with the senior cardinals and they all agree at this stage that we are going to get them. That's why you are here, Father Michael."

"I was wondering about that part," Father Michael said. "I heard I was named Bishop of Orsini today."

"Congratulations!" Imogen said honestly.

Walter grunted, though he didn't quite hide the smirk on his face.

"I didn't like the old one anyway," Dodd said helpfully.

"A bit of a horse's ass," Lex added in, also helpfully.

"The old bishop has requested to be reassigned to his estates in the north. Under the circumstances, the Holy Father approved it. So, that left a vacancy. Congratulations, Father Michael," Allegra said.

"What do you require of me?" Father Michael asked.

"I need you to convince the people to trust us. We have to put aside all animosity and be unified if we are to get through this. There will be rationing, but that means everyone will be eating the same amounts."

"How did you get the cardinals to accept that?" Walter asked.

"They haven't yet," Allegra said. "We are in charge of civilians, not the clergy."

Walter snorted. "Orsini won't survive even one food riot."

"That's why I'm trying to avoid one," Allegra said. "Serafina? You are in charge of working with Cardinal Giso's staff and Cardinal DeLancey's, including Nadira. You are now responsible for ensuring every single person inside our walls is clothed and fed. Do you understand me?"

Serafina gulped audibly.

"Can you do it?"

"Yes, Your Ladyship," Serafina stammered. "Yes. I can do it."

"Talk to Antonio, my child," Father Michael suggested. "He does for Cardinal Giso what you do for the Arbiter. My apologies, the Constable."

Allegra laughed. "I am still the Arbiter in my heart."

"Serafina? Talk to Landers, too. He's DeLancey's assistant and very reasonable. He knows a lot about housing and how many rooms we can open if necessary," Stanton said.

"Shelter, too?" Serafina asked. Her eyes were still unusually wide.

"Yes. We have a lot of damaged buildings. If we open the kitchens, I suspect we're going to get free work for two hot meals."

"Three," everyone but Cram corrected her.

Allegra sighed dramatically, but a small smile tugged at her mouth. There was so much whining when the Orsini crowd moved to Borro last year, when the worldly city folk discovered the backward routines of the abbey. "I'm sure the Almighty never meant for people to eat three times a day."

Stanton grinned. "That's because you're a tiny thing. The rest of us nearly starved in Borro."

"The healers here said I was malnourished from my time at Borro," Dodd said.

Lex nodded. "It's true, Your Ladyship. I'm not sure how I survived my injuries, even."

"All right, you've made your point. Lord, what a bunch of babies you lot are. Fine. Three. Can we make one of them something simple. Three meals a day is excessive. Soup?"

"I like soup," Dodd said rather deadpan.

"Fine. All right, Serafina? Two meals a day, plus soup. Work with the cardinals' staff, but remember: you are in charge now. Take the staff's advice, listen to Nadira, but you are the one making the decisions. Can you handle that?"

Serafina gulped again, but nodded. She managed to squeak out a "Yes, Your Ladyship."

"Speaking of food," Stanton said. "I think we need to consider stockpiling food in case of a siege."

"Doesn't the cathedral do that already?" Imogen asked.

"Beyond wine and spirits? Not really. There is the usual seasonal storage, but nothing useful. We aren't equipped to take on refugees *and* a siege. From what I've heard, we'll be starved out in a week."

Allegra made notes in her journal. "See to that, Serafina. Perhaps ask Giso…no, ask Devonshire who she'd recommend to do a total food inventory. She would know best."

"Yes, Your Ladyship."

"Nathan?"

The reedy young man jumped in his seat.

"By order of the Holy Father, you are to work with the accountants. All frivolous expenses are to be suspended until everyone is fed and clothed, do you understand? And," she scribbled more in her journal, "that now includes a stockpile of food. I don't know how much is appropriate. Work that out with Imogen and Stanton, and…who else is best?"

"I hate to do this, Allegra, but I'd recommend Vanida," Stanton suggested. "He's an awful man, but he was in the siege of Ellen's Cross. He'd have a lot to offer."

Allegra groaned, but wrote that down in her book, too. "All right, Nathan. If Vanida refuses to help, talk to Cardinal Devonshire and she'll straighten him out. You got all that?"

"Um…"

Allegra leaned forward. "Are you able to stand up to pampered cardinals or not? I need to know this now."

"I can do it, Your Ladyship. Half of them hate me anyway, after the whole bread thing. And maybe that thing about how I know the law better than they do."

"Good." She wrote herself more notes, reminders to remind herself to do things. "Nathan and Serafina. I want you both to find yourselves a *second* assistant each. Also, please find Stanton and Imogen an assistant, and get Walter a manservant and a runner."

"I'm getting servants now?" Walter asked. He shook his head.

"What's the matter, Cram?" Dodd asked. "You've been bitching that you aren't appreciated. Now that you're being appreciated, you're bitching about that."

"It feels like a trap," Walter said.

Allegra sighed. "Oh, shut up, Walter."

Walter responded with a snort.

"Stanton, we already talked about this, but I think it's time to tell everyone. Have you found me two new personal guards?"

"Rahna and Martin."

"Good."

"What's going on?" Dodd asked. "I get that Lex is hurt and all, but we're your guards."

"I'm not that hurt anymore," Lex insisted.

Allegra waved off his questions. "Officially, Lex and Dodd will be working as the new liaisons between mages and normals. Your job will be to ensure petty issues don't spiral out of control. That any member of the clergy showing bigotry will be spoken to through appropriate channels. Encouraging the lower clergy to work with the mages whenever possible. All of that."

"And unofficially?" Lex asked.

"I want you both to investigate who is causing the portals to open."

Lex glanced at Dodd and cocked an eyebrow. Lex looked back and asked, "Us?"

"Is there a problem going on between the two of you that prevents you from doing this job?" Allegra snapped. "Sorry. Sorry. I didn't mean to snap."

"I don't mind the job," Dodd said, "But we're really not investigators."

"It's fine, Contessa," Lex said. "I meant more like, um, why us? I'm still slow walking about, and I get tired easy."

"That's a great cover," Walter said.

"I'm actually hurt," Lex said, an edge to his voice.

"Calm your ass, I was there," Walter said. "I'm saying you being hurt is a good cover. You'll need to be in the healer's room, and the two of you are always together anyway, so people will just assume Allegra took both of you off guard duty. So that Dodd could get Lex on his feet and all that. Lex will be allowed to rest literally anywhere, because everyone knows by now that Lex nearly died. He can get away with loitering just about anywhere where the rest of us cannot."

"I won't be loitering," Lex said defensively. "Sometimes, I get tired and I have to sit down. I'm not doing it on purpose."

"I know! It's perfect!" Walter said with a giant grin on his face. Lex sighed.

"What do we do when we find this asshole?" Dodd asked.

Allegra took a deep breath. She hated the words that were about to come out of her mouth, but Francois said the senior cardinals all agreed. "Show them no mercy."

THE SINS WE SEEK

NOW I WAIT, Lord God Almighty, for the fist of justice to reach me. For it shall find me, of that I am certain. I have made peace with it and welcome the opportunity to explain my actions to the world. For though they will hold me up as a traitor, I will know in my soul that I acted only by Your guidance and by Your design. For you, Lord God Almighty, are who I wish to exalt above all others.

I will not resist when they come with ropes and fire. I will prostrate myself before You, Lord God Almighty, and I shall take my mortal punishment, knowing that Your will was done.

I am ready for my death and how I shall be remembered as a martyr for Your will.

EPILOGUE

"SO..." LEX SAID, just so that the silence would stop.

"So..." Dodd added helpfully.

They were sitting together on a set of wooden stairs that had, inexplicably, ended up in the middle of the courtyard and somehow survived the entire fight without so much as a spark's burn. The two friends had been sitting there off and on for a couple of days now. It's where they ate their curry lamb buns (assuming Rainier didn't get to the carts first) and fresh strawberries (from the hothouses, which cost a damn fortune), wearing their matching hats (which Lex really liked and thought made them look like an awesome pair of swashbuckling heroes, but didn't want to say because this was all fucking awkward).

So there they sat, eating, being uncomfortable, and trying to figure out how in the name of the Lord God Almighty were they supposed to find the person who was causing the portals to open? Not even Cram knew, and he knew everything. He even knew about Dodd and...

Lex made a face. Lord God, even Cram knew. Walter fucking Cram. Lex would never live this down.

You'd think I'd know, of all people, I should have known.

But, no. Lex was always the last to know about these things because no one bothered to tell Lex anything. Oh, but now Lex was supposed to magically be able to figure out who was creating the demon portals when they couldn't even figure out that their best friend was...

"How are you feeling today?" Dodd asked, casually. He asked everything casually now. Or with this longing in his eyes, like he wanted to rip Lex's clothes off. It was creepy and weird and just, well, kinda nice sometimes to be looked at like that, but definitely not by Dodd. There were rules, and Dodd was crossing them.

But it was still kinda nice. *Sometimes.*

"My wound itches now. Supposedly, that's a good thing," Lex said. Casually. Because everything they did now was casual. As opposed to friendly and fun and this was seriously bullshit. "Dodd, this is bullshit."

"What is? You not bleeding out? I'm sure we can find someone to stab you in the guts again, if that's your thing now," Dodd said with a goofy grin on his face. Lex hated that goofy grin.

"I hate that grin."

The goofy grin grew. "It's why I do it."

"I hope you're the asshole mage doing this, just so I can punch you."

Dodd punched Lex on the arm. Hard. Way harder than necessary.

So, Lex punched Dodd in the thigh. With their middle finger's knuckle sticking out just a touch. And punched, right on the edge, where it stings the most.

"Ow! Holy shit, Lex! That hurt!"

Lex smiled. "*Now* it's just like old times. Ramone said he's going to have strawberry tarts today. Wanna get some?"

Dodd grinned, and this one was genuine. "I can't solve crimes on an empty stomach."

And then things didn't seem so hopeless after all.

WALTER SHUFFLED TOWARD his bedroom door and whoever was pounding on the other side. This entire "embrace the elementals" scheme of Allegra's was really getting under his skin, because all he wanted was a good night's rest. But, everyone knew where his bedroom was now, and they kept knocking on the door.

"Yes, yes, hold on to your trousers."

The knocking continued.

"For the love of the Almighty," Walter complained. If this kept up, he was going to put a sign on his door indicating if he were accepting visitors or not.

"I'm getting my clothes on! Stop knocking!"

The knocking grew louder.

He'd drank way too much wine playing cards with Rainier and the Consorts earlier that evening. Why in the name of the unholy abyss were he and Rainier suddenly friends? And Dodd, of all people, let him win. *At cards*.

He swung open the door and was surprised by who was standing on the other side. "Father Michael? What's the matter?"

"I need somewhere to sleep tonight."

"For the love of…" Walter opened the door wider and marched back to his bed. "I thought those two were back together."

Father Michael shrugged. "I know not the latest gossip."

"Then what's wrong with your bed?"

"It's empty."

"Then why in the abyss are you here?"

"I thought maybe yours was empty, too."

A slow smile spread across Walter's face when he realized why the priest was here. "Come on in, Father."

Father Michael walked inside and made a point of latching the door behind him. "That's what I hoped."

THE END

Don't worry! Allegra and all the gang will be back in *The Sins We Seek*. Lex and Dodd have been tasked with an impossible mission: find the mage who is opening the demon portals. The suspect pool, however, leads to all the wrong places.

Did you enjoy this book? Please consider leaving a short review to help other readers know if they might enjoy this book, too.

Want to know when the next book comes out? Sign up for my new release email at **kristadball.com/new-release-sign-up/**

Want more? If you'd like to get behind-the-scenes stories, snippets from upcoming books, and plenty of cooking with corgis (no corgis harmed in these posts!!!), check out my Patreon.

...

There's **a corgi dressed as Thor** as the header...Trust me, she's cute... **http://www.patreon.com/kristadb1**

ABOUT THE AUTHOR

KRISTA D. BALL WAS born and raised in Deer Lake, Newfoundland, where she learned how to use a chainsaw, chop wood,and make raspberry jam. After obtaining a B.A. in British History from Mount Allison University, Krista moved to Edmonton, AB where she currently lives.

Somehow, she's picked up an engineer, two kids, six cats, and two very understanding corgis off ebay. Her credit card has been since taken away.

Like any good writer, Krista has had an eclectic array of jobs throughout her life, including strawberry picker, pub bathroom cleaner, oil spill cleaner upper and soupkitchen coordinator. These days, when Krista isn't software testing, she writes in her messy office.

ALSO BY KRISTA D. BALL

Tales of Tranquility Series
Blaze
Grief
Fury
Schemes
Liberate

Spirit Caller Series
Spirits Rising
Dark Whispers
Knight Shift
Mystery Night
Dead Living
Blood Family

Ladies Occult Society
A Magical Inheritance
A Ghostly Request

Collaborator Series
Traitor
Fugitive
Rebel

What Kings Ate and Wizards Drank
Hustlers, Harlots, and Heroes